ARROW OF TR

Arrow of Truth is a work of fiction and alth
third novel, it is his first "who-dun-it".

The story tells how William Hardy the third generation owner and
Chairman of a family manufacturing business, struggles to keep his
company going in the face of increased demands from his customers
and ruthless competition from his competitors as well as suffering arson
attacks, bomb threats and blackmail letters from an unknown assailant.
But as he finds business life more and more difficult he realises that
unlike his father and grandfather before him, he doesn't have the natural
business flair that his forebears did.

Meanwhile the company's bank believing that the business is on the
verge of bankruptcy installs a team of specialist business turnaround
experts to work with him to try and save the business from collapse and
then rebuild it towards its former glories and fortunes. Tensions rise
and challenges appear as the turnaround team take over from William
leaving him feeling frustrated and sidelined.

But while William is battling with these complex and demanding
business issues, he is totally unaware that his wife, obsessed with a secret
lover is betraying and cheating on him.

However in a twist of delightful irony it is also she who is betrayed by
her lover but not in a way that might be expected.

Set in Norfolk in the East of England, the story is a fast moving thriller
set within a business background where the many characters and events
interact with each other as they unfold.

Arrow of Truth - like his first and second novels – (Ambitions End ©
and Winners Never Lose ©) draws on Mike's considerable experience
and knowledge of business in general and turnaround teams in
particular and how they operate to try and save businesses that are in
difficulty.

Other novels by Mike Upton
also published by AuthorHouse
AMBITIONS END ©
WINNERS NEVER LOSE ©

To find out more about Mike Upton go to his website
www.mikeuptonauthor.com

Arrow of Truth

by
Mike Upton

authorHOUSE®

AuthorHouse™ UK Ltd.
500 Avebury Boulevard
Central Milton Keynes, MK9 2BE
www.authorhouse.co.uk
Phone: 08001974150

First published by AuthorHouse 9/22/2008

ISBN: 978-1-4389-0891-5 (sc)

Printed in the United States of America
Bloomington, Indiana

This book is printed on acid-free paper.

AUTHOR'S NOTE
It is several years since Norwich Prison housed three men in one cell. The policy now is single cells where possible, but current overcrowding within the whole prison service means most prisoners are kept two to a cell. Also parts of the old Victorian wing were condemned and are no longer in use.

Arrow of Truth is dedicated to many people:-

My wife Brenda, my daughters Catherine and Victoria and Holly my granddaughter.

Sarah, my former secretary for her help which she always gives so willingly.

A special thanks to Tom Brady - Crew Manager, Dereham Fire Station in Norfolk for his kind assistance in helping me ensure that I got the facts relating to how the Fire and Rescue Services tackle and manage a fire correct and in guiding me on the Fire Service forensic procedures. We all owe a great debt of gratitude to the brave men and women of the Fire Service who do such an important and dangerous job.

Charlotte and all her colleagues at AuthorHouse yet again for their patient and constant support and help turning a manuscript into a finished book.

And finally as always to relatives, friends and acquaintances for their unflagging interest and encouragement to me in my writing career.

To them all I say thank you very much.

This, my third book departs from the business themes of the previous two which concentrated on multi-national wheeling and dealing.

Arrow of Truth instead deals with a large family manufacturing business but also features a turnaround team – a group of experts drafted into businesses in financial difficulty to nurse them back to financial health. It is also my first venture into a "who dun it". It was fun to write and I hope it's enjoyable to read.

To all my readers, I do hope you enjoy Arrow of Truth.

MIKE UPTON

July 2008

*If you are going to shoot an arrow of truth be sure
it's tip is
dipped in honey*

Arab Proverb

Evil is sweet in the beginning but bitter in the end.

Talmud.

CHAPTER 1

8th August 2007.

The man switched off the engine and the lights of his moped and let it drift along in darkness on the slight downward slope towards the small clearing that led off the country road. Hoping that there would be sufficient momentum to reach his objective he bent low over the handlebars to reduce wind resistance to a minimum and watched carefully in the darkness as he came towards the point where he had planned to pull off the road. Gradually he came closer until finally he was able to swing the bike to the left and crunch across the flat grass verge and up to the bushes.

Dismounting he pushed through a small gap in the shrubbery and leant the bike against a tree that was part of the tree and shrub verge. Taking off his helmet he tucked it underneath the bike, unstrapped the two heavy cans from the rack behind his seat and fitted a large padlock and thick chain around the front wheel. Then taking a black plastic sheet from the pannier on the side of the bike he gently tucked it all round the machine before standing back to admire his concealment handiwork. Almost satisfied he picked up some handfuls of leaves and sprinkled them over the plastic but most slid off leaving only a few on the top. He walked away for about five yards and then turned back. The bike was to all intents and purposes invisible and as it was highly unlikely that anyone would come through this area tonight, he was certain that it would remain completely hidden.

Pulling on a black balaclava and zipping up his black jacket he picked up the two cans, then after a final check round, pushed further into the bushes away from the road. Soon he was free of the clinging branches and twigs and as his night vision improved, helped by the small amount of moonlight that shone from tonight's quarter moon but which from time to time was obscured by clouds scudding across the night sky, he could see his way forward. Stretching ahead of him was a wide expanse of grass parkland in which scattered large trees protruded majestically.

He stood quite still watching and when he was certain that nothing or no-one else was about he ran quickly to the trunk of the nearest tree. It was about fifty yards away and just beyond it stretched a three rail wooden fence that he knew ran all round this park area enabling horses to be turned out and allowed to graze without fear of them escaping. When he reached the fence he again stood absolutely still and looked carefully in all directions, then pleased that he was still alone and undetected he climbed through the wooden rails picked up his heavy cans again and made the run to the next tree and then the next until he was finally about twenty yards from the buildings which were the object of his mission.

This time he waited for at least five minutes until he stopped puffing from the struggle of running with the heavy cans. Then after another careful check around he crouched and ran the final distance to the brick walled side of the building that loomed in front of him.

The distinctive smell of horses pervaded the air which was unsurprising as he was against the stable block of Wood Hollow Hall. Working along the wall and keeping as close as he could to the bricks he soon reached the end and after carefully peering around the corner he slipped along the next wall until he reached a small archway and gate.

It was unlocked but taking a small can of oil from his pocket he squirted some of the contents onto the top and bottom hinges making sure that it ran down the inside of the upright pinions. He also dripped some onto the latch so that when he gently lifted it and then pushed the gate forward there were no squeaks and it moved smoothly and silently to an open position. He waited again listening intently but there were no sounds of voices, no barking of dogs and only the occasional snort or woofling sound from a horse.

His heart was thumping and he was breathing heavily again as he put down the heavy cans before pressing on right into the stable yard area, keeping close to the wall inside the complex. He stopped again and checked his bearings as it was a couple of months since he'd turned up on a Sunday morning when he knew that the owner and his wife were away on holiday.

He'd spoken to a woman working in the stables asking if there were any vacancies for jobs. There weren't but that hadn't bothered him as he hadn't wanted a job, just the chance to look around and get the layout of the buildings which were in the shape of a square.

On one side there was a large barn filled with hay and straw. The second side consisted of stables as did the third. The fourth and final side had a big archway in the middle through which about fifty yards away could be seen the main house. Either side of the arch which in days gone by the carriages would have used to enter and leave were some rooms. To the left was a tack room holding saddles, bridles, and all the paraphernalia that was an integral part of owning and riding horses, and next to it was a larger room which was full of galvanised bins holding oats, bran, mixed feed, horse nuts and many other different feed items. To the other side of the arch was a rest room for the stable staff to use during the day and next to it a special large stable that was used for mares that were about to foal. Closed circuit cameras linked this particular stable to a screen in the rest room so that when a mare was due to foal a rota of people could keep watch from that room to ensure that all was well without disturbing the expectant equine mum.

The man moved to the first of the two sides that had stables and taking a rope from his pocket wound it around his right hand and approached the first stable from which a large black horse stared at him over the door. It was quietly chewing some hay and showed no fear or concern just some curiosity in case some more food or a titbit was in the offing.

'Schhh my lovely' said the man quietly as he patted the large powerful black neck. Then slipping the halter over the animal's head and pulling it tight, he opened the top bolt on the door and kicked the bottom bolt free. Pulling gently and muttering 'Come on lovely' he led the trusting animal into the yard area and towards the small doorway through which he had entered the stable block area.

Much to his relief the horse quietly followed him and soon he led it through the narrow gap and onto the grass outside. Walking forward a few yards he came to a wide gate in the wooden fence which he opened and led the horse through into the field beyond.

He'd been worried about this part of his plan as his experience with horses was limited to many years ago when he'd helped his daughter with her pony at horsy events, so he was pleased that the large horse which was so much bigger than his daughter's pony had followed him so easily and he hoped the others would do the same. Also he was relieved that the clattering of the horses hooves had ceased when it got to the grass as it had sounded loud enough to disturb the entire household but from his glance through the main archway he had seen several cars on the driveway outside the entrance to the Hall and so he was sure that the family were obviously having a dinner party and thus unlikely to hear the sounds made by the horse.

He didn't give the horse a slap on the rump as would have probably happened in a cowboy film, nor did he shout at it but simply released the halter and let it wander off.

Over the next ten minutes the man repeated the process with all the horses until eventually he had released a total of nine animals into the parkland.

Now he went and collected the first of the two cans that he'd carried with him from his moped. Moving quickly to the first stable he scraped some dry straw into a pile at the back, unscrewed the cap and poured a quantity of the petrol onto the pile. Pausing and wondering if he should do the same with all the other stables and then return to light them he worried that the fuel might evaporate before he'd finished so taking out his lighter he flicked the flame into action and then touched the petrol soaked pile of straw. It ignited straight away. Carefully piling more straw onto and around the rapidly growing fire he watched for a moment as it started to spread through the rest of the straw. It also licked at the wooden walls that lined the brick built stables which having been built nearly one hundred and fifty years ago meant that the wooden lining was bone dry. It started to smoulder straight away.

Quickly making his way to the next stable he repeated the process and then he worked his way round the stable block setting fire to each stable. As he started on the second side he could see the orange glow from inside the first two stables that he'd fired while white smoke started to appear over the stable doors. By the time he'd finished firing the second side vast quantities of smoke were billowing from most of the stables.

His first can was empty so running across to where he'd left the second can he switched cans and ran to the hay and straw barn. With a grin he went in and splashed the contents liberally around making sure that several stacks were well soaked. To finish in the barn he poured a trail towards the open door and then flicking his lighter at that watched with satisfaction as the tongue of flame flashed rapidly along the trail to the first straw stack which was immediately engulfed in flames.

As he had a little petrol left he approached the tack room but finding it locked he charged it with his shoulder and the flimsy lock gave way immediately. Quickly tipping the small remaining quantity of petrol onto an old armchair chair he pushed that under one of the wall racks that held rugs and other soft items. Shaking the last drops of petrol onto the rugs he set fire to the chair then pulling the door closed ran to his small gateway where pausing for a couple of minutes to collect the first empty can he watched with great delight the increasing effects he had caused.

Flames and smoke were pouring out of most of the stables and the barn which was crackling and roaring with a terrible intensity. Some smoke was also starting to appear already from the tack room.

With a final nod of satisfaction he picked up both empty cans and left the scene of devastation that he caused. He opened and closed the small gate, ran to the wooden fence climbed through the rails and ran as fast as he could from tree to tree across the parkland until he reached the wooden fence on the far side nearest to the road.

Scrambling through he dropped to his stomach and lay there panting and watching. Flames were now appearing from the roof at one end of the stable complex and smoke now not just white but black and grey seemingly supported by the orange glow and large tongues of flames was reaching up into the night sky. At that moment the moon was clear of clouds and so the man had a clear view of the destruction that he had started.

What he couldn't see was the sudden commotion that people had started outside the house on the far side of the stable block.

***

A few minutes earlier Janie Hardy had moved from the dining room into the kitchen to supervise Annie their housecleaner who was helping with the cooking for tonight's guests and putting the finishing touches to the desserts for the dinner party that she and William her husband were holding.

Looking around the large kitchen table still laden with three different dessert dishes, and two large plates of assorted cheeses she happened to glance out of the window. Perhaps her eye had been caught by something unusual or maybe it was just habit to look across towards the stable block. Whatever it was she saw the orange glow, flames and smoke. She dropped the dish she'd picked up and ran to the dining room screaming that the stables were on fire.

Pandemonium broke out in the previously relaxed happy atmosphere. Immediately everyone leapt to their feet and rushed towards the doors. Some went out the door into the hall and then ran to the large front door and outside that way. Janie and another two guests ran back into the kitchen and then through the second kitchen and scullery and out to the yard area at the back of the house that led towards the stable block.

The one person who didn't go outside straight away was William Hardy who dialled 999 from the hall phone, gave their address and location to the fire brigade and asked them to hurry before rushing outside to see for himself.

Janie ran close to the burning buildings which were now ablaze from end to end generating tremendous heat. Other guests restrained her from trying to get closer as she screamed for the horses.

She collapsed onto the ground crying uncontrollably moaning over and over again 'Oh the poor horses, the poor horses'. William seeing his wife's distress knelt down with her putting his arm around her.

'I've called the fire brigade and they said they'd be here as soon as they could but looking at that I don't think there's much chance of saving it or the horses darling'.

This brought on a further bout of crying and sobbing while the guests stood around helplessly not knowing what to say to the Hardys, but they spoke quietly to themselves while watching the enormous conflagration.

How long they all stood watching the fire burn no-one quite knew before in the distance the faint sound of a siren could be heard which grew louder and louder until they could also see the flashing blue lights flickering across the fields as they heard the fire engine roaring up the long driveway. Eventually it came round the corner of the drive and drove straight towards the burning stable block, stopped and disgorged the team of fire-fighters.

'Shit that's well alight' yelled one of them to no-one in particular as he started to unroll some hoses.

William ran across to the man with the white helmet who seemed to be in charge. 'We don't know how or when it started, sometime after seven as it was ok when our guests arrived'.

'Anyone likely to be trapped inside?' asked the Crew Leader in the white helmet.

'No just the horses'.

'Sorry but it's too far gone for me to risk sending in my men to rescue horses sir', then seeing the anguished expression he repeated 'sorry' and ran back to the fire engine. The first jets of water were already being sprayed onto the flames when a second fire engine arrived.

The Crew Leader snapped instructions to his own men and those of the second fire engine, then walked back to William.

'We're going to need a lot of water for this. Do you have a river or lake somewhere here sir?'

'Yes the lake. It's over there' he said pointing to the right.

'Bert' yelled white helmet to another of his crew. 'Go with this gentleman and he'll show you a lake where we can get plenty of water'.

William and the firefighter ran off and then when the latter had seen where it was and gauged the distance he went back to the first fire engine and ran out lengths of hose towards the lake while William ran back to Janie who was sitting on the gravel still crying. He knew that nothing he could say would console her for now so he simply sat down next to her and again put his arm around her.

The other guests milled around fascinated at the efficient way in which the firemen were tackling the huge fire. Soon a third and then a fourth fire engine arrived the Crew Leader having radioed for additional support and they positioned themselves around the far side of stable block so that now the four fire engines could pour water onto the fire from all directions.

Watching from his vantage point half a mile away the man had seen the fire engines arrive and then heard the huge crashing sounds audible even at his distance from the conflagration as part of the roof collapsed. Myriads of sparks shot upwards into the night sky and not long after he also saw one of the end walls of the barn crumple into a heap of glowing red hot bricks as the roof timbers gave way. He could see the horses that he'd led out of the stables before starting the fire silhouetted against the flames and the terrible orange and red fire hues from the burning buildings.

The assembled guests groaned when sections of the buildings collapsed and although in many ways most of the guests thought that they ought to leave the Hardys to their private problems they were all enthralled to see such an enormous fire close up and as it was a warm dry August evening they weren't cold even without the tremendous heat generated by the fire.

The fire Crew Chief had already told William and Janie that his intention was to let the fire burn out in a controlled way as it was so well alight and he doubted if they could save the building merely try to minimise the damage. He walked around the site carefully studying the progress of his fire fighters and was pleased with what he saw as there was some evidence that the massive amounts of water that was being poured onto the burning buildings was starting to make some headway.

Approaching Janie he said 'I'm sorry that we couldn't save the horses in the stables madam but at least the ones in the field behind are alright. Were there many inside?'

Janie stared at him. 'What horses in what field?'

'The ones in the field on the far side of the burning buildings. Several of them there'.

'William quick he says there's horses in the field behind the stable block' yelled Janie as she set off at a quick run keeping well away from the still fiercely burning buildings.

The two of them skirted wide of the buildings and then ran faster to the field where sure enough standing around were several horses. Some were looking towards the fire but others were in various positions in the field grazing unconcernedly.

Clambering through the wooden fence rails they quickly went from horse to horse realising with disbelief that their beloved animals were safe.

'How the bloody hell did they get here?' asked William of no-one in particular. 'They couldn't have broken out of the stables and look the field gate is shut properly. Someone must have led them here when the fire started'.

'Well if they did that why didn't they come and tell us the stables were on fire?' replied Janie.

'No idea but at least they're safe. They're all there aren't they?' and Janie counting quickly confirmed that they were. 'We'll leave them there for the night and see about where to stable them tomorrow. Perhaps some of our friends will put them up temporarily until we get things sorted out. Hey lets go and tell the others the good news' and taking his wife's hand he led her back around the burning buildings to where their guests were still all grouped outside the house.

When it was explained to their guests that the horses were safe, following the initial relief there was much speculation as to how they could have been removed from the stables. However when the Crew Leader heard the news after saying that he was pleased to hear that they hadn't burnt in the fire he took off his white helmet and looked serious.

'This might put a different complexion on things you know'.

Seeing William and Janie's puzzled expressions he went on. 'It could be that this fire wasn't accidental because if you didn't move them who did? Was it perhaps because someone started this fire deliberately but didn't want to hurt the horses so moved them out of the way first?

I think you ought to tell the police about this and tomorrow I'll get our forensic specialists to come and have a good look around. Your insurance company will probably want to see our bloke's report in any case and they may send in their own experts. I think this is all a bit dodgy, still at least the horses are alright' and so saying he returned to continue to take charge of the on-going fire fighting operations.

Now that the incident had turned away from the potential tragedy of nine horses burnt to death and instead into simply a massive fire William suggested that everyone returned indoors as puddings, cheese, coffee and drinks were still waiting for them all.

Gradually the people drifted inside and tried to pick up the remnants of their dinner party but although everyone tried to be cheerful and were relieved that the horses were safe, nevertheless the thought that the fire may have been started deliberately led to much speculation and concern.

If someone had a grudge was it just against the Hardys or was it against people who kept and rode horses. Although hunting had been banned it was known that there was still much resentment by certain anti-hunting activists who might be prepared to cause this sort of property damage.

Most of the guests present there that night rode and many had also hunted so a feeling of unease started to spread round the table and one by one they made excuses to leave in order to drive home and check their own properties.

***

The man lying still and quiet, knew nothing of this but as time passed he heard cars starting and soon saw various vehicles driving down the Hardys long curving drive. One of the fire engines had also left while three remained to continue pouring water on the now smouldering wreck of a building from which much smoke still emerged but only a few patches of flames.

Much later when the second fire engine drove off he thought that his task was complete for now so slowly standing and with a final glance at the destroyed building but feeling no remorse, he collected his cans and made his way back to the shrub and tree verge. Pushing through he came to where he had hidden the bike.

Except that it wasn't there. Staring round in panic he moved left and right but there was no sign of his machine.

Making himself stop and think logically he realised that it couldn't have simply disappeared unless it had been stolen, but from the careful way that he'd hidden it and the stout padlock and chain that was very unlikely. On the verge of panic he pushed through the bushes onto the road and looking left and right realised that he had emerged in a different location from where he'd ridden off the road. The problem was whether he was to the left or right of where he should have been? He had no idea, nor had he any idea as to how far away he was from where he wanted to be?

Breathing deeply he quickly shrank back into the bushes as he heard a car approaching. When it had passed he again stepped out towards the road then changing his mind he pushed back through the bushes and re-approached the wooden post and rail fence. Staring carefully ahead of him he cursed quietly as the moon was temporarily hidden by some clouds but they soon passed and looking at the large trees that had provided him some cover when he'd originally worked his way carefully across the wide open space towards the stables, he thought he could work out where he'd gone wrong on his run back.

Deciding to move to his left he walked quickly crouching slightly and after about one hundred yards he thought that he had probably reached the right area and so pushing back into the bushes he cast around looking for his hidden bike. It took about five minutes but suddenly there it was.

Letting out a deep breath he quickly removed the plastic cover, folded it and put it into his bike's pannier, restrapped his two empty petrol cans onto the bike, removed the padlock and chain and then taking off his balaclava he fitted his helmet onto his head and pushed the bike onto the road. Hoping that it wouldn't give problems starting he pressed the starter button and was mighty satisfied that it spluttered into action straight away and in less than half an hour he arrived at his little terraced council house.

Wheeling the bike through his front gate and parking it in his tiny front garden he affixed the thick chain and stout padlock into place, then removed the two empty cans and went in his front door.

He walked through to the back door and went outside to the tatty wooden shed in his very small back garden and stowed the cans there before going back indoors. He took off his jacket and put on the kettle to make a cup of tea but suddenly changing his mind he switched it off and went into his sitting room and taking a bottle of whisky and glass out of the sideboard he poured a large slug and taking a deep swig he sat down in his old armchair, leaned back, closed his eyes and smiled.

'That's just the start Mr. Hardy you bastard just you wait and see' he muttered viciously but quietly.

***

Back at the big house alone since their guests had left, Janie and William sat in the dining room now cleared of plates, glasses and the other detritus of the dinner party. William was holding a large gin and tonic while Janie was sipping from a glass of red wine as they discussed the fire.

'It must have been the animal rights people or former hunt activists. I can't think of anyone else that would do such a dreadful thing can you William? You know when I first went outside and thought that the horses had all been burnt I just couldn't think straight. I could envisage them terrified, charging around their stables in panic, unable to get out oh William.......' and she burst into tears again.

'Yes I know but it didn't happen. Whoever did it at least had some compassion for them. It was us that he was trying to get at for some reason not the horses. Mind you I wish the police had shown a bit more interest when I rang them and told them what the fire chief said. I mean telling me that they've only skeleton staff on at night and as no-one's actually been hurt then they'll send an officer up here in the morning hardly fills one with confidence in our local constabulary does it.

I mean hells bells I pay my taxes, I run a big company employing lots of people, I contribute to local charities including the police Christmas appeal. It really isn't good enough'.

They sat and talked over the issues of the fire, the police and the lucky escape of the horses for ages before lightening the conversation a little as they started to discuss their dinner guests.

'I didn't think Patsy and Roger looked too comfortable with each other tonight did you? Maybe they are going through a rough patch. I mean they hardly spoke to each other did they? And as for the dress that Sue had on? Made her look like a real bag of rags. I mean I know she's lost weight but you'd have thought that she'd have bought something new or at the very least had it taken in a bit'.

'Don't be catty' replied William grinning. 'Actually I didn't think she looked too bad. After all she's got a nice figure under that dress and she was in sparkling form chatting away to everyone'.

'Especially Andy. Do you think she's got the hots for him?'

'Andy? I don't know but funny you should say that because last month at the golf club Dave said that she was a randy little thing. Maybe she has. We'll have to keep our eyes and ears open.

Now I'm just going to ask if the firemen want any more tea or coffee or do you think they'd like a beer? I'll go and see and then I think it's time for bed. This has been quite a night'.

Outside the firemen were going about their work quietly and efficiently. There were no flames now just masses of rising smoke and steam and after a brief consultation they decided that a case of beer would go down very nicely except for Bert and Fred the two drivers who would have coffee. A muttered 'thanks fellas' from the two enforced teetotallers who nevertheless grinned good humouredly.

'Right I'll bring out a large pot and the beer and then if it's all right with you guys we're going to bed'.

William having completed the refreshment supply run wished the crews good night and again thanked them for what they'd tried to do to save the building. After being told that at least one fire engine and crew would stay the night to be sure there were no flare ups, although looking at the pile of wrecked smouldering rubble it seemed unlikely, he went indoors and locked up. Walking back into the rooms used by their guests tonight he made doubly sure that there were no cigarette or cigar ends burning in ashtrays then swigging down the last of his gin and tonic he turned out the lights and walked upstairs to their bedroom.

Janie was in their en-suite bathroom and he saw that she was just getting into the bath which was covered with a thick layer of foam and giving off delightful scent smells.

'Wash your back for you darling?' he asked undoing his tie and unbuttoning his shirt.

'Umm lovely thanks' and she sank down into the water. He approached the bath and leaning forward lifted her long dark hair aside and kissed her neck softly then taking the flannel and soap from the side rack as she leaned her back towards him he started to gently massage her with the soapy soft cloth. Initially he worked all over these areas but after a little while his hands started to move more to her sides and then he worked back up towards her neck. Dropping the soap and flannel he pressed his thumbs and fingers quite hard into the side of her neck as he massaged intently before again picking up the flannel and gently rubbing her back all over.

'Feel better?'

'Yes heaps thank you. Do you want to get in and let me do the same for you?'

'No I'm just going to have a quick shower and then turn in'.

She got out of the bath dripping water and bath foam, but he wrapped a bath robe around her and then walking back into their bedroom quickly undressed himself, walked back into the en-suite bathroom stepped into the shower and stood letting the powerful water jets fire down onto him.

When he returned to their bedroom, Janie was in bed glancing through a magazine, her dark hair carefully brushed. Her breasts could clearly be seen through the flimsy nightdress that she was wearing.

'You know it's been a weird evening' he said as he pulled on a pair of shorts and climbed into bed alongside her. 'First the dinner party which seemed to be going pretty well I thought until the fire. Those firemen were brilliant weren't they eh? As for the lack of response from the police that's really appalling still thank God the horses are safe'.

Turning onto her side and propping her head on her raised left hand she agreed that they had been.

'Do you think it could have been started deliberately?'

'I don't know but the fire chaps will find out. Right it's late and I'd better be up early to see those firemen in the morning'.

She snuggled into him as he pulled her to him for a cuddle as he closed his eyes.

What a night he thought and tomorrow it was going to be quite a day what with the firemen, the police, the insurance company and of course the office. Oh God the office.

It hadn't entered his mind at all tonight and that must be the first time for weeks when he hadn't thought of or worried about the problems in his business. Mind you he wouldn't be able to go in as he'd have to be here at home to sort out the mess from the fire. Sod it. Really he knew that he should be in the office to continue trying to tackle the growing crisis in the business.

Janie lay awake in the darkness as William went quickly off to sleep her mind drifting back over the evening as she too slowly went to sleep wondering about the fire and who had released the horses.

The fire Crew Leader also pondered on that as he walked around the wrecked building checking for any potential new outbreaks of flames but satisfied that all was well he detailed one of the crews to remain on duty all night and then climbing wearily aboard the other engine told the driver to take him and the rest of the crew back to the fire station.

As they drove off he glanced up at the big old imposing house where all was dark and quiet. Must be around two hundred years old he thought and then supposed that the now destroyed stable buildings were probably of similar age. Terrible act of arson as that's what he thought it must have been to have destroyed forever a fine building in such a short time. Yes he was sure that it must have been deliberate as why else would the horses have been removed before the fire. But who he wondered?

Unless of course the owner, William Hardy had done it? Maybe some insurance fiddle. Mind you he seemed a nice enough bloke with a very attractive wife quite a bit younger than him, but that didn't mean that he wasn't a criminal, a crank, an arsonist or an insurance company defrauder. Obviously wealthy but who knows? Perhaps he's hard up? Trouble with the wealthy or apparently wealthy you could never tell.

Oh well not up to him as the fire brigade forensic teams and insurance people would soon find out if it was arson. His job had been to manage, contain and if possible put out the fire. Well he considered that he'd achieved that and contained the fire well but there had been no chance of putting it out and saving the building as it was just too well alight when they arrived. He shrugged as the fire engine drove steadily back down the drive and turned towards town and the fire station.

***

The man who'd caused such devastation having drunk several slugs of whisky decided that he'd had enough so he staggered upstairs to bed. Taking off his trousers he lost his balance and fell forward onto the bed but feeling that he couldn't be bothered to try and stand up again to undress properly he laid where he was still in his grubby shirt, pants and socks and went to sleep.

In a modern business it is not the crook to be feared most, it is the honest man who doesn't know what he is doing.

William Wordsworth.

CHAPTER 2

March 1921 - August 2007

William's grandfather, Douglas Hardy and his wife Sarah had started the business.

Douglas ran a small chemist shop in Dereham a market town in Norfolk but he was always very fond of the jams and pickles that his wife made using finest local, often hand picked ingredients and he suggested that it might be a good thing if they could sell some in his chemist shop. So using Sarah's home made recipes for Strawberry jam and Orange marmalade they bottled a few jars in their kitchen which he took to his shop and put on display on the corner of the counter.

The dozen jars that he displayed were sold within three days and so the next weekend the two of them made some further supplies which were again put onto the corner of the counter. Again these were quickly sold and soon people were coming in to the shop not just to purchase chemist requisites but to buy some jam or marmalade as they'd heard that it was so good.

At that time they lived in a little cottage and as well as making further supplies for their shop Sarah put a notice outside the gate saying

Home made finest preserves for sale

To her surprise people passing called at the cottage and willingly paid the small sums of money she asked for a jar of her preserves.

Soon the demand from the shop was requiring Sarah to make larger quantities once a week and she added Blackberry and Plum jams and Lemon marmalade to her repertoire. These new varieties proved popular but as she collected the blackberries direct from hedgerows and the plums came from their own small orchard supplies of raw materials soon became exhausted.

It was Douglas who hit on the idea of buying supplies of fruit from other local people in order to keep up with demand and it wasn't long before Sarah was spending a lot of time in her kitchen making her preserves.

Their next problem was a shortage of pans to boil the jam so Douglas asked all customers who came into his shop if they had any old boiling pans that they would sell to him. Over the next two weeks he collected several, for some of which he paid a few pence while others were given to him free mainly by customers who had bought some of the jams from his shop.

Sarah was able to keep up with demand for a while but she soon discovered that as fast as she made more supplies, so further orders were received by Douglas at his shop.

He found that as he gave greater space to the display of the products so he sold more and hence he learnt one of the first and basic lessons of selling and marketing. A good quality product properly displayed will sell and with news of these new home made jams spreading by word of mouth from satisfied customers the demand increased steadily and consistently.

Soon Douglas was helping Sarah in the evenings in the manufacture of their products. They bought larger and larger quantities of fruit from the local greengrocers, added more varieties and over the next few months their fledgling preserves business grew steadily until one evening Douglas announced that he thought that they could sell a lot more product if they went to other outlets such as grocers shops and sold it to them so they could in turn sell the preserves to their customers.

Leaving his assistant Mavis in charge of the chemist shop one morning Douglas filled the pannier baskets of his bicycle with a selection from their range of products and cycled round Dereham and one or two of the outlying villages calling upon various grocers' shops.

To his surprise and delight he soon established that the personal approach and allowing his potential customers to actually taste the products, created a ready and willing market for his preserves. It was rare if following a visit he didn't take an order. At the end of the morning he had amassed orders equal to the entire stock that they had and so that evening he and Sarah set to making further quantities of product to meet the demand.

Frankly they were both amazed at how easy it had been to sell as much product with it seemed so little effort. A simple morning's selling activity by Douglas and they had orders worth a quite a lot of money.

Over the next few weeks they both worked flat out. Douglas ran the chemist shop in the day but sharp at five o'clock each evening, except Wednesday when he closed for the whole afternoon he would close and lock up the shop and get on his bicycle to pedal around the nearby villages calling on village shops.

On Mondays, Wednesdays and Fridays evenings he would take orders and on Tuesday and Thursday evenings he would drive round those same villages in his old Morris car delivering the orders. He took out the back seat to make more room to carry supplies.

Soon they were unable to keep up with demand and so they had to bring first one and then two other people into their home to manufacturer products in order to keep up. Douglas also got a neighbour to help him build a lean to extension on the back of their kitchen and they transferred production out there where they had more room. He bought two second hand gas cookers, ran water pipes out from the kitchen, built shelves and storage cupboards and soon the production unit was working six days a week from nine in the morning until five in the afternoon. Sarah supervised and controlled the production while in the evening Douglas looked after the paperwork, invoices and other complications that started to occur as they grew their sales.

It wasn't easy to run the business as they kept running out of raw materials. If they weren't short of fruit, they ran out of sugar, or they were short of jars or they had a surge in demand and had to work through the night in order to satisfy demand. They were exhausted but happy.

One Sunday evening after they returned home from church, Douglas asked Sarah to sit down as he had something to say to her.

'I've been thinking you know. Why don't we give up the chemist shop and concentrate on the jam business. We can sell everything that we make and we're only supplying Dereham town and a few villages around within a radius of about five miles which is really as much as I can manage to cover. Every night and all weekends we are making, bottling and packing jams and yet we've only scratched the surface of this. If we really concentrated perhaps employed a salesman and opened a little factory we could make larger quantities and sell to a wider area. It would mean that we could buy fruit and especially sugar in larger quantities which should be cheaper and enable us to make more profit. Of course we don't know anything about running a factory but we could learn and also we could take on a few trusted workers to do the heavy and hard work.

You could be in charge of production and see that the jams are made properly to your recipes while I do the buying of raw materials, the planning, supervise the selling and do the books. Well what do you say?'

'It will be a big risk won't it Douglas? After all we make a good living from the chemist shop at the moment and the jam sales are just extra. If we don't have the income from the shop how will we be able to live?'

'Look Sarah, what we make out of the chemist shop is alright but I think we can make a fortune out of this jam business if we devote ourselves to it full time. It'll be very hard work for the next few years but I am convinced that it will work. We can expand the range of products we make.

I've been talking to a Wholesaler in town who will take our products and add them to his list and then his team of representatives will sell them all over East Anglia. This could be big for us you know my love'.

Sarah was still unconvinced so Douglas suggested that she slept on the idea and that they talked about it next day which as it was a Bank Holiday Monday meant that the chemist shop would be closed.

She did just that and the next morning which dawned bright and sunny and seemed to her to be some sort of an good omen she took a deep breath and told Douglas that she agreed.

So they took their momentous step forward. He wrote notifying the leaseholder that he wished to give notice on the shop and three months later he closed up on the Saturday evening, locked the shop, drove to Norwich and went to the leaseholder's office where Mr. Smith was waiting for him.

Also present was a Mr. Fox a young qualified chemist who was looking for his first chemist shop and who the leaseholder had persuaded to take over the lease.

The discussions and papers that needed to be signed didn't take long and within half an hour, Mr. Fox was the proud possessor of a chemist shop; Mr. Smith had a new signed lease and Douglas had a cheque in his pocket for the chemist shop stock which Mr. Fox had bought from him.

That money plus their small savings would be enough to last Douglas and Sarah for about six months so they knew that they had to make the business work in that time or they'd be in financial trouble.

However their plan worked wonderfully well.

They had already found a small building on the outskirts of Dereham which they could rent cheaply and so using some of the money from the chemist shop stock, together with half their small savings and enlisting the help of a couple of friends they worked to turn it into a proper little factory.

They scrubbed, washed and cleaned the whole of the interior of the old building. Douglas spent two days whitewashing the inside walls, repaired damage to the floor, fixed a hole in the roof, mended the guttering and cleared piles of rubbish from the yard area outside.

After a week they had wrought a huge change and they were ready to start installing the boilers and cooking facilities that they'd had at their home. When they had done this it took up only a small corner at one end of the building, but Douglas was undaunted and could only see how it would look in the future, not what it was now. He'd already bought some more equipment that he thought they'd need and this was installed as well.

Soon almost all was ready. He and Sarah spent a day interviewing potential employees and eventually offered positions to three women and one man.

One of his last jobs on Sunday before going to church was to fix a large sign to the outside of the building.

HARDYS FINEST QUALITY PRESERVES

On the Monday morning he and Sarah were at the factory early, ready for when their employees arrived and they were pleased when all four of them arrived at seven o'clock ready to start work.

Sarah kitted them out in clean overalls which she'd bought the previous week, made them wash their hands and then instilling into them a philosophy of quality, hygiene and cleanliness explained the process of making her preserves.

It took several hours before the first batch was made, bottled and poured into jars to cool. Everyone worked hard and soon they not only got the hang of what was required but a couple made suggestions tentatively at first but when they found that their ideas were listened to with interest by both Sarah and Douglas became encouraged to contribute more.

Weeks passed and the business grew. They took on two more employees to work in the factory and one man who had his own small van to deliver the larger quantities that they were selling and making.

Gradually over the next three years Hardys Finest Quality Preserves became available in shops throughout Norfolk and Suffolk and then spread into Lincolnshire, Essex and north London.

For Douglas a highlight was when a prestigious London food store wrote asking for a price list and shortly afterwards an order arrived for five varieties followed three weeks later by a repeat order and hence a regular business was established at this important store.

This was followed soon after by an order from some more prominent stores in London and other towns and so gradually but with increasing frequency Hardys products were to be found all over the country.

Another customer asked if they made pickles and Douglas said that regrettably they didn't but that they might in the future. That night he talked to Sarah about how pickles were made and discovering that it didn't seem to be too difficult, a few weeks later they started making small quantities of four products. They were tomato chutney and apple chutney, together with mustard pickle and a dark brown mixed vegetable pickle. To their amazement the products were an immediate success and so the company name was changed to

HARDYS FINEST QUALITY PRESERVES & PICKLES COMPANY

The addition of the pickles range quickly doubled their turnover and although they regularly installed more manufacturing machinery within a couple of years they were now exceeding the capacity of their little Dereham factory. Douglas worried about this as although he and Sarah were now quite comfortably off from the highly profitable business, he wanted to do two things.

Firstly he wanted to own his own factory and not pay rent or lease charges to someone else and secondly he knew he needed much larger premises but if he was to buy them then he'd have to borrow money to do that.

As a now well known local businessman he was listened to politely by the various banks he approached and they all offered to lend him money but only in small amounts and at high rates of interest. The problem was that they were local branches in Dereham and didn't have the authority to lend the large sums of money Douglas wanted especially when he explained that he intended to establish his new factory in the City of Norwich. They recommended that he approach banks in that City.

He did and found a wholly different approach and soon he had a loan agreed at a reasonable rate of interest which was sufficient for him to buy a piece of land to the west of the City.

He now bought his supplies of raw materials and ingredients in bulk and hence benefited from lower prices. The factory was also next to the main railway line and the railway company agreed to run a siding off the main track straight into Hardy's works.

It took nine months for his newly designed factory to be completed but as it was built from scratch everything could be designed for the precise purpose of jam or pickle making.

They offered jobs as supervisors to all their Dereham employees if they would transfer to the new Norwich factory. Some did but others preferred to remain in Dereham and find alternative local work.

So the Hardy business grew and developed. It survived the Second World War and emerged undamaged and in many ways stronger than ever. Sarah had used lots of ingenuity as sugar and several other ingredients were unavailable in wartime but she found honey or rose hip juice could be used to replace the sugar and so she bought up all the honey she could as well as establishing a large number of beehives to obtain her own honey. She also scoured hedgerows for rosehips which when crushed and boiled would produce a sweet juice.

In common with many food businesses during the war, Hardys stopped distributing its products nationally and just supplied locally. After the war Douglas drove expansion strongly and within a few years as raw materials became more freely available its products were sold in shops all over the country. A thriving export business was also established.

Hardys preserves and pickles were advertised in magazines, newspapers and on outdoor hoardings and soon became a household name.

Douglas and Sarah moved from Dereham to the City of Norwich where they bought an old Victorian house on Newmarket Road, one of the expensive parts of the City. A few years later they moved out of the City when they bought Wood Hollow Hall a country estate near Loddon and over the following years bought more land until they had nearly one thousand acres of prime country land for their estate.

But Douglas, who had taken to the role of businessman and country gentleman with ease, collapsed and died suddenly one Sunday morning on his way home from church.

The funeral was attended by hundreds of mourners. His son James who had become a director of the business a few years before and had been largely responsible for developing the export trade as well as masterminding their UK expansion now became Chairman and oversaw a period of great growth and prosperity for the company. He also moved into the big house on the country estate and Sarah moved into a small cottage on the north side of the estate where she lived quietly until she also died a few years later.

The key attribute that both Douglas and then James had brought to the business was their total dedication to the company. It was their life, their passion, their all consuming reason for being and it showed in the results that they achieved.

William though was different, very different. To start with he not only enjoyed his inherited money but he enjoyed spending it and revelled in the apparent influence in Norfolk that this brought him.

Unlike his grandfather, who while never poor had needed to be very careful with money in the old days when he just ran the chemist shop,

William had not known a time when money wasn't freely available. Whereas his grandfather had continued to use his old Morris car until it was a virtual wreck only then reluctantly buying a Rover, and his father who'd inherited Douglas's frugal approach to life was happy to drive around in an old Wolsley saloon, William used some of his inheritance to buy an MG two seater sports car. He found when he was at university that the sports car plus his apparent wealth and good looks was very useful for pulling girls and many succumbed to his charms.

Reluctant to enter the business straight after completing his university course which he scraped through emerging with a 2:2 degree he travelled the world for a year until he returned to Norfolk and started to learn the business from the bottom up.

While his grandfather and father both had a natural flair for business and people, William found business life hard and restrictive, however he realised that if he was to continue to enjoy his lifestyle then he'd have to buckle down and take a real role in the business and so he slowly worked his way up and around the business spending time in every department proving to be adequate but not outstanding in any of them.

Finally he joined the Board as a Director aged thirty four and worked alongside his father James until nineteen ninety three when the older man retired and handed over the reins to William.

He passed on a business that was profitable, growing fast, employed several hundred people, and was one of the great City institutions.

William soon found though that without his father either assisting or available to discuss decision making, the burden of running the business fell hard upon him. Nevertheless he soldiered on conscious that he was responsible for the lives and livelihood of so many people and their families.

But he lacked flair and to some extent courage. He was cautious, and whereas his predecessors had never been reckless they had both been willing to take calculated risks and most times these had paid off for them. They saw opportunities, weighed up the pros and cons and then acted.

William though would weigh up the risks and often came to the conclusion that the risk might be too great and so would either not act or take a timid approach.

It didn't take long for Hardys competitors to realise that Hardys was no longer as tough and aggressive as it had been in the past so they started to compete more fiercely.

They found that Hardys famed forceful selling and distribution operation was going soft and so were able to pick up pieces of business that in the past they would never have got. Similarly the increasingly powerful supermarkets found that Hardys were now much easier to squeeze for better prices and improved discounts and that they could play them off against their manufacturing competitors.

To start with the losses of pieces of business were not significant and William wasn't worried. After all the business had been around for over seventy years and he was sure that they could weather a few problems.

But they weren't just a few problems and they continued to hit the company from all directions.

They lost some large chunks of export trade. One of the big supermarkets delisted all their products and replaced them with a much cheaper range from a competitor. Other customers continued to pressure them for lower prices. Unions demanded higher wages and instead of fighting against those demands William caved in.

Some of their manufacturing kit was now old and in need of replacement but the cost of doing that was enormous and the problem was that the business really couldn't afford that expenditure. Well at least they couldn't from their own reserves so William arranged a loan from the company's bank to fund that replacement programme. He ought to have replaced a lot more of the kit in the cooking, boiling and pumping phases of production as well as installing new modern high speed bottling lines but his inability to think strategically meant that he only replaced part of the cooking machinery. On the positive side it meant that the loan was less but on the negative side he was piling up problems for the business in the future.

Unfortunately as the repayments and interest charges started to mount up they coincided with a continuing decline of profitability of the business. In fact it wasn't long before the financial results had declined so far that it was no longer making profit but losing money. William thought that it had been a good thing that he had only borrowed the smaller sum.

He'd only ever worked four days a week maximum in the business the other days being taken up with traditional country pursuits including hunting, shooting and occasionally fishing.

After his divorce from his first wife Dawn he'd become something of a social recluse only re-emerging back into Norfolk life a few years later. In the interim time he tried to bury himself into the business and although anyone looking at him would have thought that he was happy doing that, in reality he wasn't and very conscious that the job of Chairman of a company going through a difficult patch was a tough one indeed.

It was also one for which he was really quite unsuitable. He liked things when they were going well, decisions were not too difficult and he could enjoy the role of Chairman and the trappings that went with it as well as his country life.

But for the next few years the business struggled on however by mid nineteen ninety nine unless something significantly changed then there was no doubt that it was moving inexorably towards serious financial difficulty.

Their bank overdraft which for years had never been required was now in regular use as the cash coming in due to the loss of turnover and lower prices was a lot less than they needed to run the business on a profitable footing.

His father stricken almost immediately after he'd retired with Alzheimer's disease was unable to help and indeed now required constant nursing as his mother couldn't cope with the old man. Following in Douglas's footsteps the invalid James and his wife Belinda had moved out of the big house and into the cottage formerly occupied by Douglas and Sarah allowing William to move into the mansion.

At work William sat in the board room and contemplated the future with increasing concern. As an only child he had no other family member to whom he could turn for help. His own children from his present marriage with Janie were still at school although one day he hoped they might follow him into the business.

He knew that most of his management team needed changing to get others who were tougher and able to cope with the pressure and modern day demands of a consumer business. They'd been with the firm for many years and were now not really capable of operating satisfactorily in a modern day tough trading environment or of finding a different approach to the business.

So William watched Hardys drift downwards and after an acrimonious Board meeting they decided to lay off one hundred of their workforce something that he knew had to be done but nevertheless it troubled him as Hardys had never before in its history had to lay off any of its workforce.

The timing was bad as the decision was made just before Christmas, but he persuaded the rest of the Board to delay announcing the decision until immediately after the festive holiday. It was duly made on 2nd January 2000.

His second marriage to Janie had been like a breath of fresh air to him and he still could hardly believe that he had been so lucky as to persuade her to marry him.

He was extremely content and happy in the marriage. Unfortunately she was not, although he didn't know it.

Janie realised that something serious was troubling him. 'What is it darling?' she asked softly after supper.

'I go to the bank again tomorrow to try and get either a short term loan or an increase in our overdraft or any damned thing to get us more money but if I can't then I don't know what we're going to do. I really don't understand where it's all going wrong, well gone wrong really. When father and grandfather ran the business it made so much money. I know that I'm not as good as they were but I have done the best I can. I'm just not cut out for this rough and tumble business life you know. When I took over all those years ago everything was fine but it's all changed.

Our customers have changed. They have no loyalty to their long term suppliers, they just want more and more from us. New products, better prices, greater discounts, long term deals, new packaging and our competitors seem able to cope with this easier than we do. All in all my darling, it's a right bloody mess'.

Much to William's surprise the visit to the bank went quite well. They listened sympathetically, studied the figures that he and his finance director, Martin Fellows had brought with them, asked lots of questions and then said that they would be happy to extend and increase the overdraft in view of the fact that not only was Hardys a long standing customer and a major employer in the City, but also they felt that the difficulties that the company was experiencing were probably of a temporary nature and they were sure that in due course, given time, that they would pull through these problems.

However they passed a copy of the papers and their decision to the Regional office in Ipswich which after study classified it as **"Low Risk"** and filed it.

William was pleased with the temporary reprieve that the business had obtained and called a meeting of his board of directors to discuss a change to the business strategy.

'Look we have simply got to do better. I've got us an additional facility in our overdraft but we cannot rely on that for ever. As I see it we need to tackle our problems in three parts. Production must find ways to improve efficiency and get our manufacturing costs down. Sales have to get higher prices for our goods and find some new innovative products. Finance have simply got to collect monies owing to us quicker while at the same time being slower to pay our bills'.

This was quite some strategic statement from the Chairman who was not known for driving major change in his business.

His directors also noticed the change and went their separate ways to devise how they would carry out their own individual part of the plan and then implement accordingly.

For a while there was a small recovery in the business. Hardys got back some of the trade that they'd lost and their refound aggression seemed to be working. William and the other directors relaxed as profitability returned and so cash flow improved. Not to the historic levels that they'd enjoyed in the past but sufficient for them to start to pay back the bank, while funding the ongoing business.

Many of the people who'd been laid off before were retaken back into the company but not all and those that weren't reacted differently. Some simply shrugged their shoulders and found alternative jobs. Some started their own businesses.

***

But of those who'd been laid off, one in particular was consumed with anger and hatred. Prior to the layoff he'd already been short of money and was behind in his mortgage payments and his meeting with the Eastern Building Society had been unhelpful. They'd bluntly told him to catch up with his arrears and bring this account up to date or they'd have to consider more drastic action. When he explained that he was out of work they remained unsupportive and simply gave him 60 days to clear the outstanding monies.

He found another job as a factory worker in another factory in the City but as it was unskilled it paid much less than his previous skilled engineering supervisor rate and so although he, his wife and one daughter had just enough to live on he couldn't keep up the payments on his mortgage.

Inevitably as the sixty days came to an end the building society gave him an ultimatum. Pay up the arrears in seven days or they would repossess the house.

For his wife this was the last straw. The marriage had been under strain for some years and so she left him taking their daughter with her and moved to Huddersfield to live with her mother until she could find a separate place of her own. A year later she divorced him.

For the man this was a devastating blow and added to the resentment that he felt towards Hardys. Alright so he'd been in a financial muddle but given time and if he could have found a skilled pay rate job he could have sorted it out.

Now he was homeless, without his wife and daughter and virtually stony broke and in his mind it was Hardys that had caused the problem. A visit to the Council was the one ray of hope and they relocated him into a small decrepit two bedroom old terraced house in a run down part of the City.

From there each morning he left for his factory job filled with continuing hatred for Hardys in general and William Hardy in particular who was often pictured in the local papers hunting, opening a local fete or at a Chamber of Commerce function. Every time he saw William's picture or read an article about him his resentment grew.

He applied several times to Hardys for jobs but was always turned down and this fuelled his bitterness.

*** *

Hardys though seemed to have turned the corner. This was helped in no small way by the fact that the Ben Kilton the Sales Director having reached retirement age had been replaced with a new younger man.

John Benton initially brought a breath of fresh air to the business. He was modern in his thinking, a good manager of people, could see where change was required and had reasonably good connections with some of their major customers.

His enthusiasm and drive eventually impressed the hard nosed buyers in the supermarkets and wholesalers and over time, little by little John was able to persuade them to add more Hardys products to the ranges of products that they stocked. From there he was able to persuade them to promote the products with large displays in the aisles or at the end of shelving units or on the wholesaler's promotional lists.

The result of his hard work gradually re-built the business and although he had to accept lower prices than either he or the company would have ideally wanted nevertheless he was a major factor in steering Hardys into safer water than it had been operating in for many years. Although not enjoying the great results of the past nevertheless the business was moving back into profit and starting to grow again, albeit slowly.

But as time went on the pressure from competitors and their customers continually increased and their profit margins which they'd worked so hard to re-build were again eroded. It didn't happen suddenly but was a continuous process where little by little prices were squeezed down, or demands for promotional monies increased.

The company tried to innovate and bring out new products and some of these were successful and made it onto their customer's shelves, but many didn't.

Martin Fellows kept close to the Bank and managed their relationship which was satisfactory as the Company was paying back its loans, was back into profit and managing its cash flow.

But as the next four years went by Hardys slowly slipped from trading results that could be classed as reasonable to a position where they were starting to struggle again.

William had become happier with the way that things had been going and felt able to continue his country life spending no more than four days a week in the business and devoting more time to Janie.

The man applied again for a job at Hardys and again received a reject response not even getting an interview which further increased his bitterness.

The problem now facing Hardys though was the need to replace a large part of their machinery.

What they had was old and starting to suffer regular breakdowns. It was also inefficient, and inflexible. Their customers were demanding more attractively shaped jars and pots which Hardys old machinery couldn't pack. To do so they'd need new packing and filing lines. Frankly if William had done a thorough updating job previously when he'd borrowed money from their bank to fund renewal they wouldn't now need to be requiring to borrow a lot more money.

William and the Directors spent a considerable time preparing a business case to take to the Bank to obtain more money. It was difficult as they knew that the business was not as financially strong now as it had been due to the erosion of the profitability, but they worked hard to create a document which explained their current trading position laying emphasis on the new contracts that had been secured by John Benton, the improvement in their export trading and above all the benefits that would come from new bottling lines with the reduced breakdowns, improved efficiency and hence lower cost operation that they would generate. This coupled with the new high speed pumping machinery that they wanted to speed up the flow of finished products from boiling and cooking to bottling and packing, would transform the profitability of the business.

Additionally some major rebuilding work of the actual factory building itself would be required.

Overall it was a major project with considerable risk attached and William had agonised over it for days before finally being prepared to take the project to the Bank to ask for the money.

This time there was no quick decision. The matter was referred to Regional Office who got out their earlier file on Hardys, looked at the Company's current borrowing and repayment record and after three weeks of consideration decided to advance the money. After all the project seemed sound. It improved the profitability, helped modernise the business, removed inefficiencies and met various criteria that the bank applied to these sorts of projects.

They noted that trading was difficult but so it was with many of their clients and believing that the risk was no greater than the average for the industry sector the loan of five million pounds was approved.

While continuing to classify the business as **"low risk"** they however insisted that Hardys account was now handled at Regional Office level as that size of borrowing was quite outside the authority limit of their local branch who had handled Hardys account ever since old Grandfather Douglas Hardy had one day walked into the bank with an attaché case full of notes.

He'd said that he thought he ought to open a bank account to keep this lot safe pointing at the case of money. The branch had duly completed the formalities and Hardys Fine Preserves and Pickles had banked there ever since. It was the largest account that the branch handled and would have continued to do so, had Hardys not embarked on this expansion plan and hence taken their account requirements outside the authority limits of the local branch.

Once the bank loan was confirmed Hardys started ordering the new machinery that they needed and commissioned builders to start knocking down part of the factory and rebuilding to accommodate the new kit.

William was delighted. After all the business could soon be back making money. He'd taken a pretty major decision and got the advance that he needed and now looked forward to seeing Hardys grow to be a powerful business in the industry once again.

Much fanfare in autumn 2004 was made by the Directors to the workforce of the opportunities that lay ahead, although they explained that there would be less jobs in the future as the new machinery was more efficient, required fewer people to operate it and so a policy of non-replacement of leavers was instigated together with an offer of voluntary redundancy. As the terms offered for redundancy were generous there was no difficulty in getting the required volunteers and the workforce reduced in numbers smoothly and calmly.

But one man read about the further job reductions at Hardys and started to plot. For him it was all William Hardy's fault that he now had to live in the dump of a house that he did, that he had no wife or child with him and that he was skint. Smouldering with hate he decided that one day he'd make Mr. Hardy pay dearly for what he'd done.

The building work proceeded apace and soon the factory extensions were completed and the new machinery to go within arrived. The contractors carrying out the renovation, installation and commissioning were competent and although the whole process took about three weeks longer than planned it was eventually completed satisfactorily at the beginning of February 2005.

Hardys invited all their major customers to come and see their new capability and during the month a series of visits took place.

On each occasion the format was similar. The customers usually a buyer and buying director arrived but on one occasion a particular customer arrived in force with four of their team being present. A presentation would be made in the company's board room explaining the investment that had been made, the benefits that would accrue from it and how they hoped this would lead to more business from that particular customer. A tour of the factory lingering over the new extension and new machinery followed, after which the company team and visitors returned to the board room for a buffet lunch.

Some hard discussions then took place as Hardys team tried to persuade their customer to give them some more business but most of their visitors were non-committal at that stage and simply said that they congratulated the company on the bold updating of their factory and that they would think about how they might increase their business with them.

John Benton followed up these visits with his salesmen by visiting the customers and trying hard to persuade them to give Hardys more business. Unfortunately there were no quick favourable decisions and so the company was in the position of having spent the money they'd borrowed, was now having to pay interest on the loan as well as being expected to start to pay back some of the capital but without the benefit of the hoped for new business on which much of the financial projections justifying the loan had been based.

To start with matters weren't too serious. They were able to pay the interest and deferred the payback of capital. Their trading position remained steady not improving but the new machinery was working well reducing their production costs.

But by the end of 2005 not a single new contract had been obtained and things started to look very bleak, because not only was there no new business but once again pressure was being applied by their major customers to force Hardys to reduce their prices. Their customers had worked out that the company was now in a vulnerable position where it needed to keep supplying the contracts that it already had and although it needed new ones as well, the continuation of what it had was vital. So essential in fact that they would be prepared to supply even at lower prices in order to keep the volume flowing and the factory operating its new machinery.

The Bank started making increasingly frequent *"how are things going?"* phone calls firstly to Martin Fellows and then to William.

To start with Martin was able to keep the Bank at bay by giving relatively upbeat reports of how the business was developing but increasingly he found it more difficult to do this as really he had no good news for them at all. In fact all he had were worsening results as the pressure on their prices again forced their margins down, raw material price increases further eroded them and competitive pressure again increased.

In July of 2007 one of their major competitors launched a range of high quality products packaged in attractive new jars and at very competitive prices. Whilst all of their customers agreed to stock the new products the real blow was that three of them told Hardys that regrettably in order to make room for the newly launched competitive product range they would no longer be stocking Hardys products.

William and John did everything that they could to change this decision but to no avail. One customer agreed to give them two months before implementing the decision but the other two actioned it straight away.

Once William and Martin had calculated the effect of this on the business they felt that they had to insist on an extraordinary board meeting so that all the directors of the company were aware of the implications.

'Well have to talk to the bank immediately' William announced as soon as the meeting started. 'After all this is a major change to the business and will have serious implications on our ability to repay the loans. I mean let's be honest with ourselves' he went on quietly, 'we can't pay back the loans, not with this sort of business loss. In fact we'll be lucky to keep the business afloat at all'.

'Look we need more time to try and fight back against this decision' replied John Benton anxious that his reputation as a Sales Director was now in danger of being seriously dented as he hadn't been able to get any new business on the back of the factory investment.

'Time is what we don't have' snapped William. 'We knew, well at least I knew, that this expansion plan was a risk and it seems as though it's coming home to roost. Let's go through the position with each customer one by one again and see if we can determine any way of getting them to change their mind'.

So they did. For several hours they discussed the situation but try as they might they could find no magic bullet that would change the state of affairs in which they were.

William wrote to each of their major customers explaining how vital it was that Hardys not only didn't have its business reduced but needed more volume to support their factory expansion plans.

Two customers wrote back saying they were sorry but their decisions were made and would not be changed. One rang him and whilst expressing great sympathy for William's position would not change their decision. Two others didn't bother to respond.

William felt the weight of the business's problems on his shoulders. He looked at the photographs of his grandfather and father that were on his wall. They had been so successful. Where had it all gone wrong? They had taken chances indeed many more than he had, yet they'd always come out all right. His one big strategic move to modernise and update the factory which he'd hoped would bring lots of new business had been a crashing failure.

Sadly he picked up the phone and dialled the bank. After a brief pause he was put through to Frank Gold at the Regional Office of Foreign and International Bank who were now responsible for handling the Hardys account. Since Hardys had signalled on several occasions that it was having difficulty in repaying the loan Frank had recently upgraded the Hardys file from "Low" to **"Medium"** risk and kept a close watch on the account.

He and Frank spoke for about twenty minutes and when he finished talking William sat looking into space reflecting on the conversation.

Frank though immediately made another call this time to the Head Office of the Bank in London and asked to speak to Barry Field. He got through after a little while and spoke earnestly and quietly for some time.

'I think you'd better come and see me to brief me more fully on this as it sounds as though we might have a problem on our hands doesn't it? Could you come in on Thursday about eleven and can you let me have your file straight away so I can read it and get briefed before we meet?' asked Barry.

Shit he thought, just what the Bank didn't want. Another business going pear shaped if that was what was going to happen. Family businesses that got into trouble were difficult to turn round. Oh well he'd know more when he'd read the file in detail and then after Thursday when he'd talked with Frank Gold.

Frank sent the file to Head Office who after studying the document raised the classification from "Medium" to **"High"** risk.

William left the office at the end of that day knowing that matters if not already outside his control soon would be and it was a sad dispirited journey that he took back to Wood Hollow Hall.

Janie had reminded him to be home at a reasonable time as they were entertaining that evening and although he didn't feel like being the cheerful host he knew it was the role that he had to play. After all his position in the County and local community dictated that he and Janie gave or attended many dinner parties and it was normally something that he enjoyed.

His mood was still sombre as he bathed and changed for dinner then making his way downstairs he poured himself a very large gin and tonic, a glass of white wine for Janie and settled down to await the arrival of their guests.

Whilst worried about the business he could never have dreamed that one seriously disgruntled man was about to cause him so many problems.

Fidelity - a virtue peculiar to those about to be betrayed.

Ambrose Bierce.

CHAPTER 3

9th August 2007

The next morning William got up early trying not to disturb Janie as it was just after six when he went downstairs. He made himself a pot of tea and carried a tray of mugs out to the fire crew that were still there sitting in the fire engine. There were a few wisps of smoke drifting slowly upwards from various parts of the ruined building and as he stared at the destruction he saw that there was little left of the barn which had virtually completely collapsed and one of the stable blocks was now just blackened walls with no roof but the other was far less damaged. The tack room side of the quadrangle of buildings was the least damaged of all.

The firemen sipped their tea gratefully and told him that they thought the whole lot would have to be bulldozed and rebuilt. They said that they'd stay around for a while until their chief returned and authorised them to leave when he deemed it be safe and secure and unlikely to re-ignite. Looking up William saw the sky was dark and cloudy and thought that rain would come soon which would help with ensuring the fire was out completely.

He went back to the house and just before seven Maggie their housekeeper walked in.

'Morning Maggie you're early today'.

'Well I wanted to make an early start to clear everything up from your dinner party last night but then old Billy from the village knocked at my cottage and told me about the fire so I came straight away. Terrible isn't it? However did it happen?'

'We don't know at this stage but we'll find out. The fire brigade will come back later today to see if it was arson'.

'Arson? Goodness me. Whoever would do such a wicked thing eh Mr. Hardy? Arson well I never'.

'Well we don't know for sure at the moment but the firemen are suspicious as the horses had been let out into the field. Talking about the firemen could you rustle up some bacon and eggs for them please as I expect they're hungry?'

Nodding she walked away to get the breakfast going as requested muttering to herself 'Arson well whatever next?' intending to tell a few of her friends as soon as she could that someone had deliberately burnt down the stable block at the big house.

Janie had heard William get out of bed but she'd pretended to be asleep and after he'd gone downstairs she lay there unable to get back to sleep and thought about last night's fire but also about William who at fifty two was thirteen years older than her but already much older in his ways.

Also it was some time since they'd made love. The problem was that William had never been really very good at it and now their long sensual bouts of lovemaking seemed to have gone and it was just sex. He'd never been a very passionate man and over the last eighteen months or so it had got worse.

Maybe it had something to do with the business which she knew wasn't doing terribly well but was that really the reason? She was sure that he hadn't got a lover as he was too upright and stuffy for that and so she supposed that they had simply drifted into what they had now. A very comfortable lifestyle, but in many ways fairly sterile. Probably the same for many wealthy married couples with kids away at school she imagined.

She recalled first meeting him all those years ago at a drinks party not long after her twenty first birthday and how they'd enjoyed each other's company during the evening but it hadn't led to a date. Janie was in her final year at university where she had gained something of a reputation as a prick teaser as she was a sociable girl and easily made friends. On dates she liked arousing men but was quite choosy as to whom she'd allow to sleep with her.

She'd discovered a liking for sex and was an enthusiastic performer in bed and the fact that not only did she sleep with various men but was also known to be good in bed enhanced the desire of many others to try and get her into bed.

Graduating with a 2:1 degree in Arts and Social Science she drifted around for a while before finding work in an antiques shop in Holt a small market town in north Norfolk.

Her mother had long given up hope of her finding what she called a proper job but tolerated her "poking around with old bits of furniture" as she described her job. Actually Janie loved working with antiques and showed some aptitude for it, quickly learning what was real and what was fake.

Simon Wentworth who owned the business liked having her in his shop. At five feet nine she was tall, had long dark hair and slim with a nice figure, but her best features were her long legs which she often showed to advantage as she tended to wear quite short skirts. Bright intelligent and attractive, Simon was sure that she helped his business considerably when the old colonels and other elderly gentlemen came to browse. She seemed to easily get them eating out of her hand and sold many pieces of furniture purely through her gentle beguiling charm. Even elderly women seemed to like her. Yes he often thought she was a real asset.

Janie had a wide circle of friends in her home county of Norfolk and she was constantly in demand from various young men wanting to date and bed her, but it wasn't until she met up with William again at a friend's dinner party where he'd been seated next to her that she'd taken any real notice of him as a man rather than just a dinner companion and that evening she found that she thoroughly enjoyed his company again as she had when she'd met him before.

He was an excellent conversationalist; amusing, interesting and good looking so when the party was breaking up and he'd asked her if she'd like to meet again for dinner sometime her reply was yes.

That was the start of their romance and William had slowly captivated her with his slightly old fashioned approach to life, his impeccable manners and although not a crucial matter for her in the choice of a future husband, she couldn't help but realise that he was wealthy and that could only be beneficial for her future life.

The romance developed over time and when eventually he'd asked her to marry him she'd surprised herself and delighted him by saying yes. The fact that he was considerably older didn't concern her at the time, as she felt the benefit of his age and experience of life was part of his charm. She also realised that in some ways she was looking for a father type figure for a future husband as her own father had died from a sudden stroke when she was only ten years old and although her mother had done a wonderful job in bringing her up she had missed not having a father. William in one way provided a similar reassurance that an older father figure would have done but which a younger man of her own age couldn't.

Throughout their romance she'd refused to sleep with him and even after their engagement she told him that he'd have to wait until they were married before she'd go to bed with him.

She was unsure why she put these restrictions on him as she really wanted to have sex with him but somehow the fact that he was much older than her and his old fashioned approach to life and love not only appealed to her but just seemed to make it the sort of thing that they should do. He for his part had not seemed too put out by this and happy to accept her rules.

Janie assumed this was because of his older age approach to life and romance, whereas the younger men around her own age that she'd dated in the past all just seemed to want to get her knickers off as soon as they could. However she did insist on a short engagement and looked forward to marrying and sleeping with her future husband.

He was quite a catch being head of a large manufacturing business, known to be wealthy and lived in beautiful old Wood Hollow Hall.

The marriage was a typical Norfolk county affair with the ceremony taking place in the very small and extremely old church in the village in which Janie lived with her mother at Willowtree farm which was no longer a working farm, the majority of the land having been sold off many years ago. Now just five acres surrounding the old seventeenth century farm house, sufficient for Janie and her mother to keep a couple of horses in the paddocks.

As their farmhouse was only a hundred yards or so from the church Janie's Uncle Arthur who was giving her away walked her through the village to the church. Many of the local people turned out to wave and wish her well.

A large marquee had been pitched on the lawn of Wood Hollow Hall and the reception and post wedding lunch was held there. The speeches were witty and not too long. William an accomplished confident speaker particularly excelled with an amusing speech that had most of the invited guests, who numbered nearly two hundred, laughing uproariously. All in all it was described afterwards as a very happy occasion with the bride looking beautiful and the groom extremely handsome. The event finished in some style as a helicopter clattered into sight and landed on one of the paddocks to whisk the happy couple away on their honeymoon.

'At least no one can follow us' grinned the happy bridegroom as he helped Janie who'd changed into a pretty little dress and matching jacket clamber up into the small cabin.

The pilot congratulated them and then made sure the doors were shut before flicking the switch to start the rotor turning and soon the machine lurched into the air. Being a bit of a showman at heart and knowing that it was a special occasion he lifted about one hundred feet into the air then hovered and tipped the nose down and up a few times symbolising the happy couple waving goodbye before turning and heading for Norwich airport where Janie and William transferred to a private jet that he'd chartered to fly them to Greece.

Their first night together was spent in the bridal suite at the five star hotel in Athens and after arrival they had a drink in the bar while their bags were taken to their room. William then suggested that they make a move upstairs. Soon he held open the door into the huge room and held out his arms to carry her over the threshold. She jumped into his strong embrace giggling as they entered the room whereupon she kicked her feet to send her shoes clattering one by one onto the floor before he laid her on the bed and kissed her.

'William darling thank you, but I must go and freshen up. I'm all grubby after the travelling and I want to be nice and fresh and fragrant for you. Can you work out how the bath works and run me one that's really hot and deep while maybe you'd like to have a shower so we're ready for each other at about the same time? I've been waiting all day for you to take me to bed and make love to me, well for the last few months actually'.

Soon she heard the sound of running water and when he returned she turned her back and asked him to unzip her. He ran it down to its full extent exposing a pale pink bra strap and as she wriggled out of the dress he saw the matching pretty knickers and hold up tan stockings. Turning back to face him she moved a little way away and slowly turned round in a compete circle then blew him a kiss before repeating the turn but in the opposite direction.

'Well darling are you happy with your bride?'

'You look exquisite. I am so lucky and I can't believe that you've married an old codger like me'.

'You're not old darling, just a little more mature than me. After all at thirty eight you're in your prime while I'm a mere slip of a girl in my mid twenties' and laughing happily she'd run into the bathroom carrying a wash bag and some flimsy items of clothing.

He undressed and showered in the separate shower cubicle quickly feeling his excitement rise as he thought of their coming lovemaking. Drying himself he walked to the large bed where a moment of concern flashed through his mind as he hoped that he'd be good enough in bed for her.

He also thought briefly of his first wife Dawn. Their marriage had only lasted a couple of years until she'd run off with a vet and he'd remained single since then. He'd had the odd brief affair but nothing serious until he'd met Janie with whom he'd fallen deeply in love, amazed that such a young and beautiful girl had agreed to marry him.

It wasn't long before the bathroom door opened and his new bride emerged. She was wearing a beautiful white nightdress and negligee which were almost see through and decorated with several pretty lace trimmings. Her dark hair shone and she had only the slightest traces of makeup. As she walked towards the bed the movement of her long legs caused the negligee to move open and he could see through the nightdress where the dark triangle at the top of her legs was clearly visible. She was simply stunning and he could feel himself erecting as he looked at her.

Later he asked 'Was that all right for you darling? I mean really alright? I just want to make you so happy in every way. In our lives, in our love and especially in our bed'.

'William darling it was wonderful, thank you' she replied softly, conscious that although it wasn't the best sex she'd ever had it was certainly by no means the worst and no doubt as they got to know each other more it would get better. Later they made love again.

The next morning they took a taxi to the docks and then a chartered boat whisked them to a tiny island in the Aegean where William had rented a secluded villa. It had beautiful gardens full of colourful flowers which attracted all sorts of birds and butterflies and was situated above a little private cove where they could swim in total seclusion. Janie persuaded him to skinny dip in the warm sea and they made love on the beach. They had their own small swimming pool and spent many a happy hour lying beside it or simply rolling in to cool off and swim.

Janie spent a great deal of the time naked and gradually William did as well although he was never quite so comfortable as she was wandering around without any clothes on. She said that as it was so hot it helped keep cool and also saved time undressing when they made love which they did frequently on their little secluded beach, in the sea, by the pool, in the pool and of course in bed.

About five minutes walk away was a little taverna which offered a good selection of fish dishes as well as amazingly tender beef steaks or lightly grilled lamb cutlets. They often ate there or sometimes instead bought some simple food ingredients from the one little shop on the island to which they walked every other day. It took about twenty minutes and they made their way to where it was located in a tiny village by walking through the warm blue sea, along beaches and scrambling over some rocks.

Their three weeks honeymoon was idyllic. They were both very much in love with each other and so it continued when they returned to England and she moved into Wood Hollow Hall which had been built in the eighteen hundreds and consisted of the old house, the wonderful stable and carriage block and several hundred acres of woods, paddocks and parkland.

She'd fallen pregnant with their first child when she was twenty seven just two years after they married and then two years later had become pregnant again.

When they were old enough both sons had gone to boarding school something on which William had insisted as he wanted the tradition started by his father and then himself to be continued therefore the boys went to Stowe following in the family footsteps.

So Janie's life had evolved. In many ways she had everything for which she could want. Horses to ride around the countryside or hunt before it had been banned, a Porsche sports car and a VW Golf estate as a runabout. Plenty of money to spend on clothes or entertaining, a wide circle of friends and a lovely home. Other people looking at her would see a happy contented wife who lacked for nothing, with a loving husband who provided everything for her.

But as she lay there on that morning after William had gone down to see the firemen she felt a certain emptiness in her life and reflected on her marriage with William.

Although she felt the benefit and security of his being older than her she was also conscious that the very fact that he was older was also causing her some problems as not only was he getting stuffy but also recently often he was quite grumpy. She guessed that this was because things at his business were not going well and although she didn't know too much about the problems she did know that Hardy Preserves were finding trading conditions difficult and this was affecting William.

Maybe that's why she'd started to have an affair several months ago and she shivered as she thought of her lover with his zest for life, his carefree attitude to many things, his beautiful body but especially his wild uninhibited lovemaking which was so different from William.

It was nearly three weeks since she'd seen him and she needed him again now. Groaning she rolled onto her side and lay there for a little before rolling onto her other side then realising that it was no good and that not only would she not be able to get back to sleep but also if she stayed there her thoughts would simply get more erotic she took a deep breath, slid out of bed, had a quick shower and dressing in jeans, sweater and short brown fashion boots ran downstairs where the smell of a cooked English breakfast assailed her as she entered the huge old kitchen.

Sitting at the table some of the firemen were chatting to William and Maggie who was bustling about still tidying up from last night's dinner party.

'Morning' Janie said brightly to the room in general and smiled at the grubby faced firemen who looked tired.

'I'm going to have a good look around outside do you want to come as well?' queried William. 'You'll need a mac and some wellies as it's started to rain and there's a lot of muck about from the fire' he went on.

'Ok give me a moment' and she went to the small boot room that led off the scullery behind the kitchen, changed footwear and pulled on a well worn dark green Barbour wax jacket. William had waited for her and together they went outside to survey the ruined stable block and barn.

'William it's horrible. Seeing it here in daylight it looks so awful. It's just a pile of rubble, a complete ruin. I mean just look at those black roof beams sticking up. They look like burnt ribs' and they walked sadly around the entire devastated block amazed that the destruction was so complete. Gingerly William stepped into the ash and picked his way across the piles of brick rubble heeding Janie's cries for him to be careful. He wasn't sure what he was looking for but felt that he ought to look.

His studying of the damage was interrupted by the sound of a car crunching up the drive and as he looked up he saw a police car pull to a halt in front of the house and a young uniformed police officer get out, put on his cap and walk towards the ruined buildings.

As William went towards him Janie said that she'd check the horses and went into the parkland to look over the animals in daylight to ensure that they really were alright.

'Morning sir. I've come about this fire business as I believe you rang a couple of times last night and on one occasion reported that it had been started deliberately'.

'Not exactly. What I said was that the fire chief here said that he thought it must have been started deliberately'.

'What makes him and you think that sir?'

'The fact that the horses had been taken out of the stables. They were all bedded down for the night and if it had started accidentally then they'd have been trapped inside but they weren't as someone had taken them out into the fields at the back of the stables. There you can see them now' he added pointing at the horses.

'Could they have got out there by themselves?' queried the policeman.

'No of course they couldn't. They'd each have to have opened two outside bolts on their stable doors, walked across the yard opened a latched gate, then opened the large field gate into the park and then shut it behind them. No that's a bloody silly suggestion. Whoever set fire to the building must have let them out first. Now what are you going to do about it?' he finished aggressively.

The young officer didn't really know what he was going to do about it. If it was true that it was arson then it was a matter for CID and if not well it would just get reported as a fire. He thought for a moment and then said that he'd like to look around. William led him towards the ruined buildings where Janie met the two of them.

'The horses are fine darling but I think I'll go indoors and start ringing round our friends to find stabling for them until we get things sorted out as it's obviously going to be months and months before the stables are rebuilt'.

William nodded and then led the police officer around the outside of the devastated stable and barn blocks. Soon the firemen came out of the house and the policeman went over to confer with them before returning to William to say that he thought that he'd better refer the matter to CID and with that he went back and sat in his car.

Although he couldn't hear what was said William could see that the young police officer was talking earnestly into his phone. After a short while he re-emerged from the car to say that he'd reported the suspicions that it might be arson to his sergeant, that someone from CID would be in touch shortly and that he didn't think there was much else that he could do for now and with that he climbed back in the car and drove off.

Next to arrive was the Crew Chief from the previous evening who came up the drive in a red car and straight away conferred with the firemen who'd been on duty all night. He walked round the burnt out building before confirming to the fire crew that they could leave.

Approaching William and Janie he smiled, said how sorry he was for the destruction and advised that the fire brigade forensic team would be there later in the morning but that he was satisfied that it was now safe to remove his fire crew. However if they were worried, or in the event of any flare up which he thought was unlikely especially as it was now raining quite steadily, then they were to call them back again straight away.

When the fire car and the fire engine had gone all seemed desolate and depressing as William slouched into his study to contact the insurance company and his office.

***

At about that same time, the man was taking his fifteen minute nine o'clock breakfast break that was permitted for the early shift workers who had clocked on at six that morning.

His head ached from the whisky that he'd drunk the night before and he'd certainly felt rough when the alarm clock jerked him awake at five fifteen that morning. Sitting up quickly he'd got out of bed and gone to the bathroom where he washed and shaved before putting on a clean tee shirt, a light sweater and his work overalls. Then he'd walked downstairs made himself a cup of tea listened to the local radio to see if there was any mention of his fire raising, but there wasn't. He thought that maybe it was too early for the news reporters to have discovered about the fire which made him reflect on what he'd done.

His emotions were a mixture of satisfaction and apprehension as he was pleased that he'd finally put his plan into action but also he was acutely conscious that he'd committed a very serious offence. Shrugging his shoulders he stood up, pulled on his black leather jacket and gloves, opened a drawer of a cupboard in the kitchen and carefully took out the already sealed envelope which he tucked inside his jacket before zipping it up.

Leaving the house he unchained his moped pushed it onto the roadway outside, pressed the starter and set off for his place of work. On the way he paused briefly at a post box in the town to post his letter muttering quietly 'Now we'll see what that does Mr. Hardy' certain in his mind that there was nothing about the letter to incriminate him.

Having read that the police were able to obtain DNA evidence from the tiniest fragment of human contact, the writing pad and envelopes that he'd used had been bought from Woolworths and paid for in cash.

He'd been wearing gloves when he'd been in the shop and then when he'd put the paper in the old fashioned portable typewriter to type the short message he'd also worn gloves this time thin latex ones so he could tap at the keys. He kept them on when removing the paper and replacing it with the envelope.

The portable typewriter he'd bought a few months ago at a car boot sale, as if ever questions were asked of him he knew that had he typed the letter on his home computer even pressing the "delete" button could not guarantee that some traces of the message would not remain somewhere inside the machine which a clever policeman might be able to find and so use to trap him.

The envelope was a self sealing type so he didn't have to lick the flap to seal it. Similarly he'd made sure that when he'd bought the book of stamps they were the self adhesive type so again he didn't have to lick and betray himself through his saliva. He'd worn his latex gloves when he'd peeled one off to fix to the envelope.

Yes he nodded to himself as he rode towards his work place he was sure that he hadn't made any silly mistakes so far but he knew he would have to continue his personal vigilance to be sure that he remained the unknown perpetrator of his actions. He also knew that many criminals betrayed themselves by making just one small mistake which eventually led to their capture. The old typewriter was his big risk but he wasn't sure yet for how long he would need it. Soon it would have to go and he knew the exact place to get rid of it. There was a bridge in a deserted position spanning a river which he knew was deep and would hide forever the old typewriter when he chucked it into the water.

Reflecting as he ate his greasy bacon and eggs in the canteen he thought about the next part of his plan and realised that although he had a general idea about what he was going to do, to some extent he'd have to play much of it off the cuff as things evolved. It would largely depend on the reaction to the letter.

***

William's secretary, Mary had been the first to receive the news when he'd rung her and said that a fire last night had destroyed the stable block but that as it looked like arson he had to stay at home today and see the police and fire specialists. He asked her to cancel all his meetings and re-organise his diary as he expected to be back in tomorrow.

So that morning Hardy Preserves was alive with discussion and rumour about the fire at Mr. William's house last night. First it was said that the whole house had burnt down. Then it was said that it was just the barn. Then it was the barn and stables. Then it was house, stables and the barn. It took time before it was understood by all that it was the barn and stable block and that the house was undamaged.

'Oh bloody hell that's fuc.......err... that's very inconvenient' snapped Martin Fellows quickly correcting his expletive when Mary explained that Mr. William wouldn't be in today. He also was still irritated by the way the older people in the business referred to William as Mr. William.

It was an old anachronism stemming from a time when William's grandfather Douglas Hardy had started and then run the business. He was always referred to as Mr. Hardy but when his son James had been brought into the business to work alongside the old man, to avoid confusion of two Mr. Hardys he was known as Mr. James while the father remained as Mr. Hardy. After Douglas's death James became Chairman and hence Mr. Hardy, but when he in his turn brought William into the business then James continued to be called Mr. Hardy while William became known as Mr. William.

It was a practice often used in family firms throughout the land and seemed to work well. Therefore when William took over the reins as Chairman of the family business he was elevated to being known as Mr. Hardy and he expected that in time his sons would join the business and be known in turn as Mr. Simon and Mr. Charles. Mary however continued to call him Mr. William.

However to a modern executive such as Fellows it was symptomatic of much that was wrong with the business.

Fellows was forty five years old, five foot ten, slim, worked out in a gym twice a week, had an eye for a pretty girl, was married with three children, wore suits from M & S, and was a reasonably effective finance director. But he was frustrated with the business in general and William in particular.

When Mary had left his office he dialled two internal numbers and snapped 'My office now' to each person who answered before putting down the phone. He didn't bother with the niceties of life when in the office as he knew that the tough job he had was to try and help save the business from going bust.

If he could do it then he'd earn himself a decent performance bonus and enhance his reputation. If he couldn't not only would he not earn the bonus, but in addition his reputation would be tarnished for the first time not something that a career minded Finance Director wanted on his CV at all.

Also the workforce and staff would be out of a job. Well maybe not all as if the business couldn't get turned around then it would probably be bought by a competitor and although some of the employees would get jobs with the new employer probably not many, as any new owner would either want to close this factory and transfer production to an existing plant or would install more modern machinery here requiring far less people in this factory.

The people he'd summoned arrived in his office. John Benton the Sales Director and Geoff Hawkins the Operations Director whose responsibilities included production, warehousing and transport joined him.

'William won't be in today' grumbled Martin as soon as all were present. 'Some sort of fire at his home. Gather no-one's hurt but naturally he's got things to sort out there. Fucking nuisance though, as I was hoping to have a conference call with the bank today and really we need him here for that. However as he's not here I intend to still proceed with the call and we'll just have to update him tomorrow or whenever he's next in'.

'What caused it, the fire I mean?'

'No idea' replied Fellows in a tone that indicated he hadn't got time to concern himself with that as he looked at Geoff who'd asked the question. 'Now let's review how things are going shall we? John how are the new products coming along? Are our customers taking them and are they taking them in the quantities that we need?'

'Well it's early days yet of course but I am pretty confident that we'll get somewhere close to where we want to be but it's tough out there'.

'Of course it's tough. That's why we're paid our large salaries and get fancy company cars to produce, market and sell large quantities of our products. I have to tell you that the Bank is getting a little tired of hearing about how tough it is and then hearing excuses for why we're not hitting our sales and hence our profit targets. Look if we can't do it then the bank will either replace the lot of us, or foreclose the business. Understand?'

Turning to look at the Operations Director he snapped 'Sorted our production line six yet?'

'Not yet but we're working on it flat out and I think we'll have it back up and running later today or tomorrow'.

'I saw two of your engineers in the canteen playing cards this morning. Ok ok' he said holding up his hands as he saw that Geoff was about to interrupt him, 'I know that they're entitled to their break but I'd have thought that if they understood the urgency of sorting this breakdown they'd have grabbed a quick cuppa and a bacon roll or something and got back to the shop floor to work on the machine. Need to instil a sense of urgency there Geoff.

Now let me show you what the latest cash flow looks like....... and it ain't pretty' he added as he handed the others detailed financial schedules. 'We're not making progress as I'd like. I'm pushing back payments as much as I can to our suppliers and paying them in rotation on the basis that he who screams loudest gets paid first and he who remains silent waits. The trouble is more and more are screaming louder and louder and we're not getting the cash in quickly enough from our customers.

Whilst our suppliers are wanting payment in about thirty days although I've pushed most to between forty and forty five days, with our biggest customers not paying us for about sixty days or more then we're fighting a losing battle. Something's got to give. Either we get paid more quickly or we go bust. We've no reserves, we're almost at our overdraft limit and the Bank is making very unhelpful noises regarding our request to increase the overdraft again.

I really think that this time they're going to say no and if they do that I don't know what we're going to do. All in all therefore we are in a right fucking mess.

The trouble is guys we have problems in all the major parts of the business. That's unusual. Often when businesses get into trouble it's because one or maybe two major things are going wrong. Here we've got everything going wrong, so that means we've just got to fight harder on all fronts to survive and then climb out of this mess'.

He looked at the two other men sitting in his office as he said this and glancing from one to another he noticed the look of concern on both their faces. 'Right let's get on with our jobs shall we......... meeting over'.

Privately Fellows thought that William should spend more time in the business rather than shooting, riding or spending days fishing in Scotland. After all as Chairman he had a responsibility to the business and the people employed within it. Long gone were the times when business could be a hobby. Hardys was too big for that. It was a major manufacturer of jams, preserves and pickles.

***

At Wood Hollow Hall, William had finished talking on the phone with the Insurance Company who said that they'd logged the claim and would be sending an investigator and loss assessor out to him as a matter of urgency.

Shortly after that the Fire and Rescue Service forensic team arrived. Two men both ex fire fighters who had moved onto the special investigation section which was more interesting, and safer, than fighting live fires. They introduced themselves listened carefully to what William could tell them about last night, asked a number of questions and then said that they'd get on with their work now but might want to talk to him again later.

They worked diligently in the drizzling rain, knew exactly what they were looking for, took lots of samples and bits of burnt timber, bagged shovels full of wet ash and after several hours knocked on the door and told William that they were finished for now, but might want to return later.

'Well was it arson?' William asked.

'Difficult to be certain at the moment as we need to conduct tests in the lab, but I'd put a pound to a penny that an accelerant was used, yes'.

'An accelerant?'

'A flammable liquid used to start the fire in several places in the buildings sir. So yes, I think you can take it that it was deliberate. The question is who would have done it, but that's not our job sir. That's for the police. Well good day sir and very sorry that you've suffered such a fire, still hopefully the boys in blue will catch whoever did it. This looks like them now'.

William watched as the two fire specialists waited as the Rover police car came up the drive and then saw them speak for a while to the two people who emerged before getting into their own car and driving off.

The two plain clothes police officers walked across the drive glancing at the pile of burnt rubble as they did so.

'Mr. Hardy?' asked the middle aged man. 'Good morning sir. I'm Detective Inspector Fulton from CID and this is WPC Anne Shaw. It's obvious why we're here. Can we go inside out of this rain?'

William led the way taking the two police officers into his study. Janie looked in and asked if they'd all like coffee. They said they would.

The Inspector started by asking William to go over the details of when they'd discovered the fire and why he'd originally thought it was deliberate and listening to the point about the horses being removed and placed in the field for safety, agreed that it did seem likely to have been an act of deliberate arson. He asked lots of questions and probed as to whether William might have had any enemies who would wish to do such a thing.

'I can think of no-one who would be so wicked' replied William bluntly. 'I have no enemies. Business rivals yes of course, competitors who are ruthless in the trading environment with our customers but that's what business is all about but I simply do not believe that any of them would do this.

You know of course that my wife and I were keen members of the local West Norfolk Hunt and that of course attracted lots of people who were opposed to hunting and led them to protest, sometimes violently, but hunting was banned following that daft anti-countryside vote in the House of Commons. We now ride around following an artificial scent.

I mean if this had occurred when we were hunting foxes I could have perhaps understood it more, but we haven't hunted for ages. The anti's achieved what they wanted and got hunting banned so why attack us now?

They won and we lost. I guess that's democracy for you, even if I don't like the result'.

He was speaking strongly when he finished, a point noted by Inspector Fulton.

'What about your wife sir' asked WPC Shaw? 'Would she have any enemies?'

'No of course not. Everyone loves Janie. Naturally she used to hunt as well so the same comments apply to her but I am certain she has no enemies but feel free to ask her yourself'.

'We will sir, thank you'.

'Were the horses valuable?' asked WPC Shaw.

'Not in the sense of Red Rum or other famous racehorses, no. We have two point to pointers.....'

'Two what?' interrupted the Inspector.

'Kind of racehorse' advised the WPC. 'Usually not very top flight, sort of more middle of the road generally wouldn't you say Mr.. Hardy?'

'Well I'm not sure I'd quite put it like that but you're on the right lines certainly. Then there are the some hunters.........'

'Horses used for hunting' added the WPC looking at her superior.

'I can work out what a hunter is seeing that we've just been talking about hunting and we're now talking about horses thank you' he replied sarcastically. 'Carry on sir'.

'Err, well yes to continue in addition to the two pointers there's four hunters, a brood mare, a couple of youngsters, and a couple of old retired horses that are just quietly living out their days in retirement. That's it. Thirty thousand pounds would cover the lot of them. As I said nothing of great value'.

'To some people sir thirty thousand pounds is a fortune. People have been killed for a lot less than that you know' the policeman replied somewhat gruffly.

'Yes of course. I didn't mean that. I was simply trying...........'

'I know what you meant sir. Now then you say that the point to pointers are not particularly valuable but do large sums of money get bet on these sorts of races?'

William thought for a moment and then talked in some detail to both police officers about racing in general and point to pointing in particular. Several more questions were asked on a wide range of subjects with detailed notes being taken of the whole interview and then they asked to speak with Mrs. Hardy.

Going out into the large hallway William called for Janie who had just finished phoning a friend who'd agreed to stable the pointers until further notice, so she joined them all in the study and spent the next half an hour answering the police questions.

Eventually the Inspector said that he was finished with William and Janie for now and thanked them both for their help and co-operation. He admitted that he was at a loss at present to know who might be behind it but that they would proceed with their enquiries and keep touch. The police woman turned to Janie and asked how many staff they kept for the house, grounds and stables and whether anyone had been dismissed recently?

William replied that there was the housekeeper, her husband who looked after the gardens, grounds and woods, two stable girls and a part time odd job man, but none of them had been dismissed.

Inspector Fulton said that they'd want to see all those people and would come back tomorrow to interview them and could arrangements be made to have them all available.

William walked the two police to their car and waved as they drove off down the drive before turning back to Janie.

'How have you got on getting the horses into alternative stabling?'

'Oh fine. Everyone's been terribly helpful. To save us the hassle of taking them around everyone's coming here with their own horse lorries or trailers to take them away for us. People have been so kind and understanding'.

'Well that's how things happen in the country. Right now I need to go and ring the office again. See you later'.

During the day various horsebox lorries or four wheel drives pulling trailers trundled up the drive, and Janie helped the drivers load whichever horses it was agreed that that particular person was going to have. It was all done very smoothly and without difficulty.

When complete the place seemed strange without any horses around but at least they were safely stabled with friends until Wood Hollow's stables could be rebuilt.

Later in the afternoon Janie looked into William's study and saw that he was on the phone talking agitatedly. She stood for a while in the hallway thinking whether there was anything else she needed to do as a result of the fire or simply from having a large house to run and deciding that there wasn't she crossed the hall and walked upstairs to their bedroom.

Sitting on their bed she picked up her mobile phone and dialled a London number.

When it was answered she asked for Harry Norton.

A half-truth is still a whole lie.

Jewish proverb.

CHAPTER 4

10th August 2007 - onwards

It was the day after she'd rung Harry when Janie spoke to William over breakfast.

'Darling with the horses taken care of and the place crawling with police, firemen and insurance assessors I'm not sure that I can stand being here after the shock of the fire. I need to get away so would you mind if I went to France for a few days? You don't need me here do you?' and she smiled at him.

He looked worried and with good reason. The insurance company would pay for the fire damage so although lots of inconvenience and no doubt dozens of forms to fill in, ultimately it would be rebuilt. It was Hardys and its difficulties that really was eating into him but she knew nothing about business and couldn't help except by making sympathetic noises from time to time.

Looking up from his bacon and eggs he smiled wearily. 'Good idea. Wish I was coming with you. Maybe I could join you after a few days'.

Hell that was the last thing she wanted!

Smiling sweetly she answered softly 'Oh William that would be lovely but surely you won't be able to get away with all that's going on here and the problems at the office?'

'No I very much doubt it but never mind there'll always be another time. Mind you if I could find a day or so to get away I can always pop down and join you. I'll let you know'.

Still worried that he might decide to join her she patted his hand and replied 'It would be nice if you were there too but I'm sure you're better here in case the police or the fire service people come back. Also the insurance people will need your help. I don't think you can realistically think about going away can you?'

'Probably not. No in fact definitely not. You're right. I must stay here for the aftermath of the fire and the problems at the office. Now when will you go?'

Good that's that sorted. He's not coming.

'I'll get on the internet this morning and see what flights I can get but frankly the sooner I can get away the better. Every time I look out of the window at where the stables were I get the shivers'.

'Poor darling. Look I've got to go now. I must make some phone calls and then the insurance man is coming to assess the damage'.

'Make sure that he agrees to rebuild in old bricks. They'll probably want all modern breezeblocks and things inside but outside it would be such a shame if a modern monstrosity arose from the ashes. We must make them agree to rebuild in keeping with the Hall'.

William nodded as he left the breakfast table and wandered into his study. Looking at him she thought he'd aged in the last few weeks as a result of the business problems and now the fire had added to his pressures.

When he'd gone she switched on the computer that nestled in the corner of the kitchen and tapped away searching for her flights to France. A few clicks of the mouse and she was booked on the lunchtime flight from Stansted. Smiling happily she picked up her mobile and walked into the garden on the far side of the Hall and opposite to the ruined stables.

'Hello there' she said when the call was connected. 'I'm going down this afternoon to open up the cottage, air the beds and get some food in. Are you still coming tomorrow? Can't you get away today?'

'No I'd love to but I'm up to my eyes in work here but I'll clear my diary from tonight and join you tomorrow for a few days. Not long to wait my darling. Will you pick me up from the airport?'

'Yes of course. Don't worry I'll look after you and not leave you stranded in the middle of France all alone and lost' she giggled. 'See you tomorrow. Bye' and blowing a kiss down the phone she broke the connection.

Next she scrolled through the memory and then pressed the number she'd wanted. It rang for a while until answered by a gruff sounding Frenchman.

'Oui?'

'Est que Pierre? Ceci est Janie Hardy, d'Angleterre. Je suis c'est la notification courte main je viens en France aujourd'hui. Pouvoir vous a ma voiture prete s'I'll vous plait?'

'Ah Madame Hardy. Bien sur. Pas ce sera d'ennui. A quelle heure arriverez-vous?'

'Oh le vol part ici a obtenir d'heure du dejeuner a vous autour de trios trente, votre temps'.

'Bon, pas de probleme. Au revoir Madame'.

They kept a car in France at a small old fashioned garage very close to the airport. Having rung old Pierre who's garage it was to firstly apologise for the short notice but then to tell him what time she'd arrive she knew that the car would not only be ready and waiting for her when she got there but the boy Jacques would have given it a wash, checked the oil and tyres and filled it up with petrol as well.

Next she went upstairs and packed some clothes into a grip bag. As the weather would be much hotter than in England she put in mainly lightweight things plus slacks, some pretty undies, two bikinis and a couple of sweaters in case the evenings got chilly.

Carrying the bag downstairs she dropped it by the door then went to find William.

'You off darling?' he queried as he put the phone down.

'Yes. I'll call you when I get there. I hope you can sort out the Hardys issues'.

'So do I' he said fervently his heart dropping at the thought of the size of the problems that were facing the business. 'Have a good break. Drive carefully'.

She loaded her bag into the Golf Estate and reversed slowly out of the garage block which was a converted coach house separate from the stables and drove down the drive. Reaching the lane at the end she put her foot down and headed for Stansted arriving around eleven o'clock. The check in was efficient and impersonal then she made her way through security and emigration to wait in the lounge for the Easyjet flight to be called, which it was just after midday.

The flight was cramped, fairly full but uneventful and shortly after landing at the French regional airport not too far from their cottage she collected her bag then walked the few hundred yards to Pierre's garage.

Once smartly painted blue and white now the paint was peeling and some of the woodwork was in need of repair. Outside were stacks of old tyres, some empty oil cans, a couple of old rusting engines, some broken gearboxes and several other piles of assorted junk connected with cars. However as she walked carefully inside, the old Frenchman saw her and his face lit up in a bright cheerful smile.

Removing the foul smelling cigarette from his lips he walked quickly across to her and leaning forward to avoid brushing his grubby overalls against her smart clothes, wiped his hand on his overalls, shook her hand, bid her welcome and said that her car was all ready for her. Refusing payment for now and telling her to settle up when she brought the car back he led her through the workshop where three cars in various states of repair or dismantlement took up most of the room inside.

'Jacques' he yelled as they walked out into a back yard and a boy aged about nineteen shuffled shyly forward. Pierre asked if Madame's car was ready and receiving a nod, he led Janie round the corner to her yellow left hand drive Renault Megane convertible, clean and shiny.

Smiling at the boy Janie took a five Euro note out of her purse and giving it to him told him that he'd done a wonderful job of cleaning the car.

He grinned happily as he'd been worried as there hadn't been much notice when old Pierre had told him to stop what he'd been doing and get Madame Hardy's car ready. So he'd washed and cleaned it, hoovered out the inside, checked the tyres and water and filled it with petrol. All in all it was a rush to get it done but she must be pleased with the result otherwise she wouldn't have given him the five Euros would she, he told himself.

Pierre loaded her bag into the boot and held open the door for her then waited as she pressed the button to lower the electric roof automatically. After a few whirs and clicks the roof slowly folded itself down and starting the open top car Janie drove carefully out of the garage and onto the little road that shortly led onto the major road. Heading south she accelerated and the miles sped past.

It was just over half an hour later that she pulled off the main road and turned onto a small road that wound through the southern French countryside until the village came into sight. Slowing she drove cautiously to the far end and then turned right up a short dirt track. After a few hundred metres she stopped at the iron gates, got out of the car and taking a key from her bag opened the large padlock that kept the six foot high gates securely fastened. Propping them open she drove inside and stopped in front of the cottage. Retracing her steps she pushed the gates shut and dropped the iron fastening into the ground but didn't padlock them.

Approaching the front door she turned the key, opened the door and stepped inside. There was a slight musty smell but she knew that as soon as the windows were opened throughout the cottage that would quickly disappear.

She walked around the inside to check that all was in order. It was, as after all it had only been a few weeks since she, William and the boys had come here for a long weekend. Her next task was to go outside and check round the garden which was quite neat and tidy showing that the local man they had come in to cut the grass and trim the shrubs and plants was doing his job.

Carrying her bag upstairs she unpacked and then set to make the bed. Holding the sheets to her nose she was satisfied that they were not damp and smelt fresh mainly as a result of the dried lavender that she'd put in the drawer and the little bags of silica crystals that absorbed any moisture.

The bed was soon made and after smoothing down the duvet cover she sat and thought about tomorrow before lying back and stretching out full length relaxing and letting her mind wander. She rested for a while then getting up changed into shorts, tee shirt, sandals and went back downstairs and spent the next half and hour dusting and polishing.

Looking at her completed handiwork she smiled, went out to the car and drove back into the village stopping at the grocers shop, the bakers and the butchers. She'd soon stocked up on what she thought would be needed for the next few days and went back to the cottage where she neatly stored away what she'd bought in the appropriate cupboards and fridge.

Next she checked the pool and removing the cover was pleased to see that it was clean having obviously been looked after by the garden man during their absence.

Feeling a little grubby after the travelling, cleaning and shopping she stripped off and after checking the temperature with her hand, lowered herself naked into the water and swam slowly up and down.

The little pool here was nothing like the huge pool they had at Wood Hollow Hall but was ideal for cooling off and freshening up. Getting out she walked to the little shed, pulled out a sunlounger, spread a cushion on it and stretched out to let the late warm summer sun dry her. She lay face down for a while before turning onto her back to soak up the sun's warmth, the peace and quiet, the buzzing of the bees, the birds chirping and the general relaxation that this place always generated.

They had bought it four years ago as they both loved France and wanted a little bolt hole in the south. The opening up of budget airline flights to the nearby small regional airport had made getting here so easy whereas previously it had been a long hard drive from Calais.

When she'd come down before it had been with William or with William and the boys but this was the first time that she'd come alone.

Thinking of William reminded her that she'd promised to call him when she arrived, so going back indoors she took her mobile out of her bag and dialled. There was no answer so she left a message saying all was well then went back outside and laid down again on the sunlounger and dropped off to sleep.

When she woke the sun had cooled and giving a little shiver she went back indoors got dressed and then checking the time decided to get herself something to eat. It only took a few minutes to whip up an omelette and salad with some crusty French bread all of which she'd bought earlier, helped down with a glass of red wine.

Having eaten and washed up she switched on the TV and channel flipped for a while eventually settling to watch the BBC overseas news programme but there was nothing of great interest and so she poured herself another glass of wine and wondered once again who could have been so wicked as to set fire to their stables and especially why they'd let the horses out beforehand.

Deciding that it was too difficult to answer and no doubt the police would find out in due course she selected a CD and switched on the player, leant back and enjoyed the soft music. She allowed her mind to drift until around ten she switched off everything downstairs, walked up the narrow staircase to the larger of the two bedrooms, undressed, washed and slid into the bed she'd made earlier.

It took her a long time to go to sleep partly as a result of having dozed in the garden earlier but also through thinking that tomorrow she wouldn't be alone in this bed and it was around midnight when she finally lost herself and didn't hear a sound until the alarm jerked her awake at seven the next morning.

Knowing she had plenty of time she lay for a while looking out of the window at what was obviously a bright sunny warm morning, listening to the birds singing.

After a while she got up, made the bed, showered and dressed. First she slipped on a little lacy white thong, over which she pulled on a pair of calf length pale green tight fitting slacks. Deciding not to bother with a bra she chose a pale apricot blouse but instead of tucking the blouse tails into the low slung waistband of the slacks she tied them in a bow around her middle exposing quite a wide expanse of her flat and trim waist. A pair of light tan flat heeled slip on shoes completed her outfit. Brushing her hair she pulled it into a pony tail and held it in place with a green scrunchy. A touch of makeup and then twisting herself around she looked critically in the mirror.

'Not bad' she said out loud before running downstairs and walking into the village nodding or smiling at various people who greeted her. This was an area of France not yet invaded by Brits and so she and William were welcome as foreigners who visited the area quite regularly. Stopping at the bakers she bought some croissants and long French loaves and then wandered slowly back to the cottage. Soon the smell of ground percolating coffee and fresh bread was permeating throughout the ground floor rooms as she drank some orange juice and ate her continental breakfast.

Her eyes continually strayed to the clock. His flight was due to arrive at ten o'clock. As the journey took around an hour she decided that she'd leave by a quarter to nine which should get her there in good time.

Checking round the cottage she locked the door, got in the car and drove out of the gates leaving them open as she set off for the airport.

It was a lovely morning with little traffic on the country roads and even the main road was not too bad and so just before a quarter to ten she turned down the long road that led off the main route past Autos Pierre to the airport.

It was unfortunate that just as she was driving towards Pierre's garage Jacques had come out into the back yard to collect some old tyres which Pierre wanted moved. As he looked up he saw the yellow convertible approaching and looking at it as it came nearer he realised that it was Madame Hardy's car. Instantly he became very nervous.

Why was she coming back? Pierre had said that she wouldn't be back for several days but now she was here again. Perhaps she wasn't happy with the way he'd cleaned the car? If that was so she would probably want her five euros back, but on his way home yesterday he'd spent the money on sweets.

Her car came closer and his nervousness increased so much so that he started to pee himself. He couldn't help it as it often happened if he got stressed or nervous. The car got closer. He knew his left trouser leg was getting wet and he felt the warm liquid run into his sock and trainer shoe.

As she drove past she looked across at him, smiled and waved cheerfully. His relief was enormous, so much so that his bladder completely emptied itself and his left leg and sock were now thoroughly soaked but he didn't care. The English lady wasn't cross, wouldn't want her money back and he wasn't going to be in trouble.

Walking across the yard he untangled a hosepipe which was in a coiled muddle on the ground and turning it on he sprayed both his urine soaked left leg and his unwet right leg. He ran the hose up and down until the front and sides of both legs of his jeans were soaked. He poked the hose end into his wet trainer and flushed that as well.

No one would realise that he'd wet himself. They'd think that somehow he'd got wet washing cars. Satisfied with that thought he wandered back into the workshop mumbling, quite forgetting that he'd been sent out to do something about the pile of old tyres until Pierre yelled and reminded him, shaking his head about the simpleton he had working for him.

Jacques was capable of cleaning cars, sweeping up, tidying the yard, and doing a myriad of minor jobs leaving Pierre and his two mechanics free to get on with servicing, repairing and looking after the cars, vans and little trucks that were brought to them for attention. But if he got stressed or worried he peed himself.

Sadly Jacques was slow. He lived with his mother, his father having left them when he realised that the boy then aged two and their only son was mentally sub normal. Jacques's mother Annette had struggled to bring up the slow witted boy alone until he was old enough to try and find work but he was incapable of doing anything that was available so Pierre had taken pity on the lonely single mother and said that he'd take the boy on for odd jobs around the garage. He paid Jacques a few euros each Friday night and the boy thought that they were his wages which he spent on sweets and comics.

In addition though the old Frenchman also paid the boy's mother additional money which she carefully saved for the future and a time when she'd be too old to look after her retarded son.

She'd never got married again after the boy's father left and so from time to time she and Pierre slept together. It had started one afternoon after he'd closed his garage for the day when he'd stopped by to pass on the weekly money that he gave her for the boy when it started to pour with rain.

She suggested that he wait until the rain stopped and made some coffee but it went on for some hours and got heavier so he stayed for a meal and afterwards somehow they started kissing and eventually finished up in bed together. That was the start of a long term arrangement of convenience which suited them both whereby approximately once a week he'd call in for coffee and usually they'd go to bed.

His own wife was now really very disinterested in sex and only allowed him to have intercourse with her under sufferance and so he enjoyed sleeping with someone who was quite the opposite.

Annette had enjoyed a fairly robust sex life with her husband before he'd left her and they'd got divorced and she missed the intimacy and enjoyment that sex gave her. So sleeping with Pierre enabled her to regain her past enjoyment while he for his part revelled in the opportunity that had presented itself to him.

Janie unaware of the trauma that she'd caused the boy drove into the airport car park, found a space, checked her watch as she locked the car but left the roof down and seeing that his plane hadn't arrived walked slowly into the terminal. It was ten minutes to ten.

The monitor screen for arrivals showed that his plane would be late and was expected to arrive at ten thirty five, so making her way to the small bistro café in the little terminal she ordered a coffee and a glass of sparkling water. Sipping the coffee her mind drifted back to that time in April when she and Harry had first met.

The son of a friend of William's had been getting married and she and William had been invited to the occasion. After the wedding ceremony all the guests had made their way from the church to a large marquee set out on the lawns of the bride's parent's house.

Finding where they were to sit Janie discovered that she and William were on opposite sides of the table. To her left she had an elderly man who was partially deaf but the seat to her right was empty until just before grace was said, a tall lanky but very good looking man appeared.

'Ah here's where I'm supposed to be I think' he said to her. 'I'm Harry by the way. Harry Norton'.

She took his proffered hand smiled and introduced herself.

Harry was the sort of man who made an impact wherever he went and today this was enhanced by the fact that he was virtually the only man out of the hundred or so guests not wearing either a dark suit or proper morning dress. Instead he was sporting a light fawn suit, pale green shirt and an outrageous red and green brightly spotted tie.

'I guessed this would be a rather stuffy do today so thought I'd brighten things up a bit' he laughed seeing her staring at his tie. 'Now where's the wine?' and brushing back his slightly overlong very pale brown hair a lock of which had fallen across his face, he reached across the table, picked up the bottles of red and white wine, offered both to Janie then poured her a glass of red in response to her pointing at that particular bottle. Walking round the table he managed to introduce himself and pour wine for everyone at the same time eventually completing the circle round the table back to his own place. The bottle of red wine was empty and upending it over his own glass he smiled ruefully.

'That's what comes of being a generous soul and putting other's needs before my own. Now where's a waitress? Can't go through this entire eating and speechmaking afternoon dry can we? Ah there she is' and beckoning the middle aged woman he waved the empty bottle in her direction, received a confirmatory nod and settled back down to talk to Janie.

'Had a hell of a rush to get here today. Why is it if I leave early for things there's no traffic but if I leave it a bit fine the traffic is bloody awful?'

He was easy to talk to and although Janie turned away from time to time to talk to the old man on her other side it was a real struggle to make him hear what she said and she found herself repeating things several times to make herself heard. Harry though chattered to her on a wide range of subjects.

'So what do you do?' she queried.

'I'm a financial adviser. I tell old ladies what to do with their money' he grinned looking straight at her. 'If their husband has given them or left them lots of money then they need to be sure that it's in the best pace to earn interest or grow. Depends what they want. Some people just want their capital to build up, others need the income from high interest rates. Whatever it is they want I provide it'.

'Just to old ladies?

'No not exclusively. I do have men clients plus some corporate customers, as well as a couple of pretty young ladies like you, but mainly my clients seem to be well off older ladies'.

'Thanks but I'm not young. I'm a mum in her late, very late thirties with two kids, a husband, assorted dogs, horses and cats'.

'Being in your thirties isn't old. No I think you are definitely young and very pretty'.

'Flattery will get you anywhere'.

'Really now that sounds promising' he laughed showing off his white teeth.

'Look I didn't mean.....'

'What?' he interrupted.

'What you just said. Oh I don't know. Here come on eat and stop trying to seduce me'.

Now why had she said that? He hadn't suggested seducing her, probably hadn't even thought about it.

'Didn't think I was. It's a lovely idea though, but isn't that your husband over there?' he asked nodding across the table.

'Yes'.

'Might be rather tricky to seduce you with your old man sitting only a few feet away don't you think? Mind you it might be fun trying' he chuckled as he placed his hand on her thigh and squeezed gently.

Immediately she felt a strange feeling creep over her so she turned away and had another go at making herself understood by the deaf man so it was some time before she spoke to Harry again. When she did their conversation ranged over a wide spread of subjects and she enjoyed his company and talking with him. Later he returned to the subject of her financial affairs.

'So do you have your own portfolio of shares or savings?'

'Yes but William takes care of all that for me'.

"Hey we're in the twenty first century now so no reason why you can't manage your own financial affairs, or at least get someone like me to have a look at it for you. Tell you what. If you came to see me I'd be happy to have a quick look through and see if there were opportunities to improve. Usually there are but it's up to you. No charge for a first visit. Here's my card, think about it, talk it over with your husband and then perhaps give me a ring'.

Putting the card into her handbag she promised to think about it.

The rest of the afternoon went by fairly quickly and around five o'clock everyone started to get up to leave. Shaking hands with her fellow table guests she finally turned to Harry.

'It's been a pleasure to meet you. Thank you for your company'.

'I assure you the pleasure was all mine' he smiled pushing his hair lock back. 'Now do ring me. I'll be waiting with baited breath for your call' and he watched her walk round the table to meet up with William and then saw them make their way through the dissipating throng out of the marquee across the lawn to where they'd parked their car.

On the way home she brought up the matter of her financial affairs and to her surprise William thought it might be a good idea to have an independent expert have a look at them.

'If he seems to know what he's doing maybe he could have a look at mine as well' he mused. 'I'll get out the details of your shares and savings and let you have them'.

William was a man who liked to get outstanding things dealt with straight away so on Sunday morning he got up early before going to play golf and spent a while in his study emerging with some sheets of paper just as Janie came down to breakfast.

'Look I've jotted down a list of your financial assets here for your chat with that guy you met at the wedding yesterday. What was his name by the way?'

'Oh thanks. It was Harry but you didn't have to do it straight away'.

'Ah yes Harry. Well that should give him what he wants. You've mainly got building society deposit accounts, an ISA that's built up nicely over the past few years, some shares, a couple of unit trusts and some investment trusts. If he needs any further information you'll have to let me know. Now I'll see you later. I'll probably stay and have a spot of lunch at the golf club'.

Janie put the papers that William had prepared into a drawer making a note to call Harry next week.

It was Tuesday morning when she'd taken out his card and dialled the London number. She explained to the anonymous female voice at the other end that she'd met Harry on Saturday at a wedding and he'd suggested that she might want to visit him and soon his cheerful voice came on the line.

They'd chatted for a while and made an appointment for Thursday afternoon at two o'clock.

On the day of the meeting she drove to Norwich and caught the London train, took a taxi to Harry's offices which were in a building in one of the streets behind Oxford Street. Taking the lift she got out at the second floor and rang the bell to the side of a frosted glass door bearing the legend

HARRY NORTON ASSOCIATES

Financial Advisers

The door was opened by a middle aged lady who showed Janie to a waiting room where she read the paper for about five minutes until Harry appeared.

'Welcome. You found us alright then? Good now come along to my office and we'll have some coffee and a chat' and leading the way he took her to a large room expensively furnished in traditional style with lots of heavy mahogany furniture, thick deep pile carpets but the light colour wallpaper, pale silk curtains and large floor to ceiling windows gave the room an air of lightness.

She sat in one of the armchairs as he poured coffee into delicate china cups from the percolator on a sideboard.

'Look thanks for coming. You say your husband….err William isn't it, was quite happy for you to come here and talk to me? That's good as sometimes husbands get all macho about these sorts of things and see it as some sort of threat or challenge to their financial skills. The point is though that often although they are really good at their big jobs in business they aren't so hot at looking after their wife's financial matters. Now do you know exactly what you've got in the way of investments?'

'Yes' she smiled. 'Here's a list that William prepared for me'.

'How very efficient of him so let's have a look shall we' and he sat back in his armchair and taking a pen out of his shirt pocket carefully looked at the information she'd given him.

While he was absorbed in doing that Janie studied him. Strange she thought. On Saturday at the wedding he'd been casually dressed and quite the life and soul of the table. Here today he was wearing a dark pin striped suit and in serious mood. He was really rather good looking and the way that lock of hair fell across his face as he looked down requiring him to keep smoothing it back was intriguing. Craggy faced, longish nose, quite bushy eyebrows above his grey eyes which had deep laughter lines around them and probably a little younger than her, maybe early thirties to her late thirties. She was still studying him when he looked up at her.

'OK there's some good stuff here that I wouldn't want to change but other items I think could be improved. Look what I need to do is understand your attitude to risk and what you want from your investments then I can work out how those needs can best be met'.

So ensued a short but quite probing questioning session at the end of which he grinned at her.

'There all over. Didn't hurt a bit did it? I suggest you leave me for a week or so to come up with some alternative options and then we'll meet again and move to the next stage. Now I just need to go through a few legal matters regarding the financial advice that I'm going to give you. We financial advisers are very heavily governed and controlled you know. Good thing as it helps keep cowboys out of the business. Alright?'

He then rattled through some information that Janie didn't really either understand or care about and handed her some documents confirming what he'd said.

'Right that's that all over and out the way. Now I'll call you when I've done my analysis and got some recommendations for you'.

As she left she thought he held her hand just a fraction longer than normal as he thanked her for coming to see him. Travelling back across London in the taxi she hoped that he wouldn't leave it too long before he called her. He didn't and on Wednesday of next week he rang.

'Hi there. I've had a go at your portfolio and I think I can help you improve it quite a bit. Now we need to get together to discuss my suggestions. If you like I could come up to you but frankly I'd prefer it if you came here again as all my information and data base is here and if we need to check or look something up I've got it all at my finger tips. Now when could you get here? I can't do next week but what about Monday week? Would that be any good?'

The arrangements were made and every now and then during that next week she kept finding herself thinking about Harry. Even in bed one night after William had made love to her as she turned on her side to go to sleep she thought about the tall craggy faced financial adviser.

When the day of the second meeting arrived she travelled on an early train in order to do some clothes shopping in Bond Street before meeting Harry and happily she found a couple of outfits that she liked. The appointment was eleven thirty and just before the agreed time she was again ringing the bell feeling some anticipation and excitement as she waited for the door to open. Why she wondered?

'Ah ha already spending all the extra money that I'm going to make for you are you?' he grinned at her a few minutes later taking her parcels as she walked into his office.

After pouring some coffee he handed her a typed schedule. 'Look this is what I propose which I think will improve your earnings by about ten percent on what you're currently making. Let me talk you through it' and he explained his thinking, where he proposed to change what she had and where he suggested keeping some items unaltered. It all seemed very logical to her and he answered her several questions easily. Around twelve fifteen they were done and she folded her copies of the information and put them into he bag.

'If you're happy with that I'll get all the necessary paperwork drawn up and then we'll get everything signed and under way. I can't find the time to get away up to Norfolk for a week or so but would you be free on Friday to come down here again?

'Yes that's fine. I'm happy to come down. I love an excuse to go shopping in London'.

'Well shall we say twelve o'clock? We'll get all the boring stuff of signing papers and forms done and then perhaps you'd like to have lunch with me and we could get to know each other a bit. After all if I'm going to be looking after your financial affairs it might help if I knew more about you. What do you say?'

'That would be lovely' she replied actually rather pleased that he'd asked her.

Later that night when she showed him what Harry had suggested William seemed pleased with the recommendations and fully supported her proceeding with the changes to her financial investments again repeating that if he really could make a ten percent difference to her portfolio then he might get him to advise on his.

William obviously continued to be worried about Hardys business and for the last few days had been tetchy and so she was looking forward to seeing Harry again.

Friday morning in Norfolk dawned dull and wet so checking on the internet what the weather was likely to be in London and discovering that it was also wet Janie decided against a shopping trip. She didn't want to turn up at Harry's office all wet and bedraggled especially if they were going somewhere nice for lunch.

Dressing carefully in a matching pale blue jacket and skirt she was really looking forward to seeing her finance man again.

Just because he was going to make her more money? No she liked him as a man. He was fun, interesting and good looking, not that his appearance mattered she told herself. It was his financial skill that was important.

In his office he again explained what she was committing to and asked for her confirmation that she understood and was happy to proceed and upon receiving her confident 'Yes' he passed over the papers and documents for signing.

It was soon done then he was escorting her out of his office to the lift and down to the street where he was lucky flagging down a passing taxi almost straight away. She couldn't hear the address he gave the driver.

'Where are we going?' she queried when they were in the taxi.

'It's a French restaurant where the food is excellent, the service quiet and unobtrusive, and they don't rush you. I like to take time when eating with someone special and the French do these things so well. You do like French food I hope'.

'Love it. We've got a cottage in the south of France so William and I are both Francophiles but why did you say that I was someone special'.

'Well you are...........all my clients are'.

'Do you take them all to lunch then when you've signed them up?'

'Only the young pretty ones. No that's not true, as sometimes I take the old ugly ones but that is work, whereas with someone like you it's pure pleasure' he grinned looking straight at her.

Is he making a pass at me she wondered? Surely not.

There was a slightly awkward pause and they sat in silence for a little while as the taxi weaved its way through the heavy lunchtime traffic but it wasn't very long before his irrepressible cheerfulness came to the fore again.

He asked about the cottage in France, whereabouts it was located, how often they used it and what it was like. Any embarrassment that might have existed between them was gone.

Forbidden fruit is sweet

Proverb

CHAPTER 5

It had been quite a long journey in the taxi to the restaurant but when they eventually arrived and he led her inside it was exactly as he'd described it, very French and quiet.

He was easy to talk to and as they ate she found herself telling him all about herself. Her childhood, her upbringing, the loss of her father, her university life and her marriage to William.

'I know I'm very privileged and lucky to have such a kind husband, two lovely children, to live in a beautiful old house with hundreds of acres of grounds, have a cottage abroad and plenty of money but sometimes I wonder if there isn't more to life than all that. I don't mean going off to live in some commune or scrabble around the dirt tracks of Africa doing good deeds, but I just feel that maybe I'm unfulfilled in some way. Does that make sense? Probably not? Still I seem to have done all the talking up to now so what about you? How did you come to be a financial adviser to old ladies?'

'Young and pretty ones too' he smiled looking deep into her eyes and to her great embarrassment she felt herself blush.

God he was making a pass and it made her feel slightly peculiar. Here she was, a married woman having lunch with a virtual stranger and he was trying to seduce her. No don't be silly he wasn't doing anything of the sort. He'd simply flattered her. Yes that was it. Not a pass just simple flattery and so she concentrated as he explained his life to date.

He told how he'd been brought up in Cardiff then gone away to school at Stowe at which point she interrupted him.

'Stowe? Well that's a coincidence as William went there and it's where my boys are now'.

'As you say what a coincidence, must be fate'.

'What must?'

'Your husband and your sons and me all going to the same school. Any rate after Stowe I thought I'd like to join the Army so I did a short service commission came out with a lump sum and joined a firm of financial advisers. They were looking for chaps like me so I studied for the exams, passed them, got qualified, endured a few years with them before I left and joined up with another chap and we set up a business together. Wasn't too successful so we split up and I set up on my own. That was four years ago and I haven't looked back since'.

'Advising old ladies' she giggled.

'Yep and…….'

'Young ones' she interrupted smiling.

'Yes. So what is this feeling of unfulfilment that you have?'

She felt at ease with him and it seemed almost as though she'd known him for ages rather than such a short time. Being so easy to talk to she would have liked to say that she was finding William boring but that would have been disloyal and she didn't want to run him down to someone else especially when he was so kind and thoughtful to her. Nevertheless there was definitely something missing from her life and she told Harry that.

The speciality dessert of the restaurant was a tarte citron and with the head waiter eulogising about it they both had a small portion and had to agree with him when he personally cleared their plates that it had been delicious.

'We could have coffee here or my apartment isn't far away. I have some quite exquisite ground coffee which I brought back from Peru last year. Also lurking in my drinks cabinet there is a bottle of very old Armagnac. Now can I tempt you?'

Janie was feeling happy and relaxed. Harry was good company and there was no harm in having a glass of his special Armagnac and a cup of fancy coffee so she smiled that she'd be happy to try his coffee and liqueur.

As he paid the bill he asked the head waiter to organise a taxi and when they came out into the pouring rain there was a black cab waiting which soon pulled up outside a six storey block of apartments close to Regents Park. The lift swished them up to the top floor and he walked down the short corridor before stopping outside a teak door and inserting a key.

Once inside she was staggered at its size. It was enormous. In front of her was a very large room furnished as a sitting area, out of which at one side rose a steep open tread marble staircase. At the far end on the right some steps led down to a sunken area which contained an unusually large square black glass table with three seats on each of the four sides, clearly capable of hosting large dinner parties. Beyond that the main room led to floor to ceiling windows through which could be seen a terrace of some sort. As she walked across the room this terrace came fully into view and it was more like a patio than a normal balcony or terrace. It contained some trees in large earthenware pots, flowers in terracotta planters, a bar-b-q in one corner and several wooden sunloungers.

Turning back into the room she saw that he'd moved into the large kitchen which led off the sunken dining area so she walked down the three steps to join him. The kitchen like the rest of the apartment was ultra modern, all glass and stainless steel and had trendy black granite work tops. It was also obviously fully equipped with every appliance that any kitchen could ever need.

He smiled then turned and a loud grinding noise suddenly burst forth from the coffee grinder. When it stopped he tipped the grounds into a coffee maker, added cold water and plugged it into a socket before opening a cupboard to emerge with his bottle of French liqueur.

'Now then here you are. Coffee won't be long. I promise you it will be worth waiting for. I went on a walking and trekking holiday last year to Peru and brought back loads of the stuff. So try some of this Armagnac which is twenty years old and like a taste of heaven' he offered holding out a glass.

She took a small sip of the drink. He was right it was so smooth and soft yet beautifully warming as she allowed it to slip slowly down her throat. 'Umm that's wonderful. Like your apartment Harry. I've read about these sorts of penthouse places and seen pictures of them in magazines but to actually be in one, well it's quite breathtaking'.

'Yes I like it. Cost a fortune but it's mine, or at least it will be in twenty years or so when I've paid off the mortgage but I think it'll be a good investment. There's only two of these top floor penthouse units in this block and the other one has just been re-sold for considerably more than I paid for this so I think my money is safe. Now I reckon that coffee will soon be ready so take your drink, go and sit down and I'll bring it over'.

She walked slowly back up the steps, across the vast sitting area where she sank down into one of the amazingly comfortable settees. Looking around she saw that the whole room was beautifully furnished, but like the kitchen in ultra modern style. White leather chairs and settees, glass and stainless steel wall and sideboard units, a large plasma tv screen built into the wall, an obviously expensive hi-fi system, and therefore such a contrast to her own home with its big old fashioned well worn style of armchairs, sofas and settees, its smokey log fires, its draughty windows and its old world charm. This huge apartment had no charm it was simply a stunning statement of someone who was obviously very sure and confident of themselves.

They chatted while she drank the coffee and sipped the liqueur then she asked about the remainder of the apartment.

'Like to have a look around the rest of the place?'

'Yes please, but just let me pop to the loo first before the guided tour' and putting down her cup and the glass she looked queryingly at him.

'Oh yes sorry there's one over there' and he pointed to a door to the left underneath the staircase.

When she reappeared he offered to lead the way around and started up the stairs.

'Right here we go. First door up here is the bathroom' and he flung open the door to reveal a simply amazing bathroom fitted with trendy modern fittings and in the corner a jacuzzi.

'Next is the study then there are two bedrooms' he announced as he took her into the study then into the guest room which was large and again furnished in modern style before opening the door to what he described as his room.

'God its huge Harry' she exclaimed as she walked into the enormous room. One wall was entirely clad with mirrors and as she glanced around she also noticed that the ceiling sloped and that was also mirror clad.

There was a small terrace leading off the floor to ceiling windows. Janie looked around in amazement. 'Harry it is quite wonderful. Like something out of a fashion magazine or Hollywood. You know the sort of thing that premier league footballers or millionaires have and that bed must be a double king size. Don't you get lonely in that great thing all on your own?'

'Sometimes' he admitted 'but its one of my little extravagancies. It's a water bed'.

'Really? A water bed? I've heard of them but never seen one before'.

'Oh they're fun and fantastically comfortable. Try it'.

Gingerly she sat on the edge and found it sort of wobbled beneath her then as she gently bounced up and down she giggled at the odd sensation.

'You only get the proper effect and benefit if you lie down on it. Go on stretch out and see what you think'.

Kicking off her shoes and allowing herself to lie back and feel the bed mould itself to her shape she wriggled around trying out various positions being thoroughly amazed at the sensations the bed created. She finished in the middle lying flat on her back. Sitting up she tugged her skirt down as it had ridden up her thighs with all the rolling around.

'Well what do you think?' Harry asked looking at her legs as he sat on the edge of his bed leaning towards her. 'Look around at yourself in the mirrors' he suggested pointing to the wall and ceiling.

'God that's incredible. I've never been on a bed where I can look at myself like that and the sensations of the water bed are amazing aren't they?

This is my day for discovering new things.

First time inside a huge penthouse apartment, first time to drink Peruvian coffee, first time to drink twenty year old liqueur Armagnac, first time to see myself on a bed in mirrors and first time on a water bed'.

'Could be the first time for some other things as well' he said softly looking straight at her and moving his face closer. 'Janie you are an incredibly beautiful woman you know. Ever since I first saw you at that wedding I knew that I wanted to get to know you. I know this sounds incredibly corny but.......' and he paused looking into her eyes.

'What?'

'I think there's a sort of chemistry between us'.

'Don't be silly'.

'No really I do. Look you said over lunch that you weren't happy with William....'

'No I didn't. I just said that I felt unfulfilled'

'OK sorry, unfulfilled then'.

'And you think that you can do something about that do you?'

'I think we could fulfil each other' he said softly then leant down and kissed her very gently.

Her mind went into turmoil.

He obviously had been making passes at her after all and he'd got her back to his apartment, into his mirrored bedroom and onto his water bed. Now what? Well it was obvious what. But hang on she'd asked to look around the apartment. I mean she'd seen the enormous sitting room and wonderful sunken dining room and kitchen. What else was there in an apartment for God's sake apart from bedrooms? Bathrooms? Is that what she'd wanted to see or had she really hankered to see his bedroom after the flirting that he'd been doing over lunch. What she had to do now was quite clear. Push him away before it went any further, get off the wobbly bed, say thank you for a lovely lunch, and leave. Right now. Yes she thought looking at his crinkly eyes that's what I should do.

She pulled him back to her lips.

He responded immediately and her lips opened as his tongue pushed deep into her mouth as they kissed fiercely and passionately. Their kisses went on and on and she pushed his tongue back and then pressed her own into his mouth. She flicked around his teeth and their tongues fenced with each other for a few moments.

Suddenly easing away she looked at him and put a hand on his chest.

'Harry stop this is wrong' she said faintly. 'I'm a married woman, I'm thirty nine years old so probably older than you, I've got two kids, I............'

'And you're beautiful and looking for something more from your life' he said quietly. 'Let me help you find what you're seeking. It could be wonderful'.

He leaned down again this time kissing her forehead, her eyes, an ear and then his tongue traced its way down the side of her neck until it came level with her lips where it moved across her cheek and fluttered around her lips for ages before it slowly wandered back around her neck and nuzzled her other ear sending all sorts of amazingly tingly feelings through her body.

As she gathered his lips to hers again she felt his fingers stroking her neck down to the top button of her blue tight fitting jacket which soon popped open.

Oh stop it now. She felt a second button come loose. It's only been a couple of kisses. Alright deep passionate ones but that's all. If she didn't stop now things could quickly go out of control.

The third button opened and then the last. Moving his lips away from her he opened her jacket seeing her pretty bra, white trimmed with deep blue lace.

'God you are so beautiful. Janie oh Janie', and he kissed first one then the other material covered breast.

A voice screamed inside her head. Stop it. Push him away. Sit up, button your jacket and get off the bed. Go. Just get the hell out of here. Now. Forget the financial advice. He wasn't interested in that he just wanted to bed you. Forget Harry. Come on this is your last chance. Don't be bloody silly. Don't put everything you've got at risk for one lecherous man. Stop now.

Arching her back she reached behind and unclipped her bra for him and watching his eyes as they widened in delight she eased her breasts free for his gaze.

His mouth hovered down and fastened on a nipple where he sucked, nipped gently, flicked his tongue and kissed before repeating the activities with her other nipple which like the first went hard. His hands massaged her breasts and as he returned to kissing her lips she felt some internal waves of passion begin to develop. Pulling him down to her she kissed him as fervently as she could.

His hands now started making little forays further down her body stopping at the waistband of her skirt before returning to her breasts and hard nipples again, but each downward mission seemed to explore a little further, massaging her tummy and letting his fingers tease and slide under the skirt waist.

He moved up again and then down, this time trapping the skirt's elastic waistband between a finger and thumb then sliding around to its side he found a clip that soon popped open and a zip which slid down.

As he left her lips she glanced up and watched him in the ceiling mirror as he moved down the bed making it wobble, kissing her tummy and licking her belly button before gently easing her skirt down her legs to her ankles pausing to kiss the front of her matching panties. A final movement had her skirt off completely and she lay there nervous, apprehensive, excited and worried that he'd regret undressing her. Would her nude body still interest him?

'May I?' he asked taking hold of the elastic waist of her panties.

Not trusting herself to speak she just nodded and in seconds she was totally naked.

'I've said it before and I'll say it again Janie. I think you are utterly beautiful and I want to make love to you' he whispered undoing his shirt.

No don't be bloody stupid. Get off the bed, get dressed and go!

'Here let me help you' she said softly sitting up to peel off his shirt. She looked at his hairy chest then leaning forward kissed it letting her tongue trace its way through the hair to his nipples which she sucked in turn.

She kissed all the way up to his chin on which the first feelings of stubble could be felt while feeling him moving and wriggling she guessed that he was undressing himself.

Leaning down he slowly pushed her onto her back as his fingers found her pussy and tenderly played with her, delighted that she immediately became wet. Rubbing and stroking he expertly massaged her there while his lips alternated between her mouth and her nipples. Tentatively he started kissing his way down her body until he reached her bush whereupon he twisted round to be able to reach her properly with his tongue.

Her satisfaction as his tongue worked its way around and inside her was evident from the soft sighs that emanated from her and whenever he thought of moving up towards her lips she whispered 'Stay there please'.

She watched in fascinated delight as she moved her head to look at the wall and ceiling mirrors as he worked diligently until she pulled his face into her and shook with the effect of her orgasm. He continued to tease his fingers around and inside her as he felt her pulling gently to bring him up the bed and so sliding on top of her he kissed her hard, his tongue pushing deeply in her mouth.

'Darling I need to get something' and he part rolled off her and reached for a small drawer to the side of the bed head and then whispered 'condom' to her puzzled look. She nodded and in seconds the rubber protective was in place.

Right this is it. Your last chance. He's kissed you, ok in a very intimate way and he's licked and rubbed you to an orgasm. But that's all. It isn't too late. Push him away, get off the bed, get dressed and go.

Sliding her arms around his shoulders as he clambered back on top she gasped as he tenderly pressed himself into her extremely wet pussy. Careful to start very slowly and build up towards a faster momentum he helped her by whispering how wonderful she was.

At one stage when she reached underneath him and found his balls she squeezed them surprisingly firmly and he grunted.

He really did think she was a stunning woman so he wanted to be sure that their lovemaking was suitably memorable and therefore he took time to make it as good as he could. The fact that she was obviously not inexperienced or an unwilling partner helped.

Looking up at him she muttered his name and then glancing past him to the ceiling saw herself wrap her legs tightly around his waist and her arms fold around his neck. He kissed her breasts and lips as their movements increased rapidly and soon he was on the brink of climaxing so telling her that he couldn't hold back any longer his penis pulsed as she squeezed her pussy muscles tightly on him telling him that she was coming as well.

Groaning as he ejaculated, he kept moving inside her until giving a little scream as she orgasmed for the second time he gradually slowed down and kissed her more gently, whispering 'Janie' over and over again as he finally stopped moving.

Releasing one hand she pushed the lock of hair off his face smiling as she kissed him again when he rolled off her and lay by her side.

'Oh Janie what can I say? I didn't mean that to happen. Well I did but I didn't want to rush things like this. Ever since I first met you I knew I wanted you but I thought that a relationship would maybe develop over time, not go from flash to bang in one go' Then he roared with laughter. 'Flash to bang. I didn't mean to demean our lovemaking by calling it a bang. That sounds cheap but it's just a phrase. Means something happening suddenly, hence flash to bang'.

'I know what you meant' and she continued to stroke his hair and kiss his face, his lips and then she cuddled him into her. 'You're right about one thing though. Water beds are amazing for lovemaking. I don't know whether it was the bed, you or being a voyeur and watching us making love in your mirrors, but that was quite the most wonderful lovemaking that I've ever enjoyed. It will be something to savour for a long long time' and she closed her eyes and cuddled him stoking his chest.

So now what? You've done it now haven't you? Seduced and screwed by a man you've only met four times.

After a while she turned towards him and stroked his belly for a while before reaching for his penis which although flaccid soon responded to her hand movements.

Lifting her head and pushing her long hair out of the way she moved down to look at his stiffening penis then slid her lips over his erection and soon her head was moving up and down with an increasing rapidity as she combined the vertical movements with some strong sucking actions twisting so she could see herself in the wall mirror. Feeling him start to gasp a little too loudly at this early stage she let him slip out of her lips and her tongue traced its way up his chest to his lips where she kissed him fiercely.

'Where do you keep the condoms?'

Receiving directions she leant up and felt for the drawer, scrabbled around and then finding them, took one, tearing the foil open to release the slippery protective as she slid back down the bed. Seeing he was fully hard she asked 'Shall I do it?' and at his nod she rolled the rubber onto him then clambering on top reached down and helped him inside herself.

Leaning forward she dangled her breasts in his face while starting to move slowly up and down as he wrapped his arms around her and soon they were furiously making passionate love. Keeping her eyes open she watched him as she worked on him, enjoying the way his face wrinkled and stretched as he gasped in his rising passion. 'Oh baby I'm coming' he gasped loudly.

'Good so am I' was her panting response and almost immediately they collapsed against each other sated, happy and sexually satisfied.

They lay quietly holding each other.

God above what the hell have I done? What have I got myself into? It was crazy. This morning she came to London a loyal wife to sign some financial papers. Now she'd betrayed her husband, her children and her life. Why?

It was sometime later when he spoke interrupting her thoughts.

'Janie can we talk? You have to believe me when I say that I didn't plan this to happen. I just don't know what happened today. Well I do of course but believe me it wasn't planned. How do you feel? What do you want to do? I mean we can't just walk away from this. It's been so beautiful, so wonderful and ………'

'Schhh. I don't know. I've got to think. It can't happen again Harry. It simply can't. It was mad. A crazy mistake. A one off thing. Wonderful yes, a beautiful interlude in life, certainly. But that's all it can be, a one off event nothing serious or deep and certainly not to be repeated. Ever. To use your phrase it was a quick flash to bang. An illicit bonk one afternoon in London with a lovely man on his amazing water bed in his fantastic apartment. But it's over. Never again……..never…. understand? Now what's the time?'

'Nearly five o'clock'

'I must go. Can I have a shower please?' and feeling self conscious as she rolled off the bed she asked 'is it in here?'

Seeing him nod she walked quickly to a door which opened into the en-suite bathroom. Careful not to soak her hair and then ruefully remembering that she'd thought that morning that she didn't want to get her hair wet in the rain and now she was naked in a strange man's bathroom trying to keep it dry. Stepping out of the shower and wrapping a large towel around herself she gingerly opened the door and saw that he'd pulled on his trousers and was doing up his shirt.

'Would you like me to leave you to dress alone?' he asked quietly.

'Yes please. I feel shy now. Silly isn't it when we've been so intimate'.

'No I understand. I'll go and make some more coffee or would you like tea?' he queried in a matter of fact way.

So was that it? He'd had his way with her. Scored. A notch on the bedpost, well two as they done it twice. A couple of ripples in the water bed. Now he was offering coffee or tea.

'Tea please'.

Soon dressed she made her way downstairs, found her handbag in the sitting area so going into the downstairs loo she brushed her hair, re-applied some lipstick, mascara, eyeliner and eye shadow and walked back across the room and stepped down into the kitchen area.

They sat silently both lost in their thoughts as they drank their tea.

'I really must be going. I can get the six thirty train. I need to ring William. He'll wonder where I've got to' then her words dried up as she looked at Harry. 'Look I meant what I said. Today was a one off. Wonderful but never again. I don't know how to say good bye to you. Shaking hands seems a bit stupid so maybe I'll just wave goodbye as I walk down the corridor to the lift'.

'You could kiss me goodbye'.

'No. Harry I'm going......now. Don't kiss me just leave me'.

'Janie I can't just leave it like that. There is something between us. You felt it too didn't you? I know you did. I said earlier that there was a chemistry between us, well if it's not chemistry it is certainly something. We have to meet again'.

'No ...... goodbye Harry'.

She walked to the door, opened it, turned and gave a sort of half wave, smiled, turned away and walked off down the corridor. Feeling his eyes on her back she forced herself not to turn and look to see if he was actually watching her. When the lift doors opened she went in without a backward glance.

The rain had stopped but the pavements were wet and her pale blue shoes were soon spattered but eventually she flagged down a cab asked to go to Liverpool Street station where she bought a paper, then hunted for her mobile phone at the bottom of her bag to ring William, said that she'd be home around nine and stood waiting for the train to pull in. When it did she walked onto the platform found a first class carriage, sat down, opened the evening newspaper she'd just bought and sat staring unseeingly at it.

Whatever have I done? Been unfaithful to William that's what. Why? She'd never been unfaithful before. Never. Not once had she strayed since she and William got married. So what on earth had driven her to jump into bed with a man she hardly knew? William adored her and she loved him. Didn't she? Yes of course she did. Now she'd betrayed him. Why? She loved their children and she'd betrayed them too. What if Harry started to ring her or send letters or e-mail her? Perhaps she ought to change her password as William could log onto her e-mail address. Harry wouldn't do that though would he? No he'd just wanted to get her into bed and he'd succeeded. Mind you she hadn't put up much of a fight? Be honest you didn't put up any fight at all. Let me see the rest of your apartment she'd asked, then sat on his water bed and succumbed to his advances. You're just a right little slut she thought. Hell she even undone her own bra. Why? Had she secretly wanted to be seduced? Was there some deep psychological reason? Some deep need? Did she want to hurt William? Her mind churned round and round and the more she thought about it the more she worried as to why she'd let herself be screwed like some cheap whore. An expensive lunch, a glass of fancy brandy, a cup of special coffee and she'd been an easy lay.

She was near to tears but as there were others in the compartment she controlled herself, blew her nose and settled to read the paper. She managed for a while and then feeling in need of a drink she wobbled down the corridor as the train was thundering along at a fair old rate causing the carriages to shake around.

Shake rattle and roll she thought as she finally made it to the buffet car. Roll that's it. That's what I had this afternoon a good old fashioned roll, not in the hay but on a water bed.

'Gin and tonic please and lots of ice'.

Perhaps she ought to ask is that what tarts like me drink?'

The steward served her, smiled, gave her some change and asked if she'd been down to London for the day?

'Yes shopping but I didn't buy anything'.

Too busy being fucked by a man I hardly know.

'You know what we women are like. Hanker after a day's shopping and then don't buy anything. Daft'.

Quite happy though to undo my own bra and let a virtual stranger kiss my nipples, take my knickers off, lick my pussy and have sex with me. Twice. And I sucked his dick between lovemaking sessions!

'Ah well that's part of the mystery of life isn't it madam?'

Not as much of a mystery as to why she'd been unfaithful by letting Harry screw her.

'I suppose it is ….. thanks'.

Carefully carrying her drink back to her seat she sat sipping it enjoying the cool taste.

Picking up her paper again she read and then sat for ages staring out of the window but not really seeing anything. The country side now getting dark flashed by, the train stopped at a couple of intermediate stations and then eventually the announcement that they were arriving at Norwich had her gathering up her bag and paper and when the train stopped she left by a door already opened by a previous departing passenger.

Walking briskly down the platform she crossed the concourse, left the station, crossed the road into the multi-storey car cark feeling slightly nervous even though it was brightly lit. A middle aged man was at the ticket machine and she queued behind him. When he'd finished she spoke.

'Excuse me but would you mind seeing me to my car. I don't like walking around these places anytime but especially not at night. I'd be very grateful'.

Don't want to walk around a car park but quite happy though to have sex with someone she hardly knew.

'Of course, no problem. Which floor are you on?'

'Err......third I think' and she checked her ticket where she'd made a note when she'd parked this morning. 'Yes third'.

'OK the lift is over there'. He waited while she paid then walked with her and waited by her car until she'd got in.

'There you are. Now lock your doors and drive home safely'.

'Thanks ever so much. Goodnight'.

Perhaps she ought to add 'Oh and if you want a quickie on the back seat then I'm the one for you. After all I'm a scrubber who fucks strangers'. No I'm not. There was magnetism about Harry and she'd made a mistake. That's all. Harry was too much of a gentleman to embarrass her and if she said nothing then no-one would know. Especially William. It was all over. She'd write to Harry and tell him to tear up the forms she'd signed and leave her alone. She didn't need to see him again. That's it. Finished.

William was reading a book in the living room when she got home. The television was chattering to itself in the corner and the room looked old fashioned but cosy. This was her world.

'Have a good day darling? I must say I thought you'd be back earlier than this. Bought up the whole of London?'

'Not quite, but I found a few things. Sorry I'm so late but I checked the London weather this morning before I left and as it was raining and I didn't want to trudge around getting wet I decided to wait and leave here later than I originally planned. So that's what I did and when I got to London I went straight to Harry's office. I signed the papers then he took me to a late lunch'.

Oh and then we went off to his incredible penthouse got onto his waterbed and spent the afternoon fucking!

'Good meal?'

'Yes lovely. Nice French restaurant. The food was delicious. We talked for ages and then as the rain had cleared up I went off to do some shopping and caught the six thirty back'.

Mostly true. Just one bit missed out, albeit a rather important bit.

'All go alright with the document signing?'

'Yes'.

'Nice chap is he? I mean if you went to a long lunch you must have got to know him a bit'.

Got to know him a bit? Yes you could say that I got to know him a bit!

'Yes he's fun'.

It was really awful lying and talking about Harry like this.

'Have you eaten?'

'Yep got some cold meat out of the fridge and made myself a couple of sandwiches. I was about to make myself a coffee just before you came home. Would you like one?'

'Err no thanks. I think I'll have a whisky and then I'm going to have a bath and an early night'.

She took her whisky upstairs with her and later sitting in the bath as she splashed hot water onto her face and breasts couldn't help thinking of Harry.

I suppose every married woman is allowed one brief fling she thought. Well I've had mine now and that's an end of it.

Sighing deeply she climbed out, dried herself, brushed her hair and walked into their bedroom. To her surprise William was already in bed and from the look on his face and the fact that his chest was bare whereas he usually wore a tee shirt and shorts in bed she guessed that he wanted to make love.

Today of all days!

Turning back the duvet further than normal she saw that she was right. He was naked and already well on the way to being erect.

'Darling I'm absolutely shattered. Would you mind........' but she was unable to finish as he pulled her towards him and kissed her.

'Oh come on my sweetheart. Just relax and let me do all the work' he grinned running his hands over her breasts and down into her pussy hair.

She couldn't help it. His hands reminded her of Harry's hands. He rolled on top of her still kissing her lips and with a hand rummaging around her pussy lips which soon moistened sufficiently to enable him to enter her.

He made love quite quickly not like Harry's tender and more prolonged approach, and soon he was pulsing semen into her. She didn't usually fake it but tonight she let out a couple of soft groans and seeing the smile on his face knew he was pleased that he thought he'd made her come as well.

Nothing like the groans she'd given with Harry, but then those had been for real!

'Thank you darling. Sleep well' and he rolled off her, reached down to the side of the bed for his tee shirt and shorts, tugged them on, turned onto his back and was soon snoring gently.

She wasn't. She lay awake for ages turning over and over in her mind why she'd been unfaithful.

After all it wasn't that she was sexually frustrated. Well not really. She and William had an adequate sex life, probably much the same as most couples who'd been married for fourteen years. Not bursting with passion, just comfortable. William was kind, if a little old fashioned and not very exciting or adventurous in sex. He tended to come a bit too quickly for her liking, unlike Harry who'd pumped into her for ages before coming. But William adored her, provided everything that she wanted and would do anything for her. So why had she done what she had? Was it because of what Harry had said? Was there really was some chemistry between them?

It was hours before she finally dropped off to sleep and when she woke in the morning she knew what she had to do. Stop this nonsense now.

William had left early for work and she had another bath.

Guilty conscience? Trying to wash away your sins?

She'd come downstairs and was sipping a cup of coffee wondering if she'd ever be able to drink coffee again without thinking of Harry seducing her when the phone rang.

'Hello'.

'Janie its Harry'.

'I don't want to talk to you. I'm going to write and tell you to cancel all the arrangements and papers I signed. Now leave me alone please. I told you yesterday that it was a mistake. A one off and it's over'.

'I understand but I just couldn't sleep last night thinking about you'.

You're not the only one!

'Look Janie I just had to call you but I don't know whether to say sorry or to thank you, or both but I had to say something. If you want those papers cancelled I'll do it of course. Just drop me a quick note to formalise that'.

'Good bye Harry' and putting the phone down she cut off any further conversation and went straight into the kitchen where she had her computer.

William had his in the study but she felt inhibited in there and preferred hers in the kitchen where she felt more relaxed and homely.

Logging on she composed an e-mail.

Harry,
This is to confirm that I wish to cancel the financial arrangements that I have made with you. Please therefore will you NOT proceed with any actions that we had agreed and I would be grateful if you would confirm this in writing to me.
Furthermore I believe that it will be best if we don't meet again - EVER.
Good bye.
Janie Hardy.

She re-read it and then on an impulse instead of sending it right now thought she'd send it later in the day and switched it into "drafts".

Deciding to go out for a ride she changed into sweater and jodhpurs, drove to her friend Jackie who was looking after her favourite horse following the fire and after a quick chat went for a long ride alone through the countryside. It was a glorious morning and she was thoroughly enjoying herself when suddenly it struck her that if she cancelled the financial arrangements what on earth would she say to William?

He'd want to know why she'd suddenly changed her mind. After all up to now she'd said how nice Harry was and how helpful and what good ideas he'd come up with for her financial arrangements. William had also thought that Harry's ideas had been good and was thinking of having his own portfolio examined by the financial adviser. Now suddenly she didn't want to go ahead? William would think she was mad.

Once back home she went to her computer, called up the e-mail to Harry, deleted it then sat at the kitchen table and hand wrote a letter.

Harry
Although I'd really like to cancel the financial arrangements that I've made with you it will be difficult as William will be bound to ask why I've suddenly changed my mind especially as he thought your ideas were good.
So leave them as made but please DONT contact me again in person or by phone unless it is directly related to financial matters. Any correspondence is to be by letter, marked personal - not even e-mail.

Janie Hardy.

Yes that was better. She'd post it later. But she didn't. It sat there in a drawer of her desk for several days until one morning just after William had left for the office the phone rang. It was Harry.

'Janie please don't put the phone down. Listen to me. I fully expect you to want me to disappear and never hear from me again but I can't get you out of my mind. I must see you again…….please. Could we meet just to talk? Look I won't pester you or become a nuisance but I just had to make this one phone call. Please Janie meet me again. I really do think there is something terribly special between us.

I want to see if you feel the same way as I do. If you don't, well ok end of story. I'll go away and you'll never hear from me again I promise, but please meet me one more time ……. Janie are you there?'

'Yes I'm here and I heard what you said but what will be the good in us meeting again? I told you it was a mistake. A dreadful mistake and it's over. Harry it's over'.

'Janie please'.

'No ……. goodbye and don't ring me again'

The next few days passed. She still hadn't sent the letter and there was no call, letter or e-mail from him. Perversely she was almost sorry about that as he'd sounded so desperate to see her.

Two weeks later sitting at her computer one morning on an impulse she looked out his business card then sent him an e-mail.

If we were to meet where would you suggest? J.

His reply was almost instant.

Anywhere you want. PLEASE   H.

Why the hell had she sent that e-mail?

She ignored matters for another few days but something was starting to build up inside her and it was nagging away at her.

He was fun, he was good looking, he wasn't stuffy like William but most of all he was very good in bed. Forget it she told herself. Don't be so stupid. You've had a lucky escape. Think of your marriage, your children, your home, your friends and your life. Why get tangled up with a lover?

Another week passed before she created a new message to him and hit the "send" button.

Newmarket. Swynford Paddocks Hotel and
Restaurant. Lunch. Tuesday, 1pm. J

This time there was no immediate response. It was the following day when she logged on that amongst the several incoming e-mails she saw that there was one from him. Nervously she moved her mouse over his message and clicked.

Thank you. I'll be there. H

All through the weekend she was on tenterhooks as she was on Monday. Twice she sat down to e-mail him and cancel the arrangement but each time she created the message, when she hovered over the "send" button she moved to "cancel" and it disappeared.

She drove to Newmarket on Tuesday arriving about a quarter to one. Quite what she had in mind she wasn't sure. Perhaps she just needed to see him and tell him face to face that nothing was going to develop between them but as soon as she walked into the conservatory bar and saw him sitting in one of the wicker chairs, a glass of wine in his hand and his long legs sprawled out she knew that coming here had been a mistake.

Her legs felt wobbly. She ought to turn round and get back in the Porsche and go back home. He hadn't seen her yet so she could do that but just at her point of decision he glanced up. His face burst into a smile and leaping out of the chair he walked so quickly towards her that he almost ran.

'Janie. Thank you'.

'Look I don't know why I'm here but we have to talk'.

They did, for ages. He told her how he had been desperate to see her again and as she listened she felt again the ease with which she could talk to him. They ate a light lunch where they were sitting rather than going into the more formal dining room and afterwards sat drinking coffee until he suddenly leant forward, took hold of both her hands and looking into her eyes said softly 'I've booked a room. Will you come there with me now?'

She said nothing but didn't take her hands away. Standing he gently pulled her to her feet. 'Come on.......please' and winding his fingers through one of her hands he led her the short distance from where they were to the lovely old wooden staircase.

She was floating, feeling faint, nervous but also in some dreadful way excited, pleased, anticipating and above all wanting what he wanted to happen.

The large bedroom was lovely, full of soft colours and overlooked the lawns and grounds of the hotel and as soon as he shut the door she just fell into his arms and started to kiss him ardently and passionately.

They spent all afternoon closeted in the room and when she left at six to drive home, this time there were no protestations from her of not wanting to see him again.

She did as soon as possible. She wanted him and she needed him.

They met several times over the next few weeks, sometimes in Newmarket sometimes in London at his apartment and she found that her guilt complex disappeared completely.

She loved to be with him but most of all she loved making love with him.

Do not do what you would undo if caught.

Leah Arendt.

CHAPTER 6

The sudden raucous sound of the public announcement system crackling into life announcing that the Easyjet flight was about to land brought her back to today in France with a jolt. Watching through the windows she saw it flash down the runway and then a few minutes later it trundled towards the terminal building, turning slowly and ponderously to finish side on to the building. The door opened, the steps appeared and shortly a straggly line of passengers appeared.

Suddenly there he was, his tall figure towering over everyone else making their way down the steps. He looked at the terminal and then followed the others to disappear through a door at the far end. She walked quickly to the area where arriving passengers would appear and waited for what seemed ages but was in reality only a few minutes before he pushed through the swing doors and grinning broadly ran towards her. Dropping his bag he picked her up, kissed her and swung her round a little.

Several people nearby smiled as only the French can when they see two lovers meeting again after an absence.

It didn't seem necessary to speak, he simply picked up his bag and holding her hand walked with her out of the terminal to her car where as soon as they were both seated they kissed again but this time long deep and passionately.

'Come on let's go to the cottage' she said eventually. 'We can be alone there for as long as we want'.

Janie drove quickly until they reached the minor roads and then she slowed down partly so they could enjoy the quiet French countryside and partly because she was slightly distracted as a result of Harry leaning over and giving little kisses to her ear and neck and running his hand up and down her leg.

Arriving at the village, before going to the cottage she drove around pointing out the shops, the little restaurant and the bar where the locals gathered in the early evening to discuss the day's local events, the world, the mess the Government was making of the economy, farmer's interests, the Common Market and most things in which Government got involved. Then they'd turn to local gossip but in reality not much really happened in the little village.

She drove through the small market square then slowly towards the cottage stopping outside the front door.

'This looks lovely Janie'.

'Yes when we found it we fell in love with it. There was quite a bit of work needed doing but that's all done and we're happy with it now' she called over her shoulder as she walked down the little driveway to shut the gates.

When she turned back she saw that Harry had his grip bag in his hand and was walking towards the cottage. Taking the key out of her pocket she caught up with him, unlocked and pushed the door open.

Inside the room was cool and slightly dim due to the small windows. He dropped his bag on the flagstone floor, took off his jacket and draped it on a chair before walking slowly around the downstairs rooms. There were really only two now after the renovation and reconstruction. The major space was taken up with a large sitting room which with its limestone flooring took up about three quarters of the whole ground floor area and was furnished with a settee, assorted armchairs, an antique combined sideboard and bookcase unit, an old coffee table and some rugs. At the end of the room was a divider beyond which could be seen the kitchen which seemed to have all the modern appliances that might be needed but fitted into dark oak units. There was an old dining table and chairs in the middle.

'Janie, this is really delightful'.

'Very different from your stunning modern apartment'.

'Of course, but quite beautiful..........just like you. I can see why you're fond of it. I suppose you and William own it jointly do you?'

'No it's mine'.

'I see. That's nice'.

Looking at him for a moment she didn't know what to do.

She'd invited him here for a few days so that they could be alone and spend as much time as they wanted together, talking, getting to know each other and making love. Yes especially making love, lots and lots of making love. But now at this instant she was unsure, uncertain, nervous even. At the airport, in the car, driving round the village all that had been fine but what now? Should she take him up to bed straight away? Is that what he was expecting?

'The garden looks lovely too from what I can see' he said as he peered through the smallish windows.

'Yes it is. Come on would you like to have a look round? We've got a little pool as well if you fancy a swim' and her moment of indecision passed.

'Now that sounds a great idea. Lead on'.

He stood looking expectantly at her so she led the way through the kitchen and out into the garden. The smell of honeysuckle and other sweet scented flowers struck them both as soon as they walked outside and he held her hand as they wandered slowly around eventually coming to the pool. Letting go of her hand he knelt down, felt the water then looked up at her, brushing his hair lock away.

'It's lovely and warm. I'd love a quick swim to freshen up after the flight. Will it be ok to go in now?'

'Yes if you want'.

'Join me?'

'No, I'll just watch you for now. I'll swim later' and she sat on a sunlounger at the side of the pool.

Nodding, he smiled that intriguing smile of his and pulled off his tee shirt then sitting on one of the pool side chairs slipped off his shoes and socks before standing to unzip his jeans. Once they were off he quite unselfconsciously slid down his blue boxer shorts to drop them on the sunlounger.

Moving to the pool he sat down, looked over his shoulder to her, smiled and slipped into the water. The pool was quite short and in half a dozen strokes he'd reached the end, but turning he pushed off and swam slowly back to the other end. She watched his naked buttocks and back and then when he reached the end and stood up she stared at him watching the water drip down from his chest hairs and nipples.

'God that's better. It's amazing how grubby one feels after travelling even if it's only for a relatively short journey isn't it?' he called before floating on his back and gently paddling down the pool.

She looked at him as he swam, paddled and floated around for a while until he swam to the shallow end and climbed up the steps to come out.

As he walked towards her she looked at his penis which was similar in size to William's the only difference being that William was circumcised whereas Harry wasn't. Reaching her he flopped onto another sunlounger.

'Got a towel?'

'No sorry not down here. I forgot to bring any outside. They're all indoors ……..err upstairs'.

'Ah. Well maybe I ought to go and try to find one'.

'I'll come with you and show you where they are'.

Standing she took his hand and led the way indoors through the kitchen, back into the sitting room and to the small door behind which was the staircase. He paused momentarily to pick up his grip and then dripping water followed her upstairs.

She led the way into the bedroom and pulling open the top drawer of a large chest unit extracted a towel and held it out to him. He smiled and started to rub his hair while she stood and looked him up and down starting to feel some excitement as she studied his hairy chest and watched his penis bob about with the movements from his vigorous hair drying actions.

'Here let me do that for you' she said quietly and moving behind him gently rubbed his slightly overlong hair then moved the towel down to rub his neck, back and buttocks. Kneeling she was rubbing the back of his legs when he turned round to face her. Using the towel on his shins she looked up, her eyes level with his still flaccid penis.

'Grrrr' she growled leaning forward and nipping the end of his foreskin in her front teeth. 'Grrrr' she growled again shaking her head from side to side a little. Releasing him she giggled 'I'd like to bite it off and keep it with me always' then she slid her lips over him feeling him start to erect.

She moved her head back and forth for a little then glancing up saw his eyes closed with delight at what she was doing for him. Releasing him she stood and kissed his chest while one hand rubbed his penis and the other reached beneath him, found his balls and squeezed them gently.

He took her face in his hands lifted her chin, whispered 'Janie' and pulling her to himself, kissed her softly at first and then more passionately.

Letting go of him she could feel his erection pressing against her stomach so stepping back she sat on the bed pulling him down with her. Her hands fumbled at her blouse which was soon undone and her breasts freed. Wriggling further up the bed she slipped off her slacks and thong so as he rolled on top of her they were both naked. His penis nuzzled against her pussy which moistened immediately and straightway she felt him trying to enter her.

'Oh Janie darling this is so good' he whispered then pressed his tongue deep into her mouth and raised his hips.

'Wait. You need a condom?'

'What?'

'A condom Harry'.

'Oh shit. Ok they're in my grip'.

'I'll get them for you' and she slid out from under him, got off the bed, picked up his bag, unzipped it and rummaged around inside.

'Where will I find them?'

'In the pocket of my wash bag'.

A pause, then she smiled and handing him the packet while getting back onto the bed watched as he extracted one foil, split it open and rolled the protective down himself.

'Now where were we my beautiful Janie?' he grinned as he pushed her onto her back and rolled back on top of her again. Thrusting inside he started to make love to her. He took time, a lot of time and she climaxed beautifully, long before he muttered that he was coming. Gripping his buttocks hard she pulled him into her as firmly as she could. Concentrating on her own second mounting waves of pleasure she heard his groans of pleasure and felt him pulsing. He was still moving although more slowly now when her second climax erupted deep within her.

She clung to him silently for a while then relaxed as she felt him exhale deeply and look down on her. Neither of them spoke they just held each other until his erection subsided. He eased himself off her, removed the condom, then they lay side by side his arm beneath her as he gently nibbled her lips, eyes, neck and her still hard nipples. Responding she kissed his chin and chest.

They stayed where they were for a long time not really moving just occasionally stroking each other and kissing softly. Janie felt so happy and fulfilled with her lover as she listened to the birds singing and enjoyed the warm southern French temperatures. Turning her head she could see that the sun was shining strongly and the trees outside were just moving slightly in the gentle breeze. Looking back at Harry she saw a puzzled expression on his face.

Leaning over him she rested an elbow on his chest. 'Penny for them! What were you thinking about......me? '

'You'll be cross when I tell you'

'No I won't. What is it?'

'Promise'.

'Yes I promise. Now come on what's on your mind'.

'Well I was just thinking that it's nearly two thirty and I'm hungry. Sorry'.

'And there I was imagining that you were thinking all sorts of lovely kind loving things about me...... about how wonderful our lovemaking was. It was..... wasn't it Harry? Well it was for me but was it alright for you? You're not disappointed are you?'

'No I'm not disappointed. You were wonderful ...... but I am hungry'.

'Men! You're all the same. Sex and food. I guess sometimes it's eat then sex and other times like today it's sex and then eat. Alright let's go downstairs and I'll fix us something. I did some shopping this morning'.

She was smiling happily as she rolled off the bed, went to the bathroom then came back into the bedroom and found a pair of bikini pants which she pulled on before skipping cheerfully downstairs to the kitchen. She'd just started to lay the kitchen table when Harry joined her wearing a pair of extremely garishly coloured long swim shorts.

'Blimey no-one will miss you in those' she giggled.

'Rather fetching I think' he grinned in reply striking a pose. All the latest fashion rage I believe especially here in the south of France'.

'Maybe. Well you said you were hungry so here you are. There's pate, cheese, salad, some lovely locally baked bread, fruit and if you whip the cork out of this we'll have some of their local wine. It's actually quite good'.

So they sat happy and relaxed enjoying each other's company and their simple meal and talking. After they'd finished Janie suggested that they went outside again and soon they were stretched out side by side on the sunloungers but after a few minutes she went back indoors returning shortly with a bottle of sun lotion.

'The sun's deceptively hot here. We don't want to get burnt and be unable to make love do we, so rub some of this onto me, then I'll do you'.

'Do me? Here on the sunlounger! Yes please'.

'Silly I meant, well you know what I meant' and holding out the bottle she laid face down and relaxed as he slowly and sensuously managed the white creamy liquid into her neck, back and legs especially lingering around the area where her pussy was covered by the little strip of bikini material.

When it was his turn he lay on his back as she massaged in the sun cream working her way down his neck, his hairy chest, slowly circled around his belly which she noted was beautifully taut and flat, unlike William's which was definitely getting flabby.

Her hands moved to work their way down to his feet and then back up his shins and thighs. She rolled his long swim short legs up and massaged the cream into the top of his legs but noticing the obvious signs of an erection developing firmly pulled them down again and told him to control himself. He grinned at her.

They lay in the sun holding hands, dozing and talking. They swam, sun bathed, finished the lunchtime bottle of wine then around five o'clock made their way upstairs to bed again where they spent the next couple of hours making love. It was years since Janie had spent a really long time making love and she was just so happy. All thoughts of it being wrong were gone and as she stroked Harry's taut and very fit body she mentally contrasted it with William's which was chubby and overweight.

She amazed herself that she could lie here with her lover and think dispassionately about him and her husband, compare their bodies and not feel any guilt. Where was this all going to lead? That was the only question in her mind but refusing to dwell on it she relaxed and enjoyed her lover as he gently stroked her breasts.

'Janie?'

'Yes'.

Moving down he kissed her tummy then laid his cheek on it looking down towards her pussy. Letting his fingers entwine themselves in her pubic hair he asked 'This cottage is really lovely. You said that it's yours and not in joint names.....you know yours and Williams?'

'No it's all mine. William put it in my name for tax reasons'.

'I see'. His fingers slid lower and into her pussy.

'Umm nice, don't stop',

'Good' and he massaged her slowly. 'That may not have been such a good idea you know'.

'What?'

'Putting it just in your name' and his fingers slid deep inside her.

'Aah that's lovely.......she paused and took his hand. 'Stop a second. Why not?'

'Well it might be alright for uk income tax reasons but when it comes to Inheritance then French laws can be very complicated and strange. Some of them date back to Napoleonic times. They're not like our uk laws'.

Removing his fingers he turned and slid up the bed to kiss her breasts. 'If you die, it probably won't pass on in the way you hoped'. Stroking her hair off her face he planted a gentle kiss on her lips. 'It could be divided up by the local authorities over here with one third going to each of your children and the final third to William, or they, the French authorities that is, might decide that it should all go to the children, half each and William could miss out. As I say it can be tricky'. He kissed her again and ran a finger around her nipples.

'Oh bloody hell I didn't realise that. I'm sure William didn't either'.

'No it's not well known but there could be a simple solution. I have an off shore company called H. N. O. P. It stands for Harry Norton Offshore Property and we can take care of all the problems for you through that company'.

His hand travelled back down to her belly, circled for a little and then slid down through her pubic hair and started to play with her pussy again which by now had become very moist.

'Could you really? Aah that's so nice'.

'Yes all you have to do is sign a simple agreement know as a Deed of Ownership Trust Offshore Transfer ..... hell of a complicated title isn't it' he chuckled as he slid one finger just inside her 'then I pay you the princely sum of one euro and the property is registered in the name of my off shore company'. A second finger joined the first.

'Wait a minute' and she again took hold of his hand. He removed his fingers but left his hand lying there. 'But wouldn't that mean that I no longer own the cottage?'

'Technically yes, but that's the whole point. As it's not yours but belongs to an off shore company in this case mine, then the authorities can't do anything about it for inheritance tax'.

'But if it belongs to your company how would I or my dependants get it back? Oh and whereabouts is this off shore company?'

'Erm it's registered in the Cayman Islands. But it's simple for you to get your property back. Sign another document called a Deed of Revocation and it comes back to whoever is designated by my off shore company'.

His fingers moved to her clit which he rubbed gently. 'So it could be William or your kids, or anyone else that my company signs the agreement with. All that person or persons has to do is pay two euros......one to unwind the original arrangement and another euro to effect the transfer. As I said it's so simple. But let's not worry about that anymore. I think there is something much more important for us to discuss' and he massaged her more vigorously.

'There is?'

'Definitely'.

'What's that?'

'Which exciting position we are going to use for our next very passionate lovemaking session'.

'Any ideas?'

He had and they laughed and wriggled around making love. He suggested several different positions some of which she'd never adopted before and she enjoyed being used in this way.

Much later in the evening they bathed, dressed then walked slowly holding hands into the village to the little restaurant.

It wasn't crowded and the patron offered them a choice of a table outside on the wide pavement, or inside in the cool dark of the interior. They decided to eat inside but have a drink outside while ordering and waiting for the food to be prepared. Janie ordered one of the region's specialities, angler fish in a creamy mild curry sauce while Harry, attracted by the patron's description of his local wild boar stew decided to try that.

Two glasses of local red wine soon appeared and they sat quietly drinking slowly, enjoying the fading evening sunshine, the gentle ambience of the sleepy village street where a few people, the odd cyclist and an occasional car or van went past. Every now and then someone came into the restaurant either for a drink or to eat and each time the newcomer nodded or smiled at Janie and Harry who both felt relaxed and very happy.

'You're not worried about sitting here bold as brass with a strange man.....err your lover?' queried Harry looking at her over the rim of his glass.

'Here? In France? Good lord no. Even if people suspected they'd ignore it, or more probably admire us. After all the French expect married women to take a lover'.

'I guess so. You are lovely you know'.

'You are a flatterer, but I'm not lovely. Attractive maybe but I'm still an old married woman with two kids'. She frowned and he suddenly wondered if the mention of her children might be causing her to have doubts about her affair.

Fortunately just at that moment the patron emerged to tell them that their meal was ready and leading them to a table at the rear of the restaurant he held out Janie's chair before carefully unfurling her napkin and laying it on her lap. His wife brought a large bowl of mixed salad and a long crusty loaf after which the patron returned with two large plates brimming full of food which he set before them with a flourish.

'Voila, bon appétit'.

'Merci. Je suis sur qu'il ser a délicieux' smiled Janie.

The patron, pleased that the English lady had spoken to him in French when ordering, and not only thanking him for the food but saying that she was sure it would be delicious, decided that a complimentary bottle of house wine was called for and reappeared shortly telling her that it was "Sur la maison" and left it on the table for them to enjoy.

Once back in the small kitchen at the rear of the restaurant he told his wife that he didn't think that the English lady's dinner companion was her husband as he was a different man from when she had last been here with children and a man who he was sure was her husband. His wife nodded and said she agreed but perhaps it was a relative of the English lady who'd come to stay but agreed it was more probably her lover.

He also thought it was more likely to be her lover as he'd seen them touching and occasionally holding hands.

Ah she nodded, obviously it was the lady's lover. How nice and she made a mental note to speak to her friend Marie who was retained by the English couple to clean and tidy the cottage when they were using it and when they were away to go in once a week to open the windows, air the place, dust and generally keep an eye on it. Yes Marie would soon discover whether they were sleeping together. Mind you he was an attractive man eating with the English lady and she was sure that if they were having an illicit affair they'd be very passionate together.

Good for them she thought. Maybe he could give her husband some ideas!

The food was wonderful and the English couple quite unaware of the speculation they caused thoroughly enjoyed their meal finishing by spooning some of the salad onto their plates and taking their time to enjoy the interesting mixture of locally grown salad leaves, tomatoes and raw chopped vegetables.

They lingered over the meal and when they eventually finished, the patron cleared their plates while his wife hovered nearby ensuring that she got a really good look at the Englishman.

Deciding against dessert or cheese Harry and Janie took the nearly empty bottle of wine and returned to sitting outside where they finished it before ordering coffees and brandy and it was well past ten o'clock and dark when they paid and walked slowly, arms around each other back to the cottage where Harry declining anything further to drink led the way upstairs to bed.

So the pattern of the next few days was established. They made love when they woke, got up late, breakfasted in the garden, lazed in the sunshine, swam in the little pool, wandered into the village from time to time to shop or eat and simply enjoyed each other's company and conversation.

Harry remained at all times a gentle, considerate lover always taking time for her and never rushing their intimacy together and she concluded that he was the most skilful and experienced lover that she'd ever had.

It was on Saturday morning, their third day there and Janie was lying naked in the garden when she heard a woman's voice calling, so quickly pulling on her bikini pants she went into the cottage and picking up a wrap on the way walked across the cool flagstone floor and opened the front door.

'Bonjour Madame. Je suis venu pour nettoyer pour vous'. (Good day Madame. I have come to clean for you.) Marie stood there smiling broadly.

'Oh Marie. Merci et comment allez vous aujourd'hui? Je ne pense pas qu'il y a beaucoup à faire. (Thank you and how are you today? I don't think that there is much to do).

Janie spoke loudly hoping that Harry wouldn't suddenly appear stark naked from upstairs where he'd gone a few minutes ago but to her relief when he walked downstairs a little later he was wearing a tee shirt and a pair of slacks.

He smiled at the French woman then he and Janie returned to the garden while Marie bustled around indoors.

She washed the floor, dusted and tided, then made her way upstairs. First port of call was the spare bedroom where she immediately saw that the two single beds hadn't been made up as there were just mattresses but no bedclothes. Ah she smiled to herself going straight away into the main bedroom where it was immediately obvious that the two English people had been sleeping together.

His clothes were scattered around and the bed was rumpled and unmade. Obviously lots of passionate loving had been going on in here and she concluded that she must inform her friend Therese at the restaurant this lunch time.

Meanwhile she set to and tidied the room, made the bed, dusted around then she glanced out of the window and saw the English couple in the garden. Being nosey she quickly looked in the chest of drawers and wardrobe then pulled open the drawers on the bedside cabinets. In one she found some packets of condoms. Smiling at this further confirmation that they were lovers she moved into the bathroom where she noticed his shaving things by the basin. Another smile.

Returning downstairs she put the dirty crockery into the dishwasher then walked into the garden, said that she'd competed her work and smiled gratefully when Janie extracted some Euro notes from her bag and held them out.

'Ici. Ceux-ci sont pour aujourd'hui et pour les trios suivants. Merci do s'occuper de la petite maison pour nous'. (Here these are for today and for the next three months. Thank you for looking after the cottage for us).

'Merci Madame' and smiling broadly Marie tucked the money into her apron pocket while studying the man with the slightly overlong hair before taking her leave. Very nice and very sexy she thought walking away down the short drive. She had another cleaning job to do before she'd be able to tell Therese what she'd seen.

It was only later in the day when Janie passed the open door to the spare bedroom and saw the beds devoid of bedding that it struck her that the cleaner would have seen it too and realised that the two of them had slept together. For a moment she panicked then calmed down remembering her assurance to Harry in the restaurant a few nights ago. No-one would say anything. They were in France. Their secret would be safe.

That night when they went to the restaurant for dinner she thought that the patron's wife was particularly solicitous to them, and her questions as to whether Madame and her friend were enjoying themselves seemed a little pointed but managing to avoid blushing she said that yes they were and that tomorrow they'd drive around the area so that her friend Harry could see something of the countryside.

When they returned to the cottage she sat on the settee and checking her mobile saw that while she was out there'd been two missed calls, both from William. Disentangling herself from Harry who had plonked down beside her and was stroking her leg while nuzzling her neck, she pressed the re-dial button and moved away to the other side of the room.

'William darling how are you? Sorry I missed your calls but I was treating myself to a meal in the restaurant. You remember the one on the corner that serves such lovely food? How are things at home? Any news about the fire?'

He told her that more insurance assessors had been to the ruined stables, along with the police and the fire investigation team again. There was no doubt it was arson. He didn't mention a threatening letter which he had received the previous day.

107

Crossing her fingers she asked if he was going to be able to get down to join her for a day or so. When he said he'd love to but if she didn't mind he really ought to stay in England as there was so much going on and also things were not good at the office, she couldn't help smiling and felt a tenseness that had suddenly arisen in her stomach instantly disappear. Looking around she couldn't see Harry.

They talked for a little while longer then William asked whether the break in France was helping her feel better and when she planned to return?

'Yes heaps better thank you darling. It is so relaxing here and just to be able to get away from the aftermath of that awful fire is wonderful. Such a shame that you're not here with me though'.

Liar. That's the last thing I want.

'I thought I'd stay for a few more days and then see about getting a flight back. Tomorrow I'll ring the airline and see what's available. It would help enormously if we had the internet installed down here you know'.

'Yes I guess you're right' he replied sounding doubtful 'ok well enjoy your break and let me know when you're coming back. Love and kisses'.

'Mmm, me too' and blowing a couple of kisses down the phone she said goodbye and broke the connection.

Harry had walked into the garden as he'd thought it better if he left her alone to talk to her husband but hearing her approaching he turned and seeing a concerned expression on her face patted the sunlounger on which he was sitting.

'Everything all right?'

'Yes'. She sat next to him.

'Sure?'

'Well yes but this is wrong isn't it? There's William at home dealing with all the problems of the fire and I know he's got problems at the office as well and I am here betraying him'.

'Betray is a rather strong word. Do you want me to go?'

'No'.

'Janie really I am terribly fond of you. Ever since the first time that I saw you at that wedding there was something about you that attracted you to me. Well more than just attracted you, drew me to you I suppose.

Even in these few days together I have grown even more fond of you but I don't want to come between you and William......unless you want me to that is'.

'No. Look Harry I love William. He's totally different from you but I don't want to hurt him. What we have, you and I, is something very special but it must not break him and I up, nor can I allow it to damage him. He was so hurt when his first marriage broke up and I can't let that happen to him again, nor will I do anything to hurt my sons'.

Taking Harry's hands she looked into his eyes which she could just see from the faint moonlight since the moon had emerged from behind a cloud. Smiling she spoke softly. 'Come here, kiss me and make me stop worrying'.

He did and soon the kisses became deep and meaningful as he gently pushed her back onto the sunlounger cushions which were slightly damp from the night dew while pressing his tongue deep into her mouth where it was soon fencing with her flicking tongue.

Lifting the hem of her dress up to her waist he slid her panties off then kissed her belly button before tracing his tongue down to her pussy which he licked for a few moments before hefting her legs over his shoulders and burying his face deeply between her legs.

She quickly forgot about William, her sons, England, Hardys, the fire, in fact everything except the sensations that he was generating for her as she mewed and groaned at the intense feelings that he was inducing in her.

No-one had ever been so intimate with her as Harry and she revelled in the delightfully lewd acts that he was committing on her with his fingers and tongue until arching her back and clamping his head tightly between her thighs she exhaled loudly as her orgasm rippled through her.

Quickly he reached down to undo his belt and while continuing to love her with his tongue, with some considerable difficulty he managed to push slacks and pants down and off.

'Stay there' he commanded and ran indoors. When he returned he quickly fitted a condom, pushed her legs over his shoulders again and smiling suddenly slammed his prick deep into her.

Their lovemaking was intense and before long his soft groan told her that he'd climaxed so letting out a deep breath she relaxed beneath him as she slid her legs alongside of him.

'Hold me darling Harry, that was so incredible. Thank you'.

They lay together for a while then Harry stretched up and walking quickly over to the pool slipped into the warm water calling 'Come and join me'.

Smiling she unzipped her dress and jumped in sending a huge cascade of water over him and the side of the pool. They laughed, wrestled, kissed and played together in the water until after a while Janie thought that they should go to bed.

Climbing out they ran into the cottage locked the doors and dripping water across the floor and up the stairs Janie pulled him into the bathroom thrusting a towel in his hand and taking another for herself.

'Race you to get dry and into bed' she giggled leaning forward, shaking her hair vigorously spraying water all over the place.

As soon as they were in bed and still laughing she pushed him onto his back, climbed on top of him and leaning forward offered her breasts to his lips while gently rubbing her pussy hair up and down his penis which she felt start to stiffen.

Swivelling round she moved into a sixty nine position and took his now hard penis into her mouth whilst lowering her pussy onto his lips. They kissed, licked and chewed each other until just as she was approaching her own climax she felt his penis start to throb.

Lifting her lips off him she quickly rolled a condom down his length then re-swallowed him but after a few seconds she felt him pulsing jet after jet of semen into the rubber protective.

Just think. Only a few microns of thin rubber between his sperm and her mouth.

Later they cuddled together. Harry was soon asleep but Janie lay awake for ages thinking about William, Harry, what life would be like with a long term lover and how she'd cope with that when she was back in England?

Is this what I want? Should I, or indeed could I stop seeing him? Do I want Harry instead of William? No, That was definite. Harry was fun, very sexy, a great lover but her life with William and her children were still very important. Harry would have to remain her secret lover.

Earlier in the evening they'd discussed their lovemaking and use of condoms. Harry had said that they'd soon need to get some more as he only had a few left.

'We seem to have used rather a lot of them' he'd grinned. 'We'll either have to stop making love or find somewhere to buy some more. Do you know anywhere? Does the village shop sell them?'

She said that she didn't want to buy them in the village shop as that might strain French tolerance too much and that tomorrow they'd have to drive to another village or town to get some more.

Next morning sitting by the pool they rang Easyjet. Harry booked a flight for himself on Tuesday afternoon while she booked herself back on the Wednesday morning flight. She told Harry that she'd need time to tidy up the cottage and didn't want to waste their time together with domestic chores. Also she thought she'd like a few hours alone after he'd gone.

When they'd fixed the flights she sent William a text giving her flight time and date and then they got into the yellow convertible and spent the rest of the day meandering around the local area.

Harry was enchanted with this part of France although from time to time he distracted Janie by squeezing her knee or stroking her upper leg while she was driving. They covered quite a distance and stopped in a village as Janie said that she wanted to cook supper for them that night rather than going out to the village restaurant. So they entered the old fashioned grocers shop and soon had everything she needed.

Then they walked along the main street of this village to a little café/bar for a glass of wine and some cold meat and salad.

It was while they were drinking coffee after their lunch he suggested a walk as he said that he wanted to stretch his long legs which were still suffering from being cramped up in the car. She happily agreed and they set off and had soon left the road behind them as they wandered across a field and approached a wood but as they got to the trees he pulled her into a small clearing, took off his shirt, spread it on the ground and invited her to sit down which she did.

He didn't though and smiling he stood in front of her and stripped until he was completely naked.

'Mr. Norton whatever do you have in mind?'

'Sex with the most beautiful lady I have ever met' he responded taking his not quite flaccid penis and rubbing it.

'Harry that is so........'

'What?' he laughed continuing to rub himself 'naughty?'

'Yes but come here let me do it for you'.

'Only if you take off all your clothes as well' he laughed still rubbing.

'Harry!'

Later lying still naked she reflected that making love on the very edge of the woods was so delightfully uninhibited and sexy that it was truly wonderful. Very erotic and so natural with Harry but William would have had a fit if she'd suggested shagging naked in the woods.

They arrived back at the cottage late afternoon and went into the garden, undressed, swam nude in the little pool, kissed and stroked each other as they lay side by side on the sunloungers where they both dozed and enjoyed the sunshine on their undressed bodies.

Around seven Janie said that she'd go and make a start on the supper but he was welcome to stay and enjoy the early evening sun, so leaving him in the garden she went indoors slipped on a clean pair of panties and a short loose skirted dress and started bustling around in the kitchen.

She intended to make spaghetti bolognese and was standing stirring the large old saucepan containing the things that they'd bought that lunch time. Local minced beef, some fresh and a tin of tomatoes, fresh olives, a chopped onion, a good large splash of local red wine and some seasoning when after about half an hour or so Harry came in still stark naked.

'Hi. I got lonely in the garden so I thought I'd come and keep you company. Umm that smells delicious' he said as he peered over her shoulder at the bubbling mixture then he dropped a kiss onto her neck before adding 'and so do you'.

'Flatterer' she chuckled as slipping his arms around her waist and kissing her neck again she felt him press himself against her. His hands moved up to gently cup her breasts and he pushed his crotch more firmly against her.

'Go away .…. leave me alone' she laughed shoving her bottom back to push him away and wriggling out of his grasp. 'I'm cooking. There'll be plenty of time for that later'.

'Spoilsport' he grumbled as he walked to the fridge and took out a bottle of white wine, opened it and poured two glasses. 'Cheers'.

'Cheers and don't you think you ought to put on some clothes. It's a bit off putting for a cook to have a naked man wandering around you know'.

'Good' he grinned. 'No I'm happy as I am thank you and I think you ought to take your clothes off too so I can watch you cooking in the nude'.

'No way' she laughed. 'I might get my boobs .…. and other bits burnt'.

'I'd kiss them all better for you'.

'Yes I'm sure you would, but the answer is still no!'

He went into the sitting room area and slumped still nude onto the settee drinking his wine while she laid the table in the kitchen and continued peering at, tasting and stirring the bolognese sauce. She'd just dropped the spaghetti into a large pan of hot water and taken a little sip of the sauce when he again sidled up behind her, squeezed her buttocks, reached round for her breasts and pushed himself against her bottom where she could now distinctly feel his erection pressing against her.

Picking up the wooden spoon with which she'd been stirring the sauce she swung round. 'I told you to leave me alone while I was cooking and I meant it. Now behave yourself' and she smacked his erect prick with the spoon.

'Ouch that hurt' he grumbled 'and it was bloody hot'.

'Serves you right, now go away or you'll get another one' and raising the spoon she advanced towards him.

'Alright' he agreed 'but any chance of you kissing it better?'

'Not now .…. later maybe .…. if you're a good boy. Now go and put some clothes on as we'll be eating soon. Go on off with you' and as he turned away she landed a good hard crack from the spoon on his bare right buttock.

'Yow, ok ok I'm going. I know when to give in' and laughing broadly he walked towards the staircase. Janie watched his erection flopping up and down as he ran up the stairs but it was properly hidden when he came down a few minutes later in jeans and a tee shirt but bare feet.

Supper was a cheerful fun event and they enjoyed talking and flirting with each other, so it was late in the evening after they'd eaten, washed up and tidied everything away and were sitting cuddled together on the settee sipping some brandy, when he again raised the subject of her ownership of the cottage.

'Have you thought any more about my suggestion of putting the cottage off shore?' he queried softly smiling and stroking her neck.

'Well it seems a good idea, but is it really as simple as you said the other evening?'

Yes it is. That's the beauty of it. Look why don't I get some papers drawn up and next time we meet in London you can have a look at them then if you want to go ahead you can do so. If not, no problem'.

'Perhaps I could then talk it through with William'.

'Erm well you could of course, but a couple of things come to mind. Firstly didn't you say that he was busy with lots of problems at the office so do you want to worry him over what is in reality just a minor bit of paperwork? Secondly I am after all your financial adviser so you're quite entitled to make financial arrangements with me directly.

'Yes I guess you're right. I probably don't need to worry him about this. As you say it's only a paper formality'.

'Exactly. I'll get the paperwork drawn up when I get back'. Squeezing her hand he looked deep into her eyes. 'Now my dear Janie let's go up to bed. You just don't know how desperate I am to make love to you again but the first thing you are going to do for me is kiss better where you smacked me with that spoon .... cock and bum both need some tender care and attention' and his hand slid under her skirt and gently probed around the gusset edge of her panties.

'Oh come on then' she giggled standing and holding out a hand to pull him to his feet.

Upstairs she quickly peeled off his tee shirt, unzipped his jeans and yanked them and his pants off then as she pulled her dress over her head she continued 'Which do you want me to kiss better first then?'

He lay on his tummy as she clambered onto the bed so she kissed his right buttock then as he said that he thought she should do the same to the other she duly obliged until he rolled onto his back and pointing at his firm hard erection demanded that she now worked on that.

Holding and rubbing him gently she kissed up and down the length until as he put his hands behind her neck she opened her lips and swallowed the length of him.

'Oh baby' he muttered over and over again as she worked on him for a while until releasing him to crawl up the bed to the bedside table, found one of the condom packets they'd bought earlier that day, slit it open and soon had him covered. Slowly she lowered her pussy onto him and sitting upright moved up and down on him.

'Make it last Harry darling' she whispered as she moved a little quicker on him. He nodded and pulled her head down to him so they could kiss while at the same time he reached for and found her clit which he gently massaged enjoying hearing her groans and grunts of pleasure and satisfaction.

Several minutes later he flipped her onto her back and asking if she was nearly there and receiving a gasped 'Yes' he slammed into her fast and hard until she gurgled and groaned and he felt her pussy pulsing around his erection. It was a long drawn out orgasm that she had and as it was starting to diminish he reached his own climax.

They clung together for ages long afterwards, neither of them wanting the moment to end, or their passion to subside but finally they smiled into each other's eyes, told each other that they were wonderful and whispered thank you as they disentangled and laid quietly side by side.

She felt him removing the rubber protection and then he cuddled her into his side and they drifted slowly and fully sated off to sleep.

Tuesday dawned sunny, warm but cloudy. They made love then dressed and wandered into the village for breakfast at the restaurant before returning to the cottage where they swam, made love again this time on the warm grass, went indoors, showered, dressed and Harry packed for his return to England.

The journey to the airport was uneventful and they were soon sitting in the airport lounge which doubled as both an arrival and departure area. They talked, held hands, nuzzled until his plane could be seen taxiing up to the terminal building. The loudspeaker crackled into life again and he stood.

'I don't know what to say. Janie I have never had such a wonderful few days in all my life'.

'Nor me' she replied with a choke in her throat. 'You'd better go or you'll miss the flight'.

He nodded, looked at her, quietly asked 'May I?' then seeing her nod, kissed her softly, gave her a hug and picking up his grip walked to the departure door. He didn't look back but when she stood at the glass windows that looked out onto the apron where the aeroplane was parked he turned, smiled and waved at her. Waving back she stood watching as he climbed the steps. She thought she could see him at the window of the plane.

The steps retracted, the engines started and the plane slowly and ponderously turned and trundled out to the main runway where a few minutes later it flashed past the terminal and climbed into the air. Running outside she watched the jet as it climbed away until eventually it banked steeply as it turned north and was swallowed by the clouds.

She wasn't sure how long she stood watching the clouds where the plane had disappeared but eventually she shook herself and walked slowly to her car to drive back to the cottage.

There had been an accident on the main road and traffic was stationary for ages so it was nearly three hours later when she walked into the cool sitting room of her cottage.

The feeling of emptiness and loneliness was intense and she dropped onto the settee as the tears came. It was a long time before she stopped crying and went upstairs to the bathroom to wash her face but passing the bedroom door and seeing the still rumpled bed she flopped face down onto it and started to cry again. She could smell him on the sheets, could almost feel him there, could imagine him reaching out for her but opening her eyes she was alone and sad. Turning onto her back she lay for more than an hour letting competing thoughts start to run through her mind.

Inevitably she thought of the fire and who could have caused it. William had said that the authorities had determined that it was definitely arson. So who could hate them so much to do such a terrible thing and yet at the same time make sure the horses were safe?

Thinking about William and muttering 'Sorry' she started to cry again as she thought about her loving loyal husband. She thought of the children and her friends. What would they all say to her if they knew she'd gone to France with a lover? So her mind came full circle as Harry returned to her thoughts and smiling she let her mind wander over the last few days and the wonderful time that they'd had together as her hand smoothed across the sheets were he'd laid.

But would Harry stay faithful to her as a lover or would he soon dump her and start to play the field with other women? He was so attractive that she was sure it wouldn't be long before other women threw themselves at him, or responded to his advances. What did he want from her or with her?

He knew that she wouldn't give up William, her children and her life in Norfolk. So how long could an affair based virtually solely on sex last? He was younger than her and obviously some time, maybe soon, he'd want to sleep with a younger woman. Would that be the time that he'd move on?

Fearing that if she stayed lying on the bed close to where they'd been so intimate she'd start howling again, she got up, went downstairs and taking a deep breath started to tidy up the sitting room and kitchen. Then she went into the garden and sat for a while before having a last swim after which she looked at the grass where they'd made love that morning, shrugged and covered the pool, put the cushions away into the little shed and stacked the chairs and sunloungers to one side of the garden.

Back indoors she brushed her hair, popped on a little makeup, then walked into the village and wandered around before stopping at the restaurant for a glass of wine. Confirming in response to the patron's wife's query that her friend had returned to England she sat quietly and enjoyed the wine, the village street, the muffled conversation going on within the restaurant and the warm sunshine now that the clouds had rolled away.

Later she went back to the cottage, switched on the TV and found the BBC News channel and sat for an hour or so listening to the problems and tragedies that unfolded on the small screen.

Around the world there'd been an earthquake in northern India, a ferry disaster in China, a plane crash in Mexico and a multiple shooting in Texas. In Britain council tax officers had threatened to go on strike, a child had gone missing in Yorkshire, there was further unrest over the leadership within the Liberal Democrat party, and on the sports field England had lost yet another test match to the West Indies.

Such misery and unhappiness in so many places, contrasting with her happy life with a wonderful husband, two lovely kids and a beautiful lover.

Sighing she switched off the set and went into the kitchen to make a scratch supper from the leftovers. She settled for a ham and cheese omelette, some French bread and fruit. That about finished everything but putting any remaining perishable things into the rubbish bag, she walked down towards the village and disposed of the bag of rubbish at the refuse collection point.

Back indoors she sprayed disinfectant on the kitchen surfaces, bleached the sink, then went upstairs, ran a bath and soaked for a while before going to bed.

Climbing naked between the sheets she laid on the side that Harry had slept and inhaling his smells found her fingers moving involuntarily to her clit and pussy where muttering 'Oh Harry my love' she slowly massaged herself to an orgasm. Afterwards surprisingly she dropped off to sleep quite quickly.

She woke a couple of times in the night, the first time feeling for him then remembering that he'd gone. The second time she went to the bathroom and had a pee but after getting back into bed it took some time to drop off again.

Morning when it came was blustery and threatening rain, so getting up she made some coffee and drank it slowly downstairs. Her last actions were to unmake the bed, put the used sheets and pillow cases into the laundry basket but not before she'd held his pillow case to her cheek, dropped in the used towels from the bathroom knowing that they and the bed linen would all be washed and ironed by Marie, had a final check round that the windows were properly fastened, then locking the front door she stopped to fasten the gate and then drove to the airport.

At Pierre's garage she handed her car back, smiled at Jacques hovering shyly the background, paid for a further three months storage and walked across to the terminal.

A quick text to William to say that she'd checked in and was waiting for the flight to be called. It was on time and all too soon she was back at Stansted and making her way to the car park.

It was around six o'clock when she arrived at Wood Hollow Hall, dropped her bags in the hallway, walked into the kitchen opened the fridge, took out a bottle of white wine, poured a glass and taking it with her wandered into the large sitting room.

She expected William to be home around seven, so running upstairs she had a quick shower, did her face and hair, put on a pretty blouse and short skirt, reasonably high heels and returned downstairs to await the return of her husband.

That's it. All ready to play the faithful wife.

Sure enough at about a quarter past seven she heard tyres crunching on the gravel drive. Looking out she saw him get out of the car, stretch, look up at the façade of the house and walk slowly to the doorway. He looked tired and she felt an immediate pang of remorse shoot through her, but taking a deep breath she smiled as she walked into the hall to greet him.

'Darling' he exclaimed as he pulled her into his arms then held her away to look at her. 'Gosh you do look well. It must be the sun and French food. Seems to have suited you. Are you feeling as well as you look?'

'Yes absolutely. I feel great' she replied then looked up to kiss him. 'It was so relaxing down there and I feel so much better'.

Thanks to several days of amazing rampant sex with Harry.

"But William how are you and what's the latest about the fire? And Hardys, how are things going there…..any better?'

'No and we've had a letter'.

'Who has?'

'Well I have err, at the office'.

'What about?'

'The fire. It says that is only the start. It calls me a bastard'.

'Oh my God how horrible. Have you given it to the police?'

'Yes they've taken it away. Fingerprints and so on'.

The rest of the evening passed uneventfully. William continued to talk about the fire and the police investigation but also about how difficult Hardys was finding business.

She spoke about the cottage, the village the restaurant, the places to which she'd driven. In fact she told William everything she'd done, with the exception of Harry.

They went to bed quite early as William said he was tired. Wondering if it was a ploy to get her in bed to make love, she soon saw as she emerged from their en-suite that he was in bed wearing his night-time tee shirt and as she pulled back the duvet she saw that he had his shorts on.

Glad that he didn't want her tonight she soon heard him snoring gently and she lay there thinking over the past few days.

God what am I to do? Where was it all going to lead? And what about this horrible letter that William had received at the office?

No scoundrel is so stupid as to not find a reason for his vile conduct.

Korner.

CHAPTER 7

When she woke next morning William had already gone. Downstairs there was a note propped up on the breakfast table.

Darling,

You looked so peaceful I didn't want to wake you. I expect you were tired after your travelling yesterday. I have to be in the office early this morning and may be late back tonight. I missed you when you were away. Sorry we didn't talk about us last night. All I seemed to go on about was the fire, the police, that damned letter and Hardys. Sorry. Let's try and discuss us tonight. Love you.

William

Sod it. William was a really decent man and she'd spent several days in France screwing and betraying him. She'd used that word with Harry and he'd said it was a bit strong. Well it wasn't. That's exactly what she'd done. Betrayed him. And it was even worse as she'd done it at a time when he had all these other problems on his mind. How mean and deceitful. How low could she stoop?

Trying to snap out of her dark mood she rang several of her friends and chatted, then drove to one of them that had her favourite horse and took Jester for a long hard ride.

When she returned home after lunch she felt much better and settling down at her desk started on the pile of paperwork and correspondence which had been neglected for over a week. Then she logged on to check her e-mails and when the computer fired up the little indicator glowed

You have 39 new messages

Scrolling through, her heart started to pound as there buried towards the end of the list was one from Harry. What would he say? Noticing that her hand trembled slightly as she clicked the mouse and waited while the screen changed, she held her breath until the message appeared.

Thank you. H

Thank God. Nothing indiscreet. Could simply be a response to some information regarding her financial portfolio? Breathing out with relief but it underlined for her how careful she was going to have to be and how risky, it was having an affair. If it continued? Would it? She had no idea, but looking at the screen and visualising his face, his voice, and especially his lean fit body she felt herself drawn to him and a twinge of longing went through her as she wondered what to reply. Finally she settled for two innocuous words

MY PLEASURE. J.

Ridiculous response really. Was that all? No of course not but her thoughts were interrupted by a phone call from Fiona a former school friend who chattered on for ages during which time Janie switched off the computer and took the portable phone handset into the kitchen where she made herself some tea while talking about everything and nothing.

William arrived home around eight and slumped into an armchair. Janie took him a large malt whisky and sat on the arm of the chair stroking the hair on the back of his neck.

'Have you eaten?'

'No. I'm not really very hungry. Could you just knock me up a sandwich please?'

Leaning down and giving him a gentle peck on the cheek she said to enjoy his drink and then come into the kitchen and she'd get him something light to eat. It was about ten minutes later that he joined her by which time she had a bowl of soup steaming on the table for them both and a mixed plate of ham, chicken and cheese sandwiches.

They ate and he asked about her time in France and they chatted about a number of subjects but every time France came up she could see Harry in her mind.

William said that he'd like to find some time to get down to their cottage again soon and asked practical things about whether the pool was leaking again as it had last month, whether the woman from the village was cleaning and looking after the house and whether her husband was tending the garden to avoid it becoming overgrown. Reassured by Janie's confident assertion that all was in order he turned again to the subject of the letter and the reaction of the police to it.

Eventually he yawned loudly so they got up from the kitchen table, loaded the dishwasher together and then he smiled, stroked her bottom and said that he thought he'd go up to bed. Returning the smile she said that she'd just finish tidying up downstairs and then join him.

She dithered about downstairs wondering why she was reluctant to go to bed with her husband who'd just signalled sexual need. Before Harry she'd have stroked his bottom in return, turned out the lights and gone upstairs with him. Now she was doing everything she could to put off the moment. Stupid because she couldn't not make love to him any more. He was her husband and she wasn't going to leave him so she'd have to continue a normal full life with him and that meant making love with him.

Switching out the lights she walked upstairs to their room where William was fast asleep, snoring.

Thank Heavens for that!

Undressing as quietly as she could she slipped into bed alongside him and snuggled into his warm body. He muttered but didn't stir and soon they were both asleep.

In the morning they both woke to the alarm and she turned to him, smiled, kissed him and ran her hands over his chest.

'Darling you were absolutely zonked out last night so I didn't want to wake you but would you like to make love now? It's a long time since we did it in the morning' and she started to squeeze and rub his penis which responded straight away and soon was throbbing into an erection.

That's it. The good and dutiful wife always ever ready for sex.

Leaning over she kissed him and it wasn't long before he pushed her onto her back and was pounding into her. Although some tender and loving feelings were there, at that moment she knew that she was doing this for him and not herself so when she sensed the tell tale signs that he was about to come, she gasped loudly and apparently realistically as he groaned and climaxed.

'Thank you darling' he muttered cuddling her into his arms. 'Was that alright for you?'

Not bad but not a patch on Harry's abilities in bed.

'Wonderful. Couldn't you tell?'

'Err well yes. I thought so'.

Janie my girl, you're getting a bloody good liar.

'Good then that's alright then isn't it?' Now hold me until you've got to get up. It's so nice to be back here with you'.

Lies? Or did she mean that? Well yes in a way she did. Not for the sex with him but to be back in Wood Hollow Hall. Her home.

He soon became restless and fidgety so she said cuddle time was over and gently pushed him to the edge of the bed.

Sliding out he walked over to their en-suite emerging after about twenty minutes to dress and go to work at Hardys. His mood had gradually changed from happy after the lovemaking, to cheerful when he'd emerged from their bathroom, to miserable as he got dressed and by the time he lent over the bed to kiss her goodbye he was looking quite depressed.

Driving into the office his depression grew. The business was doing badly again and there was the worry of the fire at home. He arrived at the office just after nine o'clock.

The previous day the insurance company had agreed in principle to re-build the stables but still wanted to see the fire service and the police reports to support the information from their own assessor, but they'd told William that they'd be getting an architect to visit Wood Hollow Hall to see the site and start to plan the reconstruction of the burnt out building.

He'd been in and out of the office in the previous couple of days but unable to concentrate on the business as the fire and its aftermath took up so much of his time and thinking.

***

As he drove into the office his mind went back to the previous Monday morning when he'd picked up an unopened letter that was among his post on his desk. It was marked

CONFIDENTAL and PRIVATE

Slitting the envelope with his pearl handled paper knife, a present from Janie last Christmas, he unfolded the letter, read the few words quickly and then again more slowly.

The fire was only the start you barstid.
theres more too come

He noted the misspellings immediately but it was the sentiment that shocked him. Who on earth disliked him so much to want to destroy their beautiful home, or at least the stable block? Then there was the threat of more to come. But what? What was to come? Another fire?. He picked up the phone and rang the number that Inspector Fulton had given to him.

'Inspector good morning. This is William Hardy'.

Morning sir. I expect you are calling for an update on our investigations. Well I can tell you.........'

'No and sorry to interrupt but I've had a letter here at the office. I'll read it to you' and lowering his voice he quietly read out the short message.

'Right sir. Well at least that confirms what the fire service chaps said, that the fire was deliberate. Now look, please put the letter aside and avoid touching it as much as you can. I realise you'll have opened it and so put your fingerprints onto it, but it's important that you minimise any further hand contact with the letter, and the envelope as well. Has anyone else seen it or touched it?'

'Well lots of people would have handled the envelope, the postman of course, our post room staff, my secretary and myself, but I'm the only one that's touched the actual letter. The envelope was marked confidential and private, so that stopped my secretary from opening it'.

125

'Good and as I said just now please put it somewhere safe and I'll call by shortly to collect it from you'.

'Inspector but who would do such a thing?'

'We don't know yet sir but I'm sure we'll find out'.

William went into his secretary's office next door and asked for a plastic file on receipt of which he went back into his own office. Shutting the door he carefully, using a pencil and his paperknife, managed to slide the letter between the plastic sleeves of the file without touching it further with his fingers.

It was a little after ten o'clock when the police inspector again accompanied by the woman police constable walked into his office. William took the plastic folder and passed it across the desk. Inspector Fulton didn't touch it but put on a pair of thin rubber gloves before picking it up and staring at the letter.

'Looks as though it was typed on an old fashioned typewriter and not a computer doesn't it?' he stated tilting the folder towards the policewoman who nodded. 'Interesting that there's no demand for money, just the threat of further attacks on you. Obviously not too well educated either from the spelling mistakes. I mean three in twelve words is a twenty five percent error rate. That's good as someone like that is unlikely to be too bright and will make mistakes which should help us catch him. Any thoughts?' he asked turning to the policewoman.

'Not really' she mused 'but I just keep coming back to the fact that whoever set fire to the stables let the horses out before doing so. That means he, or she, is either an animal lover or used to working with horses, or both.

'Umm' replied the Inspector. 'Now sir have you had any further thoughts on who might be behind this attack on you and why?'

'No'.

'What about Mrs. Hardy. Has she any ideas?'

'Well she hadn't before she left'.

'Left? Has she gone away sir?'

'Yes she's gone to France to get away for a few days. The fire really upset her'.

'Was this a planned trip sir?' he queried looking at the WPC.

'No spur of the moment. She just felt that after the shock she needed to get away'.

'Did that surprise you?'

'I don't know. No I guess not'.

'Whereabouts in France?'

'We've got a cottage in the south, she's gone there'.

'Do you know when she'll be back?'

'Not really, she said she'd call me when she booked her return flights. She's only gone for a few days'.

'Will you let me know when she's back please? There are a few points I'd like to go over with her. Tell me does she often go away at short notice like this?'

'Occasionally yes. Is there anything I can help with?'

'No I don't think so sir'.

William looked at the two police officers, shrugged and then turned back to the question of the letter.

'What are you going to do with the letter? Check for fingerprints I suppose?'

'Yes and we'll need you to come down to the police station so we can take your prints and DNA sir so we can eliminate you, as it were'.

'Surely you don't think I did it or had anything to do with it do you?'

'No of course not but whatever fingerprints there are on the letter, and to some extent the envelope, may help us narrow down any potential suspects. Could you pop down this afternoon? It'll only take a few minutes of your time'.

So the arrangement was made and after asking a few additional questions the two police officers left William to his own thoughts about the fire and about his business.

He still had no idea who could possibly dislike him or Hardys so much that they'd do such a thing to his beautiful home and then have the nerve to threaten further damage of some sort.

When he visited the police station he was struck by their quiet unhurried efficiency. His finger prints were taken and his mouth was swabbed for the DNA test. It all took only a few minutes before he was back in his car and driving to Hardys again but as he entered the site his heart fell as it did every time he went there now because the business was again finding profitable trading extremely difficult. In fact they weren't making profits but losses and they were getting bigger by the month.

He chaired a planning meeting and prudently curtailed expenditure on a forthcoming marketing campaign as he just didn't think that they'd have the funds to support it.

Next he turned his attention to a plan drawn up by his team of directors for a further round of redundancies to be implemented within the next three months and reluctantly concluded that there was no option but to go ahead with the proposition when it was raised at the next Board meeting.

For the rest of the afternoon his time was spent in meetings, writing letters, signing papers and worrying about the implicit threat in the letter he'd received.

The problem was what could he do about it? Should he hire some private security guards to protect his home and Janie? What about the boys away at boarding school? Did they need protecting? Where would it all end?

Nothing happened for the next few days and gradually William started to relax. Perhaps the letter had simply been a threat and whoever had written it had no intention of doing anything. Even as he tried to convince himself that this might be the case he knew in his heart of hearts that in all probability that simply wasn't true.

It was when the fire alarm sounded on Friday morning throughout the factory and Geoff Hawkins his Operations Director burst into his office, that his heart dropped at what he'd feared but hoped wouldn't happen, had done.

'William. A bomb has been found in the factory. I'm evacuating everyone and phoned the fire brigade. I thought you might want to phone the police yourself. We need to evacuate the offices as well'.

'A bomb? Good God Almighty. Who in hell would want to put a bomb in a jam factory?' he paused shocked, unable to comprehend what was being said to him. 'Sorry silly question. Yes I'll call the police now' and picking up his phone he dialled Inspector Fulton's direct line and started to explain what had happened when the policeman interrupted him.

'I know'.

'You know? How do you know?'

'We had a call from central control via the fire service. I'd left instructions that if anything happened at your home, the factory or any other connection with you I was to be told straight away. We're just leaving now to come to you. Has the plant been evacuated?'

'Yes it's happening right now'.

'Good. You'd better get out too you know. I'll see you at the site, must go' and with that the Inspector broke the connection and hurried downstairs to his car where WPC Anne Shaw was already waiting along with two other officers. With blue lights flashing and sirens blaring they soon arrived at the factory. Crowds of people were standing around in small groups having been assembled into their fire evacuation areas.

A group of fire fighters were talking together and it was to them that the police team ran over.

'Right now what do we know? Is it a bomb?' snapped Inspector Fulton.

'As far as we can see …. yes' replied the senior fire fighter. One of the engineers says he saw a package with wires and what looked like plastic explosive strapped to part of the machinery in the factory. He called his shift manager, who contacted the Factory Director who when he saw it ordered an immediate evacuation and called us'.

'Right so three of them saw it? Where are they? We need to talk to them straight away'.

'They're over there talking to two of my blokes. I've got to decide whether to send them in or call for the bomb squad'.

The policemen walked quickly over to the three men who were being quizzed by the fire fighters.

'Hello I'm Inspector Fulton. Now I know you've probably told several people already but tell me what you saw will you please?'

'Well we haven't really' said the Hardys shift manager. Fred here called me in a right old state and said that he'd seen a bomb in the factory. I told him not to be such a silly fucker..... err sorry miss' he said looking at the young policewoman who waved a hand depreciatingly. 'Well any rate he said to come and have a look. So I did. That's a bomb all right. Seen enough of them on television to know what a bomb looks like. So I called Mr. Hawkins and he said to get everyone out quick like, so I did'.

'Can you describe exactly what it looks like please?'

'I can do better than that. Here have a look. I took a picture of it on my mobile phone and then Geoff......'

'Geoff?'

'Yes Geoff Hawkins said that clicking the phone might send a signal and set it off so I scampered out of there right sharpish I can tell you'.

'Well done. That was good thinking to take a picture and yes it might set it off so you were right to get out. Now let me have a look'.

The supervisor fiddled with his phone and then held it out triumphantly towards the senior policeman. 'Here you are. See if that ain't a bomb I don't know what is'.

The picture although slightly fuzzy, clearly showed what looked to all intents and purposes like a bomb fixed to a stainless steel pipe. There was a box of some sort packed with a grey substance. Out of this protruded a metal object with terminals and from this two wires led to a small battery. From the battery a further wire led to a small clock.

'I'd say that was plastic explosive with a timer and detonator' muttered Fulton as he stared at the picture. 'Right bomb squad it is' and he strode away to his car, wrenched up a phone and could be seen speaking rapidly and agitatedly. 'Move everyone further away from the factory and offices. I've asked for back up and traffic division are going to set up diversions to keep the area clear of vehicles. You might as well send your workforce home Mr. Hardy as it'll be hours before we can give the site the all clear. For all we know there could be other devices.

Logistically it was a nightmare to send people home. Most people from the factory were still in their overalls. Their car keys and personal belongings were in their lockers in the changing room and the blue and white tape cordon that the large number of police who had arrived were stretching around the area completely prevented them from returning to collect their personal items. The police cordon also prevented the office staff from going back to their desks. Some had had the foresight to bring handbags, or wallets with them and those that did were permitted to go to the car park areas which were well away from the factory and go home.

For the others Rod Jackson the head of Human Resources walked to a nearby office building further down the road, inhabited by an insurance broker and from the safety of there organised a fleet of buses and coaches to take people home. He also had his staff phoning as many of the night shift at their homes to tell them not to come into work.

William was quite simply devastated and just kept repeating to whoever would listen 'Who, who would do this and why?'

The police banned the use of mobile phones in an area approximately a quarter of a mile radius of the factory and police cars toured the area telling people not to use mobile phones. They didn't say why, simply that their use might cause an explosion and most people who heard thought that there'd been a gas leak but after a while the rumours started to get around. Local TV, radio and press reporters appeared and tried to interview people but they couldn't get at anyone who actually knew anything so they contented themselves with speculating on the possibility of a bomb and if it was then who might have planted it and why.

After a couple of hours the army specialist bomb squad from Colchester arrived in a truck and two land rovers and asked to see the mobile phone picture. They plugged the phone into a laptop and transferred the picture to their equipment and then having enlarged it studied it in great detail.

The fire brigade had a plan of the entire factory. All major business have to keep such a plan updated and logged with them for emergencies and although normally it was fire, building collapse or flood that was the cause of need, it also provided the information that was required in this case.

The bomb was located in a difficult area of the factory underneath hot pipes and strapped to a high pressure steam pipe. Getting at it would be hot, congested, difficult and dangerous.

The officer in charge of the specialist army unit looked grim as he spoke to Inspector Fulton and William. 'Looks like an amateur job and they're always dangerous as they tend to be highly unstable. With professionals although they're more complicated they're more stable. Right we're going in to have a look. Is there anything flammable or potentially explosive near there, apart from the bomb of course? Any gas cylinders, gas pipes etc?'

'No replied Geoff Hawkins. 'I know the layout of my factory and there's no gas near that area but that steam pipe is high pressure and would be bloody dangerous if it ruptured'.

'Right thanks'.

Turning to one of his team who had now kitted himself up in the special protective clothing and helmet that bomb disposal men use, he spoke quietly and firmly. 'Remember Chris take care, take your time and keep thinking all the time you're in there. Eyes and ears all the time. Good luck'.

The recipient of this advice nodded and then set off slowly with a plan of the factory in one hand and a bag of equipment in the other. His voice could be heard through the radio link up as he described his progress through the now deserted factory.

'OK I reckon I'm about a hundred yards away from the scene now. I'm going to radio silence'.

The army officer explained that to avoid the risk of any electronic triggering of the device no communication would occur to or from the disposal expert until he, the man at the scene, broke the radio silence.

The tension was clear to see among the rest of the army team as they listened carefully for any communication from their man inside. They also studied a blank computer screen which suddenly flickered into life and they could see the factory as the man inside carefully moved around.

The small video camera which was strapped to his helmet showed the progress he was making as he walked slowly along the factory and then he seemed to pause before turning right and walked towards some large stainless steel tanks and vessels. He approached more slowly now and then sure enough distantly at first and then more clearly the bomb came into view. The camera moved around showing it from many different angles. In close up it was eerie and frightening.

Apart from the bomb disposal team the few others that were watching were shocked, frightened and silent as they looked at the malevolent brooding horror on the screen.

Suddenly the bomb man's hands appeared in view. Gently and with infinite care he probed the grey mass of plastic explosive with a small scalpel and a tiny portion of the explosive was cut away, then the hands disappeared from view.

Still there was silence and occasional hand movements. The camera seemed to pan around the area of the bomb before a hand reappeared with a finger turned back on itself.

'He's coming back' stated the bomb disposal officer in clipped tones and he and three of the army personnel, two men and one woman, detached themselves and walked towards the factory to await the re-appearance of the brave man who'd been to the bomb. Other members of the team continued to analyse the data sent by the camera to their computers and waited for further information from the soldier who'd seen and touched the bomb.

When he remerged from the factory he went over to confer with the rest of the army team. Returning to the truck the tiny fragment of explosive was carefully placed into a small machine. A couple of switches were clicked and a dial flickered into life. They studied their computer screens intently and then suddenly seemed to relax but they remained ensconced in the truck until eventually the officer and the man who'd been to the bomb who'd now removed his helmet walked over to Inspector Fulton and William.

'We think it's a hoax. The grey substance seems to be Plasticine. It certainly isn't explosive. We're going back in now but we're pretty certain that's what it is'.

'Plasticine. Did he say Plasticine? Who would do such a thing and why' asked William wringing his hands.

'Don't know sir' replied Inspector Fulton 'but someone's really got it in for you. If the bomb people are right then this is either a warning of more trouble to come or simply an attempt to disrupt your business. Alternatively it could be a dummy bomb left in a position easily found while the real bomb or bombs are more carefully hidden. Either way it's serious and I see it as an escalation of the attacks which started with the fire at your home'.

'Yeah looks like a hoax but we'll soon know for sure'. Chris re-fitted his helmet and went back into the factory.

They watched again as the camera moved through the deserted factory and were fascinated as the disembodied hands suddenly re-appeared on the screen with some wire cutters. There was a long pause and the helmet camera moved around as Chris looked at the bomb from every direction. Finally the cutters moved forward and clipped through the single wire to the clock. Nothing happened then, nor did it when two pairs of cutters one held in each hand, gripped the two wires from the explosive if that's what it was to the battery and snipped through them both simultaneously. Now the camera again showed the scene around and under the cardboard box in which the device was held. The camera suddenly lurched as it was obviously removed from the helmet propped onto the stainless steel pipe pointing at the bomb. Suddenly a disembodied voice crackled out to the waiting listeners.

'Green one to base. Stand down. Device believed made safe. I am now removing device'.

The woman member of the team crossed herself and muttered something as everyone watched with morbid fascination as a knife held in the gloved hands cut through the sticky tape that was holding the device to the steel pipe and the box containing the bomb was carefully removed.

Nothing happened and the collective sigh of relief could not only be heard but also felt. Soon the bomb man appeared, removed his helmet again and casually carrying the device walked quickly over to his team commander.

'Fucking hoax. Look at it' he said disgustedly. 'That was no bomb, just someone wanting people to think it was a bomb. Stupid sods'.

There was an intense discussion among the army team and the police who took charge of all the components of the dummy bomb.

'Right we'll see what we can get off this lot in fingerprints or DNA' said Inspector Fulton.

'Can we go back to work now?' asked William.

'No, not until we've thoroughly searched the rest of the factory. As I said whoever did this might have planted this dummy in a pretty obvious place for us to find and remove while the real bomb or bombs could be hidden away somewhere else'.

Three army bomb specialists donned the same type of special protective clothing worn by the one member of the team that had already been into the factory. They fanned out and worked their way through the whole of the building working systematically but all the same it took several hours before they declared the building safe in that as far as they could see there were no further devices.

After that it was somewhat anti-climatic. The army team packed away their equipment and drove back to Colchester. The road diversions were removed and police blue and white "do not cross" tape wound up and taken away. Inspector Fulton accepted William's invitation to join him in his office.

'I think I need one of these' said William getting out a bottle of malt whisky and pouring a large slug into a crystal glass. 'Join me?'

'Thank you sir I don't mind if I do'.

William was about to speak when the door opened and WPC Shaw joined them, looked at the two glasses, raised an eyebrow and looked at her inspector.

'Like to join us?' asked William.

'No thank you Mr. Hardy. I'm on duty and I imagine that I'll be driving won't I sir?' she queried looking straight at her boss.

'Yes I guess you will'.

'Well who the bloody hell would plant a dummy bomb in a jam and pickle factory for Christ's sake? snarled William.

'Someone who's got a real grudge against you, or this factory. Although it was a dummy bomb they went to a lot of trouble to make it look real. Now the question is how do we find who planted it there? How many people have access to that area? From the plan it doesn't look like a general factory production part of the factory' mused the police Inspector .

'It isn't. Generally only the engineers and one or two specialists go to that part of the factory. The floor above the bomb holds the cooking tanks where the jam is cooked under pressure and superheated. The tanks are filled by the various ingredients being pumped to them, they're sealed automatically and then they are heated for some hours, the time depends on the variety before they invert, again automatically, to pump out the extremely hot cooked product into pipes where it is pumped to the filling lines next door in the main packing hall. There it is fed to the appropriate production line and squirted into the jars as they pass the multiple filling head machine.

Very few people involved and certainly extremely few in the tank area. We call it the tank farm. But if that had been a real bomb and it had gone off it would have completely wrecked our production. That is the heart of the production unit'.

'Thank you sir. I'd like to go and look at the scene for myself if you don't mind. Will you take us there and show us around please. Coming too?' he asked his younger female colleague. 'Coming to see where they make the jam?'

Kitted up in white protective overalls William, the Inspector and the WPC spent a few minutes carefully looking at and around the location where the bomb had been fixed.

'Hot in here isn't it' he muttered sweating as he crawled under a waist high pipe. 'Right now we want scene of crime officers in here to go over the place with a fine toothcomb'.

'How long will that take?' asked William anxiously.

'Don't know. As long as it takes. I realise you want to start your factory up again, but we have to examine the crime scene carefully to see if our bomber has left any clues. Usually in this sort of case they'll make a mistake and leave something that will help us find them. We might have to fingerprint and DNA test all your employees. Will that be a problem?'.

'I shouldn't think so. I'll talk to HR as they'll be the department that'll have to organise that sort of thing with your blokes'.

'Right. I also want a list of any employee that could have had access to this area. Do you have CCTV cameras covering that part of the plant?'

'No. We make jam and pickles for God's sake. We have some cameras mainly scanning the outside but very few inside and none in that area. Inspector this is a food factory, it's not some high tech secure unit'.

'Yes sir I know that but someone is starting to escalate things and I don't like the feel of it. This could get really nasty now. I don't like it at all and that's a fact'.

On the way back to the police station Inspector Fulton outlined his thoughts to the WPC. 'This is getting serious you know. Whoever is doing these things has got it in for Hardys or William Hardy himself, in a big way. I have a feeling that things are going to get worse before they get better, but eventually our villain will make a mistake and that's when we'll get him.

We ought to find out a bit more about Mrs. Hardy you know. Can you do a bit of digging and see if everything's all right between her and her husband?

Something about this doesn't add up. As Mr. Hardy said, it's a food manufacturing factory for crying out loud so it can't be a business rival. No competitor's going to plant bombs in a factory so it's got to be personal. Something about him, her, their kids, some grudge, something the business has done to a disgruntled employee. The answer's in that factory somewhere. I'm sure of that.

Get hold of all Hardy's records for current and past employees. Run their names through the police computer and see if there's anything there. Go through Mr. and Mrs. Hardys personal information, bank accounts, building societies, credit records, you know the sort of thing. There has to be something there, either with them or the business.

You'll need some help, so I'll draft you in a couple of helpers. There are those two new officers still on probation in the station. I'll give you them and they can help you. Get the work sorted into some sort of order. You organise it. There you are your first management job' he smiled at her.

'Right Gov' she replied thinking of the enormous task ahead.

Satisfaction lies in the effort, not in the attainment. Full effort is full victory.

Nicolas Boileau-Despreaux

CHAPTER 8

The man was pleased with the effect that he'd caused through his dummy bomb. Production had been stopped for the best part of twenty hours which would have damaged the company's results. Good he thought but now for something more serious. He grinned to himself as he rolled up the lino in his kitchen revealing the cracked concrete beneath.

Taking several lengths of string of different thicknesses and made of different materials, together with some short lengths of thin rope, again of different diameters, he laid them on the worktop and went out into his garden shed returning shortly with a plastic can full of petrol.

Carefully tipping some of the volatile liquid into a large glass bowl he took the first length of string, immersed it, then taking it out dangled it over the bowl until it had stopped dripping petrol. He now laid it carefully on the concrete kitchen floor. Standing at one end he flicked his lighter and touched it to the end.

Immediately the flame caught and flashed along the string to the end. It smouldered for a bit then went out.

He tried again with the other pieces of string or rope but all to no avail. What he wanted was for the rope to become a slow burning fuse but every time the petrol soaked material just flared up and the flame shot along from one end of the rope to the other. It was too quick for what he had in mind.

Deciding to give up for a bit and go and have a smoke he took the one remaining piece of thin rope out of the petrol bowl then carefully tipped the remainder of the petrol from the bowl back into the can and went into his front room where he lit his cigarette and inhaled deeply.

It was about half an hour later when he thought that he ought to get himself something to eat so going back into the kitchen he saw the piece of rope that he'd previously soaked in petrol but had left to dry and not tried burning.

More for curiosity than believing it would be any use he laid it on the floor and touched the end with his lighter. It lit but then burnt slowly along the length. It didn't flare and flash to the end but worked exactly as he wanted. Unable to contain his excitement he took another but longer length of similar rope, put it in the bowl and poured in some petrol. Putting the bowl aside he took all the rest of the things out to the shed and coming back indoors removed the rope and left it to dry for a while.

Checking his watch every few minutes when about twenty minutes had passed he stretched it on the floor. Being longer he had to lay it out in loops to get the length fully stretched out. Holding his breath he flicked the lighter and touched it to one end. Again as before it lit straight away and then burnt along the length in a controlled way. It followed the loops and twists as it had been laid out along the floor until it came to the end where it fizzled out.

Smiling happily he was convinced that he'd solved his problem. Now he just had to put it into action and then that Mr.-fucking-William-bastard-Hardy would really get what was coming to him and his fancy factory.

Cheered by that thought he got a meat pie out of the fridge put it in the oven, opened a tin of peas and a tin of potatoes and tipped them into a saucepan to heat.

When his meal was ready he ate slowly savouring what was to come next in his plan. When he'd finished he put the dirty plates and saucepan in the sink and left them there. Going into the sitting room he pulled on his rubber gloves and put the old typewriter that he'd brought in earlier onto the table and typed a message. It took three attempts before he thought that he'd got it right and then sitting back he looked smugly at what he'd created.

```
The bomb wasnt real but I bet it give you a
        frite. What come next will be.
```

Next he typed the envelope and then carefully sealing the letter in the self adhesive envelope he added a peel off stamp, then placed the envelope by the front door ready to take and post next time he went out.

Getting up he took the old typewriter out to the shed and hid it under some sacks before returning indoors. Ignoring the dirty crockery and utensils in the sink he got out a four pack of beer from the cupboard under the sink and going into his sitting room opened one, took a long swig and then sat down at his computer and logged on.

There were a few junk e-mails which he deleted and then he clicked onto one of the porno sites that he used regularly and lost himself in a fantasy world of attractive women and chat rooms for the next couple of hours.

He drank three of the four pack while at his screen until deciding that it was time to go to bed logged off, locked up and went upstairs.

Next morning he washed, shaved, dressed and going downstairs saw his letter. As he went into the kitchen he grimaced at the pile of dirty things in the sink and decided to deal with them when he got back after his shift.

He had his cornflakes and a mug of tea then added the dirty bowl and mug to the pile in the sink before dressing in his black leather outfit. Walking out the front door he shut it firmly, unlocked his moped, pushed it out of the gate and onto the road. It started first go and he rode off, stopping on the way to post his letter.

His six o'clock start shift was routine and he clocked off just after two o'clock in the afternoon, rode home, went indoors to collect some things that he'd need and then rode off again.

It took about twenty minutes to reach the garage and he propped his moped against a wall, removed his helmet and went into the office.

'Can I help you?' asked the little brunette sitting at the desk.

'Um yes. I've booked a van'.

'What name?'

The formalities were competed fairly quickly and having signed some forms he followed the girl out to the yard where she pointed out the vehicle allocated to him.

'Take care of it as it's one of our new ones'.

'Yeah I'll look after it. Now where can I leave me bike till I bring the van back tomorrow?'

'Bike?'

'Yeah. I came here on me moped. Can I leave it somewhere safe please?'

'Well I guess the best thing will be to bring it in the garage. Here I'll show you where you can park it' and as she walked back across the yard the man enjoyed watching her bottom wiggling in a pair of well fitting black trousers. 'There you are anywhere in there and it'll be OK. I'll tell Mr. Webster'.

Thanking her he wheeled the bike to where she'd suggested, padlocked it then walked back to the van, got inside, took a moment to familiarise himself with the controls and switched on the engine. He drove gingerly out of the yard, turned onto the road and before too long was pulling up at the allotments. Backing the van down the grassy track that bisected the many plots he stopped outside a run down old shed. Getting out he looked around but he was alone except for one other man working on his own allotment about one hundred yards away.

Several of the other plots were neatly tended with rows of flowers, vegetables or fruit showing careful attention. His though had lots of weeds which he ignored as he unlocked the rusty padlock and stepping inside the gloomy interior made out the shape of the two large twenty litre plastic cans full of a dark viscous liquid. Carrying them one at a time he loaded the van and then returned for an empty standard size five litre size petrol can. Lastly he collected a cardboard box with half a dozen aerosol cans that he'd bought over the last few days, each one in a separate shop.

Locking up the shed again, he shut the van's rear door and drove home. Going indoors he went through to his garden shed and collected the nearly empty petrol can that he'd used last night together with another empty can, drove off to the nearest petrol station where he filled all three cans, paid in cash and drove back home.

Parking carefully on the road outside his house he left all five cans inside the van, locked it and went indoors pleased with his preparations.

That night he took ages to get to sleep as he was both excited and apprehensive about the next stage of his plans.

He'd already decided how to handle the transfer of the money. Norfolk was criss-crossed with deserted railway lines. When Dr. Beeching had carved up the railways in the nineteen sixties the county had been particularly hard hit.

The man knew that the moment of money transfer was the most dangerous part of his plan and so he intended to tell William Hardy to drive alone to a deserted lane a few miles out of Norwich where there was an old road bridge over one of the former rail tracks. Hardy would be told to take the money in a holdall and stand on the bridge.

Then when he was certain that no-one was accompanying his victim he'd shout to tell him to throw the bag over the parapet of the bridge where down below he'd be waiting with his moped. He'd grab the bag and ride off along the old railway trackway for about half a mile where it then ran close to a lane and he could swing off the railway track and onto that little lane and away.

Smiling he started to think about all the things he could do with the money. Probably go abroad. America maybe or perhaps South America? Brazil where there were lots of dusky busty girls. Yes girls are what he'd want. Lots of them but with all his money he'd not have a problem in getting them to come with him. Maybe the Far East. Japan or Thailand. Yes he thought I bet there's some real willing girls there.

Half a million pounds. That's what he'd ask for. Easy for that rich bastard Hardy. He'd got lots of money so it wouldn't hurt to share some of it.

Then he wondered how big a bag he'd need for half a million pounds and how heavy it would be? Would he be able to fit it onto his moped? Perhaps the answer would be to hire a van again he thought, so he decided to go and have another look at the bridge and the old train trackway below to determine whether he'd actually be able to get the van along there?

With that problem solved in his mind he turned onto his side and although he tossed and turned for a while eventually he dropped off to sleep.

When he woke in the morning he felt jaded but cheered up when he thought again about the money and the girls that would buy him.

Being on the afternoon shift he spent the morning at home where he finally did the washing up, then repeated his string and petrol experiment. It worked again. He rolled the lino back into place.

At about twelve o'clock he collected one of the petrol cans from the van, took the length of rope that he was planning to use and fed it carefully into the full container. Screwing the cap back tightly he returned it to the van, and set off for work stopping on the way at a transport café where he ordered corned beef hash, chips and beans with a mug of tea.

Throughout the first part of his shift he was extremely busy and it wasn't until after nine o'clock that he could get some time to himself and at nine thirty he was able to sneak away to check on the van and its contents. Carefully taking the rope out of the can he shook off the petrol then coiled it up and put it in an empty plastic bowl that he'd brought with him. He then made his way back to his work area.

At ten he swiped his card to clock off and walked to the van. Getting in he drove it from the car park to the factory yard at the rear of the factory itself and stopped outside the box store.

This was a reasonably large room where a great deal of the product packaging was kept. Flat pre-cut pieces of cardboard which were erected into boxes automatically by the machines in the production hall, rolls of plastic film and paper and several other items of packaging material. There were lots of "**NO SMOKING**" signs as everything in here was highly flammable which was exactly what he needed.

He lugged the first of the heavy twenty litre plastic containers inside and setting up some piles of flat cardboard placed the container on top so that it was about two feet off the ground. He did the same with the second large container and then he removed the screw lids from both which he threw on the floor.

Next he brought in two of the plastic petrol cans and these were also placed on some piles of cardboard but only about a foot off the ground. He loosened their lids but left them very loosely resting in place.

Finally he carried in the last petrol can, the aerosol cans and the rope. Carefully placing some rolls of plastic film about the piles of cardboard on which he'd placed his cans he added some more cardboard, then some more plastic film rolls and buried the aerosol cans in various places in the cardboard or film roll piles.

Lastly he pulled a stool into the centre of the room and taking some plastic supermarket shopping bags out of his pocket stood on the stool to sellotape them around the smoke detector. He didn't know how effective that would be in preventing the detector working but at least it would probably delay it.

Opening the lid of the last petrol can he splashed most onto the cardboard piles before putting the unlidded can upright on the ground. Taking his treated rope he dipped one end in some of the petrol and then stretched it out towards the door. The other end he pushed into the open petrol can and secured in place with an elastic band. Finally he slid pieces of cardboard under the rope fuse throughout its length.

A last check round then getting out some matches he took a deep breath and struck it. His hand trembled as he bent down and touched it to the end of his rope fuse. It flared from where he'd dipped it in petrol but then caught fire and burnt slowly just as he wanted towards the incendiary pile he'd created about twenty feet away, in the process also starting some of the cardboard beneath it smouldering.

He watched for a little until he was satisfied that his fuse was going to work and then carefully shut the box room door, jumped in his van and drove slowly across to the far side of the yard. Parking with no lights on but the engine running he waited, heart pounding.

For a while nothing happened and he hoped the burning fuse was working alright and that it would soon reach the end of its run where it should climb slowly up towards the open mouth of the petrol can.

He didn't hear the huge whoosh or see the first flames shoot across the end of the box room, or the piles of carefully stacked cardboard starting to burn. No did he see the large rolls of plastic film start to melt and catch fire or the arid smoke rolling up towards the ceiling smoke detector which remained silent.

But soon the man did see red flames through the window.

After a little while, just as he planned and hoped the cardboard pile collapsed and the two opened large containers which were full of old engine oil mixed with a little petrol to aid combustion fell into the growing fire. As the oil and petrol mixture glugged out it ignited and fed the flames so soon more black smoke rolled across the room as the burning oil flowed around the floor burning and spreading the fire wider.

When the second pile of burning cardboard collapsed catapulting the two remaining lidded cans of petrol into the fire it took only seconds for the first to melt and the petrol exploded with such force that the window in the room shattered. It was followed almost immediately by another huge bang as the final petrol container also exploded throwing burning petrol over a wide area of the room. With the window broken, oxygen was sucked into the room feeding the fire which now burned ever more fiercely.

One by one the aerosol cans exploded scattering burning rubbish all over the room some into the ceiling one piece of which lodged in the plastic bag covering the smoke detector and started to melt it.

Unaware of the exact state of his fire but satisfied that it would now be well alight, smiling the man put the van into gear and drove slowly back the way he'd come through the staff car park and to the exit gatehouse. Normally the security guards pressed the switch to raise the exit barrier as soon as someone approached but they were busy checking in a delivery lorry and didn't notice the man waiting.

The sudden screaming siren warning them of a fire in some part of the factory was deafening and looking at the indicator board they could see where the fire was located. Precious seconds were wasted as one of them deciding that as the location was close to the guardhouse thought he'd go and see whether it was a real fire and he walked quickly across the yard but as he neared the box store he could see smoke and hear the flames roaring so he turned and ran back to the guardhouse where the more senior of the two men rang the fire brigade. He also rang the night factory manager to tell him to order an evacuation of the factory.

Still the man waited in his van until finally the gatehouse guards noticed the white van and raised the barrier. He drove out being careful to keep his face turned away from the guards but they didn't look at the van being too busy checking the procedures to be followed in case of a fire.

He drove round the corner and along beside the factory where he could see through the railings that marked the factory boundary. When he had reached a position where he could see the box store in the distance he parked, switched off the lights and settled down to watch and wait.

Soon the sounds of a fire engine siren getting closer could be heard until it swept into view and screeched to a halt. One fire fighter jumped out and ran to the gatehouse who pointed out on a large site diagram on the wall where the fire was indicated. He ran back and directed the driver across the yard just as the second fire engine arrived and followed the first into the factory.

The man sat and watched the flames and smoke pouring out of the broken window and the doorway as the fire engines arrived and stopped close to the box room. Immediately there was a hive of disciplined activity and it wasn't long before high pressure water was hissing out of the fire hoses as the fire fighters started to tackle the fire.

He stayed for a long time and while watching used his mobile phone to make a call. Eventually he could see by the actions of the fire fighters that the fire had obviously been brought under control. Clouds of smoke and steam still billowed into the night sky but it was pretty obvious that the fire was out.

'That'll show yer' he muttered nastily as he started the van's engine and drove away.

Getting home he parked outside his house, walked quickly indoors, took off his overalls and plumped down in an armchair. Pleased that he'd completed his task without being detected he decided to have a glass of whisky and getting out a bottle he poured himself a large slug and gulped it down. Pouring another he drank it more slowly before getting up and going out to his shed to remove the old typewriter from its hiding place.

He plonked it down on the table indoors. Again it took him sometime to decide what to write but eventually he finished again being careful to wear gloves.

```
Told you that next time it wood be for reel.
Hows the box store this morning? I want half
   a milion pounds and then il stop. Dont
  involve police. Soon I wil tel you how to
               deliver the money.
```

Satisfied with what he'd typed, he took the old machine outside again and coming back in poured himself another slug of whisky then wondering whether to log on to a porn site he decided against and ambled up to bed.

The next day he was on the afternoon shift again so after he'd had his breakfast he drove the van back to the hire garage stopping to post his latest letter. At the garage he waited while the little brunette, who this morning was wearing a short skirt and high heels, checked round it to make sure there was no damage then smilingly signed off the return sheet giving him a copy.

Collecting his moped he rode back home and while waiting until it was time to leave for his afternoon shift he alternated logged onto a porn site and divided his time between that and thinking again about how he spend the money.

The tricky bit would be getting the money handed over and he knew he'd have to really think that part through carefully and must re-check the old bridge and disused railway line out thoroughly to ensure that his plan would work safely using a van.

He finished his shift around ten o'clock. During the time that he was at work he joined in the general speculation as to how the fire might have started. The rumours were that it had been deliberate. He went and looked at the damage caused to the box room and was surprised at how extensive it had been, yet confined to that area. The quick response of the fire brigade had enabled them to avoid it extending to other areas of the factory.

The following day he had a day off and spent it initially at his home doing some jobs in the garden, and then having got into a horticultural frame of mind he decided to go to his allotment where he dug and tidied up his patch and planted some seeds.

That night he bought fish and chips from a nearby shop and sat in his small sitting room eating them from the polystyrene container while watching television. Before going to bed he spent an hour or so in front of his computer logged into a porno chat room.

Next morning back onto the early shift his alarm woke him at five and rolling out of bed he washed, shaved, dressed had some breakfast and then rode to work on his moped.

The day was busy and he was asked if he would put in four hours overtime that afternoon and stay on until six o'clock, so always being short of money he agreed. During one of his breaks he used a payphone in the canteen to make a phone call.

When he finally finished work it was after six, and riding along on his moped he worked out how much the four hours overtime would bring him. Arriving home he removed his leather jacket and trousers, collected some money from a tin in his kitchen drawer and then just wearing his overalls and helmet got back on his bike and headed for The Flying Eagle pub.

Riding into the car park at the back he looked around until he spotted a lamp post which would serve his need so he coasted up to it, stopped, switched off the engine and propped the machine against the pole. Taking a thick chain out of the saddlebag he wrapped it around the pole and his bike then snapped the sturdy padlock shut. Next he removed his helmet, rested it on the saddle and taking another thinner chain slid that around the pole and through the ring riveted to the back of his helmet and clicked a second padlock shut.

Satisfied that his bike and his helmet were as safe as he could make them he walked across the car park and in the back door of the pub, along a dim corridor with a chipped red tiled floor, stopped in the gents which smelt of urine and disinfectant then buttoning himself up walked into the pubic bar.

At the counter he waited while the bar maid finished serving another customer. Checking his watch he saw that he had plenty of time so he enjoyed looking at her. There was a gap of a few inches above the waist band of her trousers and below the hem of her tight jumper so he stared at her exposed bare flesh.

'Sorry to have kept you waiting. What can I get you then?' she asked turning towards him.

'Whisky please'.

'Right'. Picking up a glass she turned to the optics fixed at the back of the bar. 'Any particular one?' she asked over her shoulder.

'No, but no fancy malts or expensive ones'.

She started to fill the glass. 'Single or double?'

'Double and I'll have some ginger ale with it?'

Usually he drank it neat but while waiting he'd noticed that when serving other customers she had to bend down to reach for the mixers which were on a low shelf against the back wall of the bar so he watched her bottom as she bent forward to get the bottle. The waistband of her trousers slid down to expose the top of her bum crack and the green elastic top of her knickers. He stared, enjoying the view she unwittingly provided before she stood, whipped off the bottle cap and put it beside his whisky glass.

Pouring in the fizzy mixer he waited a moment or two and then took a sip. He paid, took his change and thought about the enjoyment that was to come shortly. It didn't take long to finish the drink.

'Like another?' the bar girl queried.

'No I've got to go now as I've a bit of business to attend to' and draining the last drop he put the glass down and walked back out into the corridor, turned towards the front of the pub, passed the lounge bar and out onto the street.

It was a short walk to the corner then he turned left into the long street that stretched ahead of him. Walking briskly, after about five minutes he looked carefully at the numbers on the gates or street doors counting his way along. 263, 265, 267, 269 and then he reached his destination. 271.

Some of the houses still retained front gardens but this one had been neatly paved. There was no gate so turning off the pavement it was only a few strides to reach the front door. He rang the bell and glanced at the tubs neatly filled with flowers on the paving slabs as he waited.

He noticed a curtain twitch and shortly after the door was opened by a middle aged lady who looked queryingly at him.

'I rang earlier'.

'Come in'. He followed her into the small hallway and then into one of the two downstairs front rooms. 'Been before haven't you?'

'Yes once'.

'Thought I recognised you, I'm Rose, remember? Glad you've come back. Now who did you see last time?'

'Gina'.

'Ah yes nice Italian girl. She's gone back to Milan I'm afraid but we've got three lovely girls here today. There's Kylie, a pretty little English blonde; Ivana, a busty brunette from Moscow; or if you'd like a really big hefty black girl we've got Violet from the Caribbean but she's just gone upstairs with a client. She'll be busy for a while so if you want her you'll have to wait'.

As she finished speaking almost as if on cue the door opened and a blonde, presumably Kylie entered, closely followed by the brunette. The man looked at them dressed as they were in identical pink shiny robes.

'Now girls show yourselves to the gentleman' commanded Rose.

The two girls looked at each other then giving a little smile Kylie took a drag on her cigarette, stepped slightly forward, untied the belt and spread her robe out wide. About five foot two, she had short spiky blonde hair, was painfully thin with small breasts, skinny legs with a dark bruise on her right thigh, several scratches on her left shin two of which were covered with sticking plaster, a thin strip of blonde pubic hair and white stilettos with four inch heels. She was chewing gum and her mouth opened wide with every chew.

The older woman pointed a finger at her and moved it in a circling motion at which Kylie turned her back, lifted the hem of her robe to briefly expose her bottom then let it drop as she turned to face front again and stepped back.

'Now you dear' said Rose to the brunette.

Ivana who had long dark brown hair that reached just below her shoulders smiled at the man, undid her belt and stretched her robe wide. She was several inches taller than Kylie with large pendulous breasts, chubby with virtually no waist as her ribcage flowed down to her hips, legs that were quite chunky and black high heeled shoes. What however riveted his eyes was her thick mass of dark pubic hair and he couldn't ever recall seeing such a thatch before.

Without being asked she turned slowly round and when her back was towards him, unlike Kylie who'd lifted and dropped her robe in seconds, Ivana pulled it high up her back then slowly leant forward and spreading her legs wide gently swayed her bottom from side to side. Standing up and turning back to face him her robe remained wide open as it rested against the outsides of her large breasts. She was also chewing gum but discretely with her lips closed.

'Her please' he said huskily pointing at the brunette. Kylie shrugged, re-tied her robe and trailing cigarette smoke left the room without a word.

'Can you remember the fees? asked the Madame.

'Umm....'

'Right, it's fifteen for just a nude all over body massage; twenty five if you want a hand job as well; thirty five to include oral and fifty for all that plus full intercourse. Longer sessions, special services and kinky things like bondage and domination are by special arrangement and price. So what's it to be then?'

'The full fifty quid job please'.

She smiled and looked expectantly at him as he reached into his pocket and counted out one twenty, two tens and two five pound notes.

'Thanks and the tip for the house? There's no fixed amount as it's up to you. Ten percent is normal but more if you wish'.

She watched as he took out some loose change and carefully selected two one pound coins, four fifty pence pieces, and then counted out ten and twenty pence pieces into her outstretched hand until he passed across five pounds exactly. Thinking *"tight git"* as most of her clients would not have bothered to count out coins exactly but just given her another fiver or maybe a tenner, nevertheless she smiled again as she thanked him.

'Right dear, full session' she said looking at Ivana, then smiling at the man added 'enjoy yourself sir'.

'You come wiz me' the girl said stretching out a hand towards him to lead him into the hallway and up the stairs at the top of which were four doors. Three were open and showed a bathroom and two bedrooms but from behind the other, which was shut, came the unmistakable sounds of sexual intercourse.

'Beeg fucking' grinned Ivana pointing at the closed door before leading him into one of the other bedrooms which was sparsely furnished with a bed, two upright white wooden chairs, a brown painted dressing table, a coat rack and a well worn threadbare somewhat dirty carpet.

'What your name?'

'Fred'.

'Ees nice name. Where you from?'

'Here….. Norwich. I live here in this city'.

'Ees nice town. You undress I geev you good time' cooed the brunette taking off her robe which she folded neatly and put on one chair. Swaying her breasts from side to side she put her hands beneath, lifted and squeezed them together. 'Beeg teets, you like?' she grinned.

The man nodded. He kicked off his shoes then quickly removed his overalls, jeans, sweater and tee shirt. He dropped all four garments onto the other chair then pulled off his rather grubby and tatty pants which he put on top of the other clothes. Naked except for his socks which he didn't take off he laid on his back on the bed and started rubbing his penis.

Removing the chewing gum from her mouth and parking it on the back of her wooden chair Ivana moved towards the bed pausing to take something out of a cardboard box on the dressing table and pushed it beneath a red rubber band that was around her wrist. Sitting on the bed she took his hand away.

'Ivana do thees. Ees nice cock' she smiled starting to play with him managing to avoid wrinkling her nose as the smell of unwashed and un-deodorised armpits wafted at her as he stretched his hands behind his head. Putting her other hand on his balls she jigged them up and down.

'Ees nice balls' then smiling at him she let go of them and ran her hand over his belly and chest. 'Ees nice body. You want I massage you or just have vank, suck and sex?'

'Umm just vank….. sorry wank, suck and sex. Don't waste time on massage'.

'OK no massage. First I rub cock to make hard then I give leetle blow job then we have fuck, ok?'

Quickly she rubbed him to full erection. Taking the condom foil from under her wrist elastic she slit it open with a deep red fingernail, rolled the rubber down his erection and taking his hands placed them on her breasts.

'You play with beeg teets' she grinned and reaching up and behind her head she ran her long hair through her hands, twisted it into a pony tail and slipped the red elastic band from her wrist around her extensive hair tresses. A further twist of the hair and it was tucked under the elastic again so that it was piled high up at the back of her head.

Leaning down she planted a kiss on his rubber covered penis then started to rub him again. He let go of her breasts and laid back to enjoy what was happening. Ivana varied the movements and speed of her hand before sliding her lips over him instead of her hand.

Her head moved up and down then letting him slip out she looked up at him. 'Ees good sucking?' and seeing him nod resumed her activities. One of her hands played with his balls while the other gripped the base of his penis and squeezed rhythmically in time with her head movements.

Feeling himself start to get too aroused he reached down and pulled her head up and off his penis.

'Ees problem?' she queried.

No problem but I think I'd like to get on with the sex now'.

'No more suck? Start fuck?'

'Yeah'.

'Ok. How you want do it?'

'You on top'.

'Like this?' she asked moving up the bed and lifting his penis lowered herself onto him. 'Ees ok? Ees what you want?'

'Yeah great' and he reached up again for her large breasts but as Ivana started moving on him he realised that his climax was approaching and desperate to prolong the session he tried to delay things.

He thought of Norwich City football team and tried to remember the scores of their last three matches but that didn't work as he felt himself continuing to move rapidly towards his climax. He next tried to count backwards from one hundred but getting to eighty realised that was too easy so he attempted to think the alphabet backwards. Z, Y, X, W, V then he got stuck and had to count forwards from P to find the next letter but as he got to U he knew it was no good and resigned himself to coming.

It happened so often like this. It hadn't been so bad when he was married but even then his wife had frequently grumbled that often he'd come too quickly for her. It had been just one of the many problems that had led to his marriage breaking up. That and the lack of money as a result of that bastard Hardy kicking him out of a job.

His breathing got louder then as he groaned Ivana felt his penis twitch. Surprised that he'd come so quickly she kept moving for a little while before clambering off him.

'You come much quick' she said sadly using her hands to squeeze him from root to tip a couple of times.

'Yeah, sorry'.

'Ees not problem for me. For you ees ……. how you say……err……. ah yes….. for you ees disappoint'.

'Yea a bit'.

Sitting next to him she smiled sympathetically as she ran her hands over his chest and belly watching his penis deflate. As it collapsed she pulled off the rubber, knotted it and walking across the room dropped it into a large battered Quality Street chocolate tin on the floor. Pulling a couple of tissues out of a box on the dressing table she gave them to him.

'For wiping cock' she said.

He squeezed himself and mopped up the small seminal emission that appeared and then sat up. Ivana held out her hand so he gave her the tissues which also went into the tin on the floor.

Putting on her robe she fastened the belt then peeled the chewing gum off the chair back and popped it into her mouth. From a pocket she took out a packet of cigarettes and lighter, extracted one and lit it inhaling deeply.

The man started to dress.

'You come back other day and pay lady for more long time' suggested Ivana and seeing his puzzled expression continued 'first I give you quick vank to empty cock. Then you rest and play with Ivana's beeg teets. I give nice massage all over zee body and lots of cock suck. When cock ready again we fuck. That way you get longer fuck as cock not fire quick second time when fucking. Ees good idea?'

'Yea right' he muttered.

'Yes will be much good time. I very good fucker'.

'I'll remember …….. sounds all right'.

'Ok when you come back you tell Ivana cock fire much quick. I help make go more slow for you. You get real nice fuck'.

Nodding at her offer he carried on dressing and when she asked if he was ready to leave he nodded again.

Opening the door she led the way onto the landing. He looked back to make sure he'd not left or dropped anything in the room and as he passed the Quality Street tin he saw that there were several used condoms in there, along with some tissues and a couple of cigarette buts.

On the landing he noticed that the other bedroom door was now also closed. Ivana leaned her head against the first closed door from which not so long ago there was the sound of sexual activity. 'All finish fucking' she giggled then she listened outside the other door and turning gave him a thumbs up sign.

'Kylie much beeg fucking' she chuckled then she started down the stairs. He followed. At the bottom Rose appeared frowning.

'That was quick. Was everything satisfactory sir?'

'Yeah'.

'Oh good. Well come back soon won't you?'

Ivana opened the front door and squeezed his bottom. 'Goodbye Fred. You come back see Ivana again. I make good long time slow fuck for you'.

He walked out without another glance and turning right started back along the road. It seemed to take longer going back but he realised that not only had he had walked more quickly on his way there fired up with excitement and anticipation, but also that going the way that he was now it sloped uphill very slightly.

Eventually, puffing a bit he came to the corner, turned right and passed the chemist shop run by Raj Patel; the Spar food store next to it run by Raj's brother Vijay; the launderette run by Raj's parents; the newsagents run by his cousin Manoj and into The Flying Eagle pub run by Martin Wilkins, originally from Dagenham but now happily settled in Norwich.

Going again into the public bar the bar girl smiled at him. 'That didn't take long'.

'Eh?'

'Well you were in here a little while ago but you left saying that you had a bit of business to take care of. I just meant that your bit of business didn't take you long'.

'No it didn't'.

'Did it go alright then?'

'Yes thanks pretty well' he replied wondering what she'd say if he explained what his little bit of business had really been.

'Same again? Whisky wasn't it?'

'No I'll have a pint this time please........that one' he finished pointing at one of the beer pumps 'and have you got a meat pie and a packet of crisps please'.

'OK won't be long'.

He paid and stood sipping his beer, eating his stodgy pie and crunching through the crisps slowly reflecting on his brief time with Ivana. Yes he would go back soon and have another session with her and wondering how much extra it would cost maybe he might try her longer time idea. He drank his beer slowly watching carefully whenever the barmaid bent over or reached down and on two or three occasions he was rewarded with a flash of her knicker elastic again.

'Another pint?'

'No just a half and then I'd better be off. Thanks'.

It was about fifteen minutes later that he walked out of the pub to the nearby newsagents where he stood and studied the porno magazines on the top shelf for a while. Browsing through several he finally selected two, paid, and went back to the pub car park, unchained his helmet and bike and rode carefully home.

Indoors he looked at the clock and saw that it was nearly nine so he switched on the TV and watched for a while before going to his computer and logging onto his favourite porn site which kept him amused for a while.

He went to bed just before eleven and read his girlie magazines for an hour or so before turning out the light and sleeping through until his alarm woke him at five the next morning.

A legal kiss is never as good as a stolen one.

Guy de Maupassant.

CHAPTER 9

William had rung the police after receiving the second letter threatening another attack and demanding money. They had come and collected it straight away, told him that they'd not been able to pick up any unaccounted for finger prints or DNA samples off the previous one but that they hoped they might from this one.

They also confirmed that at the moment they remained mystified as to the cause, reason, person or persons that were doing this.

'Whoever it is seems to be upping the anti now. This is getting serious sir. You need to take care'.

'How? What do you suggest that I do?'

'Err that's a bit tricky to advise at the moment but just take sensible precautions. Check your car doesn't seem to have been tampered with, you know nothing obvious. And perhaps install some closed circuit tv at your home. Ask your wife to take care too'.

'That's all a bit bloody vague. How do I know if the car's been tampered with? And what should Janie look out for? Come on Inspector we need more concrete recommendations than that?'

'I understand sir but it's difficult to advise you at the moment. I don't think you or your wife is at risk. He hasn't made any threats against either of you and all his attacks....... real and false have been against property. I don't think he wants to harm you or your wife, just frighten you both a bit. Nevertheless take care' and with that he left.

The truth was Detective Inspector Fulton had no idea who was carrying out these attacks or why and frankly he was at a loss to know where to look next in the police investigation.

There was a large team of detectives and uniformed officers working on it but now after several days work they were no nearer to solving the matter than they'd been at the start. Still his experience was that eventually either the whole thing would fizzle out or there'd be some sort of breakthrough usually when the criminal made a mistake. In the meantime it was just good old fashioned police work, slogging away until they got that vital break in the case.

When Janie had returned from France they'd interviewed her in some detail. It had added nothing to solving the case as they were convinced in so far as they could be, that she was entirely innocent of any involvement in the crimes.

Janie for her part knew that William was worried not only about the attacks but also about the business which seemed to be going from bad to worse in it's trading performance.

However she was desperate to see Harry again and telling William that there were some sales on in London and she wanted to pick up a few bargains she waited until he'd left for the office and then made arrangements to go to London to see her lover in a few day's time.

On the morning of her trip she'd finished showering and had put on a bright red bra and panties when William, who she thought had gone as he'd given her a perfunctory goodbye kiss a little earlier and galloped downstairs came back up as he'd left his gold pen on the dressing table

'Good heavens. A scarlet woman' he grinned looking at her. 'Thought you were just going to the sales?'

'I am....umm but I'll need to try on some outfits and the better shops like to have an assistant help, you know fittings and so on. I want to look good if I have to parade in my underwear in front of some old biddy' she reposted quickly.

'Well you look lovely and very sexy. Wish I could stay and ravish you for a while'.

'Oh I wish you could too darling that would be lovely' and she moved a knee forward and pouted at him. 'Go on off you go' and blowing him a kiss turned away.

Good Lord no. The last thing I want is William changing his mind and getting amorous this morning. Today was for Harry.

'Yes I really must go to the office. Have a good day darling' and he left clipping his pen into his inside jacket pocket.

Red underwear for a scarlet woman she mused. Good choice of words although William had no idea of how apt it was. Buttoning herself into a light grey blouse she finished dressing with a fairly short dark green skirt but before putting on the matching jacket she got out a pair of hold up stockings and was about to pull them on when she grinned. No not hold ups, suspenders.

158

After all men loved stockings and suspenders didn't they? She hadn't worn a suspender belt for years but she was sure there was an old one somewhere but a good rummage through her underwear drawer failed to find it and then seeming to remember that she'd thrown it away she settled for black hold ups. Next best thing she smiled to herself as she smoothed out the lacy tops and made a mental note to buy a couple of suspender belts some time soon.

Her arrangement with Harry was that she'd arrive at his offices about three thirty but deciding to surprise him she caught an earlier train planning to get to him about lunch time and attempt to persuade him to leave off work and go make love to her in his apartment all afternoon. So it was a little after twelve thirty when she rang the bell at his offices.

There was no answer. She rang again this time holding in the bell push button for ages. Still no answer. She rang a third time.

'Alright alright just bloody wait will you' came his agitated voice from the other side of the door and jerking it open he continued 'what do you.........' there was a pause. 'Janie what the hell are you doing here? Our appointment is this afternoon'.

He looked tousled. His hair was untidy, his tie unfastened and she noticed that a shirt button was undone in the middle of his chest.

'I thought that I'd surprise you and come early. What about lunch? Where's your secretary by the way. I rang for ages before you came?'

'Oh erm she's out for a couple of hours. Look I can't do lunch I'm in the middle of a meeting. Can we leave it at as arranged for three thirty this afternoon? Then we'll have lots of time together. Alright? Good. Look I must get back to my meeting. Rather a crucial stage I'm afraid..... till this afternoon then my love. See you later eh?' and leaning forward he gave her a quick peck on the lips and turned away closing the door in her face.

For a moment tears nearly came to her as she stood in the corridor staring at the closed door. He'd simply rejected her out of hand. Walking back to the lift she made her way down and out of the building and after a short walk found a wine bar where she ordered a large glass of Chablis and a tuna salad and sat reflecting on the distressing encounter which had just occurred.

Didn't he want to see her? Surely the lovely time they'd spent together in France meant something now? Or was it all in the past? Why had he so abruptly sent her away? Was he going off her? No surely not.

Then she started to rationalise the situation. Their arrangement was for mid afternoon and it was to be expected that he'd be busy during the rest of the day. Of course she couldn't just barge in and expect him to drop everything for her. He had his business to run and if his secretary was out on some sort of errand, then pressing the door bell for ages as she'd done when he was in an important meeting would have really irritated him. Yes she nodded to herself she'd been silly to interrupt him as she had. She shouldn't have come to see him early.

Having settled her mind she ordered another glass of wine and sipped it slowly. Finishing her lunch she found a taxi and went shopping in Bond Street then wandered onto Oxford Street where passing a lingerie shop on impulse went in, quickly chose two suspender belts one red, one black and some non hold up fishnet stockings.

As she paid she asked the cashier who was probably seventeen or eighteen at the most, if she could use a changing room.

By three thirty she was back at Harry's offices where his secretary opened the door almost as soon as she rang the bell, smiled said that Mr. Norton was waiting for her and led her straight through to his office. He jumped up from his chair and almost ran across the room to her.

'Janie how lovely to see you again. Can we have some tea please Margaret?'

As soon as she'd left the room he pulled her to him and kissed her fiercely. 'I'm so sorry about this morning but I was into something important and I couldn't get away. Forgive me?' he asked moving away from her.

'Yes of course. I just wanted to see you so much that I didn't think'.

'I've been so worried that you'd be cross with me. Ah thanks Margaret just pop it down over there and then no interruptions please. Mrs. Hardy and I have some detailed discussions to explore'. He walked to his desk and sat down. His hair was neatly brushed again, his tie properly tied and his shirt was done up.

'Now look Janie I've drawn up the documents for you to sign for your cottage. I'd like you to sit down and read them through carefully'.

'Boring. I don't want to waste time with silly documents. I want to spend time with you. Can we go to your apartment now to make love?'

'No we can't. Now come on let me give you the papers for you to read'.

She walked across the room and sliding in front of him perched on the desk facing him, carefully crossed her legs then leant down and kissed him.

'Documents are boring. I want to make love. Could we do it here in your office?'

'No'.

'Why?'

'Well we just can't. Suppose Margaret came in?'

'You told her no interruptions. Don't your staff do as they're told?'

'Yes of course but look you need to read those papers. Janie please read them...... and then maybe let's think about making love'.

'Kiss me first'. Puckering her lips she leant forward pulling his head towards her. Their kissing was protracted until leaning back she uncrossed her legs, kicked off her shoes and put one foot in his lap rolling it around his crutch area while at the same time taking off her jacket and undoing her blouse to expose her scarlet bra. Reaching inside she lifted each breast in turn out to hang outside their previous support. Smiling when she saw his eyes stare at her chest she swayed them from side to side for a moment or two before leaning forward again. Moving her foot aside she undid his zip then slipped her stocking covered toes inside his now open fly pleased to feel as she wriggled around that he had an erection starting.

'There now Harry isn't this better than stuffy old papers?'

Emboldened by the lunch time wine she deliberately allowed her knees to drift outwards until at about eighteen inches apart not only were they were stretching her skirt as far as it would go, but also they gave him a clear and erotic view of her red knickers, red suspender straps, black fishnet stocking tops and white thighs.

'And what about this?' she asked. 'Better than boring documents?'

161

'Darling of course' he replied softly sliding his hand under her skirt and stroking her stocking tops. 'Oh Janie' and he gently pinged a suspender strap 'these are lovely but I really do want you to read and sign this document in relation to your cottage'.

'Where is it then this document that's so important?'

'You're sitting on it' he grinned. 'I had it on my desk all ready to discuss'.

'Give it to me and I'll sign it' she said holding out her hand.

'You need to read it'.

'No I don't. I trust you. Just tell me where to sign'.

'Well if you're sure, lift yourself up and I'll give it to you'.

She did trying to ensure that she stretched her knees even wider apart. As he gave her the file she looked at him.

'All right where do I sign?'

Giving a deep theatrical sigh he smiled as he replied 'Initials on page seven, nine and ten and full signature on page twelve. But you really should read it first'.

'Harry there's many things I should do, and lots that I shouldn't but wasting time on reading what is I'm sure a complex legal document isn't one of the things that I think I should do. I said just now that I trust you. After all you're my financial adviser so if you advise that I should sign, I'll do so. Give me a pen'.

It took only a few seconds but as she twisted round on the desk and signed or initialled where he'd said, she didn't see the smile of satisfaction on his face.

'Right is that all?'

He nodded smiling happily at her as he took back the document. 'Thank you very much. I'm sure you've done the right thing. Now is there anything else on your mind Mrs. Hardy?' he asked as his hand stroked the outside of her knickers.

'You bet there is. Sex. Lots of it. This afternoon. Now shall I take my knickers off or are you going to do it?'

His fingers teased under the elastic and touched her pussy lips.

'Hell you're wet down here'.

'Shows how much I want you'.

'You are a wicked woman you know but I can't resist your charms and demands. Alright I'll pack up early today. Look you leave now and

I'll follow you as soon as I can. Here's a key to my apartment and this is the address'. He scribbled quickly on a notepad, tore off the sheet and handed it to her.

'Harry I promise I'll make it worth your while giving up an afternoon's work' and giving him a quick kiss she took the sheet of paper, grinned, wriggled her foot again inside his fly, slid off the desk, pulled her skirt down, tucked her breasts back inside her bra, slipped on her shoes, refastened her blouse and jacket, walked across the room and opened the door.

'Thank you very much for your advice Mr.. Norton. I find it so reassuring to have you handling my assets' she said slightly over loudly for Margaret's benefit as she walked out of his office.

It wasn't long, once back in the street, before she managed to get a taxi to his apartment. Unlocking the door she went inside.

Being on her own she thought that she have a nosey around and spent the next half an hour peering and poking into cupboards, wall units, and finding out a little more about her lover.

Slightly disappointingly she found nothing out of the ordinary so remembering an old film she'd seen years ago, she took off a shoe and placed it just inside the front door. Then she unclipped and peeled off one dark stocking and laid it on the floor a little further in where it made a clear contrast against the white carpet. She put her other shoe on the bottom stair. Unzipping her skirt she carefully laid that on the third step. Her jacket went across the sixth stair and her blouse was dropped a little further up. The second stocking draped down from the top step and her red bra was hung over the balustrade at the top of the stairs. The suspender belt went onto the landing floor and finally her knickers were hung on the door handle of his bedroom.

Going into his bathroom she entered the shower cubicle, took the nozzle out of it's holder and turning it on full blast soaped and sprayed her pussy then dried herself and flapped some of his talc onto herself.

Reapplying her makeup and dabbing perfume onto her wrists, inside elbows, behind her knees and ears, down her cleavage and finally into her pussy hair she went into the bedroom and rummaged around in his wardrobes and cupboards for a while.

He certainly had many suits, jackets and trousers as well as an extensive collection of other clothes. Hearing his key in the front door and deciding to be a compete slut for him she lay down naked on top of the duvet cover, wobbling slightly with the underlying movement of the water bed as she waited with eager anticipation what was about to happen.

Peering round the bedroom door he grinned. 'Hello there. I followed the trail that you left which seems to have led me to you'.

'Well now that you've got to the end of the journey I suggest you take advantage of the prize that's waiting for you' she smiled softly in return.

He did but it took him a very long time to reach his climax. Indeed he stopped a couple of times and appeared to have to re-gather his breath before starting to move again inside her. She didn't complain as it enabled her to come twice but he did seem to have to work quite hard to come himself.

Later completely sated sexually she walked downstairs collecting her clothes while he made some coffee in the sunken kitchen.

Dressed again she sat next to him. He was wearing just a bath robe and he nuzzled into her neck.

'Janie you are wonderful you know. As a person, a woman and especially in bed. I've never known anyone I enjoy being with more than you. I'm so lucky to be able to have you. Thank you for coming today' then he roared with laughter.

'What?'

'Well what I said just now' he grinned. 'Thank you for coming. You did didn't you? Twice I think? Nice?

'Umm wonderful' then pushing her hand inside his robe to take hold of his flaccid penis she continued 'and was it wonderful for you? You seemed to struggle a bit today. Is anything wrong? You're not going off me are you?'

'No of course not. I'm just a bit tense. Got a lot on my mind.…..even when making love to you, but you were amazing as usual darling. As I said just now I'm so lucky' and as he kissed her gently she felt his penis twitch and start to lengthen. Leaving her hand on him she nodded.

'No Harry it's me that's the lucky one. I really ought to be going now but if you wanted me to stay a little longer……….' she left the sentence hanging while squeezing him.

'No you've exhausted me. Time you went you randy little minx' and he gently removed her hand and kissed her again.

Her journey back to Norwich was uneventful and finding that William had left a message on their answer phone at home that he'd be quite late, she had a bath and went to bed.

Although not quite asleep when her husband returned and joined her in bed, she pretended to be so and soon she heard William's rhythmic breathing as he slept.

She lay for a while wondering just what was happening to her life. Here she was a married woman with two lovely sons, a devoted, if slightly boring husband, and yet she was throwing herself at her lover and behaving like a slut. After all, sitting on his desk and flashing her knickers wet with pussy juice at his face less than two feet away was hardly the action of a happy faithful wife, was it?

But it had been fun today though. Mind you Harry had been really niggled when she'd arrived early. Silly of her to have done it, but she'd thought he might have enjoyed seeing her sooner, but he hadn't as she'd interrupted his meeting. She couldn't help feel a slight nagging doubt about why he'd turned her away so abruptly, still he'd been happy enough later in the office and then in bed at his wonderful apartment and smiling in the darkness as she slowly drifted off to sleep she enjoyed again the memory of their lovemaking. Nevertheless it was odd as to why he'd struggled so hard to reach a climax. Even though he'd denied it was anything to do with her or that he was going off her.

Oh I hope not she whispered to herself I couldn't bear the thought of that happening.

Next morning, William was off early and although hearing him get up and dress she pretended to be fast asleep as he slipped out quietly to avoid waking her.

Later in the morning she rang Harry's office but Margaret said he was out and she didn't know when he'd be back, so she rang his mobile but that went to voicemail. Deciding against sending him a text she switched on the computer and sent a quick e-mail.

Thank you for your advice and excellent attention yesterday. J.

In the afternoon there was still no reply from him so she spent an hour or so e-mailing friends. Checking before she logged off she couldn't avoid a twinge of disappointment that there was still no reply from him. A call to his mobile again elicited no reply just a voicemail invitation to leave a message, and finally another call to Margaret confirmed that he was still out of the office but she'd ensure he got her message as soon as possible.

Briefly she wondered if he might be in bed with someone else but then she put that thought out of her mind as she returned to household matters and pondered what to get for supper that evening.

The next day passed with no word, call or e-mail from Harry but the following morning when she logged on there among seven new e-mail messages was one from Harry.

Excitedly she clicked on it and read

Thanks. It always gives me the greatest pleasure handling your personal affairs. H.

A discrete message, so she replied

I am always happy to put my personal affairs in your hands. When is our next review? J

God was she pushing too hard? She wanted him but did he really want her as much or was she just a randy client who wanted sex with him? Maybe he was going off her. The reply pinged back almost immediately.

Got lots on this week but as I think that a further extremely detailed review of your assets would be extremely beneficial could you make a progress meeting next Monday perhaps starting with lunch and then getting down to the nitty gritty?   H

Her heart bounced with joy as clearly he wanted to see her again. Thinking for a moment to compose a discrete reply she finally typed

Yes Monday will be quite satisfactory. I am glad you suggested a further asset review as I have a number of areas that I would like to put to you for your attention. Shall I come to your office and if so what time? Janie.

Wondering how long it would take for him to reply she soon found out when a quarter of an hour later her screen indicated an incoming message.

No not the office. Let's meet at the restaurant near Regents Park that we went to before. Have you still got the address? I seem to remember you picked up one of their cards as you left. Harry.

Now the question was which handbag had she taken that day but after a few seconds she remembered and going up to her bedroom she rummaged through it and sure enough there was the little card so skipping happily back down to the computer she tapped a reply.

Yes. Would 1 o'clock be about ok? Janie

He was obviously still logged on as the reply was almost immediate

Great – look forward to it. See you then. Bye. Harry.

Four days to go. She felt her stomach give a lurch and hugging herself tightly she sighed. Four long days to wait. God she was getting randy already just thinking about him and his body.

Picking up the phone she rang her friend Jackie and suggested that they went for a ride together. Jackie was delighted as she had planned to ride today but always preferred to do so in company rather than alone. So when Janie drove up and parked on the drive of the old rectory that she and her husband Mathew had refurbished from a tumbledown wreck which the estate agents had described as "being in need of some renovation" she was not only already dressed for riding but had got her own and Janie's horses saddled up ready to go.

They cheek kissed and then walked to the stables, led the horses outside and taking it in turns to use the mounting block were soon both aboard, with girths tightened, reins gathered and heading off down the drive.

'Nice long one or just a quickie?' queried Janie.

'You sound like Mathew when he gets into bed feeling randy but thinks I'm tired' laughed Jackie. 'That's what he asks'.

'And what do you say?' chuckled Janie.

'Oh quickie of course! I just want to get to sleep so I let him get his rocks off and that's that. Saves me having to get properly involved. Just lie there, smile, make some encouraging noises, a few grunts, one deep groan when he comes and it's all over' she laughed.

Jackie was fun and one of Janie's oldest friends. In fact if she was ever to confide in anyone about having an affair with Harry it would be to Jackie as she was the sole of discretion, amusing but sensible and as they turned out of Jackie's driveway onto the country lane the more she thought about talking to her about Harry, the more she liked the idea.

Shortly they carefully eased their horses through a narrow open gateway and onto the edge of a field without crops and effectively lying fallow to comply with EU set aside regulations. They checked with each other that they were ready to go and kicked their horses into a canter and then up into a gallop.

It was exhilarating riding fast across clear open country like this and the two of them thundered along. Soon a reasonable sized hedge came into view and side by side they flew over it, landed safely and galloped on to the next. Jumping that hedge they slowed and swung right handed to the edge of this third field as there was still a standing crop waiting to be harvested but the edge was uncultivated and they could gallop along there.

A post and rail fence marked the end of this field and they moved into formation one behind the other with Jackie leading to jump the fence, again landing safely but now slowing to a canter they went along the edge of this fourth field but instead of jumping the hedge at the end when they reached it Jackie swung left and led the way still along the uncultivated margin uphill along the second side of the field.

At the top there was a gate leading to a track into a small wood and slowing to a stop Jackie leaned down unclipped it, beckoned Janie through, followed and then refastened it.

'Whew that's blown a few cobwebs away' exclaimed Janie puffing happily.

'Yes sure has. Come on then' and she led the way along the track which was just wide enough for a motor vehicle although with the extremely uneven ground, mud and lying water only a four wheel drive would have been able to make it along there.

They set off at a canter and were soon exiting the wood onto the edge margin of another field with standing corn so they slowed to a trot and proceeded at that slower pace for some time until they regained the lane. Having gone round in a giant circle they reined back to a walk and so made their way back to Jackie's house and stable yard.

Her stables were not like the grand old building that had graced Wood Hollow Hall before being burnt down but were much smaller comprising a row of single story brick built buildings with a taller double story building attached at one end.

Originally the stables and carriage shed for the rector who would have lived here, they'd over the years been used for a variety of purposes finishing as pig sheds but Jackie and Mathew had converted them back and they now made a very effective block of five stables with the old carriage shed now their feed, hay and straw store.

Dismounting they tied the horses up outside, unsaddled them, washed them down, and throwing a light rug across their backs led them into their respective stables. Jackie had given Janie's horse the end unit next to her daughter's little welsh mountain pony's stable. Her own came next in the row, followed by the one for Mathew's horse and the end one was empty.

'You'll stay for lunch won't you?'

'Thanks' smiled Janie.

'Great. I'm sure we've lots to talk about' said Jackie as she led the way across the stable yard and into the large kitchen. 'Now let's see it's just gone twelve so time for a drink I think. Wine?'

'Lovely'.

'Red or white?'

'Either'.

'Ok a nice cold white perhaps?' and opening the fridge she took out a bottle, handed it to Janie with an opener. 'Open that will you while I get the glasses? I've got a quiche in the fridge. With some salad will that be alright?'

'Sounds lovely, thanks'.

The two of them bustled about and were soon sitting in the conservatory sipping their wine as they ate their light meal while chatting about things of interest to them both. When they'd finished Jackie said she'd get some coffee and left Janie alone for a few minutes. Looking round the conservatory she was reminded of the conservatory restaurant at The Swynford Paddocks in Newmarket where she'd been with Harry several times and suddenly decided that she would confide in Jackie about her affair.

When they were both seated again and drinking their coffee Janie looked at her friend.

'Can I ask you something, well tell you something really?'

'Of course. Is it some juicy secret that you're hiding?'

'Why do you ask that?'

'No reason it's just that you sounded a bit mysterious that's all'.

Janie paused and sipped her coffee. 'Have you ever thought of having an affair?'

'An affair? Good grief yes lots of times especially on those occasions when Mathew's been beastly but I've never done anything about it. There was silence for a moment or two then with a slight smile playing around one corner of her mouth and looking straight at Janie she went on 'Why?'

'Oh I just wondered that's all'.

'Funny thing to wonder, now come on Janie my girl we've known each other for too long for an odd question like that. What's this all about?' then pausing again she sat up with a start. 'You haven't have you?'

Janie just looked at her.

'You have haven't you?'

Janie nodded. 'Yes'.

'God. Does William know?'

'No of course not. It would kill him if he found out'.

'When was it?'

'Not was ...... is. It's now. I'm having an affair now. Hey you won't tell anyone will you?'

'Of course not. It'll be our secret. Do you want to talk about it? I guess you do as otherwise you wouldn't have mentioned it. So come on is he all hunky and gorgeous. Have you actually slept with him?'

'He's lovely and yes I .... I am sleeping with him. In London ..... erm and at Newmarket'.

'Newmarket?'

'Uh huh in a hotel there and recently we went to our cottage in France for a few days. We travelled separately but were together down there'.

'You went to France with him for a few days?'

'Yes'.

'Christ you are a dark horse aren't you. Still come on what's he like then? Have you got a picture?'

'No but he's tall slim light brown hair, fun and good looking'.

'And you're having sex with him. I mean not just kissing and cuddling but full on sex'.

Janie nodded.

'Blimey. Is he good in bed?'

'Wonderful. He's got this incredible apartment near Regents Park in London. All stainless steel, glass and minimalist with huge rooms, an enormous balcony and in his bedroom he's even got a water bed. Have you ever made love on one of those? They are amazing. The sensations are just indescribably wonderful'.

'Wonderful sensations? Yes I imagine they are'.

'He's also got mirrors in several places in the bedroom so you can see yourself ..... you know ..... doing it'.

'Good God. How very decadent but is it nice being able to see yourself ..... umm well and him I guess .... you know see yourselves at it?"

'Yes it is ..... rather fun and erotic. Are you shocked?'

'Not shocked but surprised. I never had you down for such a randy little bitch' Jackie admitted. 'So how long as it been going on? Where did you meet? Come on I want to know everything. Now you've started to tell me I want the lot. Everything. Absolutely everything. All the disgusting dirty detail'.

So Janie explained about the wedding then going to London for Harry to review her finances, then how he seduced her and their subsequent meetings.

Jackie listened enthralled asking the odd question for clarification but not wanting to stop her friend in her confession.

Finally Janie sat back smiled ruefully as she said softly 'So that's it, all of it and I'm glad I've told you. It was getting to me a bit and I needed to confide but look you promised you wouldn't say anything. You won't will you?'

'No of course not. Relax. Your naughty secret is quite safe with me. Well well well. Hey this calls for another drink' and smiling she went back into the house leaving Janie with mixed feelings. Glad in one way that she'd told Jackie who she trusted completely but also at the same time nervous that in talking to her friend she'd really been rather silly.

'Here we are' tinkled Jackie as she came back holding another bottle of wine.

Janie insisted that she only wanted a small glass as she had to drive back, but pouring another good sized slug into her own glass Jackie asked with an amused expression. 'So come on then tell me all about the sex. Do you get really naughty? How does he compare with William?'

Laughing Janie said that her friend was a dirty minded lady to which Jackie immediately agreed but Janie although reasonably comfortable with saying where she and Harry had slept together, felt inhibited in providing what her friend sensing her reluctance called, the full sloppy secrets of her illicit sex.

'Spoilsport I wanted to hear all the mucky bits'.

'Well you're not going to'.

'Ok but how often do you meet up?'

'Whenever he can get time away from his business. He's so frantically busy that it's difficult for him. We're seeing each other again on Monday'.

Later as she drove home she pondered whether she'd been silly or sensible in telling Jackie and on balance decided it was neither. It just seemed to have been something that old friends who trusted each other might chat about. How strange she thought that odd things like sitting in the conservatory today had generated memories of him and triggered her to give up her secret, then she grinned remembering Jackie's look of amazement when she'd told her that she was having an affair.

The grin however would have quickly left her face if she could have heard her trusted friend who having cleared away the wine bottle and glasses sat in the kitchen and dialled a number.

'Pauline. Hi how are you? Hey are you busy? No? Good because do you know what I've just discovered?' and the conversation went on for at least ten minutes.

If you wish to strengthen a lie, mix a little truth with it.

Zohar.

CHAPTER 10

Friday, Saturday and Sunday went by at last. They had a dinner party on Saturday night and it was a lively and happy occasion but every now and then Janie couldn't help her thoughts fast forwarding to Monday and her coming next meet up with her lover.

William wanted sex on Saturday and so she obliged him but as he was pumping away on top of her she closed her eyes and imagined it was Harry's prick that was inside her.

Monday finally dawned at last and dressing in jeans and tee shirt she had breakfast with William then when he'd left she sent a quick text to Harry asking if their meeting was still on for one o'clock. It was.

Upstairs she had a bath then dressed carefully deciding to put on some sexy underwear so after her black push up bra and little thong she pulled on the black suspender belt she'd bought the other day. He'd loved her red one so she guessed he'd like this just as much.

Prancing in front of the mirror she carefully rolled on her fishnet stockings, checked that they were straight and not wrinkled then slipped into a knee length lightweight dark blue dress. Black high heeled shoes, blue handbag completed the outfit. Finally making up her face with meticulous care she gave a twirl in front of the mirror and decided she looked fine.

Trotting downstairs she checked round the house, left William a note to say she might be late home this evening, locked up and getting in the Porsche drove quickly to Norwich station and caught the London train in good time having checked that there weren't going to be any delays.

It was nearly twenty past one and she'd just started to worry that maybe he'd stood her up when he bustled into to the restaurant, full of apologies and leaning down gave her a kiss.

'Sorry my darling the bloody phone wouldn't stop, then Margaret wanted some letters signed and I had a couple of propositions to get off all of which conspired to make me late for my lunch with the prettiest client by far that I have. Still here I am, err entirely at your disposal madam' and when he grinned that lop sided grin of his her heart bumped so loudly she thought he must be able to hear her chest banging.

'Do we have to stay here and eat' she queried. 'I'm not hungry, well not for food. In fact I don't think I want to eat at all'.

'Really but if you say you're not hungry for food is there something else for which you are hungry?'

'Yes'.

'What?' and he waved away the waiter who'd just appeared.

'You know what I want'.

'Tell me' and his eyes looked straight into hers.

'I want you ……. now ……. please'.

'Then in that case and on the basis that the client is always right what are we sitting here for? Let's go and start to conduct the detailed review of your assets which I have to say are looking quite delightful today' and he deliberately stared down her dress front as he stood. 'Come on' and he walked round to pull her chair back. 'I'll just need to square Marco. I say you haven't got a tenner in your bag have you as I'll need to sweeten him as we're leaving without eating and I've only got credit cards and no cash on me today'.

He took her eagerly offered bank note, spoke quickly with someone who she assumed was Marco and soon they were outside on the pavement. 'Like to walk or get a cab' he said looking round.

'Which is quicker?'

'Cab I guess' then seeing her expression he added 'cab it is then'.

They got one almost straight away and as soon as they were seated he kissed her again, deeply and passionately before whispering 'I think this is a much better idea than sitting in that restaurant. I have been so looking forward to seeing you that I can't tell you how randy I'm feeling' and he ran his hand along her thigh, pausing for a second as he felt a suspender strap below the material of the skirt.

'Is this what I think it is?' he smiled as he felt it more firmly and when she nodded he chuckled 'how exciting'.

The cab pulled up outside the apartment block and he asked the driver if he took credit cards. The answer was no and looking embarrassed he spoke to her.

'Look I really am sorry about this but this chap doesn't take credit cards. Can you pay him for me? The one I came in from the office did and as I said I've not got any cash on me. I do feel awful asking you to come down to London and then making you pay in cash for things'.

'No problem. I'm happy to help out' and she settled the cab fare before following him into the building.

Upstairs in his apartment she said she needed to go to the bathroom and that she'd meet him in the bedroom. He nodded and said that he'd get some wine.

Once they were both in the huge bedroom there was a moment of awkwardness between them until he said softly 'Come here my darling' and held out his hands to her. She moved towards him and they melted together and it was alright.

They stood kissing for a long time and she felt his hands roving across her back and buttocks before he leaned back. 'Turn round' was his soft command and complying she felt her zip being run down and his lips kissing her bare shoulders and down to her lower back.

'Do you like me like this?' she asked slightly self consciously. 'I put the suspenders on especially for you. I don't usually wear them just hold ups or tights normally'.

'I think you look incredibly elegant, sophisticated and terribly sexy' he replied as holding her at arms length he made her shiver as he unashamedly ran his eyes up and down her body while his fingers played with her suspender straps.

She shivered even more as he walked round behind her to unclip her bra, then knelt down behind her to slide her thong down to her ankles. Turning towards him as he helped her out of the flimsy garment she gasped as still kneeling he ran his tongue around her belly and down into her bush while his hands started to stroke up and down her thighs getting closer with every upward move to her pussy until she felt the fingers of one and then his other hand start to tease and play with her there.

She stroked his neck before leaning down and kissing the top of his head. 'Make love to me' she pleaded.

'Not yet, come here' and he led her to the huge waterbed. She sat down and then slithered herself into the middle. Looking her up and down he leaned forward and kissed her bush then let his tongue trail down to her suspender straps and stocking tops all of which he licked and kissed.

'These need to be savoured' he whispered gently pinging the straps before slipping his fingers into her pussy which was soaking wet. 'Umm now who is my extremely pretty but very randy client then' he chuckled softly as he started massaging her.

'Please' she gasped trying to pull him on top of her.

'No you're going to wait a little while yet' and he kissed her bush again before removing his fingers and replacing them with his lips and tongue.

Janie was gasping quietly but as his tongue flicked across her clit she jumped and groaned. 'Harry please'.

'No baby you must wait …… and wait ……. and wait' but he added two fingers to his tongue as he attended to her ever mounting need, until arching her back and with her hands grabbing at him she exploded into a climax that rocked right through her body.

Slowly she subsided as he moved up the bed to look at her before kissing each of her nipples.

'Harry make love to me now please'.

'No my love. You need to come like that again' and as he spoke his fingers entered her pussy.

'No please make love to me properly'.

'NO'. He slid down the bed, pushed her legs apart and started to use his tongue and fingers on her again where initially she tried to object but as she felt her passion waves rising again she stopped protesting and abandoned herself to enjoy to the full what he was doing to her. The climax when it came was so intense that she thought she'd cry. Her nails raked his shoulders and she bounced and bumped up and down, groaning and squealing loudly with the ecstasy of what was happening.

He continued to stroke her clit gently and slowly as she started to come down from her peak, until moving up the bed again he kissed her lips deeply.

'Oh Harry' she gasped still unable to speak properly.

'That sounded good. Was it?' he chuckled.

'Ecstatic …. just incredible. Thank you but now please Harry I beg you'.

'What do you beg me' he teased looking puzzled.

'You know very well' she whispered.

'No I want to hear you say it'.

'Make love to me ….. please?'

'Beg'.

'I am begging'.

'No say it. Say I beg you please make love to me properly'.

'Harry. I beg you. Make love to me. Stop torturing me'.

'You didn't say please' he taunted 'or properly' he added.

'Please Harry please ….. please make love to me properly ….I beg you'.

'Your wish is my command my love. It will be a great pleasure'. Smiling he got off the bed and standing alongside her undressed until completely naked he opened the bedside drawer and taking out a condom held it out to her.

'So you want me to make love to you do you?'

'Yes' she replied slitting open the condom foil.

'Yes what?'

'Yes please. Oh Harry stop it. I have begged you. I'll do it again if you want? I beg you …. come on don't torment me like this. Please I want you so desperately. Make love to me now …. please'.

'Uh huh. Alright if that's what you want then who am I to refuse a beautiful lady in her hour of desperate need?' he mocked turning to face her swaying his hips and sporting a firm erection which twitched as she looked at it.

'But I think you should make a start with this' he said thrusting his hips aggressively towards her.

Looking at him she nodded and stretched forward, rolled the condom onto him then took his prick deep into her mouth while one hand started to play with his balls and the other stroked his buttocks. They stayed like that for quite some time as she worked on him until he gently put a hand on her forehead and pushed her away.

'Thank you. Now you've earnt what you want, so I think it's time I made love to you …. don't you?'

She nodded and whispered 'Yes' as he rolled on top of her and slid inside. The lovemaking was slow, prolonged, wonderful for her and she felt herself rising and falling again on peaks of potential orgasm as he skilfully moved within her before she suddenly pressed her crutch hard against him whispering that she was coming which grunting and gasping loudly she did.

Still he moved, all through her orgasm until sensing that she was finally complete he thrust a little more quickly and harder until it was his turn to groan as he spurted time after time into the rubber. Finally he stopped and lay unmoving on top of her.

They stayed like that for some while before he eased himself off, kissed her lips softly and lay down beside her. 'Well I think that's a good start to reviewing your assets but I am sure much more research is needed' he grinned and he took first one breast and squeezed gently and then repeated it with the other one. 'Umm much more research' he whispered as he slowly lowered his head and licked her nipples.

Janie lay there wobbling slightly on the amazing bed looking at the ceiling mirror then turned her head to the side and in the large mirror which covered most of one wall watched as Harry kissed and licked her breasts, nipples, belly button, thighs and bush. There was something very erotic about being a voyeur to herself and she resolved that next time he made love she'd make a point of watching them in action.

She for her part stroked his chest and his legs and let her hand play with his flaccid prick. Every now and then she kissed him until she folded him into her arms and holding him loosely they dozed.

It was about an hour later that almost by mutual but unspoken consent they started to stroke and kiss each other again and soon their kissing was leading to more urgent and passionate activity.

Rolling a condom on himself Harry turned her onto her tummy and kissed her neck, shoulders, back and buttocks. He slid his fingers into her pussy and finding it moistened straight away whispered 'I love wet pussy it makes things so easy'.

She gasped and moaned softly as his fingers, then his tongue worked on her until she looked round at him and whispered 'Make love to me now Harry'.

'Ok but let's be a bit naughty shall we? Come here' and pulling her into a kneeling position he slid one hand beneath her to continue his attention to her lower regions while the other roamed around her breast and pinched a nipple.

Janie pushed her buttocks back against his thigh and felt him rubbing his prick against her pussy. Several times he did it before taking himself in hand and gently slapping his erect and hard prick up against her slit before slowly entering her. Pushing in deeply he pressed against her then withdrew and she felt his hardness slide out, move a little way from her pussy lips, pause, then press against her.

'Harry?' she queried looking over her shoulder at him.

'Schh baby it'll be fine. Just relax and leave it all to me' and with that he put both hands around her waist and she felt him slowly press himself deep within her.

'Harry! I don't know about ………'

'I do'.

'I've never …….'

'Schh …. I told you just relax'.

'But…….'

'Relax my love' he whispered as he pushed himself fully inside her.

Surprisingly it was all over rather quickly and shortly he withdrew holding the condom to ensure it stayed in place.

'Umm that was lovely. Thank you Janie darling. Now come here' and pulling her down onto her side he cuddled her to him.

She lay there for a little while then patting him on the shoulder said that she'd like a bath, rolled off the bed and pouting at him in what she hoped was a sexy way undid the clips and rolled off her stockings then took off the black suspender belt.

'Good idea' he said leaning down and picking up a stocking which he held to his lips and kissed. 'There's a Jacuzzi in the bathroom. It's great fun sitting in there relaxing and letting the water jets do interesting things!' so holding hands they walked naked along the landing into the bathroom and standing side by side arms around each other, watched as the large deep bath with the many nozzles quickly filled with hot water. Every now and then they peck kissed.

Clambering in together she laid back and relaxed against his chest while his hands stroked her neck and shoulders although every now and then they made a foray round to her breasts as the foaming water fizzed and bubbled around them.

'Ok?'

'Yes thanks' and she twisted round to pop a kiss on his nose.

'What time do you have to leave?'

'Not too early. I left William a note to say that I might be quite late'.

'Good. Where does he think you are by the way?'

'Meeting you for a review of progress, although what William thinks we've been reviewing and the reality is somewhat different' she laughed 'and then shopping'.

'Ah well I think what we've been doing this afternoon is a much better occupation than shopping don't you?'

'Yes definitely much better' and reaching behind she found his prick and played with it for a moment or two before swivelling round to face him and sitting herself on his lap.

'Harry?'

'Umm'.

'When we made love just now, that second time'.

'Yes'.

'I've never done it ….. you know ….. like that before'.

'Did you like it?'

'I don't know'.

'First time is always strange but you might get to quite like it. After all it's a great British tradition you know'.

'It is?'

'Oh yes the old British Empire was built on buggery. Probably wouldn't have succeeded without it. Those pioneering chaps that discovered continents and colonised the world learnt it in the dormitories at their public schools then progressed and carried it on as they explored the world. Of course it was illegal in those days but that didn't stop them. Lots of native men and women all over the globe got themselves well and truly buggered by the Victorian Brits' he laughed.

'Really?'

'Yes really, still at least it stopped the women producing lots of illegitimate kids'.

'I guess it did. I suppose that's how men do it is it? You know gay men'.

'Yes, but look if you don't want to do it again, that's fine we won't'.

'No-o I didn't say that. It's just that it was a new experience'.

'Sure and I think that life, especially life in bed having sex, is about new experiences. I wouldn't want to do it like that all the time but every now and then it makes a nice change. Still let's forget about it for now as I'm going to stand up and you can soap me all over'.

Scrabbling around under water for the soap and then lathering up a large soft sponge she knelt up to wash him from neck down to the part of his legs that were above the water. She spent a long time on his prick, balls and buttocks then cupping her hands to collect water she washed off the soap.

Her activity had made his prick erect a little but she pulled him back down into the frothing foaming water. After enjoying the sensations for a while he asked if she'd like something to eat as they'd skipped lunch and so wrapping themselves in bathrobes they wandered downstairs into the kitchen.

'Lobster soup with some delicious French crackers followed by a toasted brie avocado and bacon sandwich. How's that sound?'

'Terrific thanks. Are you a good cook?'

'Brilliant! I can turn an M & S ready meal and accompaniments into a feast fit for a king ….. or a queen' he chuckled as he attached the tin opener to the soup can. 'Hey open a bottle of wine will you. There's some red there in the rack or some white in the fridge. Might even be some champagne if you like'.

They sipped their white wine and ate slowly, occasionally feeding each other with crackers, bits of bacon or slivers of avocado which fell off the open sandwiches that he'd made surprisingly quickly. Janie was relaxed and pleased that Harry seemed so calm and happy in her company.

Glancing at the clock she saw that it was a quarter to six so no rush to leave yet and she said so.

'Have you had enough to eat?'

'Yes plenty thanks'.

'Right I'll make some coffee and then we could wander back upstairs'.

'Could we? And why might we want to do that Mr. Norton?' she answered coquettishly lowering her eyes and looking at her hands.

'So I can' and leaning he put his lips close to her ear 'fuck you again before you have to go home'.

'Oh is that why' she giggled. 'Well unless you really want coffee right now, why not leave that till later. I think I'd prefer take you up on your suggestion instead of sitting drinking coffee'.

On the bed they kissed passionately, threw off their robes then she pushed him onto his back and sitting on his stomach found that she couldn't reach the bedside drawer for the condoms so slithering up his body she eventually succeeded, although he pulled her so that she sat down on his face where he tongue lashed her for a while before allowing her to slide back down onto his thighs.

She stroked him until he was fully hard, kissed his now erect prick several times, rolled the prophylactic on him, checked that it was firmly in place then rubbing her pussy on him slowly impaled herself on his erection.

Moving on him she leaned down to kiss him and tasted herself on his lips as she offered her breasts to his mouth, gasped as his teeth chewed on her nipples and used all her abilities to make this a ride of lovemaking that he would remember with pleasure and satisfaction for a long time.

When he finally climaxed she was nowhere near coming herself but not worrying about that she was just happy to see his satisfied face and hear his deep groans.

It was as they were lying side by side later that they looked at each other and he said 'I think we've had a thorough review of your assets today Mrs. Hardy. Don't you?'

'Yes and do you think they are in good shape?'

'Quite excellent' he smiled as he stroked her breasts.

'But I'm sure it's the sort of thing that needs reviewing regularly don't you Mr. Norton?'

'Oh yes certainly very .... very regular reviews'.

'Good but look Harry I'm going to have to be going soon. Can I have a quick shower?'

'Sure. You know where it is. In fact take your choice of the en-suite or the bathroom. I'll get some coffee brewing'.

After her shower as she clipped her suspenders back onto the stockings it felt strange to be re-dressing in her sexy underwear.

Christ whatever would William think if he saw me in this stuff?

Downstairs they sat quietly drinking the excellent coffee each lost in their own thoughts until she turned to him.

'Harry thank you for …… well for …… well you know …. everything. It was a lovely afternoon and the trouble is I enjoy our time together so much that I'm going to want to see you again very soon. In fact I think about you all the time when I'm away from you. I know we've got to be careful and you've got your business to run but please let's not leave it too long till we meet again. Can we fix a date now? What about next week?'

'Janie darling I also love being with you. Not just for the sex although that's wonderful with you' and he held her hands and smiled deep into her eyes. 'In fact I cannot think of anyone to whom I've ever made love that is so good, or who makes the lovemaking experience so compellingly outstanding, so utterly fulfilling and so exquisitely delightful as you.

I told you almost as soon as we met that I think there's something special about us, a sort of chemistry. Well I think that even more now. You and I are so amazing together that it is unbelievable. It is breathtakingly, achingly, astonishingly beautiful and I count myself as such a lucky man to have found you and to have the privilege of knowing you and making love to you'.

Tears rolled slowly down her cheeks as she whispered softly 'Harry that is such a beautiful thing to have said. Thank you'.

'Yes you see my gorgeous Janie I am so astonishingly fortunate to have found you ……. and I think ……. well the fact is my darling ….. that I think that I might be starting to fall in love with you'.

'Harry …… really? You can't be …… can you?'

'I think I may be'.

She kissed him softly, deeply but very gently then whispered 'I must go my darling, darling Harry but hold me before I do ….. please?'

'Do you have to? We must try and find a way sometime where we could be together all night?'

'Like we were in France'.

'Yes, just like that darling'.

'God whatever are we going to do? I've got to get home now but to be able to stay all night would be so lovely. One day maybe?'

'Yes let's hope so and soon. Ok well if you really have to go then come here and give me a goodbye kiss'.

So she did and afterwards they held hands as he walked her to the door where they turned and hugged tightly. She felt tears coming to her eyes again so she took a deep breath, popped a kiss on his lips, smiled and walked out the door. At the lift she turned. He was still standing in his doorway and waved as she waited for the lift to come.

Her last sight of him was of him standing in his bathrobe blowing her a kiss as she peered out of the lift doors.

It didn't take long to flag down a cruising cab and she got to Liverpool Street station where she had about twenty minutes to wait before the Norwich train left.

Walking around the concourse she first went to Boots and bought a pair of tights, then to W H Smith to get the evening paper and finally to a snack bar where she bought a sandwich and a coffee.

Clutching her purchases she boarded the train, found a first class seat and sat there staring out of the window, but not really seeing the other passengers walking along the platform or the train staff as they got the train ready to leave.

A few more people joined the train after her and she was surprised how full it was at this time of night. She heard the whistle blow and just as it did a middle aged man plonked down in a seat opposite her, smiled and puffing slightly said 'Phew just made it thank goodness'.

Nodding in return as the train jerked into motion she noticed that the man's eyes had fixed on her legs so carefully tugging down her skirt and ensuring her knees were together she opened her pack of sandwiches and took a sip of the coffee, grimacing as it was weak and tasteless so unlike the delicious stuff that Harry had.

Thinking of his coffee made her think of him and she sat reflecting on her day and running through every detail of their time together in her mind.

Wanting to cross her legs she knew that she had to be careful to avoid flashing her stocking tops as Mr. Middle Aged man opposite although holding a paperback book seemed to have his eyes more aimed at her legs than his novel.

Smiling at him she stood up to make her way to the toilet. Once inside she peeled off her siren ware stockings and wriggled out of her suspender belt then struggled with the lurching of the train trying to pull on the new tights. Finally she sat down on the surprisingly clean toilet seat and managed to get them on satisfactorily.

Returning to her seat she smiled again at the man, crossed her legs and settled down to read the paper.

Now how soon can I find a way to spend more time with Harry. Overnight would be truly wonderful.

Back in Norwich at the car park she found a young couple and asked them to see her to her car finally arriving home just after eleven thirty where William was sitting in his study looking worried.

'Wherever have you been? It's gone eleven thirty and I was really worried. You didn't answer your mobile and I was about to ring the police'.

'Oh darling didn't you get my text?'

Well of course he didn't when you didn't send any text.

'I went to London for a quick review of how things are going with Harry Norton. Everything seems fine there so as soon as that was over I looked at some of the new fashions and then I bumped into Rosemary. She was my best friend at university and we haven't seen each other since then'.

'Rosemary? Who is she? I don't think I've heard you speak of her before?'

Who's she? Never heard of her before? Not surprised as I never had a best friend called Rosemary!

'Oh surely you must. Well anyway I was in Harvey Nicholls and suddenly this woman came up and asked if I was Jane? I said yes and she introduced herself. She lives in Devon now and was up in town for a few days. Not only that she recognised me but that we bumped into each other? Isn't that amazing?

Yes quite amazing seeing she doesn't exist!

We decided that after all this time having met up again we just had to spend time together so we went for dinner. That's why I texted you to say that I would be late'.

Gosh lying is so easy isn't it?

'Well I got no text' and he picked up his mobile and re-checked. 'No nothing from you at all' he said grumpily.

'Oh sorry well I can see why you must have been worried. It's probably swilling around in the electronic ether somewhere. Now would you like a drink or coffee? Is there something I can get you?'

'I've got a whisky but if you are having a nightcap I'll have another'.

'How are things at Hardys?'

'About as bad as they could be, but don't let's talk about that tonight It'll just depress me'.

They went into the sitting room and drank their whisky. She chattered on about her fantasy meet up with Rosemary and then saying that she was tired out and wanted a bath she left him gloomily drinking his second whisky as she went upstairs, took the saucy underwear out of her handbag and tucked it at the back of her underwear drawer.

In her bath she thought again of Harry and hoped that William wouldn't want to make love tonight. In fact she decided she wasn't going to let him and got a couple of paracetamol tablets and a glass of water ready in case which she took into the bedroom.

Getting into bed William was lying there smiling. She pulled back the covers and could see that he had his night things on but as she wriggled down he leaned towards her and ran a hand over her face and then down to her breasts.

Oh bloody hell he did want to.

'Darling I am so sorry but my period started this afternoon. It's early for some reason. I've got a headache and a shocking stomach cramp so I'm going to take these' and she held out the tablets 'and hope I feel better in the morning. Sorry'.

There easy.

'Oh my poor dear. Of course and as you say hopefully you'll be better tomorrow. Good night my love. I was very worried about you this evening'.

'Umm sorry love. Night night' and she popped him a little kiss and then they turned back to back and went to sleep she thinking of Harry and also how having said that her period had started she'd have to be careful now as in fact she wasn't due for a least a week.

He, happy that nothing had befallen her dropped off eventually, still worried about Hardys.

Next morning when he brought her up a cup of tea he asked how she was feeling, kissed her and left for the office.

She showered, dressed and as soon as she was downstairs logged on and sent an e-mail.

Mr. Norton. Thank you for the extremely thorough review of my assets yesterday which I thought was a very satisfactory session and I very much look forward to our next meeting. You must let me know when you think that should be. Janie Hardy.

The reply was almost immediate.

Mrs. Hardy. Yes I agree it was a most excellent session and it gives me enormous pleasure to thoroughly review, work on and handle the assets of such a charming lady. As to our next meeting can we leave that for now and see how things evolve over the coming weeks. Harry Norton.

Over the coming weeks? God no that was too long. She wanted to see him sooner than that so she fired off another e-mail.

Wouldn't it be better to get a date in our diaries sooner rather than later instead of just leaving it vague? Janie

No instant response and feeling slightly disappointed she attended to the rest of her e-mails, wrote a couple of letters and checking before logging off saw that there was still no reply from him. Nor was there that afternoon when she checked, nor again in the evening but there was the next morning.

Mrs. Hardy. I think we really do need to leave it for 3 – 4 weeks. Financial markets don't move that quickly (except in times of crisis) and there is nothing that will need action with your assets immediately. I have quite

a lot on at present and may be away for a while but I'll
suggest a new date in due course.
Harry Norton.

A brush off? No he had his business to manage. They weren't an
item and didn't have any sort of formal relationship. They were just two
adults having a sexual affair as and when they could. Well as and when
he wanted to. He'd made it clear when he wanted to see her and she
wasn't going to spoil things between them by trying to get him to see
her sooner. If a three or four week gap was what he wanted then that's
want he'd get. She replied

Of course. Quite understand. Thanks. J

Days passed. Janie went to a business dinner with William and
continued to notice how tense he was. When she asked him about
Hardy's business he sighed and told her that things were getting really
difficult.

'The bank is completely fed up and I'm not sure how much longer
they are going to continue to support us you know. If they pull the plug
we've had it and that is a horrible thing to contemplate'.

'Isn't there anything you or your team can do to improve things?'

'We're doing all we can but we're getting killed by our competitors
and the big supermarkets and wholesalers are squeezing us all the time
for better and better prices. It all comes out of our profit margin which
has completely gone now'.

Feeling some remorse for him while she was betraying him behind
his back, she continued to discuss the problems of Hardys but she
had no ideas that could help and they both felt quite depressed at the
business situation.

Later when they went to bed she still felt guilty, so running her hand
down his chest and taking hold of his limp prick she said that although
her period was still in full flow if he would like her to use her hand on
him she'd be happy to do so.

'Thank you Janie but I'm really tired and I need to think things
at Hardys through and it won't be too long before your period is clear
will it?'

'Alright but the offer's there if you want it' she whispered letting go of him.

He nodded, kissed her goodnight and turned onto his side, but she lay awake wondering again what was to happen with the business, with her and William, but especially with her and Harry.

At the weekend she and William drove down to Stowe school and took the boys out for lunch in a local restaurant. The two lads chattered excitedly telling their parents all about latest things that they'd been doing, how their schoolwork was going, which teams and sports they were playing, and generally how life looked from the point of view of two happy sturdy growing public school boys.

Looking at her sons, Janie felt dreadful that she had been betraying them as well as William and considered whether she could stop this affair with Harry but even as she posed the question to herself and smiled at her offspring she knew what the answer was.

At the end of the month she rang Harry at his office and although sounding pleased to hear from her he parried her questions as to when they could meet up again pleading pressure of work. He suggested leaving it for another couple of weeks.

'Surely you could find a little time for us somewhere in your busy schedule?' she asked slightly petulantly.

'Janie my love. It's not that I don't want to meet it's just that I do have an awful lot on at the moment. Look please don't take this the wrong way but you're not my only client you know and I simply can't keep taking time off during the day, much as I love being with you'.

'What about an evening? Let's meet half way. How about Newmarket where we met before? Or suggest somewhere else. Would you like me to come to London? I'll find a reason and fit in with you'.

'No look Janie just leave it a bit will you. I'm tied up most evenings. I've got to go now. There are people waiting to see me. I'll ring you in a couple of weeks'.

She reflected on this conversation for ages after the connection was broken. What was it he'd said? She wasn't his only client. Well she knew that, but did it mean he was sleeping with others? No of course not. Ok maybe she wasn't the only lady client with whom he had sex, but now that he'd put her off again perhaps he didn't want to see her any more. Maybe flaunting herself in stockings and suspenders had been too much for him?

No he'd said he loved her dressed like that. Had she been simply too pushy? But she wasn't going to press now in case she started to force him away from her.

So she kept her thoughts, worries and desires to herself and tried to lead a normal life although when she rang Harry's office three week's later, having decided that more than enough time had elapsed and that she really wanted to see him again, she was surprised to hear an answer phone message saying that the offices were temporarily closed.

Closed? Why and where was Margaret? She rang his mobile but it simply didn't connect. She sent an e-mail and a text asking him to contact her but no reply came and further calls to his office and mobile failed to raise him.

It was after a further several days of trying and failing to get hold of him that she came to the conclusion that he must be abroad. After all in one of his e-mails he'd said that he was going to be away so that must be it and slightly cheered by that thought, although still with a niggling doubt, she went to answer the phone that had interrupted her worrying session. She was surprised to hear Inspector Fulton on the line.

'Good morning Mrs. Hardy'.

'Oh good morning Inspector. If it's William that you want he's at the office'.

'No it's you to whom I want to speak. Some colleagues of mine from the Metropolitan police force in London are involved in an enquiry and they think you may be able to help them so you are going to get a call from a Detective Chief Inspector Spencer and he'll want to come and see you'.

'From London? What about?'

'I don't really know the details Mrs. Hardy but I am sure Detective Chief Inspector Spencer will explain everything to you when you meet'.

'Will you be with him?'

'Probably not madam. Well cheerio then' and he rang off.

Janie sat for a little while wondering why a policeman from London would want to talk to her but shrugging her shoulders decided that it must be something to do with the fire, or the bomb scare.

Oh well she'd find out in due course.

No adultery is bloodless.

Natalia Ginzburg.

CHAPTER 11

Immersed in the morning newspaper Janie jumped when the phone rang again.

'Mrs. Hardy?'

'Yes'.

'Hello madam. I think you might be expecting a call from me. My name is Detective Chief Inspector Spencer. We are investigating a certain matter and to use that oft quoted police phrase we think you may be able to help us with our enquiries'. He laughed. 'May I make an appointment to come and see you please?'

'Yes of course but what's it about?'

'I'd rather not go into things on the phone but I will explain everything when I see you Mrs. Hardy. Now would tomorrow be convenient, say about eleven o'clock?'

'Umm wait a minute let me check my diary'. Noticing that her hand was trembling slightly she turned the pages and saw that her morning was clear. 'Yes that's fine. Is this about the fire here or the problems at William's factory because if so he ought to be present as well?'

'No it's not about that. It's quite another matter and it's just you Mrs. Hardy that we wish to see'.

'Right I'll see you tomorrow then. Thank you'.

That night she told William about the strange phone call and he was equally puzzled but said that no doubt it would all be cleared up in the morning.

Surprisingly tense Janie couldn't settle to anything the next day but just before the appointed time a large silver Volvo saloon drove slowly up to the front of the house. Two people emerged and walked to the front door.

Janie opened it shortly after they'd rung.

'Mrs. Hardy?' She nodded. 'Good morning madam. I'm Detective Chief Inspector Spencer and this is Sergeant Maggie Wagstone'. Both officers held up id cards. 'May we come in?'

'Of course' and Janie led the way into the smaller of the two ground floor sitting rooms. 'Would you like some coffee....... or tea perhaps?'

'Coffee would be nice thank you'.

'Right it won't take a minute the kettle has already boiled' and she hurried off into the kitchen returning shortly with a tray of mugs, coffee pot, milk, sugar and plate of biscuits.

'Lovely house you have madam' smiled the Detective Chief Inspector disarmingly as she rejoined the police officers.

'Thank you. It's been in my husband's family for donkey's years. We love it here. Now what's this all about? You were a bit mysterious on the phone yesterday. You say it's not connected with the arson attack here or the problems at my husband's factory?'

'Highly unlikely madam but we can't be totally certain at this stage' he replied. 'You see we' and he swept his hand to include himself and the woman policewoman 'are with the fraud squad of the Metropolitan police'.

'Fraud squad? What's that got to do with burning down our stables and setting fire to my husband's factory?'

'I don't know at this stage Mrs. Hardy. Maybe nothing, maybe a great deal but let me start by asking you a question. Do you know a Mr. Harry Norton?'

'Harry Norton? Yes he's my financial adviser'.

'Have you known him long madam?'

'No not too long. Why? What's this all about?'

If you don't mind I'll ask the questions as this stage madam. I will explain matters further very shortly. Now how long have you known him, Mr. Norton I mean?'

'Only a few months. We met at a wedding that my husband and I attended'.

'And he's now your financial adviser is he? When and how did that start exactly?'

So Janie explained how after meeting at the wedding Harry had invited her to come to London to talk about the financial services that he offered and how she'd discussed it with William and they'd agreed that based on what Harry said he could provide in better financial returns, they'd gone ahead and turned her money over to him to look after.

Both the Detective Chief Inspector and the woman sergeant asked several questions during her explanation, then when Janie again asked what the inquiry was all about the senior detective looked straight at her.

'We are investigating a large number of allegations of fraud, deception, theft, misappropriation of funds and several other offences believed to have been committed by Mr. Norton madam'.

She gasped. 'Harry. Fraud? No you're wrong. He couldn't be. Not Harry. After all he's.............' she paused.

'What is he madam?'

'Urm, well he's a perfectly respectable businessman who provides financial advice and is making me more money than I could make on my own.... err more than William and I could make on our own. That's what he does. You must be wrong. Where did these allegations come from? Who has made these awful claims about him?'

'I cannot disclose that madam but I assure you we do not investigate these sorts of things without good reason. When did you last see or speak to him madam?'

'Well not for a few weeks as funnily enough I've been trying to get hold of Harry for some time now but I've not be able to reach him. There's an answer phone on at his office and he doesn't answer his mobile'.

'I'm not surprised that you can't get hold of him'.

'Why?'

'Because he's in Wormwood Scrubs prison on remand while we continue our enquiries'.

'In prison?' she gulped. 'On remand? Harry's in prison? Why? Oh no. Surely there's been a mistake?'

'We don't think so Mrs. Hardy. Are you alright madam?' he queried seeing how pale Janie had become.

'I think I'd like a glass of water. What you've said it's such a shock'.

'I'll come with you Mrs. Hardy' said Sergeant Wagstone as she followed Janie out of the sitting room and into the kitchen. 'These things always come as a shock, don't they?' she continued, watching Janie's hands shaking while she filled a glass from the tap. Janie took a deep swallow then re-filled it. They walked back into the sitting room where she took another sip of water.

'Sorry but I just felt a bit faint'.

'Quite understandable madam' smiled the Detective Chief Inspector kindly. He was about fifty years old Janie thought, tall broad shouldered with grey eyes but a kindly overall expression, unlike the policewoman who seemed more hostile. 'Now do you feel alright to continue?'

Janie nodded, and then answered the many further questions that were put to her about exactly what Harry had done for her financial affairs. They'd been talking for about three quarters of an hour when there was a pause in the conversation. Detective Chief Inspector Spencer stood and spent a few moments looking out of the French windows into the garden then he turned and looked straight at Janie.

'Mrs. Hardy there are some other aspects of this enquiry that I think might be better discussed at this stage just between you and Sergeant Wagstone. Now seeing that lovely rose garden out there I'd like to have a wander around it if you don't mind. I grow roses myself but nothing like the wonderful display that you have here, so while I go and make myself jealous Maggie will run through these other matters with you. If you need me just call' he finished looking at the woman police sergeant.

'Right Gov' and she waited until he had opened the French window door and stepped out into the garden.

'Now Mrs. Hardy I'd like to explore a little further your relationship with Mr. Norton. You've told us about how you became involved with him and the financial arrangements that you have with him but what about your personal relationship with him?'

'My personal relationship? I don't have a personal relationship. He was a business acquaintance handling my financial affairs. I've told you and the Chief Inspector all that. What more do you think I can tell you?'

'A business acquaintance you say. Is that all he was? Or was there perhaps a more personal aspect to the relationship?'

'I don't know what you mean?'

'Mrs. Hardy. The Chief Inspector has been very sympathetic and to avoid embarrassing you he's left us alone to talk about the personal aspects of your relationship with Mr. Norton. Woman to woman. Now let me remind you madam that giving incomplete, or worse still, false information to a police officer is a serious offence. However if you wish we can go to a police station and continue this discussion under caution probably with male officers present as witnesses if that's what you want'.

Janie looked horrified.

'So let me ask you again. Was there a personal aspect to your relationship with Mr. Norton?'

Janie stared aghast at the police sergeant.

'Mrs. Hardy?'

Janie didn't know what to say.

'Mrs. Hardy let me be absolutely frank. Were you having an affair with Mr. Norton?'

Janie thought of William, of her boys, her friends, the fire, her house, and of Harry, as she stared at the floor.

'Mrs. Hardy I asked you a question. I want an answer. Were you having an affair with Harry Norton?' snapped the police officer.

'Yes' came the whispered reply.

'Sorry. Can you speak up please? Did you answer yes?'

'Yes I did'.

'You were having an affair with Mr. Norton. Is that right?

'Yes'.

'Was the affair of a sexual nature?'

'How dare you! I don't see what that's got to do with you, and I don't see how it's at all relevant to your enquiries!' Janie replied angrily, glaring at the other woman.

'It has everything to do with this enquiry and so it has everything to do with me. Now was your affair of a sexual nature?' responded the woman police officer firmly.

There was a pause.

'Well Mrs. Hardy? We can go to the police station if you prefer?'

Janie blushing furiously looked at her feet and said very softly 'Yes'.

'Did you say yes madam?'

'Yes ..... I did say yes'.

'You were having sexual relations with Mr. Norton, is that right?'

'Yes' she whispered quietly.

'Over what period of time did these sexual relations occur?'

'Does it matter? I've told you I slept with him what more do you want to know? Do you want me to tell you what he's like in bed, how often we did it, what positions we used, whether he likes blowjobs, how big his cock is, how long he can keep it up. Is that what you want to know?' she yelled.

'No Mrs. Hardy I don't want to know any of those…..err… sordid details. I just want you to answer my question. Over what period of time did you have a sexual relationship with him?' replied the policewoman calmly.

'Almost from the start' Janie yelled again tears starting to run down her face.

'Look calm down Mrs. Hardy. Shouting at me doesn't help things at all. Now you said almost from the start. What do you mean by almost?'

Janie looked at the other woman, shrugged then calming down dabbed at her eyes with a tissue. 'Sorry. We met at the wedding then I went down to London to his office to see him. He prepared some figures and I returned another day to discuss them. They seemed fine so he drew up some documents and then I went back a few days later to sign them. We went to lunch and……………' she tailed off.

'And?'

'We went to his apartment and made love. Look will my husband have to find out about this? He knows nothing about it'.

'That's not up to me madam. I won't tell him but when the case gets to court then there's no telling what will come out into the public domain. Also it depends on the others'.

'What others?'

'The other people that Mr. Norton has defrauded. Sorry has allegedly defrauded'.

'Are there many?'

'Well we're examining his files and records. It would seem that he had about fifty clients altogether. Of those, eight were companies and we're checking what might or might not have occurred with them. Another ten were male clients and again we're checking, working our way through the list, so to speak. The remainder were females, like you. We've visited twenty three so far, you're number twenty four.

What is interesting is that most of his female clients were considerably older than you Mrs. Hardy but most seem to have fallen for his charms'.

Immediately Janie remembered Harry laughing about his older women clients.

'When you say fallen for his charms. What do you mean?'

'I mean several have admitted sleeping with him Mrs. Hardy. Of those that we've seen, eleven...... no sorry twelve now including you, were having or have had sexual affairs with Mr. Norton. He appears to have been quite a ladies man. Let me see now' and she took out a note book, thumbed through the pages and then smiled. 'Ah yes here we are. I believe you are thirty nine years old madam, then with two exceptions a Mrs....... no I ought not to quote the names, but she was in her early thirties and the other, a spoilt little rich girl in her twenties, all the other women seem to have been in their late forties or their fifties. Except two who were in their sixties and one very sprightly lady who was seventy two'.

'And they all had sex with him?' Janie muttered horrified at the revelations flowing from the police sergeant's lips.

'Twelve, including you, out of those ladies that we've interviewed so far admit they have Mrs. Hardy. As I said just now he seems to have been quite a ladies man. Of course we've still quite a number of ladies to interview yet and of those who deny having sex with him we may well find as the investigation proceeds that they change their story'.

'Women in their fifties, sixties and one over seventy?'

'Yes madam. In fact the seventy two year old lady said he was the best lover that she's ever known and had made her feel years younger'.

'Oh God how could he? Seventy two ughh? That is horrid .... revolting' and she started to cry again.

'Unusual certainly I imagine. Take your time. Shall I get you like some more water?'

Janie nodded and leant forward her head in her hands.

Returning shortly with a brimming glass WPC Wagstone sat next to her on the settee, put an arm on her shoulder and said softly 'I realise that this is all a big shock to you. Sorry. Here drink this. Do you feel able to carry on now?'

'Thank you. Yes I do. Is there anything else I should know?'

'Well he seems not to have just confined himself to sleeping with women Mrs. Hardy ....' and she paused 'there were men too'.

'What do you mean ...... men too?' Janie whispered her blood running cold.

Two of the men we've interviewed admit to having sex with him'.

'Men? He's had gay sex? Oh Christ'.

Clapping a hand to her mouth and retching loudly she rushed from the room to the downstairs cloakroom where she just made it to the toilet bowl before she vomited, several times.

Finished, she washed her face, swilled her mouth out with cold water then pulled off some sheets of toilet paper and blew her nose, flushed the loo, looked in the mirror and grimacing at herself opened the door and walked back to where the policewoman was sitting drinking her coffee.

'You had no idea he liked men as well as women?'

'No. I didn't even know he had other women as well as me never mind men. I had no idea. I mean I realised that he wasn't a monk but I thought ....' she paused and looked sadly at the other woman 'I thought that at the time ..... at this time it was just me. I never dreamed he was cheating on me like that and as for being gay as well. Oh good God' and feeling sick again she took several deep breaths to get herself under control.

'You thought you were special? Is that what he told you?'

'Yes'.

'So did all of the others Mrs. Hardy. Maybe the men too' she added unkindly. 'He told them all they were special. Many of them say he told them that he thought that there was a sort of chemistry between them'.

Seeing the looking of horror on Janie's face she continued 'Is that a phrase that you recognise Mrs. Hardy?'

'Yes. He said that to me ...... and I believed him. He said what we had together was special .... that I was special. Oh what a fool I've been' and she burst into tears.

Woman police sergeant Maggie Wagstone looked at the crying woman with her head in her hands and felt no sympathy. It was the same with most of these rich women that Norton had fleeced. Mainly wives of successful businessmen, some divorcees, two widows but mainly married women, cheating on their husbands. Although she felt sorry that Norton had swindled them out of their money, maybe if they hadn't been so keen to drop their knickers he wouldn't have found it so easy.

'You were no different from all the others. There was no chemistry between you. There was nothing special. You were just a source of money to him. He used you like all the others. You were gullible and he traded on that. He fooled you ...... along with all those other women Mrs. Hardy ...... and the men' and she let her hurtful remarks hang in the air in silence for a while.

'Did he really sleep with all those other women and the men?'

'It appears over the last couple of years or so then yes he did. I understand that he has a swanky apartment with a water bed where much of the....err shall we say.... activities took place, or at his office'.

'His office?'

'Yes some of his other lady clients say that's where they had sex with him and one of the men claims he was seduced in the office one lunchtime when Norton's secretary was out'.

'At his office?' Janie repeated quietly suddenly remembering the time when she'd arrived earlier than expected and he'd come to open the door all dishevelled and couldn't wait to get rid of her. He'd said he'd been in a meeting but obviously he hadn't. He'd been screwing some other woman or maybe a man right there in his office while his secretary was running some errand or other. And that was the day he'd struggled to come when they made love. No wonder.

She burst into tears again and the policewoman let her sob for a while before speaking firmly.

'Now Mrs. Hardy we would like you to make a full statement about your relationship with Norton. Perhaps you could come to the police station to do that'.

'You bet I will. What a rat' snarled Janie 'the lousy bastard, the rotten stinking perverted .... he told me....... oh never mind, yes I'll give you a statement all right. Definitely. I hope he rots in hell'.

'Thank you' replied Maggie busily punching a number into her mobile phone.

'Gov, we've finished here'. She stared icily at Janie as she continued 'Mrs. Hardy has admitted to having a sexual affair with Norton just like the others'. She paused listening and then finished 'Right sir'. Looking at Janie she said in a matter of fact voice 'He'll be back with us in a minute'.

Janie nodded still devastated by the news, not just of Harry's swindling but of the fact that he'd slept with all these other women many of them so much older, as well as having sex with men. She still couldn't come to terms with it. She'd really thought that she was special to him.

The Detective Chief Inspector returned and smiled kindly at Janie. 'They are wonderful aren't they …. your roses? A joy to see. Now as for this other business then it's never nice is it to discover that you've been conned out of your money? Not only that but then also to have been misused in other ways. Like so many of his other victims. Ok Sergeant have you got everything that you need?' and noting her nod of confirmation he turned again to Janie.

'Thank you for your help Mrs. Hardy. We will need to be in touch again. The sergeant will call to fix a convenient time for you to come and make a statement. Well I think that's about it for today madam. Thank you for your time' and he started walking towards the door followed by the sergeant but reaching it he paused and turned round to face Janie again.

'Oh yes one more thing Mrs. Hardy. Do you or your husband own any property overseas?'

'Yes a cottage in France'.

'Ah, now you didn't sign any papers relating to transferring that property into an off shore company owned by Norton did you?'

'Yes I did. He said that it would avoid problems with French Inheritance Tax in the future. Why?' but even as she asked her heart dropped.

'I'm afraid that was another con Mrs. Hardy. What you signed effectively gave your cottage to him, or to be more accurate to his company. There is no Inheritance Tax benefit. In fact what you've done in simple terms is give away your overseas property'.

Janie collapsed onto the sofa. 'Given it away' she repeated quietly starting to cry again.

'Yes and I am sorry to have to tell you that he's probably sold it on already. You see Norton was clever. In order to keep conning his clients it would seem that what he did was take from one client to pay the others. It was a bit like a pyramid scheme. The latest people he signed up provided him with the financial wherewithal to pay out dividends to earlier clients.

He appeared to pay out quite high returns initially when someone signed up with him but those high returns dropped away quite quickly. He'd blame the stock market, or overseas trends or something quite plausible but in reality he needed new people to join him to get the funds to pay out existing clients.

Overseas properties provided him with large lumps of capital as soon as he sold, mortgaged or traded them on. They were a real benefit to him'.

'But surely he knew that he'd get found out?'

'Maybe, but criminals often become convinced of their own invincibility you know, and while there were willing victims and he could keep getting new funds and capital coming in he could maintain the charade'.

'What recompense have I got? Isn't there some sort of governing body regulating financial advisers?'

'Yes there is.......... if the adviser is licensed and so subject to proper regulation. Sadly Norton was not and so I'm afraid that there is unlikely to be any recompense of any significance for you'.

'But I signed some papers which he said were required by some financial services authority or something to protect investors like me from fraud'.

'Yet more conning madam. He asked all his clients to sign those papers but although they looked realistic they were worthless. He made the wording up and printed them himself. No, your only option will be to sue him privately for your money and property. You might want to join with other victims in a class or group action against him.

We are trying to trace exactly where he squirreled away his money but that will probably take some time as I am sure he's buried it deep somewhere. When we have found it however much it is, then some may be available to you...... but don't hold out your hopes too much. Sorry. Thank you for your help. We'll see ourselves out Mrs. Hardy. Good day'.

When they'd gone Janie stared at the floor and burst into tears again. How could she have been so stupid? How could she have been so misled? Whatever was she going to tell William not just about losing her money, but the cottage as well, and most important of all about the fact that she'd been having an affair with a man who stole so much?

For the rest of the day she was in a daze and couldn't concentrate on anything.

When William came home he asked what the police had wanted.

'It was about Harry Norton, you know the man who's looking after my financial things. He's been arrested for fraud'.

'Arrested for fraud? Good God. Are we involved? What about the money you, well we really I suppose, turned over to him to look after?'

'I don't know at this stage. There are lots of people involved. The police are checking with all his clients. We're only one of many. It seems he was defrauding lots of people but mainly his women clients. They don't know at this stage what's happened to the money.... our money. I guess they'll let us know in due course. There's something else though William'.

He looked curiously at her. She tried to find the words to say that she'd been having an affair but they wouldn't come. How was she ever going to tell him? Maybe it wouldn't come out in court. Perhaps she could keep that part secret. Yes that might be possible. Why upset William now if maybe there wasn't going to be any need. No she'd keep quiet for now. But there was the matter of the cottage to explain.

'It's the cottage. Harry suggested that I transfer it's ownership to an offshore company that he owned. He said that it would save French inheritance tax in the future. The police say though that was yet another con and he's probably sold it on already. Oh William I'm so sorry but I may have lost us that lovely cottage'.

William looked at her in amazement. 'Why didn't you discuss that with me before doing such a thing?'

'You were so busy and worried about work that I thought it was something simple and easy to do without troubling you. Harry made it all sound so plausible. I'm sorry darling. I'm really terribly sorry' and she burst into tears.

'Hey come here' he said kindly. 'That's the trouble with conmen they make everything seem straightforward and easy. Maybe it won't come to the fact that it's lost. Perhaps he won't have sold it yet. The police will find out soon and when they do no doubt they'll let us know. Now stop crying. What's done is done. Even if it's gone it's only a cottage. We've still got each other, our sons, this house, our lives together and our love. With that, especially our love for each other, then nothing else really matters does it?'

She had almost stopped crying but his kindly words and understanding but especially his comments about mutual loving were too much to bear and the tears flooded out.

Dear William, so honest, dependable, loving, and trustworthy. She'd betrayed all that. Getting up she muttered 'Sorry' as she ran out of the room and upstairs to their bedroom where she flung herself on the bed and cried and cried.

It was quite some time later that William came in and sat by her side stroking her hair.

'There now feeling better? A good cry always helps doesn't it? Look let's forget about it for now and have an early night together. Come on go and have a relaxing bath and get into bed. I'll bring you up a whisky'.

Nodding obediently she did as he said and soon was lying back in a hot bath. William came in with a tall glass of whisky and water with lots of ice.

'Here drink this and relax. It's not the end of the world you know. Now tell me about the rest of your day'.

'There's not much to tell. I haven't been able to think of anything else except Harry and the way he's swindled us and taken the cottage away' and she started to cry again.

'Schhh come on now no more crying. Out you jump and I'll help you dry and taking her hand he helped her out of the large bath and wrapping her in a warm fluffy towel he gently dried her before leading her to bed where unfolding the towel from her he reached under her pillow and took out her nightie. He held it out to her then pulled back the covers and patted the bed sheet and without a word she climbed in and lay down.

He smiled, leaned forward and kissed her forehead then bustled about getting himself undressed before going into their bathroom where she heard him having a pee then brushing his teeth. When he came back into the room he had a glass of water and something in his other hand.

'Here take a sleeping pill. You need a good night's sleep to get over the shock and worry. I know you don't like to take them but I think tonight it's pretty essential'.

Without a word she took the pill and swallowed it while he climbed into bed on the opposite side. She took a mouthful of water and as she turned onto her side facing him she said softly 'Thank you'.

'Ok now try and sleep' and he leaned over and gave her a gentle peck on the lips before turning away from her and settling down.

She lay there hearing his breathing, grateful for his kind calm approach to what she'd said and was glad that she hadn't told him about the affair. The pill had its effect and she was soon sound asleep, unlike William who quietly tossed and turned, worried about what she'd told him but also extremely worried about Hardys business. Things were now so bad that he couldn't see how they'd survive. Tomorrow he'd been summoned to another meeting with the bank and he was sure that the demands that they'd table would be unable to be met.

It really could be the finish for Hardys, unless some miracle appeared to save them at the eleventh hour, but he couldn't see that one was there.

Eventually about two he finally dropped off to sleep dreading waking up tomorrow to face the end of Hardys.

Observe the opportunity.

The Bible

CHAPTER 12

William woke early, went downstairs, made some tea, took it up to Janie and kissed her gently awake.

'Morning darling how do you feel this morning?'

'Awful'.

'Well look take it easy today. Have a lie in or perhaps go for a ride and then why don't you get involved with the builders to make sure that they're re-building the stables properly. After all we want it to look as near to how it was don't we and I'd be grateful if you'd make sure they were on the ball'.

'Alright' she smiled realising that he was suggesting some displacement activity to take her mind off the way Harry had conned her. What he couldn't know though was her deeper worry about the affair and it all coming out into the open. How the hell was she ever going to explain that to him?

William left for the office unaware of the additional turbulence in his wife's mind. He was fully focussed on this morning's meeting with the bank and he wasn't looking forward to it.

As he drove to the factory he thought of the long history of the company and how his grandfather and father had been so successful in building Hardys and then how gradually he'd allowed it to slip away. Not through any specific set of reasons it had just got more difficult to run the business, competition had got tougher, their customers more demanding, their suppliers less accommodating, and profits just harder to achieve.

In fact the business had been making losses for nearly two years now and the cash inflow was now insufficient to enable them to pay their way. They were running out of money. No correction he thought. They'd run out of money.

Their only chance now was if the bank would increase their overdraft, or grant them a loan, or permit them to find funds elsewhere. But even as he ran through these options he knew that the answer to them all was no. This morning, the bank would finish them and that would be that. All those years of history down the tubes. Hardys finished.

What would the bank do he wondered?

Sell the brands and trade to another company, sell off the machinery, if they could, and then sell the site probably for housing. After all it was in a prime location in the City of Norwich which was undergoing a housing boom.

He parked his car and walked slowly upstairs to his office, nodded to his secretary Mary, smiled when she followed him in with a cup of coffee and agreed that he was ready for the meeting with the bank at ten o'clock that morning.

'Do we know how many of them and who they're bringing?'

'No, would you like me to find out for you?' and receiving a confirmatory nod she bustled out and rang the bank's offices returning shortly to tell William that there would be five people from the bank.

'Good God they're coming in force. Right thanks. We need our full Board here for this. They all know about it don't they?'

'Yes they do' and she left him then to brood in silence.

At a quarter to ten various other Hardy's directors started to arrive in the Board room which was located next to William's office. Hearing them there he sighed, stood up, looked around his office, touched the old leather topped desk, looked at the framed photographs on the wall of his father and grandfather then straightening his shoulders walked next door.

'Good morning everyone. Thanks for being prompt. I don't know what's to happen this morning. It's the bank's meeting really so we'll have to wait and see how it plays out. No miracle improvement today I presume he asked of the room of people in general. No answer came to him. 'Thought so' and he sat down at the head of the table staring into space.

Others in the room avoided looking at William and either just sat quietly, or spoke to each other in whispers until Mary came in and announced that the team from the bank were downstairs and should she show them up?

'No I'll go and get them. Got to face the music sometime' he replied getting slowly to his feet squaring his shoulders. He walked briskly out of the board room returning a few minutes later followed by the bank visitors who nodded politely to the Hardy directors, shook hands with everyone, and then made their way to the seats that William indicated. Mary organised coffees and then both teams of people looked at each other.

The Hardy's side saw four serious looking men and one attractive woman who while also looking serious radiated charm and somehow a sense of hope.

'William' said Barry Field from the London Head office of the bank 'I think it probably better if I kick off for the bank and come right to the point. We have to say that although we have been sympathetic and as helpful as we felt able to be, we simply cannot continue to extend financial facilities any more to your business. Unless you are able to demonstrate in tangible form that the business has or is improving then we have to take whatever action we see fit in order to protect the bank's investment. I'm sure you understand that point'.

William nodded.

'This has been a great business in the past and we would like to think that it could be again, but I have to say that we don't feel that the present strategy or management team as currently structured are capable of delivering that improvement. Therefore there has to be change.

One solution for us is to simply pull the plug now, sell the business in whole or in part, sell off the buildings and seek to recover as much of our money as we can. Indeed there are many in the higher echelons of the bank that would recommend that as being exactly what we should do.

However there have been other voices who believe that there may be alternative ways to achieve a satisfactory outcome for the bank'.

Frank Gold the bank man from Regional Office now took up the conversation. 'Yes shutting you down is a clear and safe option and we've worked out in detail what we think we could get for the business now, trade and goodwill, as well as the land and buildings and it is, on the face of it attractive, in spite of what we will lose in non repayment of our debts outstanding from you. But banks are about making money and we've looked carefully at your market place, your market position, your capabilities and what we see as your opportunities.

Having done that we'd like to have one final go at seeing if the business can't be turned round before we give up'.

William could hardly believe what was being said to him and his hopes rose. They weren't going to kill him off but give another chance. He smiled and felt his spirits rising, but the next sentence caused them to collapse.

'But you see William, we feel a wholly new strategy needs to be put in place. New product ranges, new pricing plans, new export drives, and especially a completely new cost structure...... lower...... for the business. But most of all we want a new team in here to run the business.

Now I'd like to suggest a short adjournment to this meeting while we speak with you privately about our plans and then we can discuss them with the rest of your team'.

'Seems somewhat unusual but if that's how you want to play things then so be it' reposted William slightly testily. 'Will you come to my office?' and he led the way into his own office leaving the rest of the Hardy's Board team looking mystified and uneasy.

As soon as the door was shut and William was ensconced at his desk with the five bankers pulling up chairs to face him the senior bank man – Barry Field spoke.

'William. When Frank Gold here rang me a few weeks ago and said that there was a problem with your repayments of the loans we had made to you, several alarm bells went off at once. Perhaps against my better judgement the Bank had advanced further funds to enable you to expand or modernise production but Frank was of the view that with that additional financial firepower you could pull the business round. But it hasn't happened has it?

You seem to have lost your way completely. I look at the markets in which you operate and I see other companies, both larger and smaller than you making good, satisfactory...... and crucially profitable progress. But Hardys doesn't. So we ask ourselves why is that?

There is sadly only one answer that seems to spring to mind'.

He paused and looked hard at the beleaguered Chairman. 'You William. It's got to be you. You in the way that you run the business. You in the way that you decide on strategy. You in the way that you fail to get profitable pricing structures in place. We've had a couple of industry experts have a look, on a confidential basis, at what you're doing and they believe that you simply have it all wrong.

We also have some doubts about some of the members of your team. Therefore we are going to insist that the business is run in an entirely different way, starting with your own position.

You may remain here but you become Non-Executive Chairman rather than Executive Chairman. With immediate effect Steve Howard and Emily Simmons here' and he gestured towards the blonde female member of the bank team 'will be taking over as Chief Executive and Financial Controller respectively and will be responsible for running the business'. He paused to let that point sink in.

'Their decisions will be absolute and they have the full support of the bank. They will rapidly evaluate your team and decide whether any of them should stay. If not they'll be replaced. We're not fooling around here. All decisions will be made quickly and implemented immediately.

Now before we brief your direct team is there anything I can answer for you or any questions that you might have?'

William stared at Barry Field then turned to look at Frank Gold. Both were unsmiling and very determined looking. He then looked to Steve and Emily who returned his look unwaveringly but at least she didn't look so hostile and he thought she seemed a very smart attractive looking woman but could she and this Steve chap take over the tough job that needed doing here? If the bank thought so then presumably they could. In any case what choice did he have?

The bankers were right. The business was in a mess and he didn't know how to get it out of it. Maybe this new team and any new people they brought in would be able to wreak some sort of a miracle turnaround. After all the papers were full of comment about turnaround teams going into businesses that were in difficulty and creating remarkably good results. Perhaps it would happen here.

'So my role as Chairman becomes Non-Executive you say' said William softly.

'Yes that's right' replied Steve looking at the older man. 'However be clear that it'll be me, supported by Emily that'll be running this company.

I'm sure there are lots of things you can still do. Attending trade functions, charity golf days, entertaining our customers, being our ambassador ….. that sort of thing. Of course you can retain your office here but wherever I base myself is from where the business will be run. But not here' he finished gesturing around the room.

'Attending golf functions, being an ambassador' snorted William. 'How dare you come in here and demean me in that way. My grandfather started this business, my father built it up and.............'

'And you've fucked it up good and proper' snapped Barry Field. 'Don't start pontificating like some pompous puffed up aristocrat running a hobby business. You've ballsed up a fundamentally good company and the bank has had enough William. If you don't like the idea of a Non-Exec Chairman's role then there's another option. You can go completely. You're not needed now or in the future. Well at least not for the foreseeable future that is. So make up your mind but don't sit there and start to argue with us. You know that the bank is in control and we'll do it our way'.

There was a heavy silence for a minute or two until Emily smiled at William and spoke softly. 'William I do hope you'll stay on as I'm sure we'll need your advice based on all your experience and maybe we didn't quite emphasise the importance of the role that we see you performing for us. We do need you and I'm sure we'll get along fine together'.

William looked at her for a moment and then nodded.

'Right' announced Frank. 'Time to go back and talk to the troops. Couldn't do that until we'd explained things to you William but now that we have let's get on with it'.

The one member of the bank team who'd not spoken was Ian Baker and as the most junior his role was to listen, not speak but make careful notes of all that was said. He finished scribbling in his notebook and then following the others stood up and walked back to the Board room where he sat and opened his book ready to record the details of the rest of the meeting.

It was a sombre William that had led the group back into the Board room. When they were seated he looked around the table and then spoke clearly and strongly.

'You all know that our trading position has been deteriorating for some time, years I guess, and that now we've reached a critical point where we have run out of cash and are unable to carry on as a legal viable trading business. In short without further money coming into the Company immediately, we have to shut up shop.

The bank does not feel able to continue to support us any longer with the present management structure in place. The only way that they will consider not forcing us into receivership, liquidation or administration is for there to be fundamental change here in the Board room, and in our business strategy.

In the interests of the business and our employees I have agreed to those changes. I simply have no choice. There is no other option.

Firstly I shall resign as Executive Chairman and become non-executive. Steve here will become Chief Executive and will be responsible for running the business supported by Emily who will become Financial Controller.

I understand that they will also be reviewing each of you and your positions and deciding whether you stay or go. I'm sorry to put it that bluntly, but we are in the hands of the bank and it is they that are calling the shots.

May I say that I've enjoyed working with all of you and I hope that Steve and Emily and whatever team they put in place will be able to turn the business round'.

There was silence for a minute or two and then Steve looked around the table, smiled and spoke.

'We want to try very hard to save Hardys. There are many people whose jobs, livelihoods and hence families depend on us. Undoubtedly there will be some harsh decisions to make, but be clear we will take the tough decisions quickly, deal with the pain and then get on and try and re-build the business.

Now I'll need help from'...... he paused and heavily accentuated the next word 'some........ of you to do that, but believe me, do it we will. I am quite determined to succeed. Now I think the best thing will be to get a notice out to all employees explaining William's change of role and the appointment of Emily and I and then let's all get to work. There is much to be done.

I'll see each of you today and make decisions concerning all of you and your futures here as soon as possible. Please make yourselves available all day today and tomorrow. Right is there anything else?'

Martin Fellows the finance director spoke. 'Yes cash. What about cash? We're out of money now and at our overdraft limit. How do we go on from here? And what will be my role? I am Finance Director but you say Emily will be Financial Controller. How does that fit together?

'Right several questions there Martin' smiled Steve. 'Let's deal with the cash position first' and he looked at Barry Field.

'We will make an immediate transfer today of one million pounds into the Company's bank account' replied Barry. 'The terms are more onerous than your previous overdraft but Emily has all the details and will discuss them with you Martin.

That cash will enable you to pay your current creditors and remain solvent. There is more money available once Steve and Emily have decided on the new strategy and agreed that with us, but in the meantime don't commit to anything alone and agree all payment schedules with Emily. Life's going to be very tough for the next few months'.

'Thanks' grunted Steve. 'Now Martin as far as how you and Emily fit together well let's see what we can work out in the next day or so. Now are there any other questions?'

There were none, so William suggested that the meeting be brought to an end and that they all return to their respective offices. When the Hardys management team had left he turned to the Bank team.

'It's a sad day, but I hope you can pull things through' he said looking first at Steve and then at Emily' before walking out of the room and into his own office.

'Ok. Good luck you two' smiled Barry to Steve and Emily. 'Sure you can do it?'

'No but we'll have a bloody good try won't we Emily?'

She nodded. 'Yes if it can be done then we'll do it'.

'Hey you'd better with this one. My balls are right out in the open and on the block with the knife poised directly above them!'

'Ooh nasty' she chuckled screwing up her face in apparent concern. 'Well I'd hate to see them chopped off Barry so we'll do our best for you ...... and your .... err exposed assets' she laughed.

'Yes I know that otherwise we wouldn't be backing you with Hardys like we are' he smiled. 'Keep me posted, good or bad and shout if you need anything' was his final request and with that the three bankers shook the hands of the little turnaround team, went downstairs to reception and walked across the car park to their large black Audi A8 saloon which soon drove slowly out of the gates.

'Lot of responsibility on her shoulders isn't there' stated Frank Gold to no-one in particular.

'Yes' replied Barry slowly and thoughtfully 'but she's got a good track record and she's worked with Steve before as you know on turnarounds. I think they've got a better than even chance of doing it.

After all even though Steve's only forty one, he's got a lot of experience and I have full confidence in him. Whether I'm right to have that amount of confidence .…. well we'll see won't we? Mind you if they cock it up then I will be pretty uncomfortable as there were plenty at the bank in the Client Solvency Committee that wanted to give up on Hardys and pull the plug straight away'.

'Yes I heard'.

Frank knew that it had been a very acrimonious meeting in London but eventually Barry's view had prevailed but at considerable personal career risk. He'd stuck his neck out in order to back Steve and Emily's ability to turn Hardys around partly because he hated to see long established businesses pushed into receivership; partly because he genuinely thought that with a change of strategy Hardys might be able to prosper; and partly because he did have considerable faith in their abilities in a turn around situation.

'Still I agree with you about Steve. Furthermore Emily is also a pretty good operator. She's what a couple of years younger than Steve?' questioned Frank.

'No younger than that. I think she's somewhere around mid to late thirties'.

'Well time will tell but it's going to be a fairly nerve wracking few months until we find out isn't it?' said Frank with a grim expression on his face. He stared out of the car window as Ian drove out of Norwich back towards London.

As soon as they'd gone Emily went to find Martin Fellows while Steve remained in the Board room assembling his thoughts.

First he needed to talk with William on his own. He could see that understandably he was hurt and upset at being removed from his own business but he needed to get lots of background information from him.

He and Emily since being summoned by the bank a couple of day's ago had carefully studied the figures of the business and seen over the years how it had deteriorated. They'd read the past strategic documents, seen the continual expectations of performance improvement but which always failed to materialise and studied the Marketing plans which were full of promise but failed to deliver.

In short they knew a considerable amount about the business but what he wanted was to get under the skin of the company to find its soul – if it still had one.

He had to create a new strategy and quickly, get bank approval for it, sell it internally to get commitment from within the business, and then sell it to their customers and that would be the hardest part. Still he'd successfully tackled tough tasks before and with Emily alongside him so there was no reason why he couldn't succeed with this one.

To some extent he was insulated from the results. If he succeeded in turning the business round then he'd be a hero again and enhance his reputation as an effective businessman who could deal with problem businesses and make them successful.

If however he saw that it couldn't be done even after the changes that he'd bring in, then he'd simply tell the bank to stop wasting any more of their money and bring down the shutters, close the business and sell off the assets. He would be a winner either way.

This was his opportunity.

The secret of success is constancy of purpose.

Benjamin Disraeli

CHAPTER 13

At the same time that Steve was staring at the Board room door waiting for William to join him, a few miles away across the City of Norwich another meeting was taking place, this one in a conference room at Norwich main police station.

The room was quite large but there were no windows and the air conditioning was ineffective so the room soon got stuffy.

Several police officers were present and all were chatting quietly in groups of two or three as they waited for Detective Inspector Fulton to arrive and conduct this morning's briefing and review of progress. As the door opened the room went quiet. He looked around, smiled at WPC Anne Shaw who had been working closely with him as his assistant on the arson case, nodded at the rest of the room and called the meeting to order.

'Good morning everyone. We all know why were here today. It's to review progress on the Hardys arson case and see how close we are to solving it. I have to say that frankly I'm rather disappointed with the progress, or rather lack of it that we are, or are not making depending on how you look at things.

Hardys is a major employer in this city. Been here for donkey's years and now it's the subject of an amateurish attempt to burn down one of their buildings, a hoax bomb threat and a fire at Mr. and Mrs. Hardy's home. It doesn't look good if we can't find the idiot who's doing this'.

He paused and let his eyes rove around the assembled group of people. 'Right let's go round the room. Who wants to kick off?'

There was a pause and then Anne Shaw updated him on her particular enquiries and when she finished others added their parts. Depressingly at the end of the review there was little new hard fact or information.

'Has anyone studied the cctv film from the factory on the night of the fire? I know nothing showed up anywhere for the bomb incident but it's worth studying the film for that day'.

There were several groans as sitting watching flickering cctv film was one of the most boring tasks in a police investigation often yielding nothing to the police officer watching, except a headache and aching eyes. Sometimes though, a breakthrough could be made as a result of a grainy image.

'Now I'd like a volunteer to run through all the factory tapes for the day of the fire up to and for say an hour afterwards. Arsonists often come back or stick around to see the result of their evil work. Anyone?'

'I'll do it sir' came a quiet voice from the back of the room and Inspector Fulton saw an eager looking young police officer tentatively holding up his hand.

'Thanks and you are?'

'PC Collins sir just joined the team this week'.

There were cries of "creep", "crawler" "idiot" but all said in a friendly bantering way from the other officers glad that as someone had volunteered they wouldn't be allocated the videotape watching task.

'Thanks Collins. Now you'll need someone to help you. WPC Martin I'd like you to help him….alright?'

'Sir' she muttered.

'Any questions?' asked Fulton taking control of the meeting again. There were a few and some suggestions but the meeting broke up after about half an hour and as Hardy returned to his own office he was depressed.

They still had no idea who'd done it, why or whether he, she or they would strike again. He sat at his desk and went over the information that they'd gained so far and thought about the briefing that he'd had from Detective Chief Inspector Spencer and Woman Police Sergeant Maggie Wagstone after their discussions with Mrs. Janie Hardy.

The two officers from the Met had been completely open with him not only about Harry Norton's fraudulent activities but also about the fact that Janie had been having an affair with him, although Fulton had agreed not to share that last piece of information with the rest of his team. The two London police officers were of the view at this stage that there was no connection between the Harry Norton fraud case and his arson investigation and that it was just coincidence that Mrs. Janie Hardy featured in both investigations.

Inspector Fulton didn't like cases where there were few leads for the police to follow and he frowned as he thought about the case and worked through the information that the police had gathered, the statements that they'd taken, the fire service forensic report confirming arson at the Hardys stables and in the factory, the various ideas that members of the police team had proposed and his own views on why.

What concerned him was that with the critical shortage of police, the regular diversion onto what to him, an old fashioned type of copper thought of as waste of time issues, but which were fashionable nowadays in the politically correct world in which we all lived would soon apply to his team. If progress of a substantial nature wasn't forthcoming soon then some of the members of his team would be taken off him and moved onto other cases.

He worked hard all morning sifting through files, papers, statements, notes and the myriad of unconnected pieces of information until muttering 'Oh sod it' he looked at his watch and seeing it was nearly one thirty realised that he was hungry so he walked off to the canteen.

He ordered a steak and kidney pie with chips and peas. He knew he ought to have a salad or something healthy as his wife requested, but a few lettuce leaves, tomato and piece of cheese or tuna didn't seem to fill him up.

Finishing his meal he looked around and saw that overwhelmingly the male police officers in the canteen were eating sausages, beans, pies, lots of chips whereas it was the female officers who were tucking into the lighter and more healthy meals.

Sign of the times he sighed as he stood and went to the coffee bar section, bought a large black coffee and returned to his table. What they needed was a breakthrough in the case, but from where was it going to come?

Back in his office at the end of the afternoon a knock at the door announced PC Collins and WPC Martin who looked pleased with themselves.

'Yes?'

'Err we've found something on the tapes that we think you should take a look at sir'.

'What is it?'

'A van sir and I, well we that is, think it's acting oddly'.

Could this be it Fulton asked himself as he stood and followed the two officers to the main office where the video machine stood?

PC Collins fiddled with the machine for a moment and then a black and white slightly grainy image of the factory yard appeared on the screen.

'Watch down here sir' said the woman police officer pointing at the bottom left of the screen and shortly a small white van came into view and stopped. The driver couldn't be seen. 'That's outside the box store where the factory fire was sir' she added. 'Now the van seems to stay there and if you look carefully you'll see someone taking something out of the back of the vehicle, and into the box store. Too indistinct to see who or what and it may be nothing to do with the fire but if you look at the time sequencing on the tape you'll see that it's recorded as ten thirteen and that's very shortly before the fire started'

'Now if we fast forward a bit you'll see the van drive across the yard and park opposite the box store and the time is shown as ten twenty one' said PC Collins.

'Interesting' mused the Inspector.

'Yes but there's more. We've found the van on another camera waiting at the gatehouse at ten thirty eight until they let it out. We've got it again a bit later but this time outside the factory. It looks to be parked on the road to the side of the plant and it waits there for ages. This camera is a time lapse one that only takes snapshots every five minutes but we've got the van at ten forty one and it is there for quite some time. Our last sighting of it is eleven twenty six, as after that it's gone when the eleven thirty one shot is taken'.

'That is very interesting and highly suspicious. Well done you two. Now I guess there's no chance of getting the number plate is there?'

'I doubt it sir as none of the shots are front or rear on' confirmed Collins.

'But I think we may have identified the van itself sir' interjected WPC Martin winding the tape back. 'If you look carefully as it drives along the road before it pulls up outside the factory there's a flash of light, probably a street light that it drives past, and if you look hard you can make out some writing on the side of the van. It looks like a V and a figure four'.

Inspector Fulton squinted at the grainy image then smiled as PC Collins handed him a magnifying glass. 'Here sir this may help'.

'Thanks'. He paused and stared at the screen. 'I think you're right. A letter V and a number four. Well I wonder if we can trace that somehow'.

'I think we've done that sir' Collins replied smugly.

'Yes' said the young woman police officer. 'A couple of month's ago my brother was moving flats so he hired a self drive van from a firm called "vans for you" but their design is a big V a figure 4 and a large U. I think it's one of their self drive hire vans sir' she finished also looking slightly conceited.

'Bloody hell, well done. If you're right you two this is our first real breakthrough. I suppose there's no one there now at the van hire firm is there?'

'No sir. We've rung and there's just an answer phone saying they're open from eight o'clock in the morning till five at night, but if you've hired a van and broken down or had an accident it gives a number to call. We've done that but it's simply an all night garage and tow in service. Nothing to do with the van hire firm itself'.

'Right. First thing tomorrow morning, you two go to Vans for You and see what you can find out'.

The two young police officers looked at each other. After all the boring studying of video film maybe they had found something useful.

The next morning they were outside the van hire company just before eight o'clock. The premises were locked but shortly a green BMW arrived and a man got out, looked at the two police officers and asked if he could help them.

They showed their warrant cards and explained that they wanted to find out who had rented a van on a particular day. The owner of the business took them into his office, switched on his computer and as soon as it had fired up paged through some screen data. 'Yes here we are. We had four vans out at that time three Fords and one Renault. Do you know which van you're looking for?'

'Renault' replied PC Collins.

'Ah that makes it easier as most of our vans are Fords but recently we've taken on a couple of Renaults to try them out. Got a really good price from the dealer. Right here it is then. Rented by a man who picked it up in the afternoon. Didn't put a lot of mileage on it though so he must have just used it locally'.

The police wrote down the details and asked for a copy of any documentation that the renter might have signed. At that moment a young woman walked into the office and the owner asked her to get out the paperwork for the particular hire in question. She looked at the screen, wrote down a reference number and then went into the outer office, returning a few minutes later with some papers.

The police looked at them, said they needed to take them away, issued a receipt for them and then asked if the van was in the garage that morning. It was, so they instructed that it be locked and not hired out as a police team would want to examine it later that day.

They applied "**Police don't touch – potential evidence**" notices to the vehicle then radioed back to headquarters, spoke to Inspector Fulton, told him what they'd found and done. He asked them to come and report back.

Another conference was scheduled for ten o'clock that morning at which there was a definite feeling that maybe the team had got its first real breakthrough at the end of which the Inspector said that he wanted the forensics team to go to the van hire firm and impound the van immediately then take it away for a thorough examination.

Meanwhile he and Sergeant Shaw would leave straight away to visit the home of the man who'd rented the van.

When they arrived at the small run down house in one of the poorer parts of the City there was no answer to their knocking, but a neighbour came out from next door and asked if she could help?

The police explained who they wanted to see.

'Well he's at work I expect. Lives alone you know. Usually on day shifts at the factory but sometimes he works nights'.

'Factory?'

'Yes that's right. Hardys. He works there. He's an engineer I think'.

'Thank you very much Madam. We'll contact him there'.

Assuring the woman that there was nothing to worry about and that it was just a routine matter that they needed to speak to him about they smiled and left but once in the car they grinned at each other.

'Works at Hardys does he, now that's very interesting?'

'So shall we go there now and interview him sir?'

'Yes straight away. Let's get going. Drive on sergeant'.

It didn't take long and soon they were parked in Hardys office car park. At reception they asked for Mr. William Hardy and when they were safely in his office they explained what they discovered and asked to interview the suspect.

They were allocated a small meeting room and after waiting about ten minutes William's secretary knocked and showed in a man in green engineering overalls. The police asked him to sit down and explained that they were investigating the arson attack at the factory and hoped that he could help them.

After some general questions the Inspector looked straight at the man and said 'We understand that you rented a van recently from Vans for You?'

'Um yes' the man replied nervously.

'What did you need it for?'

'Err I had some garden rubbish to move from my allotments'.

'Where did you take the rubbish?'

'To a tip'.

'Which tip?'

'The one up near the airport'

'What else did you do with the van?'

'Nothing'.

'You took it into work?'

'Yes'.

'How do you normally get to work?'

'I've got a small motor bike, well moped really. Look what's this all about? I've got a proper driving licence you know even though I usually ride a bike'.

'We'll ask the questions if you don't mind sir. Now why did you use the van for work when you'd hired it?'

'Well as I had it I thought I'd treat myself to using it. Made a change from getting wet if it rained'.

'When you used it for work did you just drive it to here and then back home?'

'Yes'.

'Did anyone else drive the van while it was here at Hardys?'

'No why?'

'A van which we believe to be the one you hired was seen driving around the factory yard just prior to and just after the fire in the box store. Now do you know anything about that?'

'No'.

'Are you sure?'

'Umm…. Well….oh yes I remember now. I had some tools to drop off in the engineers store near to the box store so I did it on my way home. I got in the van then I remembered the tools so I went to the engineers store and dropped them off. It's next to the box store then I drove home'.

'Straight home?'

'Yes'.

'You didn't stop anywhere?'

'No'.

'Are you sure you drove straight home and didn't stop anywhere at all?'

'Ah wait a minute. Yes I did stop as I remembered I wanted to make a phone call so I stopped to make the call from my mobile'.

'And during that time the fire started did it?'

'No idea'.

'We think that it did'.

'If you say so'.

'I do'.

There was silence for a while and the two police officers stared at the increasingly nervous man opposite them.

'You must have seen the fire so why didn't you get out and run off to find someone, or drive off to raise the alarm? It looks from the cctv film that you sat and watched the fire. Is that because you started it and wanted to enjoy seeing the damage that you'd created?'

'No of course not, I don't know anything about the fire starting'.

'What do you mean? There must have been flames and smoke'.

'I didn't see anything. I made my phone call and then drove home'.

'Did you stop again?'

'Yes at the gate. They made me wait for ages until they raised the barrier'.

'And then you went straight home did you?'

'No. I didn't get through when I'd tried to make the call from the yard so I pulled up and tried again. You're not allowed to use a mobile phone when you're driving you know' he sneered smugly.

'Quite!' snapped the Inspector. 'Who was this that you were ringing?'

'None of your business. Private'.

'Everything to do with this arson attack is my business. Now who did you ring? We shall want your mobile by the way to look at the call log to check'.

'I deleted it. I always do'.

'Doesn't matter if you did. We'll get the list of calls you made from the phone company. So who did you ring?' asked WPC Anne Shaw now taking over the questioning.

The man shifted in his seat. 'It was sort of about an arrangement'.

'An arrangement? What kind of arrangement?'

'To meet a girl'.

'Oh your girlfriend was it. Can we have her name please?'

'Not exactly a girlfriend'.

'What do you mean not exactly a girlfriend?'

'Like I say she's not exactly my girlfriend. I was fixing up to see a girl, you know a sort of professional girl, if you get my meaning'.

'A prostitute do you mean?' she asked with a disapproving look.

'Well yes. I ain't got a girlfriend so I go to a house where there are girls'.

'A brothel?'

'Yes' and dropping his eyes he nodded.

'Right what's the address of this place?'

He told her.

'So you were making an appointment to go and see this prostitute were you? When was this for?'

'Umm today. This evening'.

'Ok, then what did you do?'

'Well the fire engines arrived. I could see them charging around the yard so I stayed where I was to watch. I could see some smoke by that time'.

'So why didn't you rush back to see if there was anything you could do to help?'

'Because I could hear the fire alarms going off and saw the fire brigade were there and I'd be in the way'.

'But you are an engineer aren't you? Wouldn't having an engineer around be helpful?'

'Dunno, maybe'.

'It seems odd to me that you did nothing except sit and watch' asked the Inspector resuming the questioning and looking intently at the man who was now sweating quite heavily. 'Wouldn't most people have got out of their vehicle and run to see whether there was something they could do especially if they were an engineer?'

At this point Anne Shaw leaned forward. 'I think you're telling us a pack of lies'.

'No I'm not. It's the truth honest'.

'Rubbish' snapped Inspector Fulton. 'You started the fire and then sat and watched it burn didn't you? Isn't that what happened?'

'No'.

There was a long silence until the female police officer asked quietly 'So why did you sit outside the factory for so long watching?'

'To watch the fire brigade in action, err and make my phone calls'.

'To the brothel? Did you ring anyone else?'

'A mate but I couldn't get through. He must have been out'.

'Really' replied the woman police officer in a voice of disbelief.

'And then what did you do?' queried the Inspector.

'I went home......in the van. Took it back the next morning. You can check if you like'.

'We have. By the way, do you own a typewriter?' asked the Inspector.

'Typewriter? No I've got a computer but not an old typewriter'.

'Why did you say old typewriter. I didn't say it was old'.

Flustered the man replied 'Well typewriters are old aren't they? I mean everyone uses a computer nowadays. Typewriters are old fashioned. Old like old fashioned .... see'.

'Not everyone uses a computer. Sometimes people type notes, or letters or messages using typewriters, even old typewriters'. The police inspector stared hard at the man for a long while. 'But you haven't got a typewriter of any sort?'

'No. I told you I've got a computer'.

'Oh yes one other thing. We want your mobile phone please. Have you got it with you now?'

'No'.

'Is it here in the factory? Your locker maybe?'

'No I forgot to put it in my pocket this morning. It's at home.

'Alright. Can you remember the number of it so we can check your story?'

'Yes' and he gave the number to the policewoman who carefully wrote it down, checked she'd got it right and then said 'Thanks'.

'Now sir I'd like to turn to the matter of the bomb that was found in this factory. You were the one that reported it I believe?'

'Yeah. I saw it and told the shift manager and he called the director. Then the police and the army arrived'.

'Good job you saw it wasn't it as it could have been a real bomb'.

'Yeah'.

'How did you come across it? I mean that part of the factory isn't often used so what were you doing down there?'

'Someone said that they thought there was a problem with a steam pipe affecting the cooking pressures. I'm an engineer so I went down to have a look and that's when I found it'.

'You sure you didn't take it down there and plant it yourself?'

'No of course I bloody didn't'.

'I don't believe you'.

'Well you can believe what you bloody well like. I didn't put it there'.

There was a pause as the two men looked at each other. Then WPC Anne Shaw spoke.

'Have you ever been to the house where the Hardy's live?'

'No. They're toffs aren't they? They wouldn't invite the likes of me' then putting on an imitation posh voice he went on 'oh do have some tea and cucumber sandwiches won't you'.

Reverting to his normal slightly nasal and whining tone of voice he added 'Another bloody stupid question if you ask me'.

'We didn't. So where did you learn about horses?'

'Eh?'

'Well someone led the horses out of the stables before setting fire to them. Was that you?'

'No'.

'I think it was. You wanted to get at Mr. Hardy but not his horses'.

'I told you I don't know nothing about horses'.

'Got a soft spot for animals have you?'

'Look' he said angrily 'I ain't been to Wood Hollow or the stables or done nothing with the horses'.

'So you weren't the one who set the stables on fire then?' snapped the Inspector interrupting.

'No'.

'I think you're lying'.

'No I ain't. Honestly I ain't'.

'I don't think you and honesty go well together'.

'You can think what you like'.

The two men stared at each other then Inspector Fulton smiled.

'Ok sir, that's it ...... for now. We'll be in touch'.

The man scuttled out of the meeting room as the two police officers looked at each other. 'He's our man I'm sure of it but now we've got to prove it' the Inspector said looking at the ceiling. 'Right come on let's go back to the station and review things there. Oh and can you ring that brothel to check his story'.

The man was very worried as he walked back to the packing machine on which he'd been working when summoned to the police. Blimey he thought to himself they're onto me. He'd been so careful up to now but he'd forgotten about the cctv cameras around the factory. Bugger and sod it he thought.

Now what should he do? He couldn't undo what he'd done and he started to panic as he considered that he might be sent to prison. Hell all he'd wanted was some money off Mr.-William-bloody-Hardy to compensate him for all the trouble that he'd caused him in the past.

The typewriter. He'd better get rid of that and quick. He'd told them he didn't have one but if they came round and found it he'd be really done for wouldn't he?

He couldn't concentrate on his work and after an hour or so he went to find the engineering manager and told him he was feeling ill and needed to take the rest of the day off.

'Nothing to do with your recent meeting with the police is it?'

'Oh no. I hired a van recently to shift some rubbish off my allotment and they….err…..thought it had been caught on a speed camera……but it wasn't when I was driving it. Bit of a mix up at the hire firm. Bloody typical isn't it these days? No I've got a gut ache and this being a food factory I think it would be better if I took the rest of the day off'.

His boss agreed so the man left and rode home quickly on his moped. Once there he went out to the shed and took out the typewriter. Wrapping it in some brown paper and tying it with some string he carried it out to his moped and tried to fix it to the machine. After trying several positions he decided that it would be best balanced on the handlebars. It wasn't actually that heavy, just awkward. Some thin rope held it in position and so locking up his house he set off wobbling a bit until he got the hang of riding the bike with this cumbersome addition.

He rode out to the east of the City into the countryside until he came to a river, one of many which meandered into the River Wensum, the main large river which flowed through the centre of Norwich. Riding along the lane that ran alongside, eventually he came to the old bridge that spanned the river. Stopping his moped he dismounted and propped it against the bridge brick wall. Taking off his helmet and gloves he stood looking at the river and pulled out a cigarette which he lit and smoked puffing hard and inhaling deeply.

To anyone looking he would seem to be simply a motorcyclist having a fag break but to Ray King and Freddie Peters he was an enemy soldier guarding a vital strategic bridge which they had to reconnoitre for the British army.

Ray and Freddie were both ten years old and enjoying their half term holiday. They'd ridden on their push bikes to this place which was a favourite play spot of theirs where they fished for sticklebacks, tried to catch frogs, watched birds and played pretend army games.

They were about fifty yards from the bridge and having heard the moped approaching decided to hide. The grass and reeds were quite long and so they managed to secrete themselves without difficulty.

228

They remained still and watched the man smoking his cigarette. 'Let's see if we can keep hidden so that he doesn't see us' whispered Freddie. Ray nodded.

The man looked at the end of his cigarette and then dropped it onto the ground, put his foot on it, paused for a moment and then immediately lit another. He walked up and down the little bridge puffing hard, looked over the opposite parapet from the one against which his bike was propped and then pushing the cigarette into his mouth he quickly untied the rope to free the typewriter which he unwrapped from its brown paper covering.

He looked up and down the lane listening carefully to see if he could hear a car but satisfied that nothing was approaching and that no-one was nearby he stubbed out the second cigarette.

'He's up to something I reckon' whispered Ray.

'Yeah. What?'

'Dunno. Let's wait and see but we could pretend he's a lookout for the enemy who are going to be coming along this way couldn't we?'

'Yeah and when we see the enemy troops we'll radio back to base and warn them so they can call in air support can't they?' replied Freddie his mind racing away in their make believe war game. 'Hey now what's he doing?'

The man had lifted the typewriter and taking a last quick look around flung it off the bridge so that it plunged into the river with a large splash. It disappeared and soon the ripples were swallowed up by the slow moving water.

'Wow. What was that?' queried Freddie quietly.

'Don't know but we could pretend it was a bomb that had dropped. Yes one of our aircraft had dropped a bomb to destroy the bridge but missed. We'll have to radio base and tell them' muttered Ray excitedly.

The man watched the river for a moment and then pulled on his helmet and gloves, got on the moped, pushed the starter and rode away back the way he'd come. The boys pressed themselves down into the reeds.

As soon as he was out of sight and the sound of his bike had faded they ran to the river bank level with where the object had been thrown.

'I'm going to see if I can get it' announced Freddie taking off his shoes, socks and jeans.

'Hey be careful. Wait I'll come in with you' replied Ray not wanted to be outdone as he too undressed.

Soon the boys were wading cautiously into the river. It was quite deep and by the time they got to the middle the water was lapping above their waists.

'Blooming cold isn't it' asked Ray as he stumbled a bit on the uneven and quite slippery bottom.

'Yeah but I don't mind' answered his companion. 'It must be about here' and bending over he peered into the water.

'No it was a bit more over this way' corrected Ray as he too studied the river bed through the streaming weeds. 'Cor loads of fish here' he added. Seeing the bottom was a little more stirred up in one place he rolled up his sleeves and felt around soaking his upper body in the process. 'Yes here it is' he called excitedly. 'Coo it's quite heavy and all knobbly'.

'What is it then' asked Freddie.

'Don't know. Here help me lift it out' and between them the two boys hauled the object to the surface. 'Look it's a typewriter'.

'Why did the man throw that away then?'

'Well how should I know? Come on let's get it back to the bank' and slipping and struggling the two boys regained dry land with their war prize. Ignoring the fact that they were soaked they stared at their trophy as it sat on the bank.

'What are we going to do with it?' asked Freddie.

'Take it home of course. Its valuable secret enemy code equipment' replied Ray importantly. 'We could pretend that we've got to get it back to base and then investigate it'.

For a while the two boys speculated on various war game scenarios and then having started to dry off they turned their young minds to the problem of getting it home.

It was heavy for them and they realised that they couldn't carry it. 'Here that enemy soldier had it fixed to his moped so we'll have to do the same' announced Ray. Rummaging through their saddle bags they came up with some string, a short piece of rope, some chewing gum which helped them to think, and an old school tie. After several false attempts they managed to fix it, admittedly somewhat precariously, onto Freddie's bike.

He wobbled off with Ray riding somewhat anxiously alongside but after a few alarming swerves as the balance became uneven eventually Freddie managed to keep in a relatively straight line and they made progress on their half an hour journey to their homes.

Arriving at Freddie's house they wheeled the bike into the garden and unstrapped the enemy code machine which they carried to the garden hose and sprayed off the mud and lumps of weed that still clung to it.

'Now what?' asked Ray.

'Dunno. Get some paper and see if it works I suppose' replied Freddie walking indoors returning shortly with some sheets of paper.

The boys fed in the paper and then happily spent half an hour taking it in turn to bang away on the keys. They found it difficult as they were so old fashioned and took time to swing forwards, make an impact on the paper and then swing back unlike the instant action computer keyboards to which they were used.

Eventually they tired of trying to type on it and the keys jamming so they decided to go indoors and play with Freddie's car racing set, putting the typewriter onto a shelf in the garage.

***

Back at his little house the man was relieved that he'd got rid of the typewriter and deciding that the only other incriminating items were the two petrol cans in his garden shed so he strapped them onto his moped and rode off to the municipal waste site and threw the empty cans into the large designated bin.

Giving a sign of relief he rode back into town to try an extra long time appointment with busty Ivana, who smiled that she remembered him and stood waiting until he'd paid Rose handing over an additional ten pounds for a longer time session.

Then grinning Ivana took his hand and led him upstairs, where in the bedroom she helped him undo his overalls then said quietly as she reached inside his pants to squeeze his prick 'I good fucker. I make fuck last long time. You have nice come tonight. I 'elp you not shoot quick. Ees good no?'

231

Hold faithfulness and sincerity as first principles.

Confucius.

CHAPTER 14

God what a set of problems they'd inherited with Hardys thought Steve as he reflected on his meeting with William. Having listened to what he'd had to say he'd then called the management team together to openly discuss the issues facing the business.

To the surprise of all he asked for their views on what exactly were the problems and what they thought should be done about it.

This created an interesting set of discussions and it was clear that there was by no means unanimity in their views particularly in relation to what should be done to solve the problems which were substantial and deep rooted.

Each of the Directors had an opinion as to what should be done and it soon became clear that they were not operating as a team but as individuals managing their own departments to the best of their ability but without thought to the bigger picture of the business as a whole.

That he decided was the first thing that needed sorting out once he had thrashed out a new strategy.

'I tell you what I think we should do' he announced having listened to all of them 'we'll take ourselves off site tomorrow to a local hotel in the country and have an away day session. Cut ourselves off from the day to day for twenty four hours and really dig into the problems and possible solutions that might be available. Anyone know somewhere that might suit? We want a good sized conference room, some small separate syndicate rooms, decent restaurant, and some recreational facilities. Swimming pool would be nice, squash court and I imagine some of you guys play golf. Well any suggestions?'

'There's one a few miles out of Norwich' said Martin Fellows. 'Sort of cross between a country club and hotel. I'll see if I can get us in there'.

'Sounds great' he smiled warmly. 'Now I'll knock up an agenda this afternoon and let you all have copies so you can get your thinking caps on before we start. I suggest we meet there at eight for breakfast then get stuck in. We'll work through to mid-afternoon then take a break for a bit of relaxation and sport before kicking off again about seven. Fix a private room for dinner and we can carry on into the evening. We'll stop the night so no-one needs to worry about drink driving and we'll depart early the next morning back here hopefully to put into practice the plethora of ideas that we generate. Any questions?'

'How radical can we be?' asked Rod Jackson the Human Resources Director.

'The more way out and radical the better' Emily replied looking straight at him having said nothing so far at this meeting.

There were a few other general questions and then he was about to call the meeting to an end when William who'd been quiet throughout leaned forward and spoke. 'Do you want me there?'

There was a sudden feeling of discomfort around the room. This was William's business that they were going to be discussing and the management team had all taken it for granted that he would be there, however Steve had a different view.

'William I think we might all find it easier to speak freely and be radical without you there so please don't take offence, but the answer is no'.

The silence was immediate and oppressive.

'But this is my business. It's been in my family for generations and you want to talk about its future and how to run it without me present?' he asked incredulously.

'Yes we do. We will do exactly that. So as I said just now, the answer is no!'

'How do you think that.........'

'No. William please don't make a scene. You asked and I've told you the answer. Do I have to remind you and the rest of the team here that you no longer run this business? Whether you like it or not the business is effectively in the control of the bank' and raising his voice and pointing a finger at the hapless former Chairman he finished 'and under that dictat I am now responsible for it. I run it and what I say goes'.

The others noticed that until this point had been reached Steve had been quite mildly spoken but now as he stared at William and held his gaze he was clearly stamping his authority on the Hardy's team in general and William in particular.

William returned the glare then looked around the room before squaring his shoulders. 'I understand .... and you're right. You will be better off without me there. I'd just be a blockage. After all it's under my leadership that the business has got itself into such a mess.

You need to be able to think clearly, innovatively and without preconception to solve our difficulties. In any case someone's got to hold the fort here while the whole management team is away. Right, well I hope you have a productive day and I look forward to hearing the results of your deliberations. Good luck' and with great dignity he stood, nodded to no-one in particular but everyone in general, and left the room.

There was a sigh of relief from several people that no unpleasant public row had developed but also a noting that Steve was tough in that he'd established with great clarity that he had made up his mind, was not prepared to change and had faced down William in front of the whole team.

'Ok till tomorrow then. Martin, can you join Emily and me now to review the draw down of some of the funds the bank has advanced? I gather we've got some suppliers who are withholding materials from us until we settle their bills'.

The meeting broke up but afterwards there were several little huddles and sub meetings as the team shared their thoughts on the tough new Chief Executive and very pretty but probably equally tough lady now running the business.

'Well guys I reckon we're in for an interesting time. I've never worked for a turnaround Chief Executive and Financial Controller before and I think things are going to get real hairy' mused Geoff Hawkins the Operations Director.

Steve for his part was pleased with the way the meeting had gone. Shame about that row with William in front of the team but it was his own fault. He shouldn't have asked if he was coming as he'd made it clear enough to him, both in the meeting with the bank, and in his private session with him before the main meeting, that he now had no executive role within the business at all so he shouldn't expect to be involved in strategic discussions.

'Emily we need a secretary of our own. Mary has worked for William and before that his father. She is a nice enough middle aged woman but too inured into the ways of the Hardys. We need a new younger woman with whom we can work without predetermined views and opinions.

'Ok let me make a call' and picking up the phone she rang their former secretary at the company where they'd worked together on their last turnaround project.

'Lucy, hi there how are you?' They talked for a couple of minutes then Emily cut the chat short. 'Look we need a new secretary here. The former Chairman and the other Directors all share a couple of girls. We need someone that can relate to Steve and me, work with us, put up with us and generally help. Just like you in fact' she laughed. 'Now how about you coming up here for a day or two and trawling the agencies, interviewing and finding us someone?'

Lucy asked some questions and then said she'd be there the next morning to start work finding Emily and Steve someone to work with.

'Great but I'm out all day. In fact the whole management team will be. We're having an away day so you'll virtually have the place to yourself. Anything you need ask William Hardy's secretary. She's called Mary'.

With that problem solved, or at least well on the way to being sorted as she knew Lucy would find exactly what they wanted, she concentrated for the rest of the day on studying the business figures in great detail yet again. Many times she went to see heads of departments and senior managers and soon found her way around the business as did Steve.

Their presence was seen as refreshing by many people as William tended to manage from his office in the old fashioned way whereas they operated a new style management – MBWA – Management By Walking About. Their view was that it was usually better to go and see people in their own department or office rather than summoning them to theirs.

The twin approach by Steve and Emily unsettled many in the business. Steve was immediately seen as tough, ruthless, unforgiving, challenging and unhappy with pretty well everything. Emily though was seen as more approachable and although soon recognised as tough it was a softer kind of toughness.

Some of the younger men were particularly taken by Emily's smart and attractive appearance and having noticed the absence of a wedding or engagement ring speculated among themselves about her love life and what they'd like to do with and to her if they had the chance.

Emily was also generally popular with the women in the business but especially so with Kelly a nineteen year old girl in the marketing department.

She'd initially seen Emily's picture in the news information page on the company website and then passed her in the corridor and smitten with how attractive this new senior person was who'd joined the business, she downloaded her picture from the website, enlarged it then on the way home that night stopped twice. Firstly to buy a picture frame and secondly for some flowers.

Back in her little bed sit she carefully inserted the picture into the frame and then put the flowers in a little vase next to it and stood both frame and vase on her bed side table and went to sleep looking at Emily's pretty face.

The management team met next morning as arranged at the hotel/country club and started to unwind over breakfast so that by the time they went into their conference room they had largely left the day to day issues behind them and were starting for the first time in a long time to talk strategically as a team about issues.

By lunch time they'd sorted the problems into four key areas:-

Finance

New Product Development

Plant/Equipment and Efficiency

People

In order to tackle these effectively they divided into four small syndicate groups and spent time in these groups trying to understand exactly what was causing their problems, how they might put them right, what additional resources they would need and finally a timescale for an action plan to implement.

Each syndicate presented it's deliberations and solutions to the rest of the team and lively and healthy debate ensued but the rudiments of some solutions were starting to emerge.

By about four thirty as often happens at these sort of occasions some tiredness had developed and ideas were drying up, debate was becoming tetchy and repetitive, and the whole process was in danger of faltering.

'OK everyone' announced Emily after the last syndicate presentation and discussion. 'Time to take a break as I think we're starting to make some progress but we mustn't let ourselves get bogged down. Let's meet for a drink again at seven but for now it's head clearing time. For those that golf you've time for a few holes. I'd like to play some squash then have a swim. Geoff you said you played I think? Have you brought your kit?'

He nodded and so did Carl from marketing who also offered to play her.

'Alright guys but not a full match against you both. Best of three games max, OK?'

Steve smiled as he was interested in seeing how the team worked together over this away time. He had to make decisions quickly on who to keep and who to get rid of and for him every minute of their time together was evaluation time and whether they were working as a complete group, in syndicates, on their own or relaxing he was evaluating, monitoring and checking to make his decisions.

It was vital that in a turnaround situation where time was of the absolute essence he had the team beside him not only that he wanted but which he thought could help him pull the business round.

Turnaround specialists didn't get the luxury of time. They had to make an impact immediately and produce results that the Bank could see and support. If not then the decisions as to what the future held would be taken by the Bank. They'd simply shut up shop and he'd be seen to have failed, unless it was he that went to the Bank and said that it was hopeless.

So it was a fine line he had to tread. Turn it round and quickly and he'd be a hero. Go to the Bank and say it couldn't be done and he wouldn't be a hero but he'd be seen as realistic. But try and turn it round and fail to do so and he'd be tarred with the stigma of failure.

The team all wandered off to fill their brief relax time as suited them. Emily was right in that several of the guys played golf so they happily changed and were soon outside on the course. Richard, another of the team just relaxed and read the newspapers, while Matt went for a walk alone in the countryside.

She tossed a coin and it was Geoff she was to play first while Carl sat in the viewing gallery to watch.

She wore her short white tennis dress trimmed with pale blue, and white frilly knickers also trimmed with matching blue. As she checked herself in the changing room mirror she looked good and felt confident.

It was soon clear that Geoff although an enthusiastic player was seriously lacking in skill and she wiped the floor with him. For a moment during the second game when she was leading seven nil she wondered whether to ease up and give him a chance but then thought "no sod it why should I?" and finished the game without him gaining a point.

Shaking hands she grinned at his very red faced, puffed out appearance while she, although breathing quite hard, was still in good shape to tackle Carl who was a different kettle of fish. Considerably more skilled but he'd also been watching her carefully firstly to admire her lithe body but also to see if she had playing weaknesses that he could exploit.

His careful study confirmed two things. Firstly she had a great figure, terrific legs and a very cute bum but secondly that her back hand return when played from the left hand rear part of the court was her weakness. At the front of the court her backhand was good as was her forehand but pushed into that back corner she was weak.

It helped him and although he lost the first game thirteen to eleven he won the second game twelve to ten. The third and final decider was hard fought but she finally won fourteen twelve.

'Wow that was good' she exclaimed as they shook hands. 'You're a great player, thanks. Now I need a swim and sauna to relax before a cold drink. Do you swim?'

Carl struck with the thought that if he said yes would be able to see her in her swim wear immediately said yes but that he'd have to borrow or buy some trunks.

'I'd buy a new pair if I was you rather than borrowing. You never know where a borrowed pair might have been do you?' she chuckled cheekily. 'Meet you in the pool in five minutes. See if you can find Geoff as he might like to cool off with us as well' and so saying she gathered up her kit bag and walked off, little skirt swinging.

In her hotel bedroom she briefly wondered whether to wear a bikini or a full costume. Her preference was the bikini but would that change the way Carl, and Geoff for that matter, viewed her in the business? Was it too provocative? Deciding that discretion was the better course of action she pulled on a green tight fitting high legged one piece costume, checked in the mirror that all her bits were tucked in, shrugged herself into a bathrobe and slipping on a pair of flip-flops walked back down to the leisure complex.

Going into and through the ladies changing rooms she hung up her robe, dabbled her feet in the disinfectant foot bath and walked to the pool where moving to the deep end she waved at Carl, dived in and swam strongly up and down the pool for a few lengths before stopping and floating on her back to relax.

Carl swam over to her so she stood up in the shallow end where he complimented her on her swimming as well as her squash skills. She noticed that his eyes though were riveted to her breasts where her nipples clearly showed through the tight fitting costume. Ducking down so the water was at neck level she thanked him and said that she'd swim another couple of lengths which she did before also having an in-water chat with Geoff after which she decided to get out.

Returning to the shallow end she climbed the short ladder flattered that Carl unashamedly looked her up and down as she left the water. Knowing she looked good but glad that she'd not chosen the bikini which was rather skimpy she simply smiled as she walked over to where she'd left her robe.

'See you in the bar at seven' she called to him and left to return to her room to shower, wash and dry her hair and dress for the evening. She close tight black trousers, pale blue blouse and black sling back shoes.

Steve with several of the others was already in the bar when she walked in just after seven and as soon as they saw her their conversation stopped.

'Hi everyone' she trilled. 'Heads all cleared ready for the next session? Good. Martin if you're buying I'll have a gin and tonic please.....a large one'. Slowly the conversation resumed and she guessed that they'd either been talking about her squash playing abilities, her body as seen in the pool, or their views about how the day was going. Seeing the slightly sheepish looks on a couple of faces she guessed it was her body that had been the subject of conversation. Well good luck to them she thought as she sidled up to Steve and checked a couple of business matters with him.

Dinner was served in the private room and they resumed their discussions. Steve banned wine with the meal as he told the team that he wanted to ensure that their minds remained focussed on the task of sorting out the business. Only water was served although with a grin he did tell them that they could choose still or sparkling.

The meal and discussions went well and by ten thirty they had a plan of sorts although it would need much refining and developing, but at least there was a plan.

'Right ho' he announced 'that's it for tonight. We've....err, you've done well and I'm pleased with the progress we've made. Now we've got to turn a paper plan into a business plan. I want each of you to take away what we've agreed today and turn it into a properly thought through departmental business plan for your own department, fully costed, timed and with a detailed implementation programme....... and I want them by the end of this week. Now I'll buy you all a night cap and then I'm going to bed'.

They all trooped off to the bar where he ordered a round of drinks including another gin and tonic for Emily which she drank quite quickly, said she didn't want another and wishing everyone 'Goodnight' went back to her room, undressed, ran a hot bath and lying there briefly thought about the business. This was going to be a tough assignment but she was sure that she and Steve could pull it off.

Getting out she dried herself, slipped on some cream silk pyjamas, re-did her makeup, applied a little perfume and rang Steve's mobile waiting impatiently until he answered.

'I've had a bath, put on my pyjamas and I'm in bed. Now the question is do I turn out the light and go to sleep like a good girl, or do I wait for a gorgeous man to come and join me and then be a naughty girl?'

'Ah well I think we'll need to discuss that in more detail and sooner rather than later but of the two choices I think the second is definitely a better option. I understand your point of view on this but you'll have to allow a little time before I'll be able to get to grips with things'.

'Get to grips. That sounds interesting! You're still in the bar?'

'Yes I think you could say that is correct'.

'Are you coming to me tonight? I'm in room eighty six'.

'Oh yes definitely. No question about that and I don't think it'll be very long'.

'Good but not being very long sounds extremely disappointing! Do you think I might be able to do something about that for you?'

'Well that might be an area that we can explore? Ok well look thanks for the call and I'll be in touch with you as soon as I can'.

'I'm waiting'.

Turning to the members of the team still in the bar Steve grinned ruefully as he said 'Bloody Bank. Never leave you alone. Now is there anything else we need to discuss this evening?'

A couple of points were raised then sensing that there was nothing that was urgent he said 'Right then I'm off. See you guys in the morning. Don't stay up too late. Good night'.

He walked out of the bar along the corridor and finding room eighty six knocked quietly. Inside he looked her up and down and said quietly as he gathered her into his arms 'Umm you look lovely Miss Simmons'.

'Thank you' she replied as she responded to his tender kiss.

'Yes very lovely in fact ….. but there's a problem' he added as he stood back and held her at arms length.

'Is it serious?'

'Well I don't think so. You see although these pyjamas are rather pretty' he continued as he ran a finger down her nose, along her lips, down her chin and neck and gently teased at the v neck, 'the problem is that they are obscuring a very lovely body which I'd much rather look at' he grinned as he felt for the top button and tried to undo it.

'Poppers' she whispered.

'Pardon?' and he kissed her again while running his hands across her breasts.

'Snap, crackle and pop. They're poppers, not buttons'.

'Ah so they'll just........' and taking the two front tails at her waist he pulled them apart popping the lowest fastener open 'pop........' and as he stretched the opening wider the next popper came undone 'like........' and the third one opened 'this.......' and the whole jacket was now open. 'That's better' he said softly as he lowered his lips to a nipple.

'Is it?'

'Umm much better' he responded as he switched nipples and changed from kissing and licking to sucking.

'You're right I think it's much better' she whispered as she stretched her neck upwards pushing her chest forward towards maximise the attention of his lips to her nipples which soon hardened.

'What about these' he chuckled as he relinquished his attention to her breasts and ran a finger around the waistband of the pyjama trousers.

'One popper and they'll be undone but' and pushing him away she took off her open pyjama jacket 'what about you getting something off too?'

She undid his shirt, helped him off with it and then rubbing her breasts with their aroused pink nipples against his hairy chest, ran her hands down to his trouser waist band. In seconds his zip was down and feeling inside she felt him already hard.

'Come on Steve let's go to bed' and popping a kiss on his nose she turned away from him and walked to the bed where she sat down, slipped off the pyjama trousers and threw them at him. 'See one popper and off they come' she laughed as she turned back the duvet and lay down to wait for him to undress.

He soon joined her and they started to kiss deeply mouth to mouth and over each other's bodies. As he trailed his tongue down her belly she stopped him.

'Not tonight just make love to me' and pulling his head she encouraged him to lie on top of her where she could feel his erection pressing against her belly as he gently ran the fingers of one hand across her pussy but feeling it instantly wet he smiled down at her.

'Ready?'

'Yes' was her whispered reply.

'I need a condom have you got any?'

'Right here' and opening her hand to him he saw the little foil. 'Lie back' and soon he was covered. 'Come on' she encouraged.

He wasn't the best lover she'd ever had but he was pretty good and better than many of the others she'd encountered. In fact the other day she'd tried to recall all the men she'd slept with and thought it was nine.

Of them she rated Steve equal third with Seamus, a ginger haired Irish folksinger that she'd met on a business trip to Dublin and with whom she'd spent several passionate evenings after he'd finished his gigs; not as good as Nick whom she'd met on holiday in Dubai and definitely no-where near as good in bed as David a flamboyant Welsh Marketing Manager with whom she'd had a torrid three month affair. But apart from those three Steve was better than all the rest of her lovers.

He for his part found Emily a very good lover. She was pretty, had a nice figure, quite innovative in bed, good at blow jobs, usually enjoyed having her pussy licked and genuinely seemed to try and make it good for him as well as herself.

Tonight he tried to make it good for them both and in the process enjoyed bringing her to a satisfactory climax before he himself came. Yes tonight was good. They'd enjoyed making love, both climaxed and afterwards cuddled together, kissing and stroking while whispering quietly to each other.

'You going to stay and sleep here tonight?' she asked stroking his cheek.

'Is that alright?'

'Uh huh'.

Giving each other a final kiss they drifted slowly off to sleep each savouring their own thoughts as they did so.

She reflected that Steve was nice and she enjoyed being with him. Good at his job and pretty good in bed he also made her laugh. Kind, warm hearted, friendly he was the sort of man with whom she might settle down one day.

Steve's though had two subjects in mind as he gradually lost himself to sleep. Firstly the lovemaking tonight had been enjoyable and secondly he was now sure that he would be able to succeed in this project. Sighing happily he soon slept.

It was six thirty when the alarm jerked them awake.

'Come on time for you to go' she chided when he put his arm around her and tried to pull her to him as she pushed him away. 'No go on, off with you back to your own room. I'm going for a swim'.

Getting out of bed she put on her bikini and robe, blew him a kiss, said 'Thanks for last night' and leaving him to dress and go back to his own room walked quickly through the almost deserted hotel to the pool.

Although none of Hardy's people were apparent, one young good looking man and one extremely fat older man were already in the water as were two females, one young and quite pretty and the other middle aged and bulging grotesquely everywhere out of her costume.

Emily swam vigorously up and down for about ten minutes then climbed out just as Carl appeared. His eyes widened in clear appreciation of her bikini clad body but she merely said a crisp 'Morning Carl, see you at breakfast' and pulling on her robe went back to her room to shower, hair wash and dry and getting dressed choosing a blue with faint white stripes trouser suit and black court shoes with a two inch heel.

Everyone was on good form, enjoyed their breakfasts and confirmed that the away day session had been useful. Most left by eight fifteen for Hardys except John Benton the Sales and Marketing Director who was off to London to see one of their major supermarket customers.

Back at the office Steve fended off William's questions as to how the away day had gone and focussed on starting to think through and then start writing up a new overall business strategy which he knew would require approval by the Bank before he could really commit to implementing the plan.

He was also delighted when after a knock at the door a grinning Lucy walked into the room, sat down and said that she'd got four candidates to interview that morning for secretary and that providing she found one that she thought would suit, could he or Emily find a little time to see the chosen lead candidate.

He said either he or she would.

It was after lunch when Lucy said that she'd seen all four candidates and thought one would suit perfectly and that she'd arranged for her to return at four that afternoon. The interview went well and Tabitha agreed with Emily that she would start work next week.

Success is a science; if you have the conditions, you get the result.

Oscar Wilde

CHAPTER 15

Freddie and Ray met up as usual after school and played on their bikes for a while then as it started to spit with rain they went indoors and played in Freddie's bedroom until they were called down for tea.

During the meal Freddie's mother Barbara asked if they'd had a good day and what they'd done. They mentioned that a few days ago they'd retrieved an old typewriter which they'd seen a man throw into the river. She questioned them a little about it and nodded when they said that they'd put it in the garage.

After tea Ray left to cycle the half mile to his home and Freddie watched television for a while until his father came home tired at the end of his shift. He ate his supper and then settled down in front of the TV and watched with his son until it was time for Freddie to go to bed.

When the boy had bathed and was settled down in bed Barbara came and joined her husband on the settee. He put an arm round her as they exchanged quick pecks. 'You look tired Dave' she said kindly.

'Yes I am a bit. We aren't getting anywhere with this arson case. We thought that we might have made a bit of a breakthrough the other day' and he told her about the cctv information 'but it all seems to have come to nothing.

The Inspector and Anne Shaw interviewed a guy and they're reasonably convinced he could be our man, but now we've got to prove it. There are a lot of loose ends that don't fit yet. So how was your day?'

They chatted for a while and then she got up to make coffee and while the kettle was boiling popped her head through the hatch that divided the kitchen and dining end of their through lounge/diner room.

'Freddie and Ray found an old typewriter the other day in the river. They said some chap threw it off a bridge. They've brought it home. Must have been difficult for them to do that on their bikes ....

hey what is it?' she asked as her husband suddenly joined her in the kitchen.

'Did you say some bloke threw an old typewriter in a river?'

'Yes. Why?'

'This could be important'. He moved quickly out of the room and upstairs where going into Freddie's room he saw that he wasn't yet asleep. 'Hey Freddie, mum tells me you found an old typewriter. Where?'

'In the river, you know the one where we often go and play. We were playing soldiers down by the bridge and this chap came up on a moped and stood there for a while. We pretended he was an enemy lookout then he threw the typewriter into the river, got on his bike and rode off'.

'Freddie this could be important. Did you get the number of the moped?'

'No. It had a P registration I'm sure of that and' he frowned as he concentrated 'I think the numbers were one six two .... or one two six. Something like that. Ray might remember more but it was red. Hey Dad we're not in trouble are we? I mean the man obviously didn't want it as he threw it away. We didn't steal it or anything?'

'No you're not in trouble old chap, quite the reverse. This could be linked to a case on which I'm working. Mum said you'd put it in the garage, is that right?'

'Yes on a shelf at the back near where you keep your old paint tins'.

'Has anyone else touched it? I presume Ray did?'

'Yes just us two and the man of course'.

'Of course. Thanks. Now you go to sleep. I might want you to tell some other people about this in the morning. Good night and sleep well'.

Going downstairs, his tiredness was gone as he picked up the phone and dialled. 'Hello this is Dave Peters. Is Inspector Fulton still there....... no well can you put me through to him or give me a number where I can get him? It's important.'

He waited while there were various clicks on the line and then the Inspector's voice came on. 'Hardy'.

'Sir this is detective constable Dave Peters'.

'What do you want Dave?'

I'm sorry to disturb you this evening but I've something that I think might be important in the arson case'.

He then relayed to the senior officer what his son had said and agreed to return to the station right away bringing the typewriter with him carefully bagged.

There was an air of excitement when the two men met but as Anne Shaw joined them she looked distinctly miffed.

When the Inspector had called and told her to stop whatever she was doing and get back to the police station straight away, she'd been cuddling on her sofa with her new boyfriend Mick, with whom she'd been going out for about a month. She liked him a lot but since they'd met he'd continually pestered her to go to bed with him. Tonight she'd decided she might agree and as the phone rang he'd just undone her bra and started to lick her left nipple.

Dave Peters pointed to the typewriter in a strong plastic bag and then pulling on some latex gloves extracted it. Immediately there was a faint smell of river and mud.

'This is it sir. My lad and a pal were playing by a river and saw a man throw this off the bridge. They thought it'd be fun to get it so they waded in and pulled it out then brought it home. They've cleaned it with a hose but Freddie says they'd not wiped it so there could still be finger prints on it....apart from Freddie and Ray's I mean'.

The two men started to discuss the matter in some detail and soon Anne joined in temporarily forgetting the semi naked man she'd left at her flat.

After about an hour the three police officers had sorted out a plan of action, e-mailed forensics to come and collect the typewriter tomorrow, written up the notes of their discussions, put the machine back in it's plastic bag, fixed a large **DO NOT TOUCH – EVIDENCE** notice and agreed that Dave would bring his son and Ray in to the police station tomorrow to tell the Inspector everything that they could about the incident.

When Inspector Fulton got home he felt they might be close to another breakthrough in the case.

When Dave Peters got home he was pleased that he'd been able to add significantly to the police effort.

When Anne got home she was disappointed to find a scribbled note propped up on the table

Sorry babe. Didn't know how long you'd be so thought I'd go. I'll call you tomorrow so we can arrange to carry on where we left off!!!!

In the morning Dave Peters and Freddie drove first to Ray's home and collected the second boy who was excited to be going to the police station. Dave had rung Ray's parents the previous evening and explained the situation then he'd rung their school to explain that they'd both be late in.

When they arrived at Norwich police station Dave took the two boys through to a small room where Anne was still pissed off that her potential lover from last night hadn't waited. Inspector Fulton joined them.

The Inspector smiled at the two boys and told them that he thought they had some vital information that could help the police with a very important and difficult case. He reassured them that there was no possibility that they were in any trouble and simply asked them to tell him exactly what had happened.

So they told him what they'd seen and answered his gentle but probing questions. When he suggested about half an hour later that they needed to have their fingerprints taken before getting into a police car to go to the scene the lads were delighted.

Seeing their excitement the Inspector suggested to Anne who was driving that this could be construed as an emergency and that they'd better put on the flashing headlights and siren for the part of the journey that took in the dual carriageway bypass. The boys were ecstatic and couldn't stop grinning as the police car flashed past other vehicles that quickly moved out of its way.

Pulling off the dual carriageway they drove slowly down several country roads as directed by the boys until they came to the narrow lane which led to the bridge. They parked by the side on the grass verge.

'Right boys now where did the man stand and where were you?' asked Freddie's father. They pointed out their hiding place where they'd watched the man throw in the typewriter. The Inspector and Freddie's father scrambled down to check out the line of sight to the bridge, then they all went onto the bridge and the boys showed where the man had stood before throwing the typewriter into the water.

Finally the Inspector asked the boys if there was anything else they could remember however small or seemingly unimportant that they hadn't mentioned.

'Umm well yes, he smoked a cigarette before he threw the typewriter in the water' said Ray.

'Two actually, two cigarettes. I think he was waiting to make sure there was no-one around' added Freddie then paused before continuing 'but he didn't see us we were so well dug in down there' and he pointed to where they'd hidden.

'Sometimes we get really lucky' smiled Anne as she bent down and taking a small plastic bag out of her pocket and using two ball point pens carefully picked up the cigarette butts and dropped them into the bag.

'Saliva and DNA tests can be taken from these' she told the boys.

The journey back to the police station also included another emergency section with headlights and sirens full on. At the station the two boys transferred to another police car to go to school and the police driver grinned when told to use his discretion over the use of sirens and headlights. He did and again the boys enjoyed watching all the vehicles in front move aside to let the police car past. At their lunch break they couldn't stop talking to each other about their involvement with the police and they regaled their class mates with all the details.

The full police team was reconvened in the incident room. The bridge with notes of its relevance was added to the transparent board on which already were pictures of the factory, the Hardy's home, photos of the hoax bomb, the fire damaged box room and the burnt down stables. Various locations were also marked out including Hardys factory, the Hardys home, the suspect's house and now the bridge. They decided that they would wait for the forensic results before pulling the suspect in for further questioning.

'Trouble is' grumbled Inspector Fulton to the room in general 'forensics can take ages. We need to get them to allocate some sort of priority to this case'.

'Err leave that to me sir' replied Anne. 'I know someone in forensics and might be able to pull a few strings'.

'Really? Well that would be very helpful if you can'.

She went into another room, picked up the phone and dialled. 'Mick you were a real bastard running out on me last night. I might not let you….umm what was it your note said….oh yes carry on where we left off. You're pushing your luck you know. Got me all fired up and then when I returned you'd buggered off'.

Listening to the protestations of apology down the phone she grinned then continued 'Well if you want to redeem yourself sweetie you could do me a little favour. We need an urgent, and I mean really urgent, set of tests done on a typewriter that your department took from here this morning and also some cigarette buts that we've just collected. I'll send them over to you but we want the full works, DNA, fingerprints, saliva and anything else you can find. We also want you to match the typewriter keys to some letters in the arson case.

Now put this right to the top of your priority list and maybe, just maybe you will be able to carry on where you left off'.

'Hey it's not that easy to switch priorities around you know' protested Mick down the phone. 'We've got a racial hatred case, a murder, some drug stuff and an unidentified dead body' replied the voice.

'Well I've got a body that's very much alive and could be available to you….. but only if you redeem yourself and get those tests done today for me. So what is it to be?' She smiled at the reply then responded 'Thank you. I'll make sure you don't regret it. Now ring me when you've got the test results and then we'll make arrangements for tonight'.

Walking back into the incident room she told the Inspector that with a bit of luck they'd have the first set of results by the end of the day.

Well done Anne. How did you manage that?'

'Oh a chap called Mick over there owes me a favour so I told him we need our results today'.

The Inspector looked at her a little strangely but said nothing, just nodded and turned back to the team to ensure priorities for the investigation were properly allocated to optimise the team's resources.

It was just before five o'clock when Anne got the call for which she was waiting. 'Thanks that's great. Can you get someone to bring the results over to us here' but on hearing that they were already on their way she added 'wonderful'. The voice continued that there were several sets of fingerprints on the typewriter, saliva results from the cigarette ends and preliminary DNA results but the full set of DNA results would take a further forty eight hours.

'OK understood. Well that's all for now then I think isn't it' and then chuckled at the immediate complaints down the phone. 'Woa calm down sweetie. Look I think we'll be working quite late here tonight so why don't I call you when I know I'm leaving and then we can meet up?'

After a further brief chat she rang off and walked back to the incident room where she was just about to announce that the test results were on their way over from forensics when a police messenger followed her in holding a large brown envelope and when she'd identified herself handed over the package.

Inspector Fulton and Anne tipped out the contents and then dividing them between themselves carefully studied the information.

It was sometime later when they decided that they would bring in their one and only suspect tomorrow for questioning under caution which would enable them to fingerprint and DNA test him. Around half past seven it seemed that there was little further that they could do that evening so having agreed on tomorrow's arrangements the Inspector said that Anne could go home.

Nodding her thanks she picked up her mobile and moving to a quiet far corner of the room dialled a number. 'Pick up a pizza on your way and be at mine around eight thirty' she said opening her desk to collect something which she slipped into her handbag.

It was just after that time when the door bell of her little studio flat rang and opening it she smiled at her visitor. They peck kissed then she took the pizza into the kitchen to cut it into slices before returning to the one main room where they consumed it, washing it down with some bottled lagers. She had one and he had two.

'Coffee?

'Maybe later but now I'd rather get back to where we were last night when you had to leave'.

'Oh would you now? Well you'd better come over here then hadn't you' she smiled moving to her sofa bed collecting something from her handbag on the way which she carefully slipped into a back pocket of her jeans. 'Hang on we might as well get comfortable' she added tipping the seat forward and flipping it down to form a bed. 'Now I seem to remember you had your sweater off' she continued tugging the article of clothing over his head 'umm that's right' she smiled leaning forward and kissing his bare chest.

'And you had your blouse and bra undone'.

'Did I? Well you're welcome to undo them again in a moment. Now close your eyes tight and give me your hand, but no peeping' she instructed. She stretched his arm towards the bed head then he felt something cold hard and metallic click into place around his wrist. As he opened his eyes and twisted to see what had happened he saw that his wrist was now handcuffed to the bed head.

'Hey' he exclaimed tugging hard 'what are you doing?'

'I'm making sure you can't run off again. Now you're going to have to take my blouse off one handed'.

He struggled but eventually managed. 'Good. Now the bra' she smiled and when he'd managed that she continued 'now I'm a detective and I need to investigate certain matters and I think you can help me with my enquiries. I'm going to start here' she grinned undoing his trouser belt.

When he was naked she admired his body and teased him for a long time before ordering him to take off her jeans and panties one handed.

He succeeded. Instructing him to lie still she got off the bed and peered into her handbag, found the packet of condoms that she'd stopped on the way home to buy, stroked him to full erection and covered him, then telling him to turn over and lie on his front she slithered underneath and wrapped her legs and arms around him.

Later she got off the sofa bed and padded to the kitchen area to make coffee returning shortly with two steaming mugs and giving him one to hold with his free hand she hunched her knees up and sipped her hot drink.

When they'd finished the coffee he asked if she'd release him from the handcuff. Putting her head on one side she smiled and told him to turn onto his back, then said that as there might be a risk that he would try and break free she thought he needed restraining more securely, which she did by handcuffing his other wrist to the bed head with the second handcuff she'd brought home. Fastened by two handcuffs he was unable to do anything but lie there on his back, naked and helpless.

They chatted for ages about their jobs, the economy, music, politics and their likes and dislikes until she started kissing him while her hands played with his limp prick. It quickly went hard so she slid a condom onto him, clambered on top telling him that depending on how he performed she might release him afterwards or keep him secured until she felt fully satisfied.

He was a good lover and earned his release spending the rest of the night happily cuddled into her as they went to sleep.

At the police station next morning she met with her Inspector who noted her bright eyes and generally cheerful expression. They drove in an unmarked car to the suspect's house arriving about eight o'clock having established that he was working afternoon shift at the factory.

The man was in bed and thinking about how his life would change when he'd got the blackmail money from William Hardy although he was still worried about the police and their recent questioning of him but having gone over and over in his mind to try and see if he'd left any clues that could incriminate himself he was fairly certain that he'd be ok.

So when the knock on the door sounded and he peered down out of the bedroom window to see the Inspector and the policewoman standing below outside, his heart dropped.

'Good morning sir' started the Inspector when the man appeared to open the front door unshaven, wearing tee shirt and pants with his breath smelling of last night's whisky. 'Fred Harding. I'm arresting you in connection with a series of arson attacks, blackmail letters and dummy bomb threats. We are going now to the police station where we have a lot more questions to ask you'.

'Why? I told you last time that I haven't done anything' he protested.

'You did but we're not convinced so get dressed. I've also got a warrant to search these premises' and he handed the appropriate piece of paper to the man, 'but you're coming with us. If you want to be difficult we'll handcuff you and take you as you are. You've got some cuffs with you haven't you?' he asked looking at Anne.

'Yes sir' she replied remembering her naked lover last night tugging in vain to try and release himself. She'd quite enjoyed having him helpless and wondered how it had felt for him. Maybe she'd try being the one in bondage next time. 'Now what's it to be?' she queried to the man jerking herself back to the present.

'Alright alright I've nothing to hide. Let me get dressed first' and with his heart thumping he walked upstairs with the police woman following him while the Inspector started to take a preliminary look around downstairs.

'Here what do you want?' grumbled the man turning to her as he reached the top of the stairs. 'Looking for a cheap thrill watching me get dressed are you?'

'Not at all. In fact there's nothing about you sir that I can think of which would give me any sort of thrill so I'll wait here outside your bedroom while you dress. We don't want you doing a little runner do we now?'

'I need a crap as well. I haven't been yet today'. Do you want to come in and watch me do it? You can wipe my arse for me if you like. Would you like that?' he sneered.

'Just do what you have to sir and then come down when you're ready and be quick about it' she snapped and walked down to wait at the foot of the stairs.

It was about twenty minutes later just as the three of them were leaving for the police station that a small forensic team arrived to examine the house. One of them walked over to Anne and said quietly 'Are you doing anything this evening?'

'Why?'

'Well I thought perhaps..........'

'We could again carry on again where we left off' she interrupted grinning. 'Maybe......your place or mine?'

'Mine if you like' he replied grinning.

'Fine ......shall I bring my handcuffs again?' then smiling she added 'ring me later' and hastening to the Inspector's call hurried from the house to the police car as they took their suspect to the police station.

The formal interviewing took place in an airless room in Norwich police station. It was stuffy and the man was soon sweating as after taking a DNA sample and his fingerprints, the two police officers asked him question after question as they accused him of being the arsonist, the bomber and the blackmailer.

The man consistently denied everything and eventually an exasperated Inspector Fulton snapped at his junior colleague 'Right take him to a cell. I think we've got as far as we can for now' then turning to the man he added 'but don't think you're off the hook because you're not. I know you did it and I'm going to prove it.'

Next the Inspector convened a meeting of the full team and ran through the information and evidence that they had so far..

'Do him good to cool his heels for a while. In fact I think we'll leave him overnight and have another go at him in the morning. I know he's our man ..... all we've got to do is firstly get him to admit it and then ensure that we've got the evidence so that no clever lawyer will get him off. I want to see that bastard put away for a long time'.

They both settled down to paperwork and it was late in the afternoon that Anne's mobile rang. It was Mick.

'Is that the bondage department?' he chuckled.

'Yes. Now might you also be interested in chains and whips?' she laughed.

'Hey you serious?'

'No stupid of course I'm not'.

'Woa that's a relief. You said to ring later so here I am doing as instructed. Can we meet tonight?'

'Yes. We said your place didn't we?'

They agreed to meet up around eight and after eating microwaved curry they watched a DVD while they finished off a bottle of cheap red wine. They were cuddled together on the settee and kissed every now and then until as the film ended Mick pulled her towards him, kissed her more passionately and started to run his hands around under her jumper and over her bra covered breasts.

'Let's get comfortable in bed' he suggested with a glint in his eye and she nodded and followed him to his bedroom.

The took their time, undressing each other slowly and when he was naked she spent ages kissing, licking, rubbing and playing with his prick until he leaned and put his mouth close to her ear to whisper 'Can we stop foreplay and make love?'

'Uh huh but………. the foreplay has all been one sided. Now before you get to do what you want Mick my dear boy you had better start playing at the fore of me' and giving a quiet dirty laugh she wriggled away from his erect prick and spread her legs a little apart. 'Here would be a good place to start' she continued cupping her breasts and holding them towards him. As his face moved on command to her chest area she added 'followed by some play down here' and she took his hand and placed it on her pussy and soon he had her breathing deeply and loudly.

'I think the time for playing is over and the time for action is here don't you' she whispered as she leaned up and kissed his lips hard. 'Condom?'

He look horrified. 'I forgot to get any. Have you got some?'

'No'.

'Oh shit what are we going to do? I suppose …….?'

'No out of the question' she snapped.

'Right' he replied miserably.

'Mick you can either go and find a shop or garage that's open and get some or it's foreplay only. Your choice'.

'Going out sort of breaks the spell doesn't it and it's pouring with rain' he replied softly.

'It's up to you lover. Go, get wet and make love, or stay, keep dry and no sex'.

'Could we, err, just for tonight ………?'

'No forget it. Go on get dressed. There's a garage not far away they're bound to have some. I'll make it worth your while when you get back' she grinned.

'Promise?' he asked getting off the bed.

'Uh huh now hurry up'.

She was right. The garage wasn't far away and it was less than ten minutes later when he came back cheerfully waving some packets.

'Got some flavoured ones. Thought that might be fun' he chuckled.

'Did you now' she smiled holding out her hand to take them as she watched him stripping off again. 'Strawberry, orange and cherry. Ah now as I'm rather partial to cherries shall we try that? Come here' she whispered holding out her arms to him and as he clambered onto the bed she took his penis which was starting to re-erect itself. Stroking and squeezing him soon had the desired effect and opening the foil and rolling the rubber protective down onto him she smiled up at him.

'I suppose you got flavoured ones because you wanted me to do this did you' she grinned swallowing his erection between her lips.

'Ah yes baby. Yes' he gasped as he lay enjoying her ministrations which she continued for a while until she stopped, slid up the bed and whispered 'Now before you went out you were going to do some nice things to me, so I suggest you get on with it ......now please. We'll come back to this shortly' and she ran a finger up and down the length of him.

As requested he returned to her breasts and nipples then she pushed him down to her pussy where he stroked, kissed and licked her for some while until she pulled him up by his ears, kissed him hard on the lips and whispered 'Thanks now let's get this fellow into action shall we?' as she squeezed his erect prick.

Swinging himself on top of her she assisted his entry into her extremely wet pussy then grunted as he started thrusting into her. They soon found a rhythm together and both climaxed within a few seconds of each other. Separating he put an arm around her as she asked 'Was that alright for you?'

'Terrific yes thanks ...... and you?'

'Oh yes' she smiled reassuringly. 'You did it very nicely thank you'.

He looked relieved and heaving the duvet covered them both up.

It was quite some time later that Mick suggested they try another flavour to which she willingly agreed.

In the morning they giggled together as they squeezed into his small shower, played with each other's bodies as they stood under the hot water, then got dressed and said they'd enjoyed the evening.

As they left to go their separate ways he took her face between his hands. 'Anne I'd like to meet again. Would that be alright?'

'Yes of course let's meet again. I'd like that too, in fact tonight sounds like it might be a good idea to me?'

'Fabulous thanks'.

They peck kissed and left, she to find her car which she'd parked in a little street next to the block of flats where Mick lived and he to get his powerful motorbike from the underground car park.

***

Over in Norwich police station earlier that morning the man had been woken after his first night in the cells. The previous day he'd been grilled by Inspector Fulton and that snotty cow WPC Anne Shaw, as he thought of her, but surprisingly he'd refused their repeated offer of a solicitor. They'd kept asking him about the arson attacks and the threatening and blackmail letters but he'd stuck to his story that he'd had nothing to do with it and they'd been unable to shake him from that position.

Today they continued going over and over again the same points, the same questions always stern, constantly accusing.

It was late in the afternoon when anther police officer interrupted the interview and called Anne Shaw out of the interview room. She returned shortly looking very smug and handed a piece of paper to the Inspector.

'Well well' he said looking at the man. 'The typewriter that we know from witness statements you threw into the river although you deny doing so, has now been positively identified as the one used to write the arson and blackmail letters sent to Mr.. Hardy'.

'So what if it has. It's still got nothing to do with me' the man replied sulkily.

'Forensics are remarkable these days aren't they?' continued the Inspector ignoring the man and looking at the WPC '.

'Yes amazing' she replied as a picture of her new boyfriend naked, erect and handcuffed flashed into her mind. 'Quite astonishing really. The things they can find out are remarkable'.

'Exactly' continued Inspector Fulton 'like for instance, fingerprints. Old fashioned, but still effective in trapping criminals. What people don't realise is that water often doesn't wash off fingerprints and that's the case with this typewriter. We found lots of different fingerprints on it but among them all are yours sir, on the sides where I think you held it to throw it off the bridge. Interestingly there's none of yours on the keys. Wear gloves when you typed the letters did you? But the ones on the side are very clear and definite'.

The man said nothing but suddenly remembered with horror how after propping his bike on the bridge he'd taken off his gloves to get out his cigarettes as he couldn't get his gloved hands into his pocket. He then must have forgotten to put them on again before chucking the bloody machine away. Sod it what a stupid mistake he thought.

'The witnesses who saw you throw the typewriter off the bridge also saw you smoke two cigarettes. Well we found two cigarette buts on the road at the bridge and surprise surprise, we've got a DNA match to you. Now how do you explain that?'

'I'm saying nothing more till I get a solicitor'.

'Getting worried now are you?' sneered the WPC.

'Piss off. I want a solicitor'.

'Right interview suspended at fourteen twenty five hours' snapped the Inspector as he stood and marched out of the room followed by Anne Shaw.

'I think we've got him you know' he said outside. 'Come on get the team together and let's review the evidence. Meet in twenty minutes'.

The incident room was buzzing when the team assembled.

'Right now listen up' started the Inspector. 'Here's where we are. I think that nasty little creep we've got in interview room three is our man. We've got a DNA match from cigarettes to him. His fingerprints are on the typewriter that was used to type the letters and they're on the van he hired. That van is also caught on cctv at the factory at the time of the fire in the box room, and cctv pictures of him unloading something from that same van right next to the box room immediately before the fire. That same van is also seen on cctv loitering in the road outside the factory. And finally he works at Hardys'.

'Err the pictures are not clear enough to prove it's him sir, just that someone unloaded something from the back of the van' corrected one of the investigation team.

'Yes all right' snapped the Inspector tetchily.

'Gov there's something else too. Forensics are checking the sample we took from him for a DNA match against samples they've taken from the van and the dummy bomb'.

'Good that all adds to the evidence. Now what else do we know?'

'I've had a trawl through his computer Gov' announced another of the team 'but there's nothing there that I've found so far that could help us. A few general things much as you'd find on anyone's computer but also loads of porn. So far there's nothing illegal just lots of very explicit stuff. He obviously logged onto porn chat rooms and down loaded mountains of the stuff but as I say nothing illegal. I'd like forensics to delve a bit deeper with one of their real experts on computer analysis but they say they're too busy at the moment dealing with computer analysis of terrorist stuff'.

'OK. I think we're getting to him as he's asked for a solicitor'.

'Sign of a guilty conscience' said someone in the room and there was a general laugh.

'Maybe, let's hope so' the Inspector responded. 'So we've got lots of information, some that you might even call evidence but what we don't have is a motive and we all know that without a motive the chance of making the case stick when it gets to court is extremely limited.

Now has anyone any ideas as to motive and how are we getting on checking his background to see if there's a link with Mr. and Mrs. Hardy, either them in person or the business?'

'We've started that Gov' replied Anne but so far we've drawn a blank. This isn't the first time he's worked for Hardys you know. He worked there a few years ago then seems to have left before coming back a couple of years ago'.

'Not uncommon that. People like him often tend to move around from one factory to another' ventured one of the team.

'Umm but worth looking into. Can you see if you can find out why he left and exactly what he did in the interim period before he came back? Now what about his personal life?' asked Inspector Fulton.

'He hasn't got one, just loads of porn' called out another team member.

'And he visits a brothel, maybe more than one' added a woman police officer.

'Nothing illegal about going to those places is there?' remarked PC Collins.

'Oh you know all about them do you. Visit some yourself?' joked another officer.

'All right let's keep sensible. Arson, planting dummy bombs and blackmail are serious offences' grumbled Inspector Fulton. 'Come on team. We know this fellow did it. We've got to find out why. So lets dig deep and find out. If he is our man there has to be a reason why he's done it. We've got to find that reason….. so get out there and discover it' he finished raising his voice.

Later the interview with the man resumed but this time he was accompanied by a young newly qualified woman solicitor who'd taken an instant dislike to him. It wasn't anything that he'd said just the way he stared at her and she imagined that he was mentally undressing her. Ugh she shuddered.

Her thought process was entirely correct as the man was wondering what sort of underwear she was wearing, what she looked like without any clothes on, when she'd last had sex and whether she was good at it.

The Inspector's question jerked him out of his dreaming.

'Look we know you did it. What we want to know is why? What had the Hardys done to you to make you want to take revenge by burning down their stables, planting dummy bombs and setting fire to the factory?'

Hillary, the solicitor leaned close to him and whispered in his ear.

'Nothing to say' said the man.

'Have you got a grudge against Mr.. Hardy?'

He looked at Hillary, leaned close to her, exchanged whispers then smirked at the Inspector 'Nothing to say'.

From then on irrespective of whatever question the Inspector or Anne Shaw put to him he simply intoned either 'Nothing to say' or 'No comment'.

Eventually getting exasperated the two police officers called a halt to the interview, refused Hillary's request for his release, had him taken back to his cell, and after the solicitor had left, sat scratching their heads to try and discover a motive.

'They'll be one somewhere won't there Gov' asked Anne at the end of the day.

'Yes. Finding it though is the key, cos if we don't we won't be able to continue to hold him' her boss replied thoughtfully 'Look tomorrow go back to Hardys and see if you can turn anything up will you? Talk to their personnel people and also any of his work mates or his immediate boss. Now I'm off for the night as it's the wife's birthday and I promised to take her out to dinner. Go straight to the factory in the morning will you?'

Nodding in reply she watched him leave then picking up the phone, dialled and when it was answered said softly 'How would you like to reverse roles tonight and put me in handcuffs?' and chuckling she rang off.

***

The next morning she arrived at the factory just after eight o'clock and in line with her request to the receptionist was shown straight to personnel department where the head of that function, Rod Jackson was happy to try and help.

'If you hang on a sec I'll get hold of his records' and he tapped his computer keys while staring at his screen. 'Yep here we are. Joined us in two thousand and was made redundant in two thousand and three. We off loaded several people at that time and he was just one of many. He applied for jobs here several times after that whenever we advertised, but he always seemed to get turned down until two years ago when he did get taken on. I see that there's a note here that he can be a bit surly and difficult to handle. Let's have a look at his annual review and see if there's anything there?'

He tapped some more keys then smiled 'Yes here we are' and he studied the screen for a while. 'I guess overall you could say that he was a reasonably competent engineer, doesn't overstretch himself but occasionally seems to slag off the management in general and Mr. William in particular. It's been raised with him and he's got two verbal and one written warning about it…..but that seems to be all on his record. Divorced….. err not long after he got made redundant…. and that seems to be about it'.

'Thanks. Nothing else?'

'No'.

'Right. I'd like a print out of his record please. Now can I talk to some of his work mates and his boss?'

She eventually finished at the factory about ten thirty and drove back to Norwich police station where she reported what she'd found to Inspector Fulton who suggested that they should interview the man again. They called Hillary and just before mid-day Inspector Fulton, WPC Anne Shaw, the solicitor and the man were sitting in Interview room two.

After saying that this was a resumption of previous interviews and stating the names of those present, the Inspector looked at the man for some time without saying a word. When he saw him shifting in his chair and a few beads of perspiration appearing on his lip ands forehead he asked 'How did you feel about being made redundant by Hardys?'

'What a stupid question. How the fuck do you think I felt? Bloody awful if you want to know. It was alright for the fucking bosses but workers like me...... well we could be chucked out whenever it suited them couldn't we? Bastards' he replied angrily.

'Why did they choose you as one of the ones to go do you think?'

'Cos I wouldn't be pushed around. They picked on me. Bloody unfair'.

'You were married at that time weren't you?'

'Yes but not for much longer. That finally did it. Things hadn't been so great between the missus and me and when I lost me job and the money dried up, well that was the end really. She pissed off up north to her mother and took our kid with her. Rotten cow' he said viciously. 'Left me with the mortgage company chasing me for arrears, a huge pile of debts while she was with her mother. What did I have? Fuck all, that's what and it was all that bloody William Hardy's fault.'

'Why his fault' queried Anne Shaw.

'Cos he chucked me out. If he hadn't I'd have still been earning a reasonable wage as an engineering supervisor and not just be the lowest grade of engineer as I am now. Then I wouldn't have had the mortgage company foreclose on me and take my house away, wouldn't have lost the wife and kid, and wouldn't be renting the little shit hole that I live in now. You've seen it. I used to have a nice house on an estate. Three bedrooms, garden, garage. I had a car and prospects. Then Mr.-bastard-William-shitface-Hardy destroyed all that' and he was so angry when he spoke that spittle flew from his mouth.

'So you decided to get back at Mr. Hardy didn't you?' queried Anne.

'No'.

'Yes you did. You were so consumed with hatred that you set fire to his stables, planted a dummy bomb in the factory, firebombed the box store and wrote threatening letters to Mr. Hardy didn't you' snarled the WPC loudly.

'I must protest. You simply cannot speak to my client in that manner' interrupted Hillary bristling with indignation.

'Your client attempted blackmail, caused thousands...no tens.... maybe hundreds of thousands of pounds worth of damage, has diverted police time and attention away from other cases and is as guilty as hell' snarled Inspector Fulton. 'I know it, WPC Shaw knows it, he knows it, and if you've any shred of intelligence or intellect you also know it'. He looked away from the solicitor to the man.

'Now we've got cctv evidence of you, fingerprints, DNA and witness statements so I put it to you that you deliberately set fire to the stables, planted the dummy bomb, burnt out the box store and sent those threatening and blackmailing letters. Didn't you eh? Didn't you?' he asked loudly.

'No.'

'Yes you did'.

'I've fucking told you. No. How many more fucking times? No I bloody didn't'.

'You're lying, and mind your language, there are two ladies present. I say you did those things .... didn't you?' and he stared at the man.

There was a long pause as the two men glared at each other.

'Alright sergeant take him back to the cells let him think on things for a while'.

Returning she said 'I'm surprised you let him off the hook like that. I thought he was getting ready to crack and confess'.

'Maybe but he might have been deciding to dig in and continue to deny it. After all he's not too bright and so I don't think his brain works things out too quickly. I'd rather that he kicked his heels for an hour or so and started to worry.

I may be wrong but I hope that he's sitting in that cell wetting himself, not literally of course' he grinned 'so that when we bring him back up here next time we'll bust him open pretty damn quickly'.

The two police officers then departed to their respective desks and worked separately for a while until the Inspector walked to Anne Shaw and waiting till she'd finished on the telephone said 'Right get that solicitor in here then get him up again and let's see if we can't get a confession out of him'.

The formalities were observed the tape started and Inspector Fulton smiled and spoke quietly to the man.

'Look we all know you did it. I know it, you know it, the police sergeant here knows it, in fact even your solicitor probably thinks you did it. Now you'd save us all a lot of time, work and hassle if you'd just admit it. Often people who've committed crimes feel better after they've faced up to what they've done and admitted it. Sort of absolves them of guilt somehow. So come on admit it and we can all get on with other things.

We've got fingerprints, DNA, cctv footage, your old typewriter and even the paper we found in your house is the same as was used in the blackmail letters. We've got evidence from witnesses who saw you throw the typewriter into the river. We've have got you lock stock and barrel.

Now if you admit it then things might, just might go a bit easier on you when it gets to court. So stop wasting time. You did it didn't you?' and he smiled encouragingly.

The man looked at the two police officers, then at his solicitor then finally he looked down at the table.

'Yes' he said quietly but suddenly he leapt up half standing, leaning forward resting his hands on the interview table and yelled 'Yes I did it and he fucking well had it coming the bastard. Serve him right'.

Inspector Fulton looked pleased.

WPC Shaw looked startled.

Hillary the solicitor looked shocked.

The man looked angry.

'SIT DOWN' instructed WPC Shaw.

The man glared at her.

'Sit down I said' she repeated firmly.

When the suspect had slowly subsided back onto his chair the Inspector spoke again firmly and very directly.

'Now to avoid any confusion later and for the benefit of the tape this is to confirm that you have just confessed to four things. Burning down the Hardys stable block; firebombing the factory; planting a dummy bomb and sending threatening letters to Mr. Hardy. Is that right?'

'Yes' the man yelled again in the highly charged atmosphere but then looking around the room he repeated more quietly 'yes I did'.

'Why and why now? If you were angry about being made redundant why wait all these years? Why now?'

'Cos there's redundancies threatened again. The factory director said so in his last briefing. He said that the business wasn't doing too well and that there'd be bound to be some more redundancies'.

'But that doesn't mean you'd lose your job does it? It might be others surely?' asked WPC Shaw

'Nah. They don't like me. I've got some warnings on my record and they're bound to pick me. Bound to' he finished.

'But is that a reason to burn down Mr. Hardy's stables, plant dummy bombs in the factory and set fire to part of the factory? People get made redundant every day. Most of them get other jobs. Surely you could have found something else to do?' queried the Inspector.

The man looked at both police officers for a short while then shrugged. 'Maybe, maybe not'.

It was all over then. The man was cautioned, made to wait while a confession statement was prepared then asked to sign the document on each page before being taken back to his cell to await an appearance at Norwich magistrate court next morning to be formally accused.

That initial hearing was short. He was asked to confirm his name and address, then the charges were read out and he was asked to plead guilty or not guilty.

He looked at the three magistrates but said nothing. As he looked around the court he gazed at Anne Shaw as the Clerk repeated the question then he turned to look at Inspector Fulton who smiled and nodded at him. The man nodded back then smirked as he spoke.

'Not guilty'.

He was remanded in custody to appear at the county court to face the charges at a future date. Then he was taken down into the holding cells beneath the court until about four hours later he was handcuffed, led out into a waiting prison van along with three others, eased into the tiny single cell compartment in the van and driven to Norwich Prison where he was processed and eventually taken to the older part of the

Victorian building where he discovered to his horror that he was to share a cell with two other men.

The prison officer apologised but said it was a result of the prison overcrowding and he hoped it wouldn't be too long before he was moved to a two man cell.

There were two bunk beds on one side and on the other side a single bed located next to the toilet. He lay down dispiritedly and told the other two to 'Piss off' when asked why he was in there.

It was some hours later after he'd eaten his sandwich tea and was ready to go to bed for the night that he started to get undressed. He was just in his underpants when Big Pete, one of his other two cell mates, walked over to him grinned then suddenly shoved him violently backwards so he lost his balance and fell onto his bed. Still grinning Big Pete reached for the waist elastic of the man's pants and yanked them down to is knees.

The man's immediate thought was that he was about to be sexually assaulted, which he was, but not in the way that he imagined in that terrifying moment.

With one hand cupping the man's genitals Big Pete clenched his other hand into a giant fist and slammed it down hard, cruelly crushing the testicles and penis.

The scream could be heard all down the corridor but no-one took any notice. Screams were common in prison.

'Hey' the man eventually gasped rolling on the bed in agony and cradling his aching balls. 'What you do that for you bastard?'

'I asked you a question'.

'What question. When?' he moaned

'Earlier I asked what you were in here for. You said piss off. Now no-one talks to me like that ...... do they Billy' he snarled looking at the other cell occupant.

'No Pete, at least not if they've got any sense they don't'.

'Hear that?'

The man nodded furiously still moaning then yelled as Big Pete stretched out one huge hand and grabbed his lanky hair and twisted hard. As the man reached up to try and remove the hand he felt Big Pete's other hand take hold of his genitals again.

'No please' he screamed. 'Please don't. Look I'll tell you just leave me balls alone'.

'I'm listening' but although the hand holding his hair was removed the other still gripped his cock and balls tightly.

'Please don't' begged the man trying now to pull the lower hand away but unable to do so he gave up. Speaking quickly and stumbling over his words in his eagerness to confess and get the hand away he explained about the fires, the letters and the dummy bomb but said he'd pleaded not guilty.

When he finished speaking he was so frightened he was almost crying. 'Look I've told you everything now so please let me go. I won't cause any trouble here. I've never been in prison before'.

'Now if you'd said all that when I asked you earlier it would have been better wouldn't it?'

The man nodded furiously. 'Sorry won't happen again'.

Big Pete still kept a tight hold on the man. 'Better not. Make sure you remember your place in this cell' but he still didn't release the man. 'Now just to be certain that you do' and he turned to Billy 'hold him down will you mate?'

The man screamed 'No please no' as Billy took a firm grip on his arms and leaning on him pressed him against the bed. Big Pete still holding the cock and balls in one hand held his other huge clenched fist in front of the man's terrified eyes.

'When I ask something you answer' but before the man could reply that fist slammed down. 'When I tell you to do something you do it' and another crushing blow landed. 'When I want something you get it. Understand?' and a third explosion of pain flashed throughout the man's body.

Billy closed his eyes and wished he could close his ears to the awful screams that ricocheted around the cell as Big Pete, on remand charged with causing grievous bodily harm, and a huge slow witted man with a fearful temper was obviously going to give this new chap a terrible time. He wished he could stop it but didn't know how and was desperate to avoid the big man tuning on him as well so he stayed there, doing as he was told holding the victim down as that huge fist slammed down.

The pain was so awful that the man screamed continuously and thought that he was going to be sick but shaking his head from side to side he just managed to keep his lunch and sandwich tea in his stomach.

'Pete I think he's had his lesson now' said Billy and turning to the crying man added 'haven't you?'

'Yes' but that was all he could say as he looked at Big Pete and begged 'please don't hit me again ….. please' and to his relief he felt himself released.

'I'll be watching you'.

'Yea ok'.

'Right' and patting the man's face Big Pete walked the two paces across the cell and climbed onto his top bunk where he broke wind loudly and for a prolonged time filling the small cramped room with his awful smell. 'Better out than in' he muttered.

Billy wrinkled his nose and went to lie down on his bunk below the big man who giggled as he let out another loud burst of wind. 'Whoops that's better' …….. then as yet another erupted added 'and that'.

The man though was rolling around on his narrow and uncomfortable bed, knees up sobbing and taking deep breaths. Copious tears of pain and fear flowed until Big Pete leaned down from his bunk and said menacingly 'Fucking stop that moaning will you or I'll and give you a proper belting then you really will have something to moan about'.

'Sorry. Right. Yes I'll try and be quiet but they don't half hurt' and he sat up and put his feet on the floor. 'Aagh' he exclaimed as the pain from his lower region shot around his body again.

He fell to his knees but moments later he started to get used to the pain which now came in waves instead of being continuous. Kneeling he leant forward and pressed his face into the rough blanket his body shaking with fear, pain and emotion. He stayed there for some time his pants still round his ankles until as some of the pain faded he clambered slowly back onto the bed, pulled up his pants and lay down but the movement sent further shafts of agony through him making him yelp.

'Sorry Pete' he said turning to look up at his huge tormentor.

'Welcome to Norwich Prison and my cell' laughed the big bully.

The man was still in agony whatever position he adopted so he lay still for a long time until standing up again and hunching over seemed to make things a little easier. He stayed like that for ages breathing deeply before eventually summoning up the courage to move again. He shuffled to the not too clean stainless steel wash basin and filled it with cold water right to the brim.

Gasping in pain he struggled to remove his pants and then pressing up against the basin he dangled his cock and balls in the cold water which seemed to help. He gently splashed water onto himself and stood there for some minutes.

'Here you wash that basin out properly when you've finished. I don't want to wash my face or do my teeth after you've been dangling your cock in there mate' warned Big Pete.

'Yea ok I'll wash it round but please let me stay here for a minute. It's helping'.

'Just as long as you do' laughed Big Pete.

Eventually the man moved away from the basin, let out the water, re-filled it and using the towel with which he'd been issued on arrival at the prison scrubbed it round observing with distaste that his towel was now covered with grime but at least the basin was clean.

Lying down on his bed he felt a little better. Billy on the other lower bunk looked across at him and smiled sympathetically.

'Oh God' whispered the man to himself as he slid under the rough blanket then turned to face the wall and gently put his hands around his swollen testicles which still throbbed so painfully that not only was he unable to get to sleep but he couldn't stop crying, but very quietly, to avoid any risk of upsetting Big Pete.

It was five days before his balls stopped throbbing and just ached; another week beyond that before the swelling had all gone and they were back down to usual size and yet another fortnight until they stopped aching altogether and everything seemed to be normal again.

Happiness is not always measured in smiles.

Anonymous.

CHAPTER 16

Steve was busy working on the plans to develop the Hardys business. He was starting to enjoy the challenge that this business presented and working out how it was to be improved. Running it wasn't difficult. Turning it round was.

He knew that the bank would be pressing for an early meeting with him to review his plans as although as Chief Executive he was in charge of the company, it was under the auspices of Northern and Southern Bank and he was not only acting as their representative and manager, but in effect was managing the business by proxy. Their business. Their proxy.

The trouble was that following the away day strategic review session there were plenty of things to be done short term to improve profitability and cut their costs, but their real weakness was the absence of a long term plan to break out of their current financial stranglehold.

They simply weren't making enough money and with the increasing competition in the supermarkets and sadly in their export markets too there was no opportunity to increase their prices. So they had to solve their problems either by lowering their costs, especially the cost of production, or by increasing throughput volume sales at their current cost base.

The difficulty with finding ways of lowering their production costs was that to do this would require millions of pounds of investment in new plant and machinery and the bank would be highly unlikely to advance more money, certainly not at this early stage in the recovery.

So without big cash injections he had to find ways of increasing their sales and to start this process he called a meeting for all the sales and marketing teams together in the main conference room.

He sat at the top table alone while Emily propped herself on a table also at the top of the room but slightly to one side.

Shortly after they'd settled themselves the various members of the two departments arrived more or less on time, but none as promptly as Kelly whose crush on Emily had grown by the day. Sitting in the front row she fixed her eyes on her dream lady listening in wrapt pleasure as Emily spoke.

'Good afternoon everybody. We've asked you here today as we want to explain some of the facts of this business to you, to help you understand where we are and what we need to do to improve the performance and results of the company.

In very simple terms we need to make more money. Hardys almost went bust but our bank doesn't want that to happen and so has provided additional funds to give us time to sort ourselves out. But we don't have much time, so speed of improving results is of the essence.

Be quite clear if we don't, then they'll pull the plug on the company. Not only is Hardys unprofitable but it is very short of cash and so control of cash is going to be a vital and on-going challenge for us all. That is my task to manage the cash and eke out what comes into the company so we can, hopefully, pay our suppliers. I will work closely with you and others, especially the finance department to find ways to solve these problems'.

'Yes' said Steve taking up the discussion. We'll need to revisit the New Product Development programme as recent launches have hardly been inspiring have they? Well that has to change. We need new ideas, new labelling, new packaging that will run on our existing production lines and above all excitement and innovation.

You in sales and marketing are at the forefront of our company so it is up to you to firstly hold onto what we've got and ensure we don't get dropped by any customers and then when we've got our new products ready you'll lead the charge forward.

I want ideas, I want innovation, I want creativity, I want action......
now! If you want to talk to me about anything my office is next to the board room come and see me. Right any questions?'

Several hands were raised and an interesting and useful question and answer session took place. Both Steve and Emily were frank with their replies. If they thought a good point had been raised they said so. Equally if they thought the idea or question was unhelpful or stupid they left the questioner in no doubt as to what they'd thought of the point.

Eventually the session came to an end and as everyone was about to leave Emily looked round the room and finished the meeting by saying firmly 'We're relying on each and every one of you'.

'Right' said Steve crisply. 'We've explained what needs to be done so let's see together what we can do. Thanks for coming today' then he and Emily left the room.

Once they'd gone the sales and marketing teams started to make their way back to their office areas. Among them was Kelly who drifted back in a daze. She'd never once moved her eyes off Emily's face or body while listening to her and noticing that she'd dropped a handkerchief in the corridor as she'd left, Kelly quickly picked it up muttering to a colleague as she put it in her pocket that she'd see it got back to Emily but arriving home that evening she carefully tucked it under her pillow.

It was about a week later when Steve had his first formal meeting with the bank. He'd decided to talk to the bank team first with just himself and Emily present before inviting other members of the Hardys team to join them.

'Now then how are you getting on?' asked Barry Field as soon as "good mornings" and other opening pleasantries together with coffee had been dispensed.

'Well gentlemen' started Steve 'there are as we know several things wrong with this business but I would classify the two most important ones as inappropriate machinery in the factory incapable of producing modern packaging and products and a dreadful sales and to some extent marketing function.

I am working on the assumption that the bank won't invest more money at this stage on production equipment so we have to work with what we've got?'

Both Barry Field and Frank Gold nodded.

'Right that's what I thought. All is not lost but I need a new Sales and Marketing Director as John Benton isn't up to it and I might also need a new Production Director to really take this factory by the balls and squeeze and shake it till it gets it's costs down and it's efficiencies up. I'll take a view on that in due course but the priority is a new Sales and Marketing Director. However I'd be grateful if you'd keep all that

information about need for change to yourselves at the moment ……..
but that's what's needed.

So I propose to use a head hunter to find me top flight people. Until
then we'll battle on with what we've got.

I'm also really unhappy with Martin Fellows the Finance Director
here and so we propose to part company with him tomorrow. Emily will
take over finance and run that department in the interim period until
we get a replacement FD. I am going to go for an experienced Interim
not a permanent appointment at this stage then when that person is on
board Emily can concentrate on Planning, Strategy and IT whilst also
supporting Finance. The rest of the team seem ok for now, but life's
tough and there are no real quick fixes'.

'Yes we can get some costs out and make a few short term sales
improvements but until we get some new good people we won't make
significant progress on change' suggested Emily.

'Ok understood. Now what about the arson problem? Have the
police caught anyone yet?' asked Frank.

'What arson problem?' responded Steve and Emily together.

'Don't you know about the maniac that's tried to burn down the
factory?'

'No'.

'Well William knows all about it. He should do seeing the stables
at his home were burnt down too. So you don't know about the fake
bomb either?'

'No I bloody well don't' came Steve's angry reply 'but I will in a
moment. Excuse me for a minute' and rising he stormed out of the room
into William's office next door.

'William what's all this about arson and fake bombs? Why wasn't I
told? If I'm to run this company I must know everything of significance
and I'd say that setting fire to the factory is pretty significant wouldn't
you?' and his eyes flashed angrily at William.

'Ah. Sorry. Yes we've had a bit of a problem but the police have
caught and charged a chap. One of our engineers, so I think it's all over
and done with. I mean one of our engineers from here? Unbelievable.
Apparently bearing a grudge because we made him redundant years ago
and as a result he ran out of money, had his house repossessed and his
wife left him taking their child with her'.

'Hang on a minute William. I know nothing about this. When did all this happen?'

'Oh sorry. Somehow thought you knew'.

'No I didn't so what's it all about?'

William then explained about the fire in the stables at his home, the dummy bomb in the factory, the fire in the box store and the threatening and blackmail letters. Steve was amazed that none of this had been reported or advised to him.

'Look William I'm very glad that this guy has been caught for your sake and the sake of the business but I should have known. I should have been told about it. You...... should have told me. Please understand that as Chief Executive of Hardys I need to know everything of importance that happens in this business. Is that clear?'

For a moment William thought about putting this newly appointed upstart in his place. How dare he speak to him like that, but he controlled himself and remembered that it wasn't his business any more and he had no longer held any sway or authority. It was being run by the bank through Steve and Emily, so he nodded and replied quietly 'Of course'.

'Thank you. Now is there anything else I ought to know about?'

'No'.

'You really should have told me' Steve snarled as he turned on his heel to return to the Board Room where he smiled frostily at the bankers and advised them that the police had caught and charged one of their engineers.

'Good. Well that's one problem less for you' smiled Barry. 'Now is there anything else we need to cover before you bring in your team and we review where the business is at present?'

'No but remember don't mention that two of them are to be replaced' cautioned Emily.

The bankers nodded then waited until the rest of the directorial team joined the meeting having been summoned by Tabitha.

'Right I propose to outline the first thoughts for revitalising the business' started Steve 'and then I'll ask each of the team to speak to their part of the plan. Please feel free to ask any questions' he smiled at the bankers as he switched on the computer projector.

Standing with a small gadget in his hand he waited until the machine had warmed up and the first slide appeared on the wall screen

PROJECT PHOENIX

'I've called it that for several reasons but now it seems to have added significance as I've just found out about the arson' he said somewhat bluntly still displeased that not only William but also not one of the team had bothered to mention it to him. 'Rising anew from the ashes. That's what Hardys is going to do'.

He pressed the button on the gadget.

'We'll start by outlining what we've identified so far as being the most important matters that are affecting the Company and then move on to outline how we intend to set about them. The first is Cash Management and Emily will outline the issues and our plans to manage this'.

The bankers stared unsmiling and unmoving at the screen as Emily started, warmed to and moved through her presentation. She was good at public speaking and indeed quite enjoyed it but she had been slightly nervous this morning.

The business was not at this early stage showing any signs of improvement although to be fair she'd only been there a few days and could hardly be expected to have waved a magic wand and created a miracle improvement in the cash position.

Unfortunately the business had actually deteriorated further in its financial performance and although she was going to share with the bankers the thoughts and ideas that she and the team had generated at the away day, she knew that in reality there was nothing in the plans that would make a dramatic difference. Improvements yes but not the turnaround that she'd and Steve been brought in to effect.

They needed more time to think through, develop and execute a new strategy while at the same time generating sufficient improvement to not only give the bankers confidence that they could do what they'd been tasked to do, but also to ensure that they continued their financial support of the business. Without that the business would collapse instantly.

Following Emily's part of the presentation which was in truth aimed not only at the Bankers but also the management team, the Bankers seemed slightly more relaxed and even made some potentially helpful suggestions regarding cash management.

Steve then invited each of the individual Directors and Heads of Departments to outline how they were going to tackle their own specific areas of responsibility. There was a common theme running through their presentation which was getting costs down, controlling expenditure and increasing sales.

When John Benton the Sales and Marketing Director spoke it seemed as though he was mouthing the words but didn't give the impression that he really believed what he was saying. Steve and Emily exchanged glances a couple of times with the bankers but beyond challenging and asking some "how" questions nothing was said to him.

'So there we are gentlemen' said Steve looking at the bankers as the last Director finished his session and he stood to take control of the meeting and presentation again.

'That's how we are starting and we will naturally keep you posted with progress on how the various plans evolve. Of course you'll see our weekly and monthly financial results and our daily cash balance'.

'Speaking of cash' interrupted Emily 'we are ok for cash at the moment but if sales don't improve quickly we might need a further cash injection'.

The banker's brows furrowed at this as they made some additional notes on the pads of paper in front of them before Frank looked at Emily and Steve.

'Thank you for a clear presentation of how you see the issues and what you are intending to do about them. We shall, as you say, watch with close interest the progress you make ......very close interest. We can only wish you the best of luck. Let us know if we can help further'.

The meeting broke up and when only Steve, Emily and the bankers were left they looked at her. 'Emily' said Barry, 'we are convinced that you can do this but you've certainly got a big task on to control and manage the cash to achieve that. I can see from this morning why you need to replace the two guys. They're simply not up to it are they?'

Without waiting for an answer he went on 'Look we are here to help you. We really want you and Steve to succeed. You both have a fine reputation in turnarounds so far and you will want to enhance it with a success here but whatever you do keep us in the picture. Tell us what's going on, positive or negative. Don't be afraid to call us with bad news. We understand that turnarounds don't happen smoothly and you'll have downs as well as ups, but overall let's hope that we can all get a success out of ....err what was it ......ah yes... out of Project Phoenix. Good luck'.

After shaking hands Steve showed them down to reception and then waited as they walked across the car park and got into their car. He walked back to his office where Emily was sitting in an easy chair.

'Well so far so good but our honeymoon period with the bank will be of short ..... very short, duration. They'll want to see improvements and quickly' he said grimly.

'How long do you think that they'll give us?'

'I really don't know but I suppose when we start to run out of cash again that'll be the crunch. If they don't think that we've got a realistic rescue or recovery plan on track they'll simply refuse to pump in any more money and that'll be it'.

'We'd better get it sorted then'.

He nodded and invited her to stay so they could plan through the rest of the day after which he checked some important points on tomorrow's payments and whether there was still enough money available to make them. Receiving confirmation from her that there was he nodded as she said she really needed to get back to her own office.

Tabitha knocked and came in with a cup of coffee. 'Thought you might need this' she smiled.

Even though it was early days he thought that he and Tabitha would work well together. Tabs, as she liked to be known was efficient, quick, used her initiative and seemed to have a really nice personality.

When he asked about her status she'd told him 'Single as there are far too many men to play with to think of settling down yet' and grinned at him.

'No doubt' he'd chuckled.

Next morning he asked Martin Fellows to come and see him.

'Martin sometimes there are difficult things that have to be done and this morning I have one such issue'.

'Yea well we all have them from time to time. Can I help?'

'Not really as it affects you. I think it is always best to come straight to the point in these circumstances. Martin we, that is the Bank and I ……. no that's not true, let me be honest. I ……. don't think you are what we need here heading up finance in this time of crisis. You are a bright Finance Director and trying to hold this mess together isn't your forte. You need to be in a proper business that has a clear strategy, is financially sound and knows not only what it's doing but where it's going. That isn't Hardys at the present. So I think you should leave'.

'Leave? Christ! Do I get any say in this?'

Steve looked at the other man, held his eyes and replied 'No. Sorry. I've got your severance package here' and he passed across two sheets of paper. Look on the bright side. At the moment we've got the cash to pay you off. If we can't turn this round and it goes bust, you'll get nothing'.

'Steve don't be so hasty. Look I can help you turn Hardys round. I don't mind working with …. for Emily. She and I could work together and help you. With William out of the chair I am sure that the changes that are required will be implemented by you'.

'No sorry. It's also not what we need, what I need. I want a different sort of Finance Director, preferably someone older who has been through this sort of cash crisis management before. You are a career finance man. This isn't a career job. This is either a collapse in a heap with your career folding with it, or possibly a long boring slow grind to eventual financial stability. That's not you Martin, so go now with your career and reputation intact'.

The shocked finance man looked at Steve who returned his gaze without flinching.

'It's for the best' Steve added soothingly.

'Ok. When do you want me to go?'

'End of the week?'

'Right. Let me study these' and he tapped the papers with details of his severance package 'and I'll come back to you'.

The meeting was over.

Steve had rung the Head Hunter on the day of the bankers visit and outlined his requirements over the phone.

Nigel Charlesworthy was one of the partners in Wright and Charlesworthy a leading City of London head hunting firm. They made their extremely lucrative living by finding top class individuals and persuading them to leave their existing employer to take up an important opportunity at another firm. There were many such head hunting firms, some large, some small, some good, some not.

Wright and Charlesworthy were medium sized but with an excellent reputation for finding exceptionally high calibre people. Their fees were very high but as they always said when challenged "if you want the best you have to pay for it".

Steve had been aware of them for some time as they'd made a point of getting to know him, something that was an important part of a head hunter's role. To seek out and watch the progress of good people so that when they were retained to find a particular person for a role they could tap into their data base of potential individuals.

As they knew each other, Nigel was able to refine the brief on the phone with Steve and agreed that he'd e-mail a formal proposal, fees and terms of business before the end of that day for Steve's approval.

When it arrived Steve blinked. The usual fees for head hunters were between 20% and 33% of the candidate's starting salary. Wright and Charlesworthy charged 40% payable as 25% up front on accepting the assignment, 10% when they produced a short list of at least three suitable candidates and a final 5% when the successful candidate started at the new firm.

He rang Nigel, told him that he'd like to give the role to him but that his fees were too high.

'Steve we don't negotiate. Those are our terms. Of course you can find cheaper but will they do as good a job for you? I doubt it. Now shall we make a start tomorrow?'

Smiling at Nigel's polite but firm refusal to negotiate he replied 'Yes please but the really urgent one is an Interim Finance Director'.

It was the next day that Nigel rang Steve just after nine o'clock.

'Do you mind an American for your interim finance chap?'

'No not at all. Why?'

'Got a great bloke and he's immediately available. Just finished a project and was thinking of going back to The States but interested in your need and would be prepared to consider staying for, well six months maybe longer depends on the project, the terms, the challenge ….. oh and you. He's quite strong minded so if he doesn't rate you he won't come and work for you'.

'Sounds ideal. When can we see him?'

'How about this afternoon say around five?'

'Hang on' and Steve checked his diary. 'Make it five thirty will you'.

As soon as Travis Anderson walked into Steve's office the turnaround man knew that here was a person he could work with. Tall, broad shouldered, short almost crew cut hair, square neck, in his mid forties, the American projected an attitude of toughness and determination. He had an extremely firm handshake, a ready smile and had just been invited to sit down which he did in the chair in front of Steve's desk when Emily joined the two men.

The discussion lasted about an hour and at the end Steve asked how soon Travis could start working with them if they invited him to join the team.

'Tomorrow morning if you like. You say that the existing finance guy is leaving on Friday so it would be helpful to have at least a coupla days with him before he's gone.

Look as far as I'm concerned Nigel will have told you my terms. I assume they're ok, otherwise I guess you wouldn't have wasted your or my time, in asking me to come here to Norfolk.

If not then that's fine. I've just finished a job in a major electrical business in Glasgow and before that I was part of the team turning round an engineering business in Manchester.

Now I've already got two new options I'm considering. One is in Düsseldorf Germany where there is a car component supplier in trouble, or there's a big project in Cleveland, Ohio which is of interest as it's in my country and I ain't been back there for nearly five years. However Cleveland is a whole long wagon train ride from North Carolina my home state, but I could hop a flight from time to time and get to see my folks again.

Then there's this job with you guys and I have to say that I kinda like the idea of jams and pickles. I've not worked in that field before so it sounds real interesting. Look I can do this job for you, no problem as I enjoy challenges like this although from what you've said it sounds a bit of a bitch of a business that you've got here. But I reckon the three of us could make a pretty good team and crack it' and he smiled openly at Steve, but especially at Emily.

'I think we could too. It'll be tough but we've got the bare bones of a new strategy, the workforce are up for the challenge, most of the senior team are ok although we've got one other change to make. We need a new Sales and Marketing Director but that'll be a permanent appointment not an Interim like you ..... or Emily and me.

Travis can you give Emily and I a few minutes on our own to have a quick word. There's the Board Room along here' he continued as he led the big man out of his office and settled him into the large room. 'We'll be back in a couple of minutes'.

'Take your time. I ain't going nowhere right now'.

'So what do you think?' queried Steve when he got back to Emily.

'Gorgeous hunk of a man' she laughed then continued 'sorry you mean is he right for the job? Grrrr yes definitely' and again she grinned.

'Get your horny hormones back in their box and think about him as our Interim Finance Director. Could you work with him?'

'Could I work with him? Is the Pope a Catholic? Does the sun rise in the morning? Is it dark at night? Is he the sort of man to set a woman's heart racing? Yes Steve I could definitely work with him' then seeing a worried look come into his eye she added 'oh don't be silly! I'm just winding you up.

I think he'll be great. He's got the experience of working with bankrupt or failing businesses, he's obviously tough, he'll command respect here and be able to manage our creditors as well as our debtors and I am sure you and I will be able to work well with him'.

'That's what I thought. Good I'll get him back in then and sign him up'.

'Grab him quick and stop him going back to America' and she got up and walked across his office pausing at the door with a little smile playing around her face 'or if you don't .... I'll grab him and that might be for wholly different reasons!' and she left chuckling.

Smiling Steve collected Travis and took him back to his office. 'Right we'd like you to come and join us'.

So they discussed and negotiated Travis's terms. Like most Interim Managers who joined companies for a specific project or for a specific time period Travis charged a daily rate the size of which had initially made Steve's eyes water but having now met the man he felt that he was going to be getting value for money. However Travis wanted a success bonus as well. An amount of money that was paid to him if the turnaround team succeeded in getting the business back onto a firm footing.

He was prepared to take Steve on trust and leave the exact detail to work out when he joined but he wanted confirmation right now that such a bonus would be payable.

Steve didn't have a problem with this, as indeed he and Emily were on such an arrangement although rather than a day rate they were both paid a fixed monthly sum for the duration of the project.

The two men shook hands and Travis said that he'd be there first thing in the morning to start work so smiling and saying that he looked forward to working with him Steve walked the man down to reception and then went to look in on Emily who was packing up for the night.

'Good day?' he asked.

'Yes actually. I've spent time working on how we implement the plan we've developed. It's going to be tough with the costs and kit that is in factory and I think we're going to struggle until we can afford some new machinery. But I know that we've got to make do with what we have so that's the planning assumptions that I've used.

Also we have to get marketing and sales sorted out. We need three things. First we need some new business. Second we need to get rid of about half the product portfolio that is unprofitable and isn't making us money but losing money with every pack we make. Lastly we need to instil in the people who work in those departments that what we want is profit, in other words profitable business, not volume for the sake of it' and she was speaking quite strongly.

'Yes it's odd but they seem to believe that a busy factory is the key. It isn't. A busy factory producing profitable products .... yes. A busy factory producing unprofitable products ..... no' he finished.

Maybe Travis and I could work on that together' she queried.

'Sounds good. Any plans for this evening?'

'Yes I'm driving to Ely right now. I've got a cousin there who I haven't seen for ages so she's invited me for supper and to stay the night so I can have a drink or two and not have to worry about driving'.

'Sounds fun, ok see you tomorrow. Enjoy your evening' and he went back to his own office where he worked until about nine thirty when he decided to go for a walk around the factory.

He liked to tour the production areas especially at night and the factory people working there appreciated seeing one of the bosses taking an interest in what was going on.

Steve found it difficult to talk easily with them and hard to engage in small talk conversation as he'd seen others do so, especially Emily. So he tended to stick to factual questions about output against target, machine efficiency, wastage and things directly related to the process itself. In this way he learnt a lot about what was going on, motivated the people by his presence but remained a little distant from them. He couldn't help it. That was just the way it was with him.

He was also disappointed that Emily wasn't there tonight. They had an interesting relationship having met on a previous turnaround assignment.

That had been for Blocksons, a large chemical manufacturer who had borrowed substantial sums of money from their bank to fund a rapid expansion programme which initially had gone well, so they had borrowed further monies to build a new warehouse and packing complex in the Midlands which would significantly lower their operating costs.

Unfortunately two things had then conspired almost simultaneously to put the company in financial peril. Firstly they lost a large overseas contract, while at home a newly re-energised competitor had cut prices and so forced Blocksons to cut their prices. Both of these put serious pressure on their profit margins.

But things were then compounded by a serious delay in getting the new warehouse and packing unit operating satisfactorily which meant that they were not getting the planned cost savings from the new unit and had to also continue running their old production and packing plants.

And if those three things weren't enough, interest rates rose.

The company was therefore squeezed in all directions. Its sales had dropped and what it did have were at lower margins; it's costs had shot up instead of coming down; the money it borrowed was costing much more than it had budgeted. All of this was unsustainable and the company teetered on the edge of bankruptcy.

Their bank called in Steve to take control as he'd worked on a couple of successful turnaround projects for them before. The first of these had been a big project where he'd been the number two and the second one was much smaller but he'd led it and successfully turned the company involved from loss to profit with a strong positive cash flow.

As a result of that success he'd been given charge of the bigger Blocksons project and had achieved a stunning success which really established his reputation as a highly skilled turnaround expert.

While working at Blocksons, in one of the regular reviews with the bank he'd said that he needed a good planning manager to work with him and a few days later Emily had arrived.

The two of them got on immediately and worked well as a team and it was about three months after they started working together that he'd asked her out to dinner one night. She'd accepted and subsequently about once a week they went out for a drink or for dinner until about six months after they'd first met they slept together.

It was a happy pleasant experience which they both enjoyed. There were no great crashing violins in their minds or rose coloured skies in their eyes. They had dinner, went to his room in the hotel at which he was staying, tenderly undressed each other, went to bed, kissed a lot, made love and went to sleep. In the morning they kissed again, made love again and went their separate ways, she back to the flat she was renting on a temporary lease for the duration of the project to get changed and he to shower and get dressed.

They met up again an hour later at Blocksons, worked at their respective roles, went back to her flat that evening and made love again.

Steve had got divorced four years before. Since then he'd had an on-off relationship with a girl but there was nothing fixed about their relationship.

Emily previously had almost got engaged to a young man she'd originally met at University but she and her fiancé gradually grew apart so one evening after talking for ages and concluding that actually they didn't want to marry each other, they mutually called it off.

She'd had one reasonably serious boyfriend since then, a couple of less serious relationships and a number of one night stands, but nothing permanent.

Working together at Blocksons she and Steve had become quite close and enjoyed each other's company both in the office at work as colleagues, but also out of work as friends. The added bonus was that they slept together from time to time.

They were both happy with this slightly odd relationship, ensured that their personal life didn't interfere with their work commitments, but enjoyed their lovemaking when it occurred. It was a casual affiliation forged on mutual respect and need when it might arise, but they both knew that one day they'd probably meet a partner who would mean much more to them and that whatever happened in their business life, the sex life between them would cease. But they hoped that they'd still remain friends.

For the time being though it suited them both to know that when they needed a friend to go out with for a drink or a meal the other was there and that sometimes it would lead to bed and sometimes it wouldn't.

Tonight had been one of those nights when he'd fancied taking Emily to dinner and then making love with her and he had to admit to the slightest touch of jealousy at the way she had so overtly played up being attracted to the big American finance man.

Oh well he sighed to himself, no nookie tonight then and after his walk round the factory he drove himself back to the hotel in which he was staying, had a late supper in the bar where he could relax and be casual rather than the more formal arrangements in the dining room, took a half bottle of red wine up to his room where he sipped it slowly while watching the film Apollo 13, the story of how the American Space Control centre managed to bring back the crippled space craft after the onboard explosion which led to the famous phrase *"Houston we have a problem"*.

Again marvelling at the portrayed ingenuity in solving the problems in deep space he found himself thinking that if mankind could solve that sort of problem which was literally a matter of life and death then he ought to be able to solve the problems of Hardys and tomorrow he'd have a thorough review with Emily of exactly where they'd got to so far.

When the film finished he switched off the tv, undressed, got into bed and was soon asleep although again regretting that it wasn't after making love to Emily.

***

She however having enjoyed her evening chatting and laughing with her cousin had gone to bed quite early but clicking the poppers shut on her pyjamas remembered how Steve had recently popped them open and decided that she'd like him to pop them open again, sooner rather than later.

She too slept well.

To confess a fault freely is the next best thing to being innocent of it.
Publilius Syrus.

CHAPTER 17

Janie couldn't sleep and had no appetite. She desperately needed to talk to someone but dare not discuss it with William. Ok she could discuss the cottage and the fraud with him but not Harry. Not how she felt about him.

How did she feel? She missed him. No she didn't just miss him she wanted him. In spite of everything that he'd done, she wanted him - desperately.

She wanted to feel his arms around her. She wanted to have him kiss her in that wonderfully deep passionate way that he did. She wanted to see that long lock of pale brown hair flop forward onto his forehead and brush it back for him. She wanted to put her arms around him and hold him tightly. She wanted to hug him. She wanted him to undress her in that slow teasing way that he did sometimes. She wanted to undress him and reveal his lovely firm, trim, fit body. She wanted to lie beneath him as he made love to her. She wanted to feel him inside her. She wanted to straddle him and move on him looking down on him while he kissed her breasts and loved her nipples. She wanted to lie quietly next to him with her arms around him just cuddling and listening to his breathing. She wanted to smell his manly aroma. She wanted to inhale the musky scent of his aftershave. She wanted him, all of him and she was distraught to think that she wasn't going to have him any more.

Never mind what he'd done. No that was stupid she thought. Of course she minded what he'd done.

She minded that he'd conned her. Her and William. She minded that he'd stolen from her. She minded that he'd taken all her money. She minded that at a time when William was having such problems with his business, Harry had brought this additional set of problems down onto them. She minded that he'd taken their cottage in France away from them. She minded she'd been so gullible that he could easily get away with it all. She minded that he'd obviously not meant any of those sweet nothings that he'd whispered to her in bed. She minded that all his wonderful words of affection and endearment were nothing but false and part of the con trick.

She hated the reality that she'd been so stupid. She hated the fact that he'd slept with all those other women. She particularly hated the knowledge that he also had sex with men. She hated everything about him. She hated the lies that she'd told William and indeed was still doing so. She hated not making love with her husband but somehow not being able to bring herself to do so.

Yes. She missed Harry and everything about him.

This morning, before William left for the office he'd brought her up a cup of tea and sat on the edge of the bed to enquire kindly and solicitously about her health.

'Apart from this Harry business is there something else worrying you?'

This Harry business? What else was there to worry about?

'No darling I just can't get it out of my mind that's all'.

'Well I understand but I just wonder if there's anything else. Are you feeling ok? It's just that you don't look your usual cheerful self. In fact you look pale, drawn and almost as if you're ill'.

'No really I'm ok. Well except for my wretched period which started earlier than usual and seems to be going on for ages'.

'Ah maybe that's it, on top of the Harry thing then. Perhaps a trip to the doctor would be advisable?'

'Yes possibly. I'll see how I feel today and if things aren't improving I'll make an appointment. Now go on off you go. Are things getting any better at work?'

'Well not really but I'm sort of on the sidelines now. It's Steve and Emily who are running things and I just do what I'm told. Very frustrating but I suppose it's the only way. Short of me stumping up a few million quid to clear the debts and so on, then it'll have to be like this. Alright darling I'll see you tonight. I should be back around six thirty. Would you like to go out to dinner somewhere? Might cheer you up?'

'Can we see how I feel?'

'Of course, well goodbye darling. I do love you'.

'Mmm and I love you too William. See you tonight'.

They kissed. He went. She rolled over in bed. She started to cry.

Later when she stopped feeling so sorry for herself she got up and had a bath but as she lay back to soak for a while she thought of the jacuzzi bath she'd enjoyed with Harry and this set her mind rampaging around all the times that they'd spent together.

'I've simply got to talk to someone' she muttered aloud and getting out she dried, dressed and sitting on her bed dialled Jackie.

'Hi. Are you doing anything this morning?'

'Nothing special, why do you want to come and ride?'

'No. I ...... I'd like to talk'.

'About Barry your secret lover?'

'Yes and it's Harry not Barry. Would around ten thirty be ok?' It was and so just before that time Janie was walking into Jackie's kitchen.

'So how are things with Mr. Wonderful then? Come on I want to know everything you two have been getting up to. Everything you hear. All the dirty details you naughty girl' Jackie chuckled.

Janie looked at her friend and burst into tears.

'Hey what's up? Oh Christ .... William hasn't found out has he?'

'No' she sobbed. 'It's Harry, he's in prison'.

'Prison? Why? What the hell has he done?'

Jackie's kitchen was large and led straight out into the conservatory but in the corner was a two seater sofa so Janie plumped down into that and then looking up, slowly at first and then more quickly told her trusty friend everything.

She spoke for ages and Jackie didn't interrupt just letting her friend pour out her heart while hoping that she'd be able to remember all the details to pass on to Pauline when she rang her with this latest instalment of Janie's secret lovelife.

Janie explained how Harry had defrauded her and William of her money along with all the other people; probably stolen the cottage in France; about the other women who'd apparently slept with him and how some of them said that they'd done it at his office; about the time when she'd arrived early and found him dishevelled and desperate to get rid of her and how that afternoon he'd struggled to climax. Still feeling shocked she explained how old some of the other women that Harry had slept with had been. Finally she looked at Jackie and said sorrowfully 'There's something else too'.

'On top of all that?'

'Yes' she nodded. 'He' she gulped. 'Apparently he's also ..... umm he's also been sleeping with men ...... you know having sex with some of his male clients'.

'Christ how awful for you'.

'Yes'.

'Are you sure about that?'

'Yes ...... well as sure as I am about all if it. It's what the police have told me but in a way I suppose it didn't surprise me'.

'Why? Did you .... you know .... suspect that he was gay?'

'No I don't think he is. Well he can't be can he? I mean .... when we were together he was ...... he was a brilliant lover. If he was good like that with me and presumably with all the other women then he can't be gay'.

'He could be bi, you know likes women and men'.

'Oh God do you think so?'

'Well why did you say you weren't surprised to find out that he sleeps with men?'

'Because' and her voice dropped and became very quiet forcing Jackie to lean forward so she missed nothing of what Janie was about to say. 'He did .... umm he ..... err that is to say .... we ..... we did it like that. The last time I spent the afternoon with him, the second time he made love to me ....' her voice tailed away 'he did it ......' then whispering she finished 'like men do it........ up the bottom' and she hung her head and sobbed loudly.

'Oh my poor Janie' soothed Jackie moving to sit next to the distraught woman and putting her arms around her. She tried her best to comfort the crying woman although also she really wanted to know whether her friend had enjoyed sex like that but thought that she'd better not ask. Maybe Janie would say. She herself had never done it that way. Mathew had suggested it one night when he was drunk but she'd refused point blank.

Amazed at these latest revelations from Janie she waited to see if there was any more juicy information to come out which she could pass on to Pauline.

'Go on have a good cry it'll help' and she cuddled and calmed her, stroking her hair and holding her tightly. They stayed like that for some time until Janie sniffed loudly and easing herself away looked for a tissue in her handbag.

'Here' offered the other woman grabbing some kitchen roll. 'Have a good blow' and smiled as Janie nodded and did just that. 'Right now I'll make some coffee'.

'Thanks.

Janie sat still staring into space watching as Jackie bustled around rattling cups and waiting while the kettle boiled.

'I guess you haven't said anything to William?'

'Not about Harry no. He knows about the fraud and the possible theft of the cottage but not about Harry. I wouldn't know how to tell him. It'll break his heart. He's a good man and never done me any harm. He'll be so hurt when I tell him'.

'No chance that you can keep it a secret I suppose?'

'No as it'll be bound to come out in court. Or some newspaper will find out. I mean it's a great story isn't it. Lots of rich wives having sex with a fraudster who stole their money and property while shagging them. Think of it. A procession of us in court having to tell all. And then there are the men. It's got everything that a tabloid could want hasn't it?' Money, sex, scandal'.

'I suppose so. Oh you poor thing. When are you going to tell William then? And how? '

'I just don't know' and she looked miserably at her friend as she was handed a mug of coffee.

'Look hold that I'm going to pour in a drop of brandy. It'll do you good' coaxed Jackie and Janie watched as the brown liquid glugged into the mug.

'The trouble is' Janie said quietly 'I can't bring myself to sleep with him, William I mean. I've cheated on him so badly and he's done nothing wrong but I just can't let him'.

'Why?'

'I don't know. Somehow I feel I've defiled myself and so I don't feel it's right to let William into me …. into my body. I know it's silly but I just can't. I suppose I am ashamed of what I've done'.

'You say you've defiled yourself. Isn't that being a bit over dramatic? I mean lots of women, and men for that matter have affairs and if all of them stopped having sex with their husbands or wives the world would collapse. I mean presumably you took precautions, you know condoms and things especially as ....'

'Especially as he was shagging men up the arse as well as me?'

'Exactly'.

'Yes we did, thank God'.

'Well that's good. You've not noticed anything wrong with yourself though have you? Down below I mean. Any signs that things aren't as they should be?'

'No. Oh God do you think I ought to go and have some tests?'

'Might be a good idea. I don't know. Maybe not necessary if you used protection. That's what they're for after all'.

'Yes but they're not infallible are they? And ....' she paused.

'And?'

'We had .... that is I gave him ....' she paused again 'oral sex. Not all the way just as part of, well part of getting ready to make love but sometimes I did it before we put on the condom'.

'And did he, you know do that to you?'

'Yes' she whispered.

'Then it might be a good idea if you went for some tests'.

'But now that you've suggested this until I know the results I won't be able to sleep with William and he's going to get suspicious. We don't have a particularly intense love life. Once a week sometimes twice but that's about it. It's ok and quite enjoyable and he's not bad at it but I've put him off for a few days now and I don't know how long I continue to do that to him?'

The two women continued to talk and gradually Janie felt better.

'Do you want to stay for lunch?'

'No. Thanks for listening. It really has helped just talking to someone I can trust. I'll ring the doctor and get those tests organised' and she gave a little laugh. Seeing Jackie's querying expression she continued 'William suggested this morning that I go and see the doctor. I'd told him my period had started early and was going on for a longer time than usual which was why we couldn't do it'.

'Well there you are then. Make an appointment, then tell William you've had some tests and are waiting for the results. That should keep his ardour under control for a few days until you know the results. If it doesn't then you could always give him a quick hand job. Probably though once you get the all clear, you'll feel able to make love with him again'.

'If I get the all clear' mumbled Janie mournfully.

'Oh come on. I'm sure you'll be ok. Now do let me know if there's anything that I can do won't you and feel free to call round or ring up for a chat anytime'.

'Thanks' and with a little smile Janie gathered up her bag and walked to her car with Jackie beside her.

'Bye. Now Janie, chin up. I'm sure it'll be alright. Remember I'm here if you want me'.

Janie had only just got to the bottom of the drive when Jackie, telephone receiver in hand said 'Pauline. Listen you are not going to believe what I'm about to tell you'.

Janie drove home slowly and as soon as she was indoors rang the surgery to make an appointment for that evening. She was fortunately able to book one of the two lady doctors at the practice as she didn't really want to have to explain why she wanted to be tested or be intimately examined by a male doctor. It would be bad enough having to do it with a woman doctor.

The rest of the day she couldn't concentrate or settle to anything. She checked her e-mails and instinctively looked for one from Harry even though she knew there was no possibility of that happening now. She double checked her "in", "sent", "drafts" and "delete" boxes to ensure there was nothing there, to or from him.

She drank a cup of coffee for lunch and ate a tasteless banana. In the afternoon she wandered over to the stables to see how the rebuilding work was going on.

Eventually she saw that it was four thirty and with her appointment at ten past five she went to the bathroom, squatted over the bidet, washed herself thoroughly, dried carefully and flapped on some talc then in the bedroom pulled on some clean panties, didn't bother with hosiery and getting in the car arrived a few minutes early at the surgery.

Desultorily flicking through an out of date woman's magazine she waited until called to go through to the doctor.

Doctor Sally Hopkins was smart, mid-thirties and generally approachable but Janie found it difficult as she stuttered and stammered at the start of the explanation of why she was there.

Seeing her patient's obvious difficulty and embarrassment the doctor smiled and said 'Look if it is some sort of personal problem you have, don't worry as everything you say in here is utterly confidential you know. Now how can I help you?'

Unable to look at the younger woman, Janie stared at her feet blushing as she explained that she'd had an affair which was now over but she thought she ought to have a check up for sexually transmitted diseases.

'Is there any particular reason or worry that you have about the partner with whom this occurred?'

'I have found out that I wasn't the only one with whom he was sleeping although I didn't know that at the time'.

'I see. Did you take precautions? You know did you use condoms?'

'Yes every time when we had …. umm when we had intercourse'.

'That's good and although not infallible they usually provide a high level of protection' the doctor said reassuringly.

'Yes I know but there were ….. other times ……. erm, other things that we did with each other where we didn't use protection …… well we couldn't …. doing what we did'.

'I assume you mean oral sex?'

'Yes' she said quietly.

'Both ways?'

'Sorry?'

'You performing oral sex on him and he with you?'

'Yes' she whispered blushing furiously.

'That's not so good. Still don't let's worry at this stage. You've no reason to suspect that your partner has any sexual disease have you?'

'No but ………'.

'But Mrs. Hardy?'

'It might be ………'

'Yes? she smiled encouragingly.

'It's might be that he also sleeps with men. I didn't know that either at the time I was involved with him'.

'Umm. Now I have to say that I don't like the sound of that….. but don't let's jump to any unpleasant conclusions at this stage'.

Then she asked several more questions which Janie answered although she still found it difficult to look the doctor in the face, who sensing Janie's continued embarrassment spoke reassuringly.

'Look I've told you that everything is confidential. Furthermore we don't judge people here. We are here to provide advice and medical support. For how long has this relationship been going on?'

Janie told her then answered some more questions about her normal state of health and confirmed that she had not discovered anything untoward and no soreness, swelling, discharge or itching.

'Those are all good signs. Now is this the only non-marital relationship you've had or have there been others either recently ...... or in the past?'

'No it's the only one .... ever ..... since I got married years ago'.

'Good. Now this man with whom you've been having the affair? You say he has been seeing other women and men as well as you?'

'Yes I believe so' replied Janie bitterly.

The doctor pursed her lips. 'Well look I expect everything will be alright' she said quietly 'but someone who has multiple partners does expose themselves and those with whom they have sexual intercourse, to a much higher level of risk. Especially someone who sleeps with men and women. Ok we'll start with a mouth swab. Open wide please'.

Janie did as asked and the doctor wiped a small swab around the insides of her mouth after which she carefully pushed it into a narrow tube.

'Right now I'll have a look at you so slip off your undies and hop up onto the couch will you please. When I've finished examining you I'll take some swabs, a urine sample and some blood to test'.

Taking a pair of latex gloves out of a box she continued as she pulled them on 'Right now I'm going to have a good look around so just relax if you can please'.

The doctor stretched a wide elastic round her head on which a small light was fitted, then put on a pair of special magnifying spectacles as she examined Janie extremely thoroughly. She didn't hurry and while she was having her lower regions pulled gently this way and that Janie just turned her head aside and stared at the wall utterly ashamed of why she was having to have this done.

The last thing she felt was two swabs being taken one of which seemed to probe really deeply inside her. The doctor put them both into special tubes then carefully removed the gloves she'd been wearing.

'Well the good news is that I can't see anything untoward at all. No sores, irritation, warts, lesions, scars or evidence of discharge.

That's good, as if there was anything there that shouldn't be, then something would be showing by now. So far so good. But unfortunately not all possible diseases or infections show up in an obvious physical way at all. That's why we need the swabs, blood and urine samples. Ok you can sit up now'.

Putting on a new pair of latex gloves the doctor took some blood from Janie's arm and then asked her to go to the toilet next door and produce a urine sample.

When she came back carefully clutching the little bottle, the doctor smiled. 'Thanks. Now you can get dressed while I just finish labelling these' and she pointed at the four blood filled vials 'and that' pointing at the urine sample bottle.

Janie pulled her panties back on and smoothed her skirt down as the doctor finished writing on the labels.

'I'll contact you as soon as we get the results through. They'll probably be in three batches. The first two will enable us to rule out everything except HIV. That test will take the longest time, the rest we get pretty quickly. Now try not to worry. One thing though. It might be advisable not to have intimate relations with your husband for a while ..... just until we know for certain. Have you had sex with him since you were involved with this other man?'

'Yes' she replied then added 'but not very often'.

'The number of times doesn't matter. If this man has infected you then once is enough for you to have passed it on to your husband, so my advice is to refrain from now on until we know for sure. I see from your records that you're on the pill so you obviously don't use condoms with your husband'.

'No we don't'.

'Well as I said I do strongly recommend that you refrain from sex with him until we know the situation for sure'.

Janie nodded. 'Yes I understand. Thank you doctor. Erm you won't leave a message or anything will you if I'm not at home when you ring with the results will you?'

'No of course not' Sally laughed.

Driving home Janie was glad that she'd seen the doctor and relieved that she hadn't condemned or passed any form of judgement on her and once home she thought that she'd take up William's offer of supper out and rang a local restaurant to book a table.

Then she rang Jackie and told her that she'd been to the doctor. They chatted for a minute or two and then rang off each to await the arrival home of their respective husbands although Jackie immediately rang Pauline to update her. She in turn promptly passed on the latest information to her friend Tanya who told her husband Gerald when he got home from work.

William looked tired but cheered up when Janie said that she'd booked a restaurant for them and it was as they were relaxing over their main course that she told him she'd been to the doctor.

'Everything alright darling?' he asked looking quite concerned.

Oh yes everything's great. I'm probably riddled with all kinds of horrible sexual diseases, am going to die slowly and painfully from aids, almost certainly will have infected you and when I tell you all about it you'll be distraught and horrified with me.

'Yes she examined me and has taken a swab and some blood and urine samples. She should have the results soon. In the meantime I'm afraid sex is out of the question for a little while longer. Sorry darling'.

'Oh I quite understand. Just as long as you're ok that's all that matters' and he smiled kindly at her.

'Thanks' and she covered his hand with her own and squeezed. 'I am so lucky to be married to you'.

Bloody right you are, but for how much longer when he finds out what a rotten filthy slut you are. Really You're nothing but a dirty little whore.

The rest of the evening passed pleasantly enough and she even felt able to converse with him on a number of subjects until he drove them home to Wood Hollow Hall.

'I'm going to have a bath and then go to bed if that's alright' she said as he poured himself a malt whisky.

Being careful to continue the deception she again left the Tampax box in an obvious position in the bathroom having removed several towels. He'd be sure to see it and hopefully continue to accept her reasons for no sex.

Her last thought before dropping off to sleep was what she would do if the tests revealed that she was diseased and worse still if it then transpired that she'd passed something on to William as a result of her affair with Harry.

Next morning William was in the office early as he wanted to attend the weekly review meeting of progress held by Steve and Emily. They were doing their best to manage his feelings by including him in certain meetings and hence making him still feel part of the business but things were becoming more difficult for him as he missed not being Chairman and felt a bit like a spare part as he listened to discussions and watched decisions being made about his business.

No, not my business any more he had to keep reminding himself. It was the Bank's business now and although he hoped that one day it might come back into his personal control he also frequently reminded himself that business life was tough now. He admired the way Steve seemed to take every set back in his stride, not be fazed by problems and with the support of Emily handle in a calm competent way the myriad of issues that flowed onto his desk.

And issues there were in plenty. The Bank was a hard demanding taskmaster and rang daily to check on progress and the cash situation. Steve started to visit customers himself alongside John Benton the existing Sales and Marketing Director as it was proving a slow process to find a suitable replacement.

***

The difficulty for Nigel Charlesworthy the head hunter was that really top flight candidates were reluctant to take on the role at an ailing consumer business that was teetering on the brink of bankruptcy. Unlike Travis Anderson who had already made the switch out of permanent employment and into Interim management as his career choice, hot shot Sales and Marketing Directors were always especially careful about managing their careers and wanted to be sure that each and every move they made was not only good for them personally but was seen by their industry to be a good move.

For this reason above everything else, all the candidates Nigel had seen when told of the company and it's difficult circumstances, shied away as the last thing they wanted was to try and defend a potentially dying business from going bust as if it did collapse they didn't want themselves or their careers associated with it. Connection with failure was not an attractive career option for them.

Nigel spoke again to each of his researchers and re-briefed them. To all of them he finished by saying 'Look, somewhere out there in the big wide world is someone who will see this not as a potential blot of their career, but an opportunity to shine. Now just find me that person'.

***

Travis Anderson though had settled in well and immediately started to make an impact. On the morning of his second day he'd travelled to London for a meeting with the key people in the Bank, confirmed the strategy to which the business was working, impressed all of those he'd met, leaving them with confidence that here was a tough, effective Finance Director who was just what the business needed.

In the afternoon he visited one of the company's major suppliers who had been pressing hard for payment of their outstanding bills and threatening to withhold further stocks unless the account was settled. In a calm yet extremely firm way he outlined the new business plan, agreed to pay immediately half of what was outstanding, and pay off the remaining balance over the next two months in weekly instalments. In return he wanted continued supplies assured, longer payment terms, a return to more normality in the relationship between the two businesses including a cessation of the hostile attitude that they'd been adopting towards Hardys.

While they thought about that he reminded them that as they were one of Hardys key and major suppliers whose products were essential manufacturing ingredients if they didn't help then the business would probably go bust and they'd probably not get back any of their outstanding monies. They agreed to his proposal and he drove back to Norfolk highly satisfied with his day's work.

Equally Emily and Steve were delighted with the news of the re-negotiated terms with the supplier and suggested some more of their suppliers who were also pressing hard for clearance of their outstanding accounts for him to tackle.

'No problem. We've gunned one down, now we're gonna round up the rest of 'em' he grinned. Emily noticed that when he grinned his mouth went slightly lop sided which she thought was very attractive.

Next day Steve had a meeting with the Trades Union for the site as he intended to freeze the annual pay round. This was likely to be a difficult meeting and it wasn't helped by the fact that William before had been seen as soft and something of a pushover when he was negotiating with the Union.

William's grandfather had always refused to negotiate with or even recognise trade unions and had managed to maintain this stance over the years, because he treated the workforce fairly and they knew it.

However when the old man died and William's father had taken over the reins he'd seen the way that the tide of industrial relations was moving and realised that to continue to refuse to recognise the Union would lead to continual strife and a gradual reduction in good relationships between the company and the workforce.

So reluctantly at first but then with increasing willingness he had fully supported his workers right to belong to a Trades Union and had embraced the opportunity by seeing that rather than the Union being an enemy of the company, if workers rights, grievances and demands were handled properly and sensibly then the Union and especially it's shop stewards, could become useful as the company and workforce worked together.

That didn't mean that he was easy to negotiate with and he had quickly established a reputation for taking a tough uncompromising approach to negotiations with the Union especially when it concerned wage rates.

Although they hadn't liked it they did respect him and his ability and they knew that at the end of the day whilst it certainly wouldn't be a generous outcome, it would be fair to both parties.

That approach lasted for the years that William's father ran the business. He faced down unrealistic wage demands, refused to give in to threatened strike action, forced change and modernisation through when required and generally found that providing he and his Personnel and Human Resources people worked hard at industrial relations then there was little that they couldn't do.

He used to tell his directors and managers 'Remember that although our work force may have different horizons, different goals and objectives from us here in the Boardroom, at the end of the day they want four things out of their working life.

Firstly, security of employment. Next a fair days pay for a fair days work. Thirdly to understand where the company is going, what it's doing and why. Lastly to be treated fairly, honestly and as you would want to be treated yourself if you were in their shoes. That' he would boom 'is the secret of good industrial relations'. Generally he was right.

William though was different. Without the strength of character of his father, nervous of standing up to tough union negotiators, frightened of what they might do if they went on strike or go slow, instead of facing them down he gave in. Time and time again.

But now as three shop stewards and two full time union officers entered the Boardroom they were uncertain of this new chap Steve. Of course they were aware of the company's difficulties. They weren't fools and realised that the most important thing at the moment was for everyone to work together to keep the company afloat. This was not the time to screw the company to the wall. It was already there with its back firmly jammed against it with no room to manoeuvre.

However concessions made now had to be paid for at some stage in the future. They expected the company to say that it couldn't afford any pay rises and to some extent they were prepared to go along with that for the time being as long as they got some agreement to correct and catch up at some designated time in the future.

What they weren't expecting though was after the opening pleasantries and short presentation by Emily on the parless state of the business, for Steve to open the discussions by asking for everyone at shop floor level to take a ten percent pay cut. He added that he was also going to be asking for all office staff to take a similar cut, for all managers in both officers and factory to take a twelve and a half percent cut, for all senior managers to take a fifteen percent cut and for directors to take a twenty percent cut. While the union team were digesting that he continued with his list of changes.

'Next I want to discuss overtime and the changes that I need to bring in there. At the moment anything above eight hours on a shift is classed as overtime. I want to move that to nine hours. In other words the first additional hour is paid at standard rate and not time and a half.

As far as the actual overtime pay rates are concerned, then I want to change away from all overtime being paid at time and a half, to the first two hours being paid at time and a quarter and overtime only paid at time and a half from hour three onwards'.

'Hang on' grumbled Clive Higgins the senior union man. 'What you're saying is that the normal eight hour shift is to become nine hours and all those hours paid at ten percent less than now. Then hours ten and eleven paid at time and a quarter not time and a half, and my members have got to work for twelve hours before they get back to time and a half. Is that right?'

'That's about the size of it ………. for weekdays'.

'Weekdays?'

'Yes as weekend rates also have to come down. Saturdays will be paid at normal weekday rates with overtime as just explained and Sundays will be paid at time and three quarters not double time'.

The union team looked dumfounded.

'That's for starters'.

'Starters? There's more?' asked one union man incredulously.

'Yes. I also need a small redundancy programme to reduce the workforce by around eight percent. Then I've got some other things I want to re-negotiate and get rid of some of the strange and inefficient practices that exist here. But the redundancy, main pay reduction and lower overtime rates are the most important of the changes that we are going to have to implement.

Now I realise that this will have been a bit of a surprise to you fellows so if you want to go away and think about it for a little while, please feel free to do so and then let's reconvene to discuss it'.

'Yea I think we'd better have a break 'cos what you've proposed will be wholly unacceptable to our members'.

'As unacceptable as us closing the business and them all being out of work?' asked Emily staring straight at Clive 'because that is the alternative'.

'It might happen in any case if we can't do three things' added Steve. 'Get our sales up, manage our scarce cash inflow and crucially lower our costs and that's why these pay cuts are so important. In fact in the very short term the cost reduction is the most important of all'.

The union team stared at Steve, Emily, William and Travis who sat silently saying nothing so far but when just the four of them were alone he grinned his lop sided grin as he spoke to Steve.

'Do you play poker buddy?'

'A bit sometimes yes. Why?'

'Thought so. I reckon you're like those old time hustlers on the Mississippi steam boats who were the best darn poker payers there were at that time as they learnt that bluff if done convincingly, worked. They also knew when to dig in and when to fold. Now I reckon I'm a pretty good poker player and I'll play you sometime mister but I'll be mighty careful how I call the cards when I'm up against you!'

Steve grinned. 'Well come on then odds on us succeeding. Em?'

'Forty percent'.

'Ah hah. Travis?'

'Sixty, maybe seventy percent that you'll get some of what you've asked for but not all'.

'We'll see' mused Steve quietly. 'William?'

'I just don't know, I really don't'.

It was about an hour later when the five union men returned to the Board room looking unhappy. Clive spoke first.

'We came here today to discuss the future of the company and how we could help. We also wanted to talk about pay rates for our members and were expecting the company to say that because they were in difficulty they couldn't give our members a full or proper pay rise. We could have understood that and would have been prepared to discuss it.

What we didn't expect was to be told that there was to be a redundancy programme and that our members pay was being cut. In all my years of negotiations with employers I have to tell you Steve that this is the first time that I've come in to discuss a pay rise and been offered a pay cut. I've been offered pay freezes before. I've been offered delays in pay increases. I've been offered stage payments but not a bloody pay cut' and his voice had risen angrily.

'First time for everything' Travis said quietly.

'No need for smart arse comments like that' snapped Clive.

'Not being smart arsed, just kinda making conversation' smiled the big American.

'Well it ain't helpful' continued the union man now thoroughly riled. 'We are just not accepting what you say Steve. If you want to discuss a pay freeze well ok we don't like it but we're realistic. We know the company has difficulties and we'd like to help in some way. We are a responsible Trades Union and not here to damage or add to the company's problems but a pay cut just ain't on' and he glared across the table.

'Pity' Steve replied leaning back. 'I am glad to hear though that you want to help the company through it's current difficulties, but you see if you guys don't help us by accepting that we have to cut our costs then the future is bleak. Very bleak. In fact I can't see that we'll survive so I will have to ask for another meeting with the bank and tell them that sadly we aren't going to be able to cut costs sufficiently to turn the business round and therefore they'd better start planning to wind the company up'.

'You're not serious. This was a good business once and surely it can be again?' but although spoken strongly there was a look of real worry on the face of Phil Grayson the number two union man.

'Was is the operative word' said Emily. 'Was. In the past. Not now and if we don't sort it out then not in the future either....... as it won't be here. Then where will your members be eh? Out of work and I would remind you this is a big workforce here and jobs in Norwich and Norfolk are not two a penny. I doubt whether many of them will get back into comparable employment or if they do it'll take some time. So think very carefully before you push Steve into such a tight corner that he has no option but to call the Bank'.

There was silence for a while.

'Look the last thing we want is our members out of work. You don't either but we simply can't go back to them and say that we've agreed a pay cut' muttered Clive.

'Go back and tell them then that they'll all be out of work in three months then!' warned Emily.

'Seems to me fellas, that you ain't gotta lot of choice. Now we don't want to cause you problems but you have to understand that we are not joking here. What you oughta do though instead of getting all kinda steamed up and saying you can't or won't accept it, is to ask Steve about pay rises in the future when ……. if …….. we turn this motherfucker around. That could be a more fruitful approach to this issue than us all sitting here banging away at each other' drawled Travis in a relaxed manner. 'Yea that's what I'd do if I was you' he finished.

'Well you ain't me are yer?' grumbled Clive 'but ok if, and I say if, we were prepared to consider what you've suggested how do you see things panning out for the future?'

That was the turning point of the discussions. Emily outlined the strategic business plan, was open with the union team as to the risks and opportunities that were within it, explained the timescales by which improvements had to happen.

Travis took the union team through the current and future predicted finances and they could see just how precarious the company's position was.

Steve then rounded up and summarised what Emily and Travis had said. 'Look you've heard from all of us now. We've been totally open with you and held nothing back. We need those cost savings but I will commit here and now to three things.

Firstly we'll meet with you weekly to update you on progress good or bad. Secondly we'll rework our numbers to see if we could manage maybe to cut a point or two off the percentage reductions we've proposed and lastly I guarantee that if we succeed in turning this business round as soon as we are able to do so we'll embark on a programme of restoring the wage rates firstly back to where they are right now and secondly to start a process of increasing them.

The redundancies we've proposed will be voluntary and not compulsory at this stage and with your help we'll probably get the numbers of people that we want putting up their hands to volunteer.

So can we do a deal on that basis or are we going to dig in for a long fight? Your call'.

'We need another recess'.

'Take all the time you need'.

Alone again Steve, William, Emily and Travis discussed the position. Both Emily and Travis raised their percentage estimates of likely success but William remained gloomy and refused to commit to a figure.

'By the way Steve' queried Emily 'you never said what you think are the chances of success? What is your estimate?'

'Same now as earlier, ninety nine percent. I'd say one hundred but there's always a tiny element of uncertainty in these things. Tell you what though we ought to bring in Rod Jackson now for the final session. After all he is head of Human Resources and Industrial Relations and he'll be the key person in maintaining contact and also monitoring and briefing our progress to the Union fellows. I'll call him'.

Rod joined them and was quickly briefed. 'Well if you pull that off it'll be a very useful first step forward won't it' he commented when he'd understood the proposal that the union team were considering.

'Steve we're going to take you on trust' stated Clive when he and his colleagues returned. 'We are prepared to put your proposal to our members. It'll be up to them to decide whether they are prepared to accept it or not'.

'Will you recommend it's acceptance though?' asked Emily.

There was a pause as Clive looked at her then glanced quickly at his team who nodded. 'Yes we will recommend that the company's proposal be accepted but we would like you to address the workforce first and give them a potted version of what you've told us about the company's financial position? After all if we're going to work together to solve this problem it would be seen as a bit of solidarity between management and union. Then when you've done that we'll take over, outline the offer, propose acceptance and deal with the problems'.

'That's a very positive approach. Thank you' replied Steve. 'Yes we'd be happy to talk to the workforce. Now you'll need a day or two to get things organised so let us know when and we'll do our bit. This could be an interesting Industrial relations co-operative venture. Management and workforce working together to save the company'.

'Union and Management working together' corrected Clive.

'Yes ok union, management .... and workforce working together.

There were nods and smiles all round as everyone shook hands. The union team left to organise their side of things and the management team sat back to review the successful meeting.

William who had been given strict instructions in private by Steve not to enter the discussions and that apart from saying hello and good bye he was to remain silent throughout, had been amazed at the audacity of Steve's approach and even more he was astounded that the union seemed to have accepted it. He also knew that he personally would not have been able to force through such a radical programme.

However he was glad that it seemed that it might be accepted, as he knew enough about industrial relations to know that normally, although not always, if a union recommended their members should accept a proposal then generally it was accepted by the membership when they came to vote on it.

***

At about the time that Steve, Emily, Travis and William were reviewing the outcome of the meeting Janie received a phone call.

'Mrs. Hardy?'

'Yes'.

'Hello Mrs. Hardy. This is Doctor Hopkins from the surgery. I thought I'd ring you straight away as we have the first set of results from your tests'.

Janie's heart plummeted as she waited with baited breath for what the doctor said next.

'It is good news I'm pleased to say. All the results we've got so far are negative. That means there is no infection for those things for which we've got the results. There is a second batch to come tomorrow and then the HIV results by the end of the week. Now do you want me to run through the ones for which you are clear?'

'Yes please' she gasped then listened with some revulsion as the doctor called out several horrid sounding diseases, the names of some of which she recognised but many she'd never heard of before. 'Presumably if this lot are clear then the likelihood is that the others will be too?'

'No I'm afraid I can't say that Mrs. Hardy. Each potential disease is distinct, separate and able to infect you in its own right, but let's say it's encouraging. It is good news so far'.

'Right thank you. You'll call me as soon as you get the other test results?'

'Of course as soon as I have them I'll ring you, good or bad. But let's keep our fingers crossed shall we? Goodbye'.

Janie sat holding the dead telephone receiver staring at it and seeing the doctor's face as she absorbed the news. So far so good then and although her spirits lifted a little she was still dogged by a feeling of dread that something horrible might be within her body.

'Oh God Harry' she muttered softly, 'how could you?' then she realised the oddity of what she'd just said. How could he what? Swindle her? Sleep with other woman? Sleep with men? Infect her?

But he hadn't infected her. Well not on that list of diseases the doctor had read out and he'd never promised to be faithful to her. He'd said lots of lovely things to her and about her, often when they were cuddled together after making love but he'd never made her any promises of her being his only woman.

Nor had she for that matter. He'd never asked her if she was having an affair with anyone else.

'Oh God' she whispered 'what a mess'.

The body of a sensualist is the coffin of a dead soul.

Christian Nevell Bovee.

CHAPTER 18

The next day the doctor rang Janie to say that she'd got the next batch of test results and they also were all clear, so now there was just the HIV result to come.

***

Clive rang Steve to say that they'd set up the various meetings with the workforce for tomorrow, one in the late morning at the end of the morning shift, one at the start of the afternoon shift and then one at ten o'clock in the evening for the night shift. Steve confirmed that he, Emily, Travis and Rod would be there.

The following day three meetings with the workforce duly took place at the factory. The management team from Hardys spoke clearly and concisely about the problems of the company and how they planned to work to put things back on course. They also said that they had a cost cutting programme that affected the workforce which they had discussed with the union representatives and that it would be they that would outline that plan to the workforce.

Steve, Emily, Rod and Travis then withdrew back to Steve's office and waited for the outcome.

The meeting was in the large staff canteen and was a noisy affair. When Clive Higgins outlined the proposed redundancy programme there was not too much dissent but when he put forward the management's proposals for wage cuts there was uproar and it took several minutes of Clive and his colleagues shouting 'Brothers listen' before eventually the noise died down and he was able to continue.

'Brothers look. I don't like this proposal at all ………'

'Well why didn't you tell them to fuck off then' yelled someone from the crowd and several voices joined in agreeing with the sentiment.

'Because brothers it is the only option. The Management have shown us the numbers. They've shown us how seriously this company is in trouble. If the costs aren't lowered then the company will go to the wall and none of you will have jobs'.

'Bollocks. Just Management bullshit' yelled another meeting attendee.

'No brothers. This isn't just Management bluff. I repeat that we've seen the books and I cannot bring myself to be party to seeing the business collapse and all of you out of work.

We've got an undertaking from Management that as soon as things get better then they will restore wages, maybe not all in one go but gradually to where they are now and then they plan to increase them. But brothers and it is a big but .... the company has to become successful and you can help in that process.

Now we're going to be watching and monitoring the progress. The Management have offered us a weekly meeting to review the results. We'll be right up there fighting for you, your jobs, your rights and your wages.

You know me and you know that you can trust me. I am telling you that if you don't accept the motion that we will put to you shortly then within a couple of months at the outside you'll be out of work here, all of you.

Now are there any questions?'

There were several but they mainly fell into three areas. Why had the company got into the mess that it had? How good were this new management team to put it right and could they be trusted? When did Clive think that wages would get restored to current levels?

Finally there were no more questions so taking a deep breath Clive Higgins took a firm grip of the microphone and asked for a show of hands on the motion before the workforce.

It wasn't overwhelming but it was a lot more than half who put their hands in the air to accept and when he asked for those against it was a noticeably smaller display of raised hands.

'I declare that the motion is carried' he boomed. 'Right brothers thank you for your support and we will be working day and night with the management to protect your interests'.

When the afternoon shift went to their meeting, news had already filtered through of what it was all about, nevertheless Steve and his team made the same presentation as earlier and then left Clive and his colleagues from the union to repeat their session.

When asked to vote on the motion again it was favourable but the margin of acceptance showed a larger majority than from the morning's meeting.

'Well there you are Steve' said Clive as he walked into Steve's office after the second meeting. 'We've got two of em through for you'.

'Yes thank you. Now what do you think about the night shift?'

'They'll know all about it of course from phone calls and discussions with the morning and afternoon lot but it's important that you and your team also come and present tonight. We mustn't be seen to treat them any less importantly than the other two shifts. Also they are a more difficult bunch so I am less relaxed about them. Still we'll know in a few hours.

We're counting the ballot forms now. Shows of hands are one thing but it's ticks on the ballot papers that matter. Sometimes blokes are reluctant to stand out against their comrades in an open meeting but a secret ballot, ah that's another thing'.

'You don't think there's any chance that it won't go through on the ballot forms do you?'

'No. It'll go through alright with that show of hands and if roughly the same number as put their hands up in favour of supporting the company tick the boxes then we'll only need a small majority of the night shift to vote yes and we'll have an overall majority in favour. See you at ten then ok?'

Steve nodded and bent his head to some papers on his desk but he looked up again when Clive stopped at the door and said 'Course if the entire night shift vote against ….. then the overall majority will be less than fifty percent ….. and then we're fucked. So you'd better lay it on thick tonight with the risks and all that'. With a cheery grin but that worrying thought he left.

It was about seven o'clock when Emily walked into Steve's office.

'What you doing about eating tonight? I've spoken to Travis and he was going to work here till about eight then go and find somewhere for a meal then come back here for the ten o'clock session. Haven't spoken to Rod yet'.

'Yes that sounds sensible. Look round up Rod and see if he wants to join us for a meal somewhere. Tonight of all nights we'd better find somewhere cheap and cheerful as if we are seen stuffing our faces in some swanky restaurant when we're asking the workforce to take a pay cut we'd probably get lynched ...... and quite right too'.

So it was about nine o'clock when the four of them were sitting in a burger bar not far from the factory having eaten their meal and were drinking coffee when Rod acknowledged a couple of men who came in and ordered cheeseburgers and large fries.

'Couple of our night shift supervisors' he said quietly.

Sharp on ten Steve stood up in the canteen and started to repeat the presentation for the third time that day.

It was almost eleven when a weary Clive walked into Steve's office and said 'Ok you've got your majority ...... just. Less than thirty percent of the night shift voted in favour ...... but it's enough when added to the morning and afternoon shifts.

Now my neck is on the line for you lot so don't you let me down. My Divisional Officer at the Union thinks I'm mad to have agreed to this deal but I am prepared to trust you. However I warn you ...... all of you' he said menacingly as he pointed his finger at Steve, Emily, Travis and Rod 'if you bugger me around, try and play me for a monkey or fuck me up in any way at all .... I'll have that workforce out on indefinite strike quicker than you can say union. Clear? Right now I'm knackered and it's time to go home. Good night all'.

'Come on I could murder one of your English pints' announced Travis when the union men had left. 'What say we all go to the Shepherds Arms down the road for a quick one before we go home?'

It was nearly twelve in the pub after first Rod and then Travis had left that Steve turned to Emily.

'Well done today. I thought you did your part of the presentations extremely well'.

'Thanks. In a funny way I enjoyed it but it was a bit stressful though. In fact I still feel a bit tense even now. Good result though isn't it?'

'Yes it is ...... and I know an ideal cure for stress'.

'You do' and with an intriguing smile she continued 'and what's that? Wouldn't have anything to do with bed and sex would it?'

'I didn't say that but if you're suggesting it and trying to seduce me?'

'Oh come on Steve. Let's stop playing games. Would you like to come to my place tonight?'

'Yes if that's alright'.

'Uh huh I think I'd like that'.

They each got into their own cars and drove in convoy to her rented flat. When they were inside they kissed and then ever practical Emily stroked Steve's face feeling the day old stubble before asking 'Do you want to play all kissey cuddle or shall we just go straight to bed ….. right now'.

He kissed her again, leant back, smiled and said softly 'I think going to bed right now sounds a perfect idea'.

When they were in bed she ran her fingers around his chin. 'Umm now be careful with that prickly chin. I don't want you to make me sore'.

'I'll be careful'

'You'd better be' she chuckled as she pushed him onto his back, twisted herself round to face his feet, lowered her pussy onto his face and said quietly 'now be very careful down there. I want you to tease and excite me, not scratch or make me uncomfortable'.

'And what will you be doing while I do that? he asked after he'd run his chin over her pussy lips once.

'Yes that's it. Just like that. What will I be doing? Well I think I might amuse myself with this' she muttered as she slid her lips over his erection.

So while she did that he used his prickly chin extremely gently before switching to using his tongue and fingers. They sixty-nined for a long time until swivelling back round and sitting on his chest she leaned down, popped a kiss on his lips told him that he'd got her nicely excited then she leaned over, opened the bedside drawer, took a condom, slit it open, rolled it over him then slowly lowered her pussy to engulf him deeply within her.

They moved well with each other and it was a prolonged, satisfying session of lovemaking until Steve pulled her face down to his lips, kissed her hard then muttered 'I'm about to come baby'.

'Good because I am too' and almost immediately he felt her pussy gripping and releasing his prick as she shuddered into her orgasm which triggered off his ejaculation.

Later they lay cuddled together in each other's arms, told each other that it had been good tonight, said thank you to each other and were soon asleep, happy and contented.

***

Not so far away in Wood Hollow Hall, William had gone to sleep frustrated as he had really wanted to make love to Janie but she'd said a very firm no explaining that she wasn't yet free from her period but she did lie there for ages worrying and recognising that sometime soon she'd have to let him. The odd thing was though that she'd almost felt a twinge of desire tonight when he turned towards her and stroked her shoulder but she simply had to wait for the last test result from Doctor Hopkins to know if she was HIV positive or not.

Next morning was Friday and it dawned cloudy, windy and pouring with rain which she hoped wasn't an ill omen.

William was up early as he was going to London to represent Hardys at an industry conference. He wasn't speaking there just socialising and playing his role as ambassador as outlined for him on the day that his role as Chairman had been made purely nominal and Steve and Emily had taken over.

Janie went back to sleep after he'd left but when she did get up she saw that the team of workmen were sitting in their hut as it was obviously too wet to work on the stable block rebuilding. This was starting to come along well and all the footings were complete and the walls were starting to be rebuilt using old materials in keeping with the house itself and ensuring that when finally complete it resembled the original as much as possible.

***

When Steve woke he couldn't see Emily but he heard sounds of running water from the bathroom so he padded into there where she was bent over the hand basin washing her hair. He stood for a few moments admiring her long legs but also her cute backside which was wiggling around under her nightie.

Quietly he sidled up behind her then putting his hands around her waist he squeezed gently and leant forward to drop a kiss on her neck.

'Get off' she spluttered twisting round to look at him.

316

'You look really cute like that with your bum wiggling about' he laughed as he slid a hand under her nightie and lifted it up. 'Umm' he murmured staring at her exposed bottom 'very cute'.

'Leave me alone' she laughed flapping a shampoo covered hand at him.

'You could just stay there and carry on while I ……..' and he rubbed himself against her.

'I told you leave me alone.'

Turning round to face him she flipped a wedge of shampoo foam at his face. 'I'm sorry if I woke you but my hair needed a wash so I decided to get up early and do it this morning. I had planned to do it last night but other things seemed to take place which prevented me. Any rate what time is it?'

'Did they?' his morning erection still standing out strongly and pressing against his shorts. 'To answer your question it's just after seven, so why don't you get that hair finished and dried and then come back to bed?'

'Will we have time?'

'Depends on how long you're going to be fiddling about in here with your hair' he replied pushing his crotch forward so his erect prick pressed against her.

'Alright go and keep that ready for me then' she said patting him. I'll be as quick as I can'.

Sure enough it was only a few minutes later that she returned to the bedroom, took her hairdryer out of the dressing table, knelt down to plug it in giving Steve a wonderful view of her naked bottom as the nightie rode up when she leaned forward then sat down in front of the mirror and started to dry her long dark hair.

He watched for a while then sensing that she was nearly finished got out of bed naked, walked to her and putting his arms around her started stroking her breasts.

Her nightie had a high neck and she was sitting on the hem so try as he might he couldn't get inside it so he contented himself with playing with her breasts and nipples from outside until suddenly she put down the hairdryer, switched it off and turning put her arms around him and kissing him hard pushed her tongue deep into his mouth.

He half carried, half pulled her to the bed where he lifted up her nightie as she held up her arms to help him take to off. Kissing her he handed over a condom foil which she rapidly opened and rolled down him.

Gently he pressed her onto her back, rolled himself on top of her and checking that she was moist and ready for him slid deep within her.

She grunted as she felt him fully engage with her then she wriggled to get more comfortable, wrapped her legs around his waist, looked up and smiling said quietly 'Let's see what you are like after a good night's rest then'.

He concentrated on making it good for her and when he heard her breathing getting louder and her arms held him much more tightly he knew she was close to reaching her climax. The problem was that he was too, but gritting his teeth he kept moving within her until he felt her nails dig into his shoulders as she let out a long soft moan which seemed to go on for a considerable period of time. As she quietened down he pistoned into her more quickly and also groaned, as he exploded into the rubber.

They lay with their arms around each other for some time until by mutual consent they eased apart and lay side by side.

'So verdict?'

'Ok'.

'Only ok? Come on Em I really tried to make it good for you'.

Laughing loudly she leaned across and kissed his nose. 'You did Steve. I'm teasing you. Actually it was great, thanks but .... and she twisted to look at the little bedside clock 'we ought to get up now. Do you want to shower first or second?'

'Can I go first then I'll shave and go. I need to be in a bit earlier this morning. You can swan in whenever you feel that you are ready to grace us with your presence!'

He got out of bed just quickly enough to avoid the slap that she aimed at him and laughing while blowing a kiss he walked towards the door paused and said, his face suddenly serious 'It was great for me too you know. Thank you'.

It didn't take long for him to shower and shave and back in the bedroom he dressed while she was in the shower carefully avoiding getting her hair wet again. She had just stepped out of the shower when he stuck his head into the bathroom.

'Umm you are lovely you know' he commented openly looking her naked body up and down. 'Right I'm off. Catch up later in the office. Bye' and with that he was gone.

As she dressed she reflected that she was really getting to like Steve and for a moment wondered if maybe more might develop in this relationship than just work colleagues, friends and occasional lovers as the mood or need suited them. It was a long time since she'd had any sort of serious relationship. Could Steve be the person with whom she might start one again? Still pondering this happy thought she drove into work arriving just on nine.

She went straight into a planning meeting with the sales and marketing teams where Kelly blushing furiously, offered to take the notes of points discussed and actions agreed when Emily asked for a volunteer.

Steve started his day by sitting down with Travis and together they re-established a priority order for suppliers to be paid then he went and walked through the whole of the factory stopping frequently to talk to people on their own or in little groups. He went everywhere and into every department and sensed that although some clearly resented the fact that next week their pay was being cut, many others were happy to know that they'd still got a job and philosophically accepted that if the price of the hoped for long term survival of Hardys was some short term financial pain, then they'd put up with it.

It took him more than three hours as he deliberately didn't want to rush or to be seen to be afraid of talking to people or responding to challenge or arguments.

Although he didn't know it, his actions were much appreciated by the workforce and they decided that for the moment they'd give him the benefit of the doubt and log him as a good bloke who really was trying to sort out the company.

***

Janie felt lethargic but decided that in view of the two lots of good news from Dr. Hopkins she should snap herself out of it. After all there was only the HIV test result to come.

Ah yes! Only the HIV result? Oh nothing to worry about there then. Forget the fact that if it was positive she'd eventually die a slow lingering death from some awful aids related illness.

She rang Jackie and said that she was coming over for a ride but preferred to go out on her own if she didn't mind. Although trilling lightly 'No of course not' actually she was disappointed as she wanted to find out the latest instalment of Janie's private life and what was happening.

Janie enjoyed her ride and returning after a couple of hours felt brighter, fresher and more relaxed. Riding did that to her. She was a good rider and enjoyed it whether just ambling along country lanes, chasing a pack of fox hounds although now that hunting had been banned that was illegal and the hunt had to follow a scented rag, or just galloping fast across country.

Today had been fast galloping and cantering across countryside she didn't know well and that added to the enjoyment.

***

Rod had organised a meeting for twelve o'clock in the canteen for all the office staff so that he, Steve, Emily and Travis could explain how they needed to cut their salaries in line with the factory operatives.

They were listened to in silence. At the end there were a few questions but everyone trooped off either to the food counters or back to their offices.

The company had prepared letters for each of the managers and senior managers and Rod and his team spent most of the afternoon hand delivering them around the offices and factory advising them the specific details of their pay cuts.

The Bank was pleased to hear the good news of the acceptance by the workforce of the redundancy programme and the pay reductions.

Travis finished the day satisfied with the progress he'd made in chasing customers for payment of outstanding bills and offered some discounts for payment to be made in future within seven days and to his pleasure several of their customers had accepted.

Steve finished the day pleased with this week's work and results and not only felt right on top of the job but more and more convinced that this was a project in which he would succeed.

Emily finished her day happy that the planning session had gone well but made a note that Steve really must chase up that head hunter to get them a new Sales and Marketing Director.

Rod finished the week surprised but full of admiration for the way Steve had managed the wage reduction exercise and realised that the business was now being led by an extremely competent individual and he could understand why the Bank had given him the job.

William finished the week sitting in a first class compartment on the way back from a conference in London having played his ambassador role well and had learnt to parry the odd pointed question from various people as to what was happening at Hardys.

Janie finished the week still desperately worried about the outstanding HIV test and also how she'd ever be able to tell William about Harry.

Kelly finished her week absolutely ecstatic. She'd taken the notes at the marketing and sales meeting as agreed and when the meeting finished had hurried to get them typed up on her computer, carefully checked them then printed off a copy and taken them to Emily's office.

'Oh you needn't have rushed them out today. Monday would have done quite well then you could have e-mailed them to me but as you've brought them I'll have a quick look through them now shall I?'

The smitten young woman stood watching as her idol carefully read the papers, made a couple of changes then smiled and handed them back

'Thanks very much'.

'Oh it was no trouble. I'll e-mail them out to everyone before I go this evening. Umm I think your hair looks lovely today. You've styled it differently haven't you?'

'Not intentionally but I was in a bit of a rush this morning after I'd washed it so it probably hasn't gone quite right. Still the weekend is coming up so I'll probably have another go at it. Are you doing any special?'

'I'm going clubbing tomorrow with a group of friends. Nothing else organised yet though. Probably just play things by ear'.

'That sounds fun. Hope you enjoy yourself. Don't get too drunk' cautioned Emily putting on a mock serious expression.

'No I won't. Actually I don't drink much. Well I can't really. If I have more than a couple I get piss ….. err sorry, sloshed. Have you got anything nice organised … for the weekend I mean?'

'No. I've not made any real plans yet. Probably just chill out and relax but I might go out with a friend for dinner tomorrow if he's free'.

'Will that be with your boyfriend?'

'No I don't have a boyfriend' she laughed 'well no one special that is, but it might be with a man who is just a friend of mine. It's Kelly isn't it?'

'Yes' she replied blushing as Emily smiled straight at her.

'Right Kelly well thanks again for those notes and for doing them so quickly. Enjoy your weekend. You must pop in on Monday and tell me all about your clubbing night and whether you find yourself a hunky man eh?'

Kelly just nodded. She was too overcome to speak and turning walked quickly out of her dream lady's office and back to her own work station where she made the couple of changes that Emily had marked then e-mailed it to all the meeting attendees before sitting staring at her computer screen doing very little more work and running through in her mind every moment in Emily's office until it was time to go home.

Back in her little bed sit she sat for ages holding the framed photo and couldn't wait for Monday to come when she'd been invited to go and tell Emily all about her weekend. It was a little after ten when she showered and put on a pretty pink nightie and got into bed.

Once again she picked up her idol's picture and smiling moved it towards her face and kissed the glass covered lips then putting the frame back on her bedside table and without taking her eyes off Emily's picture she raised her bottom to enable her to lift the nightie free and sliding one hand onto her bush and the other into her pussy she slowly and gently massaged herself to a climax. Her eyes never wavered once nor moved away from Emily's picture.

***

William got home about seven and Janie kissed him, trying to act as normally as she could. He was just pouring her a gin and tonic before getting his own whisky when the phone rang. He picked it up and listened for a moment said 'Hold on please' and handed the instrument to her.

'It's a doctor Hopkins for you'.

'Oh thanks' she replied calmly before walking into the hall but her heart was thumping so strongly she thought her rips would crack.

'Hello?'

'Mrs. Hardy?'

'Yes'.

'Good evening this is Doctor Hopkins. Look I'm sorry to ring you in the evening but on Fridays I don't go to the surgery as I run a clinic at the hospital but I usually pop in on my way home to pick up messages and so on. When I did so tonight I saw that your HIV test results had come through so as I know how worried you've been I thought that you'd like me to call and give you the good news'.

'Did you say good news?' gasped Janie.

'Yes you're clear'.

Janie nearly collapsed at the news.

'Mrs. Hardy are you still there?'

'Yes. Yes I'm here. Thank you. Thank you for the news'.

'My pleasure, so that's the lot now. You are clear and free of any sexually transmitted infections'.

'Thank you very much and also for not criticising or judging me'.

'That's not what we're here for. We don't judge people we just mend them when they're ill or hurt' and she laughed. 'Good night and enjoy your weekend'.

'Oh I will, believe me I will'.

Her legs felt wobbly as she walked back into the sitting room and made herself smile at William.

'Everything alright darling?'

You bet it's alright. I've got my life back. I'm not raddled with disease. I am safe to be with. I am safe for you to have sex with again. Now all I've got to do is extract myself from this fictitious prolonged period problem.

'Yes that was my doctor with the results of my tests. They've found out what's wrong with me. Apparently it's a hormone imbalance and although quite rare it's not unheard of in women of my age. She wants me to pop in to the surgery and pick up some tablets tomorrow. She said once I start to take them it'll clear up very quickly, in fact it could be as quick as a day or so'.

Blimey that sounded good. Hormone imbalance. Need some tablets. Clear up quickly. Day or so. Brilliant.

'Oh good, I'm glad that it's nothing serious then darling. Come here' and when she went to him he put his arms around her and gave her a gentle kiss.

'Right now come and talk with me while I get the supper ready' she went on. 'I've got some lovely sea bass and I thought I'd grill it with some parsley butter, new potatoes and some French beans. How does that sound?'

It was after they'd eaten that he said she looked better than she had for some time. She replied that as she now knew what the matter with her was, she suddenly felt heaps better in herself.

They listened to some music and then went to bed where they lay in each other's arms listening to an owl hooting as they drifted off to sleep.

Saturday morning Janie left at nine to drive into town ostensibly to collect her pills. She'd found an old empty pill box at the back of the medicine cabinet which had her name and the instruction to take two tablets twice a day on it so she'd tucked that into her handbag.

In town she went into the first chemist that she came to and bought two packets of aspirins then returned to the car where she spent a few minutes popping the pills out of their plastic and foil protective packaging and tipping them into the empty pill box.

Back home she put the now filled pill box on a shelf in the bathroom in a prominent place and reminded herself that she would have to remember to remove four pills each day for the next few days. Satisfied she walked back downstairs reflecting on yet another piece of subterfuge.

This spreading falsehoods is easy isn't it? Association by sight. William would see the box of pills, see them reducing in number, she'd tell him in a couple of days that her long running period was over, that her hormones were back under control and they could start to have sex again. Easy peasy.

She rang Jackie and gave her the news that she had no infections or disease and the two women chatted for a while before ringing off.

William had gone out to play golf so he'd be away for most of the day. Feeling brighter and happier than she had for some time Janie decided to go for a long walk in the lovely countryside around where they lived. It made a change to be walking along she thought rather being on horseback and she stopped at a little pub for a half of lager and a sandwich before setting out to return home where she arrived mid afternoon.

He returned around tea time having played well and so he was in a good mood. It was strange as normally he was such an even tempered person but when he played golf badly he was irritable for hours after he got home. Shooting or fishing didn't affect him in that way just golf.

***

Emily spent the morning shopping and tidying her flat but mid afternoon she thought about the evening and tomorrow, so on an impulse she dialled Steve's mobile.

'Hi. Are you doing anything this evening? No? Good. Do you fancy coming round for supper? I've got some steaks that I picked up today when shopping. I'm not a great cook but I can do steaks ok and we could have some salad and micro-chips with it. I've got some prawns which would make a nice starter. If you brought a bottle of wine or two maybe it could be fun and ……. err, you'd be welcome to stay the night if you like to save worrying about drinking and driving. What do you say?

He said that he really didn't have anything planned and had been intending to go to the cinema but prawns, steak, salad and micro-chips sounded much more fun, so yes thanks he love to come for supper and stay the night.

***

Janie and William had been invited to friends for dinner and were having an enjoyable evening even though Janie had felt a jolt of apprehension when she saw Jackie was one of the guests but nothing untoward happened as they were all standing around chatting with pre dinner drinks and she started to relax. Even when as they started to go through to dinner Jackie took her arm and in a voice so quiet that no-one else could hear said she was so pleased all Janie's tests had come back clear and then asked whether she'd heard from Harry to which Janie muttered 'No thank goodness'.

Janie had offered to drive home so William was happily tucking into the red wine as was Jackie who'd persuaded husband Mathew to drive tonight.

It was as they were nearing the end of eating the main course when Janie tensed as Jackie commented on a very recent newspaper report of a premier league footballer caught cheating on his wife with another woman. Unfortunately this seemed to be a topic of interest to most people round the table and the discussion widened to adultery in general and then moved onto to how mistresses managed to juggle their secret life with a normal open life.

Janie kept sending dagger looks at her friend who just smiled and kept the conversation rolling along on this subject and it was at the point of running out of steam when Jackie spoke in a voice slightly overloud obviously bolstered by red wine.

'I wonder how many married men have affairs, or married women for that matter. I bet it is lots if we did but know'.

You cow. Stop it. Shut up.

Hardly able to look at her friend and worried what was going to come out next, especially as she saw her top up her glass and take a deep swig.

'I read the other day' continued Jackie 'that something like thirty percent of married people have had affairs at some time in their marriage. That's one in three. Now there's sixteen people round this table, eight men and eight women so if the national statistic applies that means that five of us sitting here have had, or are having an affair. Isn't that amazing?

Now I know that I haven't so that reduces the odds, although when Mathew gets beastly sometimes I dream of some gorgeous man whisking me away …. so remember that Mathew darling' she laughed pointing across the table at him.

So go on is anyone going to own up to having had or indeed now having an affair? Isn't that a wonderful word, affair? Conjures up visions of romance, illicit lovemaking, raw passion and deep down dirty sex'.

There was some general laughter and Janie was about to try and change the subject when Jackie started again.

'Right let's go round the table'.

No please for fuck's sake don't do this Jackie. Why are you being so awful? I trusted you and thought you were my friend. Everything was getting ok again and now you're doing this.

'So Graham have you ever had an affair?

'No Jackie I haven't and I don't want to'.

'Better bloody well not' interjected Graham's wife Caroline 'as if he did I'd be down to the divorce lawyer quicker than you could say bonking'.

More laughter then Jackie moved to the next guest and the next and then she smiled as her somewhat unfocussed gaze rested on Janie.

'So Janie have you ever cheated on William?'

Take a deep breath, keep calm, relax, join in the fun. Fun? Some fun!

'No of course not. Why would I want to? William is everything I want in a man and I wouldn't do anything to hurt him ….. ever'.

As she finished speaking she walked to where her husband was sitting further down the table on the opposite side, leant down from behind to put her arms around him and planted a kiss on the top of his head.

God that went well and sounded brilliant even if it was a pack of lies.

'And although you haven't asked me Jackie I haven't either' said William. 'I know it sounds a bit corny and old fashioned but Janie and I happen to love each other very much don't we darling' and twisting round he looked up at her and smiled, then turning back to look at Janie's tormentor added 'and I think this is a particularly stupid discussion so I suggest we change the subject'.

To Janie's immense relief there was a chorus of 'Hear hears' and taking her seat again she stared at Jackie wishing that she'd turn to stone and was relieved when the conversation turned to politics and the matter passed.

Later in the hall as everyone was getting ready to go home Janie seeing Jackie looking somewhat glassy eyed and wobbling unsteadily, hissed in her ear 'You bitch. I thought you were my friend and you do that tonight'.

'Bit of fun sweetie and no harm done is there?' and she hiccupped.

'Might have been though. I shan't forget this in a hurry'.

As she drove them home William sat cheerfully engulfed in red wine, and brandy. 'Not a bad evening was it?'

'No quite fun'.

'That was a funny do though wasn't it?'

'What was?'

'That business with Jackie asking whether anyone had had an affair?'

It wasn't a funny do at all. It might have been a fucking disaster.

'I mean I thought it was all in rather bad taste especially as no-one is going to sit there and admit it if they have are they? Bloody silly really. Don't know what came over the woman' and he lapsed into silence for a minute before sitting up and saying 'Hey you don't think that she's been having one do you and got some sort of guilty conscience?'

'What an affair? No I'm sure she hasn't. After all she's probably one of my best friends and I'm certain she'd have confided in me if she had'.

And if she had said anything I'd have kept my mouth shut not teased and tormented her in public like she did to me tonight.

'Hmm, odd though. Oh well doesn't matter. Now where are we?'

'Nearly home darling just sit back and relax'.

'Will do. By the way I thought you looked lovely this evening. I do like that dress'.

'Thanks'.

'How are you feeling? I mean are the pills you got from the doctor doing any good?'

'Do you know I think they could be? I've only taken two lots of two tablets so far of course and have to complete the full programme but hopefully things will be back to normal soon'.

Maybe tomorrow night she could say that big improvements had occurred. Tell him her period was over and she was ready to make love to him again. After all that's what his question was about just now. Yes of course he wanted to know if she was getting better but what he really wanted was to know when he could have sex with her again. Yep the deception had gone on long enough. Tomorrow she'd let him get back into action.

He nodded and smiled at her.

***

Steve was also smiling. Emily had cooked the steaks to perfection. The prawn cocktail that she'd made had been good too and having cleared away the plates and dishes they'd been cuddled on the sofa kissing and stroking. He was minus his shirt and she, naked apart from a pair of pink and white panties, was gently nibbling on his nipples.

Her own nipples were now fully aroused and hard as a result of the careful, gentle and prolonged kissing, licking and sucking to which he'd subjected them over the past quarter of an hour. That was the nice thing about Steve she thought. He took time to arouse her properly and didn't just rush to get her knickers off and screw her.

Slipping a hand inside her panties he found her pussy and started to stroke the lips and clit until by mutual consent they made their way to the bedroom and soon were making love more vigorously than they usually did.

They both climaxed and afterwards lay relaxing. 'Marvellous things dicks aren't they' she commented later as she played with his flaccid appendage. 'Small, limp and floppy but a little stimulation and they change out of all recognition. Good thing too as they're not a lot of use to us girls like this are they?' and she chuckled as she jiggled him around. 'These are great as well' she added as she took hold of his balls and massaged them for a moment or two.

'You know usually we make love and then go to sleep. What say we don't do that tonight and maybe see if we can't do something about this little fellow' and her hand moved from his balls to this prick which she gripped and started to rub. 'That's it my little beauty up you go' she encouraged as she saw his erection starting again. 'Come on now let's have you all nice and big'.

He did and as they jostled around at the start he pulled her into a kneeling position pressed her head down then having checked that she was wet and ready for him, he rolled a condom tightly onto himself and slid deeply home into her pussy while his hands reached round for her breasts. He started to pound into her and she tried to move in time with him but as he shuffled forward a little to adjust the angle of penetration his prick slipped out of her.

329

'Sod it' he muttered as he took hold of it and re-inserted himself. Moving more quickly now and holding her hips tightly he rammed in and out while she moved back and forth in time with his movements until suddenly groaning loudly she stretched up to try and maximise the effect of her orgasm. Unfortunately this action caused him to slip out again.

'Sorry' she gasped as she quickly helped him back inside where a few more quick thrusts resulted in his own climax.

Finished he withdrew and collapsing beside her onto his tummy grinned at her as she also lay down on her tummy.

'Ok?'

'Umm ok for a change but I prefer either being properly beneath or on top so I see you and kiss you. Some of the other positions can be fun for a change too but doggie fashion is a bloke thing really'.

'Oh I'm not sure it's just a bloke thing?'

'Of course it is. It plays to your dominant role. It's the hunter gatherer returning to the cave grabbing his woman bending her over or shoving her forwards and exerting his rights to sex. It is ok for you men, you can see what you're doing and can enjoy looking at the woman's back, bum, neck and even lean down and kiss some of those places.

But what does the woman see? Not a lot unless she twists round to look over her shoulder getting a nasty crick in the neck. No, I'm not sure many women would choose to be bent over or made to kneel while being screwed if they had a choice.

The other problem is that your dick can slip out too easily as you discovered a few minutes ago' she laughed. 'So although I'm not complaining just remember' she said wagging her finger at him 'that it's not a lot of fun with my face pushed into the pillows and my bum in the air'.

'It is a very nice bum though' he said softly running his hand across her buttocks.

'Thanks. Probably my best feature, that and my long legs'.

'Oh I don't know. These are nice too' he said as he slid a hand under her chest'.

'They're ok but a bit small. I wish I had more there up top'.

'No they're lovely. Turn over' and when she had he leaned over to kiss each breast in turn. 'Perfectly shaped and nice sized'.

'Thanks but I'd still prefer to be a C or maybe even a D cup rather than just a thirty four B. Still as I don't intend to waste any of my hard earned money on a boob job they'll just have to stay as they are' and putting her hands around them she squeezed them into higher mounds and said 'go on kiss them again for me'.

He did spending time on her nipples, then with a goodnight kiss on the lips they put their arms around each other and went to sleep.

In the morning Steve woke first and lay for a while just looking at Emily as she slept and decided that she was really rather pretty, interesting to talk to and fun to be with. She was also good at sex and he lay there hoping that she'd wake sooner rather than later as he wanted to make love with her again. Fortunately it wasn't long before she opened her eyes, looked at him, smiled and whispered 'Good morning' as she folded her arms around his neck when he rolled on top of her.

'Umm now I think this is going to be a nice way to start the day' she muttered slowly wrapping her legs around him enjoying the feeling of his erection pressing against her.

When they'd finished she peeled the used condom off him, knotted it and dangled it in front of him.

'Yuck, you mucky beast' she chuckled.

'You had as much to do with producing it as me' he protested softly.

'Mmm so I did ...…. and ..….. you ..….. enjoyed ..….. every ..….. moment ..…..of ..…... it ..….. didn't ..….. you?' she smiled tapping his nose with a forefinger as she articulated each word, then swinging her long legs out of bed she went into the bathroom where she had a pee, washed, did her teeth, brushed her hair, popped on a little lipstick and then came back into the bedroom and sat on the bed looking down at him stroking his chest.

'Shall we spend the day together or have you got things you need to do?'

'Well I want to go into the plant this morning and have a look around but apart from that I've nothing planned. You could come with me if you like? What about you? Got anything in mind?'

'I usually go to the gym on Sundays. I go a couple of evenings during the week as well but Sundays is my day for a good long hard work out. What time do you want to go into Hardys?'

'Oh no special time, say about nine thirty. Look what do you do about breakfast?'

'Cereal and maybe a slice of toast but I bet you like a big cooked breakfast do you?' she laughed.

'Yes. I get up and swim for a while in the hotel pool then go and ruin it all with a monster breakfast but I tell you what. A light breakfast will do me good. So how about we have that here, then go to Hardys after which we can call at my hotel so I can collect my gear then trog off together to your gym.

For lunch we could find a nice little pub on The Broads. Maybe get a boat out for the afternoon? How does that sound?'

'Rather good actually'. Looking at her watch she continued 'It's just gone eight now so shall I shower first and let you stay there for a few more minutes then while you are showering I'll get the toast on'.

Several people were surprised to see Steve and Emily as they walked round the factory and frequently they had to reassure worried questioners that there was nothing wrong but they were simply taking an interest in how things were going and so the message started to get round that the new management were alright and even prepared to get off their backsides at weekends to see how things were coming along.

Emily had a real ability to get people chatting and between them with her relaxed approach to conversation and Steve's slightly more pointed questioning they learnt a lot about how things were going. They also received several suggestions from various members of the workforce on how improvements could be made and they duly noted those and promised to look into them on Monday.

They made their way from the factory to Steve's hotel where he dropped off the little overnight bag he'd taken with him to Emily's flat, grabbed his gym kit and then they drove to her gym, signed him in as a temporary guest member and worked out together for the next couple of hours.

She looked very attractive in her leotard and she had been right this morning. Her bum and legs were definitely striking features of her body and every now and then he glanced at her as she worked out.

Steve though was also in good shape and pounded hard on the various pieces of equipment and it was almost lunch time when they agreed that they'd done enough fitness work.

Showered and changed they met in the bar and while she slowly sipped at a half of lager shandy he downed a pint.

They went back to her flat dropped off their gym kits and then drove out of Norwich to Wroxham where they hired a motorboat and puttered off to find the pub which the boat hire man had said was only a few minutes down the river.

He was right and they managed to moor up without problem and sat in the sunshine sipping some more shandies and enjoying some freshly made ploughman's lunches.

They spent the afternoon mooching along in the boat tying up a couple of times for a kiss and cuddle, laughing at the shouts and cheers from people on other boats. On one occasion Steve, while not detracting from kissing Emily held up one finger as the catcalls were particularly raucous.

Back at her flat in the late afternoon Emily suggested that they went to the cinema in the evening as there was a film that she wanted to see. Steve said that he'd like to see it too but as there was plenty of time before they had to go out how about they spent the next hour or so in bed? So they did.

They enjoyed the film, stopped for a burger afterwards and then returned to her flat where they made love again after which he left to go back to his hotel as he had his suit there and his other work things like laptop, files, briefcase and other documents and he didn't want to rush around the next morning. As he left though he kissed her gently, said he'd had a great time and maybe they could do it again.

'I think that I'd like that Steve' she replied and when he'd gone she said quietly 'yes I'd like that very much'.

***

As Steve was driving back to his hotel, Janie was getting out of the bath and after drying she flapped talcum powder around herself, took one of William's favourite scents which she'd taken into the bathroom with her and applied a little behind her ears, traced a scented finger down her cleavage, wiped a little onto her wrists, put on a touch of eye shadow and some mascara, did her lipstick and slipping into a white see through nightie walked into the bedroom where he was in bed reading a golfing magazine.

333

Silently taking a deep breath she slipped under the duvet.

Ok here we go. Time to try and get back to normal.

She turned to him. 'Do you really want to read that boring old magazine or could I tempt you to something perhaps a little more interesting?' and she ran her hand down his chest and inside the waistband of his shorts.

'I am sure you could but only ….. you know…… only if you are feeling well enough. I mean are you alright?'

'The doctor said that these pills might work very quickly and they certainly seem to be doing with me, so therefore I think that the answer to your question is yes. I am alright now thanks, so come here my darling William' and she pulled him towards her as her lips closed with his.

They kissed for a long time as one of her hands played with his penis inducing an erection while the other stroked herself until she was wet.

This is it then. Get on with it. Forget Harry. Forget what might have been. Forget all the worries of possible disease over the last few days. You are fine. Be a true wife and satisfy your honest, faithful and loving husband.

'Make love to me darling' she whispered crossing her arms to remove the nightie and pulling his face to her breasts where he nibbled and kissed her nipples before pressing her down and sliding on top. He paused before entering her and raising his eyebrows whispered 'You are sure you're ready?'

'Yes very sure darling'.

You'd better be. No going back now is there?

Afterwards as they lay beside each other and he had said "thank you" and how "wonderful" it had been, she reflected that William had been his usual careful, gentle, thoughtful self when making love to her, quite unlike the wild, erotic and often abandoned sessions she'd enjoyed with Harry.

But that's in the past now. Forget Harry. William is what you have.

She lay awake for ages thinking about William, Harry and what might come out in the trial that was so long ahead that she was able to put it to the back of her mind for now. However when she thought of Harry although she still experienced a little jolt of lust, she knew that somehow her mind was putting that time with her lover away into a compartment well removed from daily use.

It was very comforting lying there listening to the breeze, the owls, the night and to William's gentle deep breathing. Dear William.

She slept.

Still desiring we live without hope.

Dante.

CHAPTER 19

Steve's week started well. First thing on Monday morning Nigel rang to say that at last he'd found a candidate who was not only an outstandingly good Sales and Marketing Director but was also prepared to take on the risky job at Hardys.

Furthermore he was available at short notice having just finished an assignment in Japan for a major consumer goods company. On successfully completing that and returning to the uk, rather than immediate promotion to Managing Director of one of their divisions as he thought that he'd been promised when he took the Japanese job, he found that it was likely to be at least two years before they thought that a suitable vacancy would become available through their internal succession plans. Accordingly he was disgruntled with them and wanted to leave as soon as possible.

'So the career planning bog-up with him is their loss and your potential gain' boomed Nigel Charlesworthy down the phone. 'See him quickly if I was you as he'll be in demand this guy and won't be hanging around on the job market for long' so although he had a very busy week planned Steve freed up a slot on Tuesday afternoon and the arrangements were duly made for him to meet with Greg Morrison.

Emily started the week by having discussions with Hardys computer department investigating how they could produce improved analyses of the factory performance. This took until about eleven o'clock when returning to her office Tabitha said that Kelly from marketing had come along twice to see Emily.

'What about?'

'To tell you about her weekend. Apparently you asked her to call by and do that. When she was with you on Friday?'

'Oh yes I remember but it was only a sort of throw away line at the end of a conversation when she'd told me she was planning to go clubbing'.

'Well she's keen to tell you all about it'.

'Look I'm pretty busy today. If she comes by can you put her off?'

'She'll be upset'.

'Why? She was only going clubbing'.

'Because I think she's got a bit of a crush on you and she'll be hurt if you brush her off'.

'Oh don't be silly. She's a grown young woman of what twenty two, three. She's not a schoolgirl with a crush on her games teacher'.

Tabitha raised an eyebrow. 'You'd be surprised. Go on find her five minutes. Can I slot her in after lunch?'

'Oh alright if you must but just in case you're right, come in and rescue me after five minutes will you?'

'Might do ..... might not' laughed the secretary as she handed Emily some documents and walked out of her office.

'Please?' Emily called after her.

Steve had his start of the week call with the bank and was surprised that in addition to the usual team there was someone else on the conference call. He introduced himself as Henry Wilkinson and said that he was Head of Special Situations.

Whoa thought Steve. They were bringing out the big guns now. Were they getting nervous about his ability to turn Hardys around? Well if so he'd better reassure them and pretty quickly.

'Oh well in that case I'm glad you are on the call today' said Steve in a very positive tone of voice 'as things are really starting to go rather better here.

I guess you will have been told of the deal we've done with the Union. It is an important start as it shows firstly that we're not going to have industrial trouble as we hammer through our cost reduction plans, and secondly it makes a significant difference, in a positive way, to our financial results.

If you hang on a second I'll get Travis to join us and he can give you our latest estimate of the improvement that it will generate' and putting down the phone he walked quickly to the outer office, told Tabitha to get Travis and returned to the phone.

'Now I can also tell you before he comes that Travis is a great addition to the team. Also tomorrow I'm interviewing for a new Sales and Marketing Director and I believe that with him in place plus Travis and Emily who is proving to be a great member of the turnaround team, as she was on the last project, then I think we have the skills, and firepower to get things turned.

Now you guys will be wanting to see improvements and quickly. The good news on that front is that our cash flow is better than our previous forecast mainly as a result of Travis's re-negotiated terms with some of our major customers and a couple of the deals he's done with our key suppliers.

I can also see several other areas where we can cut costs further without damage to the products, the brands or the business overall. Ah here's Travis' and waving him in he went on 'so I'm actually starting to feel slightly optimistic about things'.

'Good' was the only word that came back up the phone line from Henry.

Steve quickly explained who was on the line to Travis and scribbling on a note pad he pushed it in front of his finance man.

BE BLOODY CAREFUL WHAT YOU SAY WITH THIS NEW GUY. DON'T PROMISE ANYTHING THAT WE CAN'T DELIVER.

Travis nodded as he started to speak. 'Hi folks. Right let me start with cash flow. I guess Steve's told you the good news. I'm going to e-mail you a new schedule this morning and you'll see we are way ahead of our forecast so I don't think we'll need to draw the last tranche of the emergency funding just yet. In fact with a bit of luck we might be able to hold off that for some time'.

There were sounds of approval down the phone which Steve had put onto speaker so they could both hear everything that was said.

'Now as far as the profit forecast' and then Travis laughed 'always sounds funny describing something as a profit forecast when it is a loss not a profit but there I also have good news'.

'I'm glad to hear it but it doesn't sound funny to me. Not at all funny' replied Henry dryly.

'Turn of phrase' commented Travis grinning at Steve as he scribbled three words on the writing pad.

What a jerk!

'Sorry Henry, us colonials sometimes get the Queen's English a little wrong but putting that aside what I can tell you is that I consider our negative profit' and he grinned again at Steve 'is going to be maybe fifty thousand better than forecast when we've finalised this month's calculations.

If we can continue that trend then we might be up to a half a million better than forecast by year end and that would put us in the black again, but it's early days and I'm not promising that'.

'Sounds encouraging but how solid are your forecasts?' came the disembodied voice down the phone.

Travis grinned as he wrote again on Steve's pad.

Shall J say J've just made 'em up?!!!

'Oh they're pretty darn watertight. We've worked on them very carefully and as long as we hit the sales numbers then they're ok. We need that new Head of Sales though and darn quick'.

'Steve I thought you said that you had someone in mind for the role'.

'No I said that I was interviewing tomorrow for someone who incidentally comes highly recommended. That only happened this morning and I haven't had a chance to brief Travis, or Emily for that matter yet'.

'I see. Now on a scale of one to ten with ten being absolutely certain that you'll pull things round and one being total failure and let's put the business into administration straight away, what are your feelings about your chances of success?'

Travis wrote 5-6? on the pad and looked at Steve.

He nodded and said 'Somewhere between five and six at this moment. That's my feeling right now'.

'Travis do you agree?' queried Henry.

'Yeah I reckon that's about the size of it'.

'Ok. Good luck. I'll leave you now with the rest of the team here as I've got to go to another meeting. In fact I should be there now but I wanted to have a word and get a feel for the issue. Lot riding on your shoulders up there so I'm glad we've had this conversation'.

There was a sound of shuffling from the speaker and the other team in London were obviously re-arranging themselves around a table or desk down there as Henry left.

'Yea I ought to be going too so unless you really need me I'll leave you now' said Travis.

Steve agreed as did the London team so Steve was left alone to talk with the faceless men from the bank in London which he did for the next half hour or so before the conversation came to an end.

He felt like stretching his legs at that point so he wandered along to Emily's office where she having returned from her computer meeting and also being told about Kelly's possible feeling for her was just reading her morning's e-mails.

'Hi' he started as he walked in and propped himself on the edge of her desk. 'Thanks for the weekend. I really did enjoy it'.

'Glad to have been of service'.

'No I don't just mean that' he smiled 'but the whole time we spent together'.

'Mean what?'

'Oh come on you know perfectly well what I mean'.

'Yes I enjoyed it too ...... and not just that either' she laughed showing her even, extremely white teeth and pink tongue.

'Maybe spend another weekend together sometime?'

'I'd like that, thanks'.

'Good. Now I tell you what I've come to see you about' and he briefed her on the interview tomorrow but also on the telephone call with the Bank.

'I think he could be a nasty piece of work this Henry Wilkinson chap so we'll have to watch our step with him. If he calls you be very careful what you say to him'.

She agreed that she would do just that then after a couple more minutes chat, he left and went back to his own office.

The rest of his day went quickly as he was busy in meetings, phone calls, writing reports, checking reports from others and poring over sheaves of figures from Travis's finance department.

Emily also had a busy day except for the little interlude when Kelly knocked on her door and asked if she could come in as it was two thirty and that was when Tabitha had told her to come back.

'Yes come in and sit down' invited Emily walking to one of the two easy chairs in her room and pointing at the other. 'I haven't got a lot of time but how did you get on clubbing? Did you pull then? Find some hunk who swept you off your feet?'

'Oh no' Kelly giggled nervously as she sat down, crossed her legs and tugged her short skirt down as far as she could 'but I did have a good time' and she gabbled away for a couple of minutes explaining that she and some friends had visited three different clubs in Norwich on Saturday night and that she'd eventually got back to her bed sit around three in the morning.

'You naughty little stop out' chided Emily.

Kelly protested that nothing untoward had gone on.

'Oh really? I bet you pulled some handsome bloke and spent the night ravishing him!' she chuckled.

'No honestly I didn't' she exclaimed.

'Hey calm down. I'm sure you didn't. I was just pulling your leg'.

'Oh I see' mumbled Kelly blushing furiously. 'Did you have a nice weekend then? Did you go out to dinner with your man friend like you said you might?'

'No we didn't go out to dinner. On Saturday he came round to my flat and I cooked for us then on Sunday morning we went to the gym together and in the afternoon we had a boat out on the Broads. It was very enjoyable'.

'A boat on the river. Just the two of you?'

'Yes just us two'.

'Ooh that sounds so romantic' sighed the infatuated young woman but before the conversation could develop into what Kelly thought about romantic boat trips Tabitha knocked and put her head round the door.

'Emily sorry to interrupt but Steve's on the warpath. Some report he is expecting from you or something?'

'Oh God yes. Thanks. Sorry Kelly. I'm glad you had a nice time at the weekend but we'll have to cut this short now. The boss is calling'.

'Yes of course. Thanks for talking with me. Bye' and as she stood up and walked out still blushing Emily just stopped herself saying 'Anytime'.

When she'd gone Tabitha came in. 'Well?'

'Well what?'

'Well can you see now that she's got a crush on you?'

'I don't know. Maybe?'

'Maybe? Rubbish, she's mad about you. I mean not many junior staff come out from your office and tell me that you're really wonderful do they? You'll need to let her down carefully though'.

'Ok thanks for the advice. You work for a woman's magazine or something on the advice page in your spare time do you? Write to Tabs and tell her all your problems. Instant solutions dispensed' and both women laughed but as Tabitha was leaving she stopped laughing.

'I mean it Emily. Be nice to her. I don't know if you've ever had a crush on another woman but I did once ….. years ago, and it hurt so much when she rejected me'.

'Alright miss agony aunt. I'll let her down nicely, not that I've done anything to encourage her'.

'That's just it, you don't have to' and with that somewhat enigmatic comment she left Emily to her paperwork and e-mails.

Kelly back at her desk was in a daze of happiness as she relived the meeting remembering every word of the conversation with her lovely hero. So Emily went to a gym? If she found out which one she could join too and then see her beloved outside work.

But later that night in bed she suddenly put two and two together and realised that Emily's man for whom she'd cooked dinner had probably slept with her on the Saturday night. Of course she hadn't said that they had. Well she wouldn't would? But if they were together at her flat having a cosy dinner on Saturday and then spent Sunday morning at the gym before going on to the river, the chances must be high that they'd spent the night together.

Looking at her pin-up's picture in its frame she whispered 'Oh Emily why when I'm here for you?' and she cried herself to sleep.

***

Janie and William watched the ten o'clock news on tv then she said she was going to bed. She saw the expression on his face which was a cross between puzzlement and interest but she said nothing more and went upstairs and into their en-suite. When she emerged William was sitting on the bed in his undershorts. Smiling at her he went into where she'd just been and when he came out still wearing his pants she was undressed and sitting up in bed.

His eyes fastened onto her naked breasts and as he approached the bed she flicked back the duvet revealing that the rest of her was also naked.

Patting the sheet she said quietly 'Come on darling'.

'Janie is it ....?'

'Definitely' she interrupted softly. 'The doctor said those pills should work quickly and they are so take those pants off and come here'.

He did and as he leaned towards her she pushed him onto his back. 'Lie still' she whispered into his ear then pushed her tongue deep into his mouth which opened willingly to accept it's probing entrance. Rolling on top of him she slowly rubbed her bush on his penis as it erected and while continuing to kiss him she felt her own arousal starting.

Tonight she felt horny and wanted to fuck and be fucked.

'Relax darling' and easing her hips up a little she reached down and pushed him inside her. 'Take time there's no need to rush' she muttered as she leaned forward and dangled first one and then the other nipple to his lips before leaning down and kissing him again.

When she started moving on him she was careful to do so slowly at first and then building some momentum before slowing again. Repeating this process time and again the lovemaking was lasting well and she knew that her orgasm when it did arrive would be good but she worried that he wasn't going to last too much longer, so she completely stopped moving on him just lay still on top leaving him buried inside her unmoving.

'Janie' he said looking up at her as she felt his prick start to twitch within her.

'Schh just keep absolutely still. Can we make it last a bit longer?' She remained unmoving as she ran a finger around his face, eyes and across his lips but feeling him twitch again she watched as he struggled to keep himself under control.

'Umm that's it. Hold back my darling' and to her great delight he did and sensing that he had got himself under control she smiled then kissed him again before squeezing her pussy muscles and starting to move on him again moving increasingly quickly. Sitting upright she bounced energetically on him running her hands through her hair and moaning loudly and with greater frequency until suddenly she felt him explode inside her. Continuing to move she gave a prolonged groan as she too experienced a most satisfying climax.

Staying above him and still moving as she wanted to extract the maximum effect from her orgasm she gradually slowed and flopped down onto him before rolling slowly onto her side and turning to face him.

'There was that alright darling?' she asked as she took hold of his slippery and still erect prick and rubbing it slowly felt a little more of his emissions leak out. She wiped her palm on the sheet.

'Wonderful thank you'.

There we are then. Back in the business of marital see and two nights running. Whoa! Wasn't difficult was it? Not really a problem after all and without Harry now she'd need it with William.

***

Greg Morrison was of medium height, thirty eight years old, slim but possessed of an intensity and earnest approach that instantly impressed Steve.

Their discussion lasted over an hour and Steve could see why Nigel had recommended him. He took him to see Travis who after half an hour's conversation took him to Emily who like the other two was impressed with their possible new Sales and Marketing Director. When she'd exhausted her questions she walked him back to Steve.

'Ah come in. Emily can you round up Travis and then both of you come and join Greg and me will you?'

He and Greg small talked until the other two joined them whereupon Steve leaned back in his chair and looked straight at Greg.

'There is one question which I haven't asked and although I don't know whether Emily or Travis did I'd like to ask it now. Why on earth do you want to take on this job?

The business is in a mess, we're struggling to keep afloat and the cash situation is critical. We've lost big chunks of trade and some of our major customers; the plant is not as flexible as we'd like which restricts how accommodating we can be to our customers needs; we've had some sabotage; morale is crap although improving; we ..... that is Travis, Emily and me are all here on temporary contracts to try and sort out the mess and then we're off to the next project and I can only tell you that we told the bank yesterday that we have a fifty to sixty percent chance only of pulling this off.

'Oh' smiled Greg. 'I thought Nigel said there were problems here' and he roared with laughter.

The others joined in then listened with increasing interest as Greg spoke.

'Look my career so far has been onwards and upwards in multinational companies. Good standard stuff. Do a good job and get promoted. Do that next job well and get promoted again. Go off on assignments like I did to Japan.

Leaving aside that I consider I've been shafted by being told it'll be a couple of years before I get my next move and effectively I'm being parked during that time, I need a job ...... but not just any job.

I have for some time thought that I want to branch out of the standard corporate career ladder climb.

Doing what? I don't know. Maybe it's just itchy feet. Corporate life is very cosy. You are confined within guidelines. You are controlled and developed down set pathways.

Maybe being in Japan for two years opened my eyes to a different set of values and a different life style.

Perhaps I want to chuck it all up and be a missionary? Maybe I want to go and save the rain forest? Possibly I would like to start my own company. Perhaps if I can find someone to lend me a million or two, I'd could buy a business or buy into a business. I really don't know.

Now you are probably starting to wonder if I am the guy for you as I've got all these doubts.

Well I suggest that I am because while I am trying to sort out in my own mind what my long term life is going to hold for me, I will do a fantastic job for you here. We can agree a fixed contractual period, two, three years and I will commit to it, absolutely one hundred and one percent.

Whatever thoughts I might have about my long term future will not, I assure you, affect my performance in the job you need doing. In fact it might help me shape my future.

Could be that if ……. no not if …… when we sort this company out and turn it into profit could be that I'd like to buy it or buy into it. I think that there are plenty of opportunities for Hardys.

I've done my research since seeing Nigel. Ok Hardys has been battered recently and over the past couple of years has lost out to its competitors but that is no reason to give up' and his voice got a little louder and his face took on a determined expression.

'We can put that right. I'll talk to the supermarkets and wholesalers to find out what they want. There are always opportunities if you look hard enough and have the right sort of dialogue, are prepared to listen to their needs and then find a way to fulfil that requirement.

Even though I've been on the other side of the world I still have good connections here. I also know several exporters and I have several ideas of how we could develop that trade.

So what have you got to lose by taking me on? Nothing. I'll bet you've struggled to find anyone else who is good and prepared to step off the corporate ladder to take a risk like this. They'll all be too worried about wrecking their upward career path.

Go to a failing business? Oh no far too risky. What happens if it all goes tits up? ….. whoops sorry Emily' but she inclined her head indicating that she wasn't offended so he continued 'if it goes belly up? Where would that leave me they'd think? A risk that on their precious cv which so far has had only successes now has a sodding great failure.

No. They won't come, so you'll be left with has-beens; failures that have already happened; or those that are inexperienced and will not succeed in what you want to be done.

My guess is that you really need me. Yes you need me a lot more than I need you, but …… actually I do need you …. or something like you.

I need something to do that is challenging, interesting and could be fun. I want something into which I can immerse myself totally. I am a very intense person. I don't do frivolity. I don't do time wasting. I don't do buggering about. I work. Hard, long hours and very effectively. So I think your risk in taking me on is minimal but the reward I can give you will be high. Make me an offer and let's get on with it. Together.

There now I know that was a long winded answer and that is not normally me as I tend to be concise and to the point but I felt you were entitled to a full explanation of why I want to come here so does that answer your question Steve?'.

It was an impressive piece of presentation spoken from the heart. He was right. They all knew that but to have it laid out like that so clearly and so effectively and with such determination together with his conviction that he not only wanted the job but was confident that he could do it, swayed them all.

Steve looked round the room at his two other colleagues, smiled and then turning to Greg said quietly 'Well I guess the only thing to say is welcome aboard the good ship Hardy!

Now look this is what we thought about in terms of a salary and benefits package' and he passed over a single sheet of paper with the details clearly laid out.

'You might feel it's a bit on the mean side and maybe it is in the short term but we thought a bonus equal to one year's salary payable on us successfully turning the business round might be an incentive that would make the whole deal worth while. What do you think?'

'I think it looks fine. I'm quite happy to take a risk that although I could undoubtedly get a better package elsewhere, as I have explained you offer the sort of challenge that I think I'm looking for. So thanks ..... I accept and look forward to working with you.

I've got a few things to clear up and I'll start next Monday if that's ok.' and standing he shook hands with them all. 'Can someone fix me with some accommodation for then please?'

'Right I'll get Tabs onto it' said a delighted Steve. 'Now we are four and I really think that now we do stand a chance of success here'.

***

Janie and William made love again on Tuesday night.

Three nights running! We haven't done it so frequently for years. Hope he doesn't want to keep this up. On the other hand this was the first time that I didn't think of Harry while we were doing it .... only now afterwards.

***

The rest of the week seemed to go by quickly for Steve. He found that he was increasingly busy as did Emily and Travis, but the three of them had started having a short end of the day meeting at six o'clock to review what had happened during the day, check what issues were coming up tomorrow and generally ensure that they each knew what problems they each had and how they were tackling them.

'We'll have to get Greg into these meetings' suggested Emily after they finished their discussions on Thursday evening. 'After all his contribution is going to be so important. If he really can get some new sales going and quickly it will make such a difference to the business won't it?'

Leaving the office that night as she trotted down the stairs she caught up with Travis who was moving in his usual slow purposeful way. She'd never seen him hurry but had noticed that with his long legs he covered the ground pretty quickly in spite of not seeming to rush anywhere.

'Hi' she smiled.

'Hi yourself. Had a good day?'

'Uh huh. You?'

'Yep' and as they'd reached the bottom of the stairs he held the door of reception open for her to go through first.

'Thank you kind sir. Nice to see that some men have manners'.

'Yes mam' he drawled. 'You going home right now?'

'I am, why?'

'Well I wondered if you'd like to come for a drink. Been meaning to ask you for ages but never kinda got round to it'.

'Thanks I'd love to. Where do you fancy going?'

'Nice little pub down by the river. Now the question is do we take two cars or go in one, and if one which?

'I'll drive us'.

'Sure?'

'Yes. leave your car here and I'll drop you back afterwards. Ok?'

'Sounds good to me'.

Travis was fun. He talked about himself and his upbringing in America. His parents divorced when he was eleven but fortunately they not only remained good friends but didn't live too far apart and so he would happily spend time with each of them.

After he'd finished high school and college he joined an accountancy firm and quickly made his mark not only as a hard worker but also someone with flair and as he climbed the corporate ladder he developed a reputation for finding innovative and creative solutions to problems.

Posted to some of the firm's overseas offices he did stints in Mexico, Australia, Paris and London which was where he got involved with one of the major banks on a corporate rescue project.,

Deciding that this was an exciting and more interesting field of activity than straight accountancy he joined the bank's corporate recovery team and spent the next three years on various European projects during which time he built up a good reputation and a significant network of useful contacts.

Approached one day by a different bank to handle a recovery project for them he decided that he now had enough contacts to risk branching out on his own and so he took the new project from the rival bank but working on his own as an independent rather than being on the new bank's payroll.

From then on for the next four years he moved smoothly from one project to another being called in by Banks, Venture Capital Groups or Accountancy firms.

When he'd finished his last project he'd been thinking of going back to the USA and had explored his network of contacts there but as he was about to accept an assignment the Hardys opportunity arose and seeing that this would only be for about a year, maybe less he decided to take one last project before going back to America.

'That's a really interesting life you've had then isn't it?' asked Emily fascinated by Travis's life story but intrigued by him making no reference to women 'but what about the softer side, the non business side? Never thought about getting married?'

'No. I enjoy my freedom too much and with my somewhat nomadic life I am not sure it would be fair on the lady. That doesn't mean that I haven't enjoyed the company of ladies. I sure do and I have had some very pleasant liaisons, but nothing permanent. Maybe when I go back Stateside I'll find me a nice lady with whom I can settle down. Perhaps buy a little log cabin in the woods and sit on the porch smoking a pipe and raising a large family' he laughed.

Emily joined in the laughter and although not wanting to develop any sort of relationship with him nevertheless could imagine that good looking Travis would be a real catch for the right woman.

'So what about you? Emily is a very British name and conjures up visions of delicate sweet lace charm set in quintessential English countryside. A chocolate box cottage with roses up the walls in a little village with a stream running outside and fruit trees in the garden'.

'Oh nothing could be further from the truth I'm afraid. My parents lived in Southampton. My Dad was the manager of a large department store there and my Mum worked part time as a secretary in a solicitor's office. They still live in Southampton. I had a good upbringing. Went to school at a convent where we were taught by nuns then University in Hull before going into industry.

I joined a corporate recovery division of a bank and had been there ever since until the project before last where I met Steve. When we finished that one he suggested that I join him as he'd set up on is own. Bit like you really. So I did and we worked on that last project together and then came here to this one'.

'Tell me ...... are you and Steve an item ..... outside work I mean?'

'No not really. We enjoy each other's company and spend some time together but there's nothing fixed or permanent about it. Arrangement of convenience I guess' she smiled.

'Ah' he said looking at her. 'Another drink?'

Having had one glass of wine she elected for just a glass of sparkling water while he had a half of bitter to follow on from the pint he'd already drunk.

'I limit myself to one and a half pints and no more if I'm driving' he said seriously 'but if I ain't gonna drive then I might have a few more' and his smile made her insides flutter a little.

It was around nine when he said that he was hungry and did she fancy staying and having a meal with him so knowing that she didn't have much in the freezer and bearing in mind that she'd planned to go to the supermarket to stock up on food she said she would love to.

The evening was enjoyable. Travis was an interesting and fun companion and he made her laugh several times with a ready supply of jokes and stories about people he'd met, projects he'd handled and his approach to life which once away from columns of figures, balance sheets and profit and loss schedules was surprisingly light hearted and quite carefree.

Around eleven they drove back to Hardys where he smiled as he thanked her for a nice evening. Getting out of her car he grinned 'Adios amigo'.

'Thanks for a really enjoyable evening and for the meal. It's good that there are a few gentlemen left in the world' she smiled.

'My pleasure mam. Do it again sometime?'

'Yes I'd like that' and starting the engine she gave him a wave and a smile and drove off. He followed but at the first set of traffic lights while she went straight on he flashed his lights and turned left.

She drove home had a quick bath and getting into bed lay there reflecting on the evening and decided that Travis was a really nice fun guy.

***

Janie some miles away was also lying in bed but feeling somewhat frustrated after William had again this evening made love to her but it had been too quick and although he'd climaxed, she hadn't. Nevertheless she'd let out a couple of false moans when he'd asked 'Was that alright darling as things happened rather quickly I'm afraid?'

'Yes it was lovely thank you' she reassured him stroking his face and giving him a little kiss before pulling her nightdress back on.

This is getting a bit much. I mean we used to do it once, maybe a couple of times a week, but ever since I said I was well again he's wanted it every night. Mind you with Harry we were at it like rabbits. She giggled as she wondered who having studied rabbit's sex activities had passed the phrase into the English language.

William stirred at the sound of her chuckle. 'You ok only you sounded as though you were laughing or something?'

'No not laughing, little cough. Got something stuck in my throat' and giving another gentle throat clearing type of cough she continued 'there that's better. Good night'.

But she lay there unable to go to sleep wondering about Harry.

Maybe I ought to go and see him? Can you do that? Can you just turn up and say you want to see prisoner so and so? No surely not. Presumably there are designated visiting days and times? And if she did go would he see her? Do you have to apply for a permit or something to visit a prisoner? Can you force him to see you? Probably not as it would breech his human

351

rights or something? How would he be taking to life behind bars? Harry liked the good things in life. Good food, wine, smart restaurants, trendy modern clothes. Now he'd be eating dreadful food, no wine and wearing prison uniform. What about his cell? How different from his huge palatial apartment with its water bed, fancy bathrooms, terrace and jacuzzi? God it's no good I must stop thinking about him. Remember what he did. Stole my money. Stole the cottage. Screwed all those other women including some real oldies. Shagged men too. No I don't want to see him.

Eventually she drifted off to sleep but woke up again around four o'clock and feeling wide awake and being careful not to disturb William she got out of bed and went downstairs to make a cup of tea. Sitting in the kitchen she sipped the hot drink.

She gazed out of the windows and by the light of the moon could see the partly re-built stable building. It would be a long time before that was fully re-constructed. Then her mind went to the cottage in France. Had Harry really stolen it off them? Surely not? She loved that little cottage and she'd loved being there with him. In spite of it being a warm night she shivered as her mind flicked over the time they'd spent there together.

I must find out. We've just assumed from what the police said that he'd stolen the cottage off them. Maybe he hadn't? Perhaps he hadn't actually done that. Could it be that he had feelings for her and that might have stopped him? Or if he was planning to do it then maybe he hadn't had time. Perhaps it was still theirs? I could pop down to France to find out. Either way it was going to be heart breaking. If the cottage had gone then she'd be devastated but if it was still theirs she'd see him everywhere in the building. They'd had such a happy time and had made love so many times. I've got to find out. I need to go there. I could also go and see him in prison. I need to see him.

A sudden wave of sexual longing seeped through her.

No I don't need him, I want him. I want him to take me to bed. I want him to tease and please me. I want to bounce around on that water bed with him. I want to sit in that Jacuzzi with him. I want to watch myself making love with him in his mirrored bedroom. I want to go to the cottage with him and lie in bed listening to the birds chirping and feel warm, loved and totally satisfied sexually. I want him in spite of everything. Never mind the other women, the men and the theft. I just want him.

Growling slightly she finished her luke warm tea, crept upstairs and slid into bed without disturbing William and finally slept. Friday was the day that she rang Jackie and said she was coming over for a ride and arriving noticed that her friend didn't look her in the eyes. She'd been wondering when she could face her former friend, as that's how she thought of her now, and on the way over in the car Janie had pondered what to say to Jackie about her outrageous comments at the dinner party and how nearly she seemed to have come to breaking the confidence that Janie had shown in talking to her about Harry and from the shifty look that Jackie gave and the fact that she wouldn't look straight at her she knew that her friend felt uncomfortable.

'I think I'm going to move the horses from you' snapped Janie.

'Ok. Look Janie I'm sorry. Mathew said that I made a real fool of myself at that dinner party. He was so cross with me as we drove home. I don't know what came over me. Well I do it was the wine. I had too much. Sorry'.

'Sorry? That hardly covers it does it? You bloody nearly told everyone that I'd had an affair. I told you about Harry in the strictest of confidence. I thought I could trust you and then you go and start to play stupid games like that. Fortunately William didn't smell a rat but I don't know whether anyone else did?'

'I'm sure they didn't'.

'You haven't told anyone else have you?'

'God no of course not. I know I was silly at that dinner but no-one else knows about you and Harry. Trust me. Look, take your horses if you want to but please accept my apology. Come on Janie we've been friends for years. Don't let my stupid semi drunken antics spoil that. We all do silly things at sometime in our lives. Friends?'

Janie looked at Jackie's worried face. 'Oh alright, but don't you …. look if you ever ………'

'I won't ….. ever' interrupted the other woman, 'promise'.

Giving a deep sigh Janie forced a smile and then pulled the other woman close and gave her a little hug. 'Friends' she said quietly although knowing that their relationship would never be quite the same again.

They saddled the horses and went for a long ride and as the countryside passed her by Janie felt her irritation with her friend slowly disappearing and by the time they got back to the house, un-tacked and washed down the horses and turned them out into a paddock she felt calm.

'Coffee or maybe some wine?' asked Jackie.

'Coffee would be good'.

So the two women sat in the garden drinking coffee and chatted about unimportant things until Janie leaning forward stated 'I'm going down to France to see if the cottage is still ours?'

'How will you know?'

'God I hadn't thought of that. I've no idea. Well presumably if there is some other person living there I'll know that it's gone'.

'Yes but if it is now owned by, oh I don't know say another English family they might not be there and plan to use it occasionally as you and William did .... err and Harry'.

'I'll ring the police and see if they know anymore but look if I do go would you come with me. I think William is too busy at work at the moment and I really don't think I can face going there on my own. Will Mathew mind if you come away for a day or so?'

'No but what can I tell him? I can't for example very well say that you think your lover might have stolen the cottage can I?' and she looked apprehensively at Janie to see the reaction to her slight joke.

But she needn't have worried. 'No hardly' Janie smiled in response.

'What about saying that you were thinking of redecorating and refurnishing and wanted a second opinion?'

'Yes that sounds good. Let's say that' and she sat looking pensive.

'What's up? Something else on your mind?'

'I want to see him'.

'Who .... Harry?'

'Yes. I've got to see him. I'm going to find out how you get to see someone in prison'.

'Is that wise?'

'No it obviously isn't but I can't help it. I must see him face to face and ask him about all these allegations. I need to know for myself not just what the police have told me'.

Jackie studied Janie then taking her hand said softly 'You've still got the hots for him haven't you?'

There was silence until Janie whispered 'Yes'.

'Good God Janie. After all that he's done to you?'

'I know but I can't help it. What we had was so wonderful and I think so special. I mean he said such lovely things to me and our lovemaking was so beautiful. Jackie you have no idea. It wasn't just a fling. I mean it wasn't love or anything but it was so much more than just an affair. It was exquisite. It was as if I had another life'.

'Well I don't think you should go and see him. What good will it do? If you really still do want him you'll only get frustrated as you can't have him. He's locked up. He's is prison and if he's done all these things to you and the others then he'll be locked away for years.

Are you going to mope around like some love struck teenager waiting for him? How do you know he'll want you? To him you were probably just another daft nearly forty something that he seduced. He's had your body, now he's got your money and probably your cottage as well. Well that's what he wanted and shagging you was just a means to an end ……. and he got the end he wanted didn't he?

You are probably history as far as he is concerned. Look you said that he didn't answer your calls or e-mails towards the end. You were already getting the brush off. You were discarded and you had better face up to that fact my girl'.

Janie looked at her friend and as a tear rolled down her cheek she muttered 'Maybe but maybe not'.

'Oh come here you silly thing' and the two women hugged for the second time that morning. Jackie held her tight as Janie sobbed for ages until pulling away she sniffed.

'Sorry it's just all so emotional and I can't talk to anyone about it. I obviously can't talk to William about Harry although at some time I'm going to have to tell him I suppose. I can talk to him about the money and the possible loss of the cottage but not Harry. That's why I was so hurt when you did what you did at the dinner party as I was terrified it would come out there and then'.

'I've said I am sorry about that'.

'Yes I know and I'm not raking that up again. You will come to France with me won't you?'

'Yes I will'.

Janie suddenly sat upright. 'Would you come to the prison with me when I go to see Harry?'

'You really are going then?'

'I have to'.

'Umm well I don't know'.

'Please. I don't mean to come inside the place and meet him, but would you come down with me to keep me company? You could wait outside in the car while I go in? I'm not sure I can manage it all on my own'.

Jackie looked at her friend and took a deep breath. 'Alright, yes I'll come with you'.

'Thank you. Hey he's in Wormwood Scrubs. That's in London somewhere isn't it. We could perhaps go there and then go on to the airport and get a flight to France. Sort of do it all in a round trip'.

'Ok. Well you find out when or if you can go and see him and fix things up. Let me know when you are ready to go. I won't mention the prison thing to anyone and we'll stick to the cover story of checking out the interior of the cottage shall we?

Come on let's have a glass of wine. These are momentous times you know'.

Before Janie had got home Jackie had picked up the phone to Pauline and breathlessly opened the conversation with the words 'You'll never guess what now'.

Back home Janie rang directory enquiries and a few minutes later was speaking to an employee at Her Majesty's Prison Wormwood Scrubs who explained the procedure for obtaining a permit to visit a remand prisoner.

She also rang the Metropolitan Police and got straight through to Detective Chief Inspector Spencer who asked how she was, sounded very friendly and said that they were making excellent progress on the case.

'Oh that's good. Look I've two reasons for ringing you Chief Inspector. First of all do you know when the case will go to court as there are certain issues that I need to think through in case they come out'.

'Quite, but I can't say at the moment. Fraud cases are always complex and this one seems particularly so. Probably not for at least nine to twelve months I would say'.

'Right. Now the second thing is about our cottage. Do you know yet whether Harry ...... Harry Norton did steal it. I mean has he sold it on to someone else yet?'

'I don't know I'm afraid. Although it is important for you, to us it is only one of many pieces of the clever and difficult jigsaw that Norton managed to weave that we're trying to unravel'.

'So when do you think I might know?'

'I can't say at this stage. Sorry'.

'But it's awful not knowing whether it's still ours or not. Isn't there someway I can find out?'

'You could try going there. If the locks have been altered or the furniture changed then the probability, nay pretty well certainty, is that you've lost it but if neither of those things have occurred and bearing in mind that it wasn't long before we arrested him that he got you to sign it away then you might be lucky and discover that he simply didn't have the time to move it on'.

'I see. So going there is probably the best thing to do at this stage?'

'I would say so yes. The other thing that comes to mind is this. Did you pass over to him the deeds or any other documentation that you hold for the property?'

'No it was something that he asked for but they were lodged at our bank for safekeeping along with certain other of our documents and papers. I kept meaning to write to the bank to ask them to retrieve the cottage deeds but I never got round to it'.

Well that's good news. Now look I don't want to raise your hopes falsely Mrs. Hardy but as the papers that he produced and you signed passing over the cottage to him were worthless and false and as you've still got your actual deeds, you might be alright. I can't say for certain but I think it might be hopeful for you'.

'Thank you' she said gratefully.

'Is there anything else?'

'No thank you Chief Inspector'.

'Right we will need to see you again soon so you can give us some more details of your business relationship with Norton.

'Erm more details about my business relationship with him? Just the business side' and her heart started thumping.

'Yes. I understand what you are getting at but at this stage I'm only interested in the financial side of things ...... not any other relationship issues'.

'Thank you'.

'But look we also need to discuss your official statement with you in some more detail'.

'Oh right. When?'

'I'll get Maggie Wagstone to ring you and fix a convenient time for you to come down and see us'.

'Ok thank you and thank you for your time this morning'.

'No problem. Any time you think I can help or there's something you want to know just call me, or Maggie. Goodbye Mrs. Hardy and I do hope that you've still got the cottage. Will you go there, to France I mean?'

'Yes'.

'Fine well let me know the outcome will you, good or bad?'

'I certainly will thank you, good bye'.

Happiness is a choice that requires effort at times.

Aeschylus.

CHAPTER 20

The weekend had gone rather boringly for Steve. He'd been hoping to spend some or all of it with Emily but she had a long standing arrangement to go home to her parents and had left work on Friday evening to make the long drive to Southampton where she arrived around ten o'clock.

He ate in a pub on Friday evening and went into work on Saturday staying there all day, some of the time in his office but he made two tours of the factory, one in the morning where he chatted with many members of the day shift and then again mid afternoon after the shift change where again he talked and listened.

Returning to his hotel he threw a few things into a small grip bag then drove up to the North Norfolk coast and meandered along enjoying the scenery, realising that Norfolk was far from flat as so many people thought.

He stopped at the Blakeney Hotel right on the quayside in Blakeney and asked if they had a room for the night. They did so he took it then walked along the coastal path past Morston to Stiffkey and back.

Back at the hotel he went up to his room had a hot bath and then after sinking a couple of pints of local ale enjoyed an excellent dinner sitting at a window seat watching people wander along the quayside in the warm early autumn sunshine. He was fascinated seeing the boats which were moored at the quay rising up as the tide came in.

Next morning he was up early, tucked into a huge breakfast then went for a walk for a few miles in the opposite direction from yesterday before returning, checking out and continuing his drive along the North Norfolk coastal roads.

He'd heard of a pub called The Walpole Arms with an excellent reputation for food located in a tiny village close to Blicking Hall, one of the great stately homes of England and after a few false turns found it.

The reputation was not wrong and he enjoyed a pleasant lunch there in the olde worlde charm of the pub absorbing the interesting mixture of clients, some clearly locals and there just for their Sunday lunch time pint while others were tourists like himself, or people who had bought property locally and commuted to the area at weekends from London or the Midlands.

Back at his hotel in Norwich late afternoon, he lay down on his bed and dozed for a while, then watched tv eating a sandwich sent up by room service finally going to bed around eleven.

***

Janie was feeling horny and so was pleased that on Friday night William instigated sex but on Saturday night when they went to bed around one o'clock after holding a dinner party which had gone well he went straight to sleep.

However when he came back into their bedroom on Sunday morning after showering she was surprised to see that he was naked and sporting an erection.

She'd been just about to get up but seeing the glint in his eye she stayed in bed, smiled and enquired 'Where did that come from? Have you been playing with yourself in the shower you naughty boy?'

'Janie really!' he responded quite shocked at her remark, but he got back into bed, helped her off with her nightie and rolled on top of her. It was all a bit quick and although he grunted into his climax she was a long way away from an orgasm. After it was over he cuddled her into his arm.

'Long time since we've had a lie in and a bit of fun on a Sunday isn't it? We must do it more often'.

Must we? Hopefully not, especially if you're going to come off so quickly and leave me high and dry!

'Yes that would be nice but not next weekend darling as the boys will be home from school. They're coming on Friday evening and go back Sunday night so you'd better put on your thinking cap to decide on what to do with them. Maybe some shooting and I'll take them riding if they'd like.

Now' she chuckled as she fiddled with his not quite completely flaccid prick 'time to get up. I want you to help me in the rose garden this morning. I have some ideas for re-arranging one of the paths'.

***

Monday morning William, Steve, Emily, Travis and newcomer Greg met at the office.

Steve outlined where he saw their priorities and said that he was very keen to ensure that Greg understood the opportunities but also the limitations of the factory. What they could do and importantly what they couldn't.

'William no one knows this factory and it's capabilities better than you do. Could you please spend this morning showing Greg around? Every piece of kit, every production line, every boiling and cooking tank. How products are made, production speeds, the labs, the development areas and crucially can you impart to him from your enormous knowledge, the key facts about preserves, pickles and sauces.

I want him pumped full of information and knowledge as it will be essential that he has a really in depth knowledge when he goes out to fight with our customers and try and get us new business.

Then this afternoon Travis can you take him on and get him through the numbers so he can see just how much we need profitable new business. Finally mid afternoon or so when Travis has finished with him, Emily I'd like you to take him under your wing and run him through the Planning, IT and other areas that you look after.

Should have you up to speed by tonight Greg and with luck by then you'll be an expert on the business'.

William was delighted to help in this way. Steve was right. In spite of the fact that he wasn't a very good businessman he did know an awful lot about the factory and the products and he'd been feeling somewhat lost recently as this turnaround team had taken everything under their control, were making the decisions and running the business, his business. No he chided himself again, the Bank's business now. Maybe one day though he'd get it back.

He started by telling Greg about the history of the company then spent time explaining the different products and showed diagrams of the factory production processes and the layout of the site.

Greg absorbed information quickly and could retain detail well so William enjoyed his role as teacher to such a willing and clearly apt pupil and by the end of the day the new member of the turn around team really felt that had received a good grounding in the basics of the business as a result of William, Travis and Emily's teachings.

Tabs took him to the flat that she'd rented for him and he pronounced himself happy with it. It was in a Georgian house in Lime Tree Avenue one of the best parts of the City. The old house had been beautifully converted into four flats and his was on the first floor with a delightful view over the long garden and immaculate lawns.

'Hey having to mow that lot isn't part of the rental agreement is it?' he laughed pointing out of the window.

'No I believe that there is a gardener who comes in regularly to look after all the garden. Now you sure this is ok for you?'

'Yep it's fine' he replied bouncing on the bed 'just fine. Thanks for finding it'.

She drove them both back to the factory where he walked into Steve's office.

'Right, day one complete. William was a good teacher, as was Travis and Emily. Tabs has found me a highly suitable flat. So tomorrow I'm going to meet the Sales and Marketing team and then off we go. Now what about John Benton. He's still here I believe?'

'Yes but first thing tomorrow we're parting company with him. I've arranged to see him at eight so if you keep out of the way till about nine we'll have done the deed. I'll then take you along and introduce you to your team then it's up to you'.

Right I'll be off then' he replied quite unfazed that his predecessor was to be fired next morning. These things happen he thought. One day it might be him.

'Hang on' said Steve. 'I thought you and I might have supper together. We can chat about the business and get to know each other a bit'.

They did and it was a useful and successful evening and by the time that Greg found his way back to his flat and started to unpack the few things that he'd brought with him he was tired after a day of relatively little action or decision making, simply being a sponge and absorbing information at speed from several sources. He liked the team though and was sure that they would be able to work well together.

***

'Hi' started John Benton as he sat down in Steve's office at eight o'clock next morning. 'You wanted a meeting with me now?'

'Yes. Look I believe in coming to the point when there is something unpleasant that needs doing so that's what I'm going to do. The fact is that we don't believe that you are up to this job and although I don't blame you for all the ills that have befallen Hardys, as head of Sales and Marketing you control the front line and that front line has been letting us down.

Now we could have all sorts of debates about it, but I don't intend to do that. I have a severance package for you here and I'm happy to agree a mutually acceptable form of wording to release into the business and the outside world about why you've left and been replaced'.

The Sales Director looked stunned as he picked up the piece of paper Steve put on the desk then shaking his head he asked 'Your mind's made up? Any point in discussing it?'

'No'.

"Well obviously I am disappointed and don't agree with the decision but if that's the way it is, so be it. Can I see the details of the package and when do you want me to go?

'Yes here they are ……. and right now. This morning. Your replacement is already here. He spent yesterday getting to know the business and as soon as you've left site this morning then I'll introduce him to the sales and marketing teams'.

'Bloody hell you're not hanging around are you?'

'Haven't got time to do that I'm afraid. Look I know this is a blow but a young chap like you will get another Sales or Marketing job pretty quickly I think and you'll have a whack of money to tide you over until you do. I know it's not all about money, but pride, prestige, your own esteem and having a responsible job are what matters but at least you'll have a good financial cushion to give you the time to find that.

Now go and clear your office say your goodbyes and give me a look when you're ready to leave'.

'Ok so you're not going to march me off the premises then?' he said sarcastically.

'No of course not. Now go and clear up and I'll see you when you're ready'.

'Can I at least say hello to my replacement?'

'Sure I'll have him here when you go'.

John Benton left Steve's office in something of a daze. He hadn't expected this and it had come as a complete shock. Yes sure sales had been bad and many of their new products that his development and marketing people had created had failed to sell sufficient volume once in stores or had simply been rejected at the outset by the big supermarkets. But to get fired without warning was one hell of a shock.

However Steve had been generous and the severance package would last him and his partner Sandy for at least a year which was more than enough time to get another job and if he got one quickly he'd have some money to put away into savings.

The only thing was that he'd have to broach it carefully with her as she'd told him last night that she was pregnant about which they were both very pleased. How ironic he thought. Last night they'd been overjoyed that in a few months they were to be parents for the first time. Now a few hours later he was out of work.

Nevertheless John was a professional manager and as he went round his team to say goodbye he didn't slag off Steve or Emily and Travis but just said that it had been felt better for the business if a new Sales and Marketing Director was appointed.

His team were sorry to hear that and to see him go, as on the whole he'd been a good boss to work for but now there were varying degrees of apprehension about who would replace him.

After he'd packed his possessions into four boxes a couple of them helped him carry them down to his company car which the terms of his severance deal allowed him to keep for six months or until he got another job, whichever came first.

Finally he looked in on Travis and Emily to say goodbye then went back to Steve's office shook hands with him, met Greg who said 'Best of luck' then squaring his shoulders walked out of the room stopping at the door.

'I mean what I'm about to say. I do hope it all works out and that you manage to turn the business round. It is a great company and deserves to survive. Good luck and I'll watch progress with interest. Good bye'.

Steve stared at the empty doorway for a moment, then nodded, looked at Greg and stood up. 'Right come on, time to meet your troops'.

Although still shell shocked at the sudden and quite unexpected departure of their former boss the sales and marketing teams were pragmatic people and all they wanted to do now was size up the new guy and get on with their jobs.

Greg called them all into a small meeting room and spoke about his business philosophy of hard work, effective decision making, freedom to operate and results orientation.

'Get me good results and we'll all get along just fine. Screw up or fail and you're going to have problems. So let's not do that eh' and although he smiled there was no warmth in his eyes and his face was set like granite.

His team knew that this new man was going to be a much harder task master than his predecessor but they weren't necessarily afraid of that and indeed some of them looked forward to working in the new more demanding regime.

During the day he spent time with each of them, questioned a lot, challenged much, suggested alternatives, listened carefully and was free in complimenting where he saw good, cajoled where he saw room for improvement and generally at the end of the day had made a positive impact on them all.

Over the next three days of the week he accompanied the Sales Managers on their visits to customers where his open approach and willingness to listen to what those customers thought about Hardys, the products, the shortcomings and interestingly the opportunities that still existed made those hard nosed buyers think that maybe here was someone who might just succeed in creating and developing products that they needed to build and increase their business.

It was a busy week which he enjoyed and on the Friday evening he sat in Emily's office reviewing with her what he'd done and what were his thoughts.

'I think there are masses of opportunities out there. We've just got to think them through, decide where our priorities are, not try and be all things to all men, focus, get sharper and slicker and if we do that I think we just might get some new business.

Quality and decent margins for our customers that is what we need, coupled with some innovative packaging and new products.

Next week I want to try and understand two things. Firstly what we can do on the production lines which is different from what we do now but isn't going to cost a fortune to implement and secondly I want to have a look at our export business because that's where we ought to be able to pick up some big lumps of business quickly which will help cash flow and profitability.

I've got a few contacts and I'm going to squeeze them hard and see what happens. Well that's me for the week now I'm nipping over to Amsterdam for the weekend. I've discovered that there's a KLM flight out of Norwich direct to there'.

'Amsterdam? City of vice and goodness knows what else' laughed Emily. 'Now you behave yourself Greg' she said sternly wagging her finger at him.

'Yes Miss, but no vice. My best mate lives there and he's invited me for the weekend. He married a Dutch girl a few months ago so I'm certain she will ensure we behave ourselves' he grinned. 'You got any interesting plans?'

'Going boating for the weekend ...... with Steve'.

'Great. Have fun. See you Monday'.

Emily walked to Steve's office. 'Ready captain?' she smiled.

'Yea hang on I just need to update this spreadsheet' and he tapped away at the keys for a few minutes before exclaiming 'Done'.

Logging off he locked his desk and taking her hand led her out of his office and into the corridor just as Kelly, chatting on her mobile phone came by and seeing Emily holding Steve's hand muttered 'Good night' and scuttled off.

'Tabs says she's got a crush on me' Emily said quietly.

'Tabs fancies you?'

'No silly, that little marketing girl that just passed us. Her name's Kelly'.

'Has she? Well I've got a crush on you too'.

366

'Really?'

'Yes sort of. I really do rather like you and I am so looking forward to this weekend'.

'Me to'.

They'd decided that having enjoyed their recent afternoon boat trip it might be fun to hire a small cruiser for the weekend and meander around the Norfolk Broads, one of the great and beautiful areas of rivers, lakes and marshes of England.

Driving out to Stalham they completed the various forms that were needed by the boatyard, paid, received the ten minute instruction lecture, then were handed the keys to their boat, shown how to start and stop the engine, shown where the anchor and mud weights were stowed, warned not to exceed the speed limits to avoid the wash from the boat damaging the banks, and with a cheery 'Enjoy yourselves' from the boat man they were ready to go.

Deciding to change out of their office clothes into casual gear suitable for boating they explored below decks. Their boat was designed to take four people so there was what was grandly called the "master cabin" which was right at the front of the boat and featured a large double bed which tapered into the angle of the bow.

Next to this cabin was a bathroom with toilet, washbasin and full sized shower cubicle but no bath. Then came a second cabin with twin bunks, a reasonable sized saloon sitting area which also contained the kitchen, although Emily chided him when he referred to it as that and laughingly told him that on boats it was known as a galley. The saloon opened into the open cockpit at the rear of the vessel.

All in all it was cosy, well equipped, clean and they both thought as they changed that they were going to have a great weekend.

Now dressed more suitably they walked to the local supermarket close to the marina and stocked up on tea, coffee, wine, beer and whisky.

'You thinking about getting any food or just booze?' she queried.

'Well just something for breakfast. We're bound to find some waterside pubs for lunch and supper' so now adding bread, milk, cereal, bacon, eggs and tomatoes they staggered back to the boat and stowed everything away.

'Right off we go' said Steve as he pressed the starter button. The engine throbbed into life and as Emily untied the ropes to release them from the dock he gingerly eased the craft away and into the little cut which led to the main river.

Standing on the foredeck she coiled the front rope neatly and then nimbly walked along the narrow side strip of deck which ran beside the cabins until she gently jumped down into the cockpit where she stowed away some fenders and coiled the second rope.

'You look as though you know what you're doing?'

'My Dad had a boat when we were kids. It was smaller than this one but we had lots of weekends on it. He called it Harem' and she laughed.

'Interesting choice of name'.

'Well it was an amalgam of Hillary, my sister's name and Emily. Mum used to hate it but he thought it was fun and when we were small we didn't realise the significance of it.

Strange though that coiling the ropes came straight back to me. I guess it's like learning to ride a bike, you never forget. Dad always insisted that ropes were coiled neatly. Not only does it look neater but it's safer as having ropes draped all over the place is a risk on a boat as you could catch your foot and trip overboard'.

They pottered along enjoying the evening sunshine. Emily opened a bottle of red wine and poured two glasses then handing him one she sprawled on the cushions in the cockpit watching the water, wildlife and reeds drift gently by.

They'd been going for about an hour when what was obviously the edge of a village came into sight and seeing several boats moored there he suggested that maybe now they could find somewhere to tie up for the night and then walk into the village and get a meal.

'Sounds good but remember we are going downstream and the current is flowing out so when you decide to come alongside the bank turn round so you're heading into the water flow'.

He looked puzzled as he headed the boat in towards the edge of the river, slowed the engine down as he approached the grassy bank, put it into reverse and revved it up. The boat slewed sideways, thumped into the bank and then slid away out into the river again.

Frantically muttering while either revving or slowing the throttle and wrenching the steering wheel this way or that the boat kangarooed along near the bank every now and then brushing against some reeds or banging into the grass bank itself.

Hearing Emily hooting with laughter he turned and grinned. 'Making a balls of it aren't I?'

Yep. Shall I have a go?'

'Sure' and stepping aside he let her take up position.

Giving a quick look around in all directions she swung the wheel to the right, accelerated into mid river, turned to face upstream and then steering in towards the bank, slowed the throttle then cut the power right down allowing the boat to slowly drift in to the side coming to a perfect halt as it gently touched the bank. She flipped the wheel so that it stopped parallel to the bank and putting the throttle into neutral leapt out of the cockpit with the rear rope in hand, ran lightly along the side deck, collected the front rope and jumped onto the bank holding the two ropes and with the boat held fast.

'Can you bring the two metal spikes and the mallet to bang them in and hold the boat here please?'

He scrabbled around in the locker under a seat, found what she wanted and jumped less agilely then she had off the boat and banged in one and then the other spikes. Quickly she fastened the ropes and stood up.

'There we are'.

'Most impressive. You obviously haven't forgotten what your Dad taught you'.

'You tried to do it the hard way running with the current. It can be done but you need a bit more practice. Coming alongside into the current is much easier as it stops the boat for you'.

'Proper little Miss Ahab aren't you?'

Pouting she leaned forward popped a kiss on his cheek and then running a finger down his chest to his waist band said softly 'Like all things Steve .... practice makes perfect'.

'It sure does' he grinned pulling her towards him.

'Not now' she laughed easing herself away. 'Supper. Come on let's find somewhere to eat'.

They locked up the boat and walked arm in arm into the village where there were two pubs, both busy. The first said they'd have to wait about an hour before they could be served but the other a little further away from the river said they'd serve them in about ten minutes. Good as their word almost exactly on ten minutes a waitress took their order, allocated them a table outside on a little grassy area, quickly brought them a bottle of wine and said she'd bring their meals as soon as they were ready.

Emily and Steve leaned back in the metal rustic style chairs, drinking their wine, enjoying the sound of happy people all around them, the screams of the swifts as they swept overhead, the chirping of some hedge sparrows and the glorious sound of a thrush singing its heart out in the now dimming ready for night evening sky.

'This is lovely Steve'.

'Umm if only there weren't all the other people around it would be perfect'.

They talked about the village where they were, the boat and had just turned to talking about work when Tina their waitress arrived carrying a huge tray which she carefully balanced on the edge of the table and then unloaded their meals. Emily had chosen "scampi a la mexicaine" while he'd gone for the home made steak and kidney pie".

'Do they eat scampi in Mexico do you think?'

'Never been there but I don't see why not. Looks good though'.

They ate, talked, relaxed, drank the bottle of wine, had coffee and then he suggested that as it had by now got dark they ought to think about paying and going back to the boat.

All was fine as they wandered through the village and back towards the river but although some tied up boats had lights from the cabins showing it was actually quite difficult to pick their way along the bank in the darkness to where they'd moored up.

They were close to their destination when suddenly Steve tripped over something and went headlong onto the ground except that there was a cut away part of the bank at that exact point and his right arm, shoulder and head plunged into the river. As he tried to get up his foot slipped and his legs slid into the cold water.

'Oh shit!' he spluttered standing in four feet of cold water. He quickly scrambled back onto dry land.

'Are you alright?' she giggled.

'Fuck I'm soaked' and for a moment he didn't see the funny side of things.

'Hey come on we're nearly back. Now hold onto me. I'm not sure that boats, rivers and you are too well connected at the moment' she laughed.

Reluctantly he joined in the laughter and did as she suggested cautiously holding her hand as they made their way back to the boat.

They'd not put up the cockpit cover so jumping down into it he unlocked the door to the cabin and switching on the lights peered in the mirror where he saw a very bedraggled looking person staring back at himself with bits of weed and mud all over his face, hair and neck.

'Fuck' he repeated.

'Later maybe' she chuckled but for now I suggest you strip everything off and go and try out the shower'.

Which is exactly what he did and soon he re-emerged looking quite cheerful, wearing some clean dry jeans and tee shirt with nothing on his feet.

'Better?' she giggled.

'Yes' and he joined her in laughter.

'Oh Steve you did look funny' and she chuckled 'then when you tried to get up and slipped right in' and this time she simply howled with laughter. Rolling on her side she hugged herself as she lost control roaring with laughter. Eventually she managed to stop laughing and turning saw that he was looking possibly a bit miffed, so trying hard to control herself she offered to make some coffee while he poured out the whisky.

'Suppose I did look a bit of a twit' he suggested but this set her off again and it was ages before she finally stopped laughing.

They chatted about work. She said that she thought Greg had made a good start and he agreed and they both confirmed that they were pleased with the work that Travis was doing.

There came a point in their conversation when it just seemed to stop and they looked at each other, moved closer and kissed.

'I think it might be a good time to try out that slightly odd shaped bed don't you?'

'Yes please' and taking his hand she led for the short distance from the saloon into the main cabin, where they undressed and scrambled onto the bed.

'Emily' he said softly as she climbed onto his chest and looked down at him.

'You did bring some protection didn't you?' she asked softly.

'Of course. In fact if you stretch over there you'll be able to reach that little bag and if you hunt around in there I think you'll find what we need' and when she found and fitted one to him he gently rolled her onto her back and entered her.

The sex was good. Languorous, tender, gentle, deeply satisfying and took a long time and afterwards she whispered as she held him close that it had been good.

They slept enjoying the gentle rocking movements that occurred from time to time and when they woke the sun was shining brightly. Pulling back a curtain they blinked at the intense light then Steve clambered out of bed and put on the kettle to make some coffee.

While it was boiling he heard her in the shower and as he poured the coffee she emerged wrapped in a towel.

'Umm' she said picking up a mug and inhaling deeply.

He left her as he went and showered then pulling on a pair of shorts and flip flops he joined her in the cockpit. They sat side by side enjoying the warm morning sun relaxed and happy in each other's company as they slowly drank their coffee and watched the river come to life. Eventually he spoke breaking the quiet.

'Right I'm going to cook some breakfast and you young lady had better go and put on some clothes'.

'Aye aye captain'. Smiling she saluted and stood dropping the towel off one shoulder then switched to do the same with the other shoulder before walking into the cabin where she removed it completely, posing naked with one hand on a hip, the other hand behind her head and one knee in front of the other. She giggled, blew him a kiss then ran inside towards the bedroom cabin.

Finding the bacon, eggs and tomatoes that they'd bought yesterday he soon had delicious smells permeating the whole boat so when she emerged just wearing a bright yellow bikini she asked if she could have some too.

'Not just your usual cereal today then?'

'No that smells too good to pass up'.

They set up a small table and ate in the cockpit enjoying the food and the morning sunshine. Other boats passed them and they waved back to the various people who acknowledged them.

Around ten o'clock they cleared away, washed up made some more coffee and set off down the river.

The rest of the weekend passed lazily and happily. They ate in pubs, they drank beer sitting on grassy lawns, they relaxed in the boat and they made love several times.

We are never deceived – we deceive ourselves.

Jahann Wolfgang von Goethe

CHAPTER 21

Janie was exhausted by the end of the weekend. Having their two sons home was wonderful, but they were constantly on the go and wanting attention.

They'd arrived late on Friday afternoon after William had driven to their school to collect them for their weekend exeat.

Friday evening they all sat around the dining table chatting non-stop until it was time for the boys to go to bed and their parents stayed at the table discussing their sons and the various things that had been talked about over supper after which William had poured them both a drink which they savoured quietly.

They'd had sex every night this week except last night and Janie was hoping that she'd have another night off so she said that she had a couple of things that she needed to do before coming to bed so why didn't he go on up and not hang around for her?

She fiddled around tidying and putting things away then read the local paper before logging on to her computer to check her e-mails until seeing that it was just after midnight she hoped he'd be fast asleep by then.

He was but naked, so he'd obviously been expecting some bedroom action this evening. Being terribly careful to avoid waking him she slithered quietly into bed and managed to go to sleep straight away.

In the morning the boys bounced in wanting to know what the plans were for the day.

William said that he'd arranged to take them to a clay pigeon shoot in the morning and then they'd all go to a local pub for lunch. In the afternoon Janie was taking them to a friend where their ponies were stabled and they could have a ride and then in the evening some other friends with two boys about their own ages would be coming over so that all eight of them would have supper together.

So that's how the day went and Janie pleading a headache managed to put William off again as he rolled towards her once they were in bed.

What the bloody hell is the matter with him? He never used to be like this. Stopping him from a bit of nookie for nearly three weeks hadn't turned him into a constant sex demanding husband, surely?

Sunday they lazed around as a family in the morning with the boys giving snippets of information about the latest goings on at school then they all went for a walk in the afternoon, had tea for which Janie had baked a huge chocolate cake. She suggested that the boys took the remains of it back with them. Around six William drove the boys back to school.

When he got back they watched tv for a while, discussed some articles from the Sunday papers, had a snack supper with which they drank a bottle of wine and later she had a gin and tonic while he tucked into a malt whisky.

'Right come on then old girl, bed time I think' and from the way he spoke and brushed his hand over her buttocks she guessed what he had in mind. When he walked out of the en-suite completely naked and partly hard she knew she was right.

Ok get on with it and don't worry about me. Just get yourself to come then we can get to sleep as I'm really tired.

'Thank you darling' he whispered a little later as he lay beside her.

'My pleasure entirely …. alright for you?'

For Heavens sake don't say no and can we do it again!

'Wonderful ….. and for you too?'

'Yes darling and a lovely way to end a great weekend'.

Oh you creep! Just listen to yourself!

'It was nice seeing the boys wasn't it? I thought they both looked very well but they've grown haven't they?'

He grunted agreement and turned over to go to sleep.

Monday morning Janie having bathed and dressed collected the post from the hall floor and took it into the kitchen. After putting on the kettle and dropping a couple of slices of bread into the toaster she started separating the mail into two piles. One for William and one for herself.

After dealing with her post she switched on the computer and quickly typed a letter to Harry asking if he would see her. Addressing it to Her Majesty's Prison Wormwood Scrubs she sealed it then going out to the car, drove to a local post box and posted it.

***

Greg had enjoyed his weekend in Amsterdam and was now anxious to follow up on some of the customer discussions that he'd had last week as well as going to visit some more of their major customers. He was keen to generate some new business and so he settled down in his office and rang some of the major customers that he'd met for the first time last week. They were open to ideas that he put forward and by the end of the morning he had several possible avenues of new business opportunities. He summarised them in a document then e-mailed it to the senior sales managers and said that he wanted to discuss with them that afternoon.

Steve wanted a root and branch review of costs with Travis and where they could make more savings.

Emily was unhappy with the planning systems that they were using and had arranged for a selection of the Sales and Marketing teams plus a couple of junior accountants from Travis's finance department, together with an IT expert to get together with her in one of the meeting rooms to thrash through the faults and limitations in the present system and decide how it should be improved.

Travis needed to begin the preparation of a new budget document for the Bank. This was an onerous task and one to which he wasn't really looking forward but it had to be done, so telling Tabs he didn't want anyone to disturb him he started working on it.

Later Emily was pleased with her meeting that morning with the group of people she'd summoned. They had identified many ways in which the planning systems could be improved and several individuals had been tasked with follow up actions. Among them was Kelly who had again volunteered to take the notes.

'I see this as urgent so although I know you are busy please allocate some priority to completing your parts of this improvement activity' Emily demanded as the meeting closed.

Kelly considered that this applied to her as well and so she skipped lunch in a rush to get the meeting notes to her superstar which she did by just after two. Knocking on Emily's door she handed her the notes and asked when she should return to collect them.

'I don't know. I think the best thing will be for you to e-mail them to me, I'll check them through, make any changes that I consider necessary and then I can issue them from here. Thanks for doing them so quickly'.

'You won't want me to come back then?'

'No I'll take it from here' and looking down she picked up some computer print outs and studied them until Kelly quietly muttering 'Oh right' had left her office.

Emily quickly read the neatly prepared notes, made some amendments then put them aside to await the e-mailed version but no sooner had she done that her terminal pinged and checking she saw that Kelly had done as asked. She made the changes on screen then issued the document to everyone who'd attended the morning's meeting but also decided against sending a "thank you" to her admirer.

The week progressed seemingly at varying speeds for the main characters now running Hardys.

Greg spent more time visiting major customers but also turned his mind to how to get some quick easy wins. He considered that export might give him that opportunity. The business needed some big lumps of new business and quickly and his view was that the best way to achieve that might be to crack some contracts for overseas supply.

'I need to call in a favour' he started when phoning to the first of his export contacts. 'You remember how I got you supplies a year or so ago of that soft drinks product when you were in a muddle and needed stock quickly? You do? Good because now it's payback time ..... please'.

He explained his new job, talked through the product range said he'd e-mail some prices and would they come back to him today?

They did with an order for ten container loads of assorted preserves subject to some haggling over price.

Two other exporters also came good straight away and another said he might be able to do something in a few weeks.

Bouncing into Emily's office he grinned at her. 'Hey madam planner. Do you want the good news or the bad news first?'

'The good'.

'Ok. I've booked orders for a total of twenty eight containers of product for export'.

'Crikey that is good. Well done. And the bad news?'

'Got to be shipped by the end of the month'.

'Christ that's less than three weeks'.

'Yep that's what I worked it out to be' he chuckled.

'Thanks a bunch Greg. Standard export packs or any special labelling or requirements?'

'No I try and make things easy for you planners' he chuckled. 'Standard stuff so straightforward. Nice and Easy does it' he sang parodying the old song.

'Got any more bombshells like that up your sleeve?'

'Could be' he smiled 'leave it with you then .... ok?'

Nodding she picked up the phone and summoned two people to her office and when they arrived the three of them started to reorganise production schedules, plan overtime and check labour availability and one way and another find a way of doing what was required.

It was an enormous boost to the business and just what they needed.

Steve was delighted when he found out about it and went to see Greg.

'That's really great' he enthused.

'Hopefully just the start. I know I've only been here for a little while but I am convinced that there is plenty of business out there for us however we are going to have to be more flexible on some of our packaging constraints. Can we get a meeting of you, me, Emily, Travis I guess, maybe William and whoever runs the factory? That's Geoff Hawkins isn't it?'

'Yes'.

'Right well if we all get together let's really see what we can do? My experience is that usually lying around in some basement or other, most factories have a glory hole full of old pieces of machinery that are no longer in use but which are perfectly serviceable along with brand new kit that was bought but for one reason or another was never installed.

With a bit of ingenuity and a will to make it happen, you'd be surprised what can be achieved whereas at first sight seems impossible'.

Steve saw the logic in what was suggested and asked Tabs to set up such a meeting as soon as possible which she did for Wednesday afternoon being the only time that she could get them all together as their diaries were crammed full of appointments, meetings, review and planning session, phone calls to the Bank and generally working flat out to try and not only save Hardys, but turn it round back into a successful and profitable business again.

William was pleased to be invited to attend the meeting and was looking forward to it as not only did it give him something positive at which he might be able to contribute but he was becoming bored with being Chairman in name but barred from making any decisions or taking action within the business.

Knowing there was nothing that could be done about it though also didn't help. He'd represented Hardys at a couple of trade golf tournaments which he'd quite enjoyed as he was a reasonably good golfer with a low handicap, and he'd attended some trade dinners, helped with entertaining some customers but he felt underused and to quite a large extent undervalued.

However he could see that the team of Steve, Emily, Travis and now Greg were doing good things with the business and were making decisions that were clearly right but which he'd have struggled to make.

They were unencumbered by family or company history. They were here to do a job. Fix the problems, turn the business round from crushing losses leading to the brink of collapse into a profitable enterprise, hand it over all fixed and then move on to the next lame duck.

Odd life for them but he knew that good quality turnaround experts or teams were increasingly in demand. Sign of the tough times for British industry.

The positive side of this for him though was that he wasn't constantly struggling to make the business work, grappling with problems that he found hard to deal with, battling with the Unions over a whole range of issues and being chased by management for decisions.

Frankly not really being very busy work meant that he wasn't tired or exhausted now like he had been for the last few months. He felt fitter, more alert and so able to spend more time with Janie. Also he had to admit that he felt able to initiate sex more often than he had for years and frankly he was enjoying re-discovering the joys of making love with her so much more frequently.

In fact he thought looking at his watch and seeing that it was just gone four *I'll go home now and suggest to Janie that we spend the rest of the afternoon and all evening in bed like we used to when we were first married.* Although unable to hide the feeling that he was playing truant in some way he closed his office walked into the car park got into his Range Rover and arrived home about twenty to five.

'Darling you're early. Something wrong?' exclaimed an extremely surprised Janie as she looked at the large very old grandfather clock in the hall.

'Not at all. I hadn't got much to do so ....' and he walked over to her gave her a peck on the lips as he slid his hands around her waist 'I thought we might spend some time quality together. Maybe have the rest of the day in bed' he added as he squeezed her to him.

Oh Christ. The rest of the day in bed? Surely not. What the hell was getting into him? Was he secretly taking Viagra or something?

'Darling that would have been such a lovely idea but I have only just this minute promised Jackie that I'd pop right over to see her. She's worried about one of our horses. Says she thinks it's got a sore leg'.

'Oh dear. Shall I come with you?'

God no, especially as the whole story about Jackie and the horse's sore leg was a fabrication made up on the spur of the moment. How the bloody hell can I stop him?

'No look it's probably nothing serious. What I think you'd be better doing is going and checking on the work on the stable re-building. I am not sure that the workmanship on some of the brick work is up to the right standard. Some of the brickies seem ok but there are a couple who seem rather slapdash about things and I think it needs a man's approach.

I really do think that as you are here and the site foreman is as well that it would be worth you two getting together to review how they're getting on and importantly discuss how they are going to install the beams for the roofing.

After all we want it to look internally as well as externally just like it was before the fire, don't we?'

'Absolutely, yes that sounds a good plan in the absence of a little bout of activity upstairs' and he chuckled as he squeezed her hips.

'Plenty of time for that later my love' she smiled in reply popping a kiss on his nose.

'Yes hurry back. We could still have a nice early night and plenty of time in bed'.

Phew. Narrow escape – for now at least. Later though was another problem.

Getting in the car she immediately dialled Jackie's number on her mobile and when the call was answered said 'Ah good you're there. I'm coming over to look at my horse with bad leg'.

'You haven't got a horse with a bad leg'.

'Jackie listen to me. I have got a horse with a bad leg and I'm coming over to look at him right now'.

'Okay' came a very sceptical reply.

When Janie arrived a worried looking Jackie came out of the house to greet her.

'Hi. What's all this about one of ....'

'No I know there's no injured horse. I needed an excuse to get away and frankly it was the first thing that came into my head'.

'Why what's happened?'

So Janie explained about William's sudden rejuvenation and increased demands for sex.

'God you shouldn't complain. Wish I was so lucky. Mathew and I get it together once or twice a week usually Friday and Saturday although occasionally he gets a glint in his eye mid-week'.

'Well that's how it used to be with William, one or two times a week and that was fine but recently, in fact since I put him off for those weeks while I was having the tests after the Harry thing, he seems to want it every night. Today for example he's come home from work early and suggested we spend the rest of the day in bed. I mean I ask you. Rest of the afternoon and all evening? I don't know what's got into him. Whatever am I going to do Jackie? How I am going to cool him off?'

'Do you want to?'

'Yes I bloody well do'.

'Why'.

'Because we're too old for all that banging away every night malarkey' she sighed.

'So it was alright to get shagged senseless over and over again by Harry but it's not alright with your husband?'

'Ouch that's cruel and below the belt'.

'True though isn't it?'

'Maybe but it's different somehow'.

'How?'

'Oh I don't know. Just different. I suppose it's what people taking a lover do when they're together. Shag shag shag. It's all part of the illicit thrill. Would you for example want Mathew to suddenly start squeezing your bum in the kitchen and suggest you spend the afternoon and evening in bed?'

'You bet I would' she laughed.

Janie joined in the laughter and the two women now firm friends again sat and talked for a while until Jackie asked 'Coffee or wine?'

'You sure I'm not keeping you from something?'

'No. Mathew will be home around seven so you are welcome to stay till then. You never know when he arrives he might rush in, throw me over his shoulder and carry me off upstairs to bed. Or perhaps sweep everything off the kitchen table and ravish me there. Then again he might not and instead walk in slowly, say he's knackered, pour himself a drink and ask what's for supper?'

Janie stayed till she heard Mathew's car come up the drive and swing round to the side of the house. Shortly he appeared looking weary.

'Hi Janie, phew I'm knackered. Want a drink?' and he poured himself a large gin and tonic, walked over to Jackie and gave her a little kiss on the lips and dropped down into a comfortable armchair. 'What's for super my love?'

The two women exchanged glances as Janie responded 'No thanks Mathew. I must be going. I just came over to see Prince as he had a bit of a leg but it seems fine now'.

'Oh right ho. How's William?'

'In fine form thanks'.

'Good. Look if he fancies a game of golf tell him to give me a call. Some while since he and I battled it out over eighteen holes'.

'I will as I'm sure he'd like that. Bye' and giving him a little wave she walked with Jackie back to her car.

Getting in she started the engine then grimaced as Jackie leaned down to say 'Now go back home, have a nice bath with lots of scented foam, pop on some sexy undies, whisk William up to bed and spend the rest of the today shagging. I'll keep looking at the clock and wondering how many times you've done it!' then roared with laughter at Janie's horrified expression. As she watched Janie zoom off down the long drive she thought she must tell Pauline this latest episode in the love life of her friend

Arriving home Janie saw William over by the stables. He waved and walked over to her.

'Hi you're back. Good. Everything alright with the horse?'

'Yes seems to be improving. She'll keep me posted'.

'Good. Hey I'm glad you suggested that I catch up with that foreman chap. They had it all wrong round the back there. You remember that little series of indentations along the back wall? Well they'd missed those out completely. Here and look at this' and enthusiastically he held her hand as he led her onto the building site and pointed out some of the foundations. 'Got this in the wrong place .... and this .... and look over here. This doorway is quite incorrect. It was a single doorway that's needed for the tack room not a double.

It is a damn good job that you spotted that things were going wrong you know. Another couple of days and there would have had to be a major piece of taking down and re-constructing. Well done'.

Now that was a stroke of luck. Sheer fantasy thought of mine that there was something amiss with the building and it turns out that there is. Hey maybe I could get him focussed on that. After all the builders are going to be here for ages and he could hound the life out of them and while he was doing that he wouldn't be pestering me for sex. After all when William gets a bee in his bonnet about something he's like a terrier. He'll not let go of it. Yes this could be where he can burn off some of his mental energy which might result in his physical energy and sex drive diminishing as well.

'Thanks. Look I don't think that they really understand the plans properly and I'm sure that they'll be making other similar errors. You said the other day that you were much less busy at work now that turnaround team were in there helping you. So why don't you devote time to project managing this rebuild? Hardys could manage with less of your time for a while.

You could get the plans up on the walls of your study and check and double check everything that they do both before they do it and then again after they've done it. I think your input will be invaluable. After all not only do we want it right, we want it to look just like it did before the fire. I think without your personal attention there is a danger that it might not happen'.

He looked at her and nodded seriously. 'You know Janie I think you're dead right. It needs a proper project manager not just the foreman roughly guiding things along. I'll do that. Thanks for the suggestion. In fact I think I'll go and make a start on getting some drawings out and checking what they've done so far right now. Will that be alright?'

'Yes definitely it will' she said with much emphasis and watching him disappear off towards the workshop which was the one tiny piece of the original building that hadn't been burnt, pulled down or collapsed he emerged shortly with a spirit level, a long surveyor's tape measure and some pegs.

'I'm going to bloody well check everything that they've done so far. Call me when supper is ready will you?'

Agreeing that she would she watched as he bounded into the centre of the construction site and started to stretch out his tape. Walking indoors she smiled as she poured herself a gin and tonic and sat down to watch the BBC News to catch up on today's world events.

William came in at eight fifteen when she called him for supper and chatted enthusiastically about several mistakes that he thought he'd found and as soon as he'd finished eating he was off back out there again where he stayed until it was too dark to see, at which point he came indoors and went into his study.

The phone rang just after ten and he called out 'Janie ...... it's Jackie for you. Probably about your horse I imagine. If you pick up in the sitting room I'll put this extension down'.

'Right William thanks I've got it now' and she waited until she heard the click as he put down the study extension.

'Hello, Jackie?'

'So how many times?'

'Pardon?'

'So how many times have you done it then? I keep thinking of you two rutting away. Go on make me jealous'.

'Five and I'm absolutely shattered'.

'WHAT! Really?'

'Yes. We're just having a breather before we have a final shag and go to sleep'.

'Christ Janie, I never knew William was such a horny sod'.

'He isn't'.

'Eh?'

'I'm joking you fool. The real answer is none thank God. William's been out at the stable reconstruction' and she quickly filled in her friend on how well her plan had worked but as she'd almost finished explaining William walked in holding a glass of whisky.

'Ah well it's good that the cold water bandaging seems to be working'.

'The man himself has come in I guess?'

'Yes quite right. Well thanks for telling me about Prince. Let me know tomorrow how the leg is will you please? Must go now, bye' and she rang off, turned round and smiled at William. 'Prince seems to be responding quite well to the treatment'.

'Oh good. Look I imagine you'll be going to bed soon but do you mind if I stay on down here for a bit. I am just not happy with some of the things they've got on that plan and I need to spend some time understanding it'.

Are you crazy? Do I mind?

'No darling, stay as long as you like. It is so important to get it right isn't it?'.

She had a quick bath and then stretched out in bed smiled and was soon asleep and didn't hear him wriggle in beside her around one o'clock.

In the morning William was up early and back out at the construction site where he waited for the foreman and the brickies to arrive. When they did he marched them all into his study in the house and lectured them on where he considered the work was incorrect or of unsatisfactory quality and where he believed that they needed to make changes to their future plans.

Then they all trooped out to the site and Janie could see William pointing to things as he was followed around by the foreman and some of the workmen.

It was nearly ten o'clock when he drove off to Hardys.

***

The meeting to discuss production machinery that might be available started at two o'clock sharp and there was quite a group of people gathered in the large meeting room for the event. William, Steve, Greg, Emily, Travis, Geoff Hawkins the Operations Director who'd also brought along his engineering manager and two production managers.

'Blimey, cast of thousands' grinned Steve as he arrived and sat down. 'Now what we want to find out is what machinery we've got available that is either mothballed, spare, taken out of service, used to be in use but for one reason or another is no longer? In short what have we got that we don't use but we could do so to give us some more flexibility and enable Greg and his team to get us some new business? Has anyone got an inventory of what's lying around?'

'As a matter of fact yes we have' said Geoff. 'I pulled off a computer print of all spare kit, unserviceable or unused machinery and frankly there's a hell of a lot of it tucked away in the basement on this site. Here it is' and he dropped a computer print out that was about two inches thick onto the table and slid it across to Steve.

'Good grief' he said flicking through it. Does anyone know what all these mean. They are identified by asset numbers not by what they are. I know it's ok for the finance boys' he grinned at Travis 'to have all the numbers but it would be more helpful if instead of ..... err for example just stating 76P1L3MPF/14768 we knew what it actually was'.

'Means bought in nineteen seventy six, production unit one, line three, multi purpose filler and then it has its own unique identification number' explained one of the Production Managers.

'Crikey. Do you know what they all mean?' asked Geoff Hawkins clearly impressed at the knowledge of his senior manager.

'No but many of them I do'.

'We ought to be able to get something sensible out of the computer' suggested Travis looking at Emily. Couldn't we get some sort of translation into English rather than just numbers.

'Don't know' she relied making a note 'but I'll get someone onto it straight after this meeting'.

'We could always go and look' suggested William. 'Its ages since I went down to that basement and don't forget we've got that old warehouse up on the trading estate which is full of old junk. I don't think there is anything useable there but it might be worth a quick look'.

'God yes I'd forgotten abut that place' muttered Geoff.

'If you like I'll go in there on my way in tomorrow and see what's there and if any of it is any use ….. err if you'd like me to that is' William finished slightly diffidently.

'That would be very helpful thank you' replied Steve.

So the meeting wound on and at the end just before three thirty there was an action plan and the feeling that somehow they probably could find some kit that might be able to be brought back into use which would enable different shaped jars or packs to be run down the production lines.

***

Having checked with Steve that he wasn't needed any more that day and promising to check on the forgotten warehouse on the trading estate William left Hardys and was back home by five o'clock where after giving Janie a quick and very perfunctory kiss he changed into some old gardening clothes and was soon out on the building site.

He worked alongside the builders until they finished for the day around five thirty and then he spent the next hour and a half walking all over the site checking what they'd done during the day.

As it got dark he came in for supper but straight away afterwards he was into his study where he checked and re-checked the plans against the notes that he'd made on his site inspection.

He also spent some time reading through the papers and schedules in an old file that he had in his office where there was a list of machinery and other items stored in the old warehouse. Years ago some of this old kit had been lying around getting in the way at the factory or cluttering up their main machinery storage areas and so he'd insisted that it be moved off site to avoid confusion and disorder. Why he had the file in his office at home he couldn't remember but he put it by his briefcase ready for the morning.

Yawning he made his way upstairs where Janie was in bed reading.

He told her what he'd been doing then as he undressed said he was tired and after spending a few minutes in their en-suite he slid into bed, smiled as he leaned toward her and kissed her.

Hopefully this is going to be just a good night kiss and not a prelude to anything else.

'Nite Janie. I'm off to that old warehouse of ours on the trading estate tomorrow, then I've got a lunch at the Chamber of Commerce in Norwich, and I'll be back mid afternoon as the builders start to put up one of the ceiling beams and I want to be sure they get it right. Sleep well' and he turned onto his side facing her and although he threw one arm around her shoulders it was for comfort and companionship, nothing else.

'Good night darling. Sleep well'.

Are things back to normal? The test would be when they next did it whether that would start him off wanting to do it every night again?

Slowly starting to drift off to sleep her mind turned to Harry in prison and she wondered how long before she'd hear from him as to whether he'd let her visit. It was up to him. She couldn't force him to see her. He had to send her something called a Visiting Order which would permit her one visit.

Thinking about him locked up in his cell, probably sharing with someone else as she'd read that prisons were full and most prisoners were now forced to share cells made her mind run over some of the times they'd spent together and unable to stop herself she couldn't help thinking with pleasure of the sex which had been so exciting, stimulating and wonderful.

'Oh Harry why, why?' she muttered softly.

'Did you say something?' queried William sleepily.

'No darling, go to sleep'.

'Thought you spoke?'

'No you must have dropped off and been dreaming'.

'Ah good night'.

William left around eight next morning armed with the box file and the keys to the old lock up warehouse which was in the corner of the trading estate.

The door creaked as he opened it and going in took him back years as he saw some of the old machinery and remembered how some of it had been used. He wandered around the dusty building seeing, touching, remembering and then taking out his mobile phone he started taking photographs which he thought would be helpful.

It took him around an hour to complete his examination then locking the place up again he drove to Hardys. Going into Steve's office he was pleased to see Geoff Hawkins there too so he explained what he'd seen and handing over his mobile suggested that someone download the pictures onto a computer and print them off.

'Not sure how to do that' he admitted sheepishly.

'Oh we'll soon find someone who can. Thanks' smiled Steve. 'We've already found some kit here that we think could be brought back into operation which might give us the chance to run some different jar shapes down the line.

So meetings took place throughout the factory. Old designs were uncovered from various locations Greg became interested in some of them as he thought that a retro look range of premium quality preserves and pickles might appeal to their customers.

Deep doubts, deep wisdom.   Small doubts, little wisdom.

Chinese Proverb.

CHAPTER 22

On Thursday morning Emily had just settled into her office, fired up her computer and was starting to sip her first cup of coffee machine coffee when the door was pushed open and Steve marched in.

'Have you finished revising those planning schedules?' he snapped clearly irritated by something.

'No not yet I'll try ………'

'I said I wanted them for first thing this morning, so where the hell are they?' he interrupted

'Steve I'm sorry but I have been tied up on other things…….'

'Not good enough' he grumbled. 'When I say I want things by a particular time then that's when I want them. Now stop whatever you're doing and get on with it. I need to study them and then discuss them with Travis as it'll affect the draw down of the last chunk of the money the Bank's putting up for us and I have a call scheduled with the Bank just after lunchtime'.

'Look if I can just explain. You see …….'

'I don't want explanations. I want the numbers' and with that he stormed out of Emily's office banging the door shut as he went.

'Bastard' she muttered then closing down the data she had on her screen she pulled up instead the latest planning schedules of forward demand and settled down to update and complete the information for which Steve had been waiting.

So ok, she was late getting it done but it didn't warrant all those histrionics from him this morning surely?

It was a demanding, time consuming and very detailed task fitting together all the various production and purchasing requirements to meet the varying customer demands for product, packaging and timescales and it was something that to be honest she'd put off on a couple of occasions as it was such a boring and difficult task but it was one that had to be done.

Previously some of Hardys people had handled this but since she'd reorganised the planning process and installed new working methods it was now something which she managed herself. In due course she'd train others to do this work but for now it was her own job but it did take time and she regretted not having started the training process with others already.

Her phone rang at ten thirty. 'Are they ready yet?' demanded Steve.

'No but nearly finished, won't be long'.

'Come on hurry up I'm still waiting' and he put down the phone.

It was about an hour later that she walked along the corridor to his office and went in. He was talking on the phone but as soon as he saw her he said 'Hang on a sec' to whoever he was speaking and cupping the hand piece glared at her as he said 'planning schedules?'.

'I've just e-mailed them to you. Do you want me to stay while you open them?'

'No I'm sure I will be able to manage to understand them after waiting so long'.

Without responding to him she turned and muttering 'Well fuck you then' but so quietly that only she heard, left his office and returned to her own where she put her head in her hands but stopped herself from crying.

'Come on' she said to herself. 'You're a business woman don't get all weepy just because you've had a bollocking. These things happen and it'll blow over'.

She saw Steve later in the afternoon at a production review meeting where he was irritable to everyone and at the end she stopped him as he was leaving. 'Were those planning numbers ok? How did the phone call to the Bank go?"

'Badly but if I'd had more time to study them and longer to talk with Travis about them we ….. I, might have done better on the phone. We got clobbered. The Bank isn't happy with the speed of recovery and think we need to do more to get the turnaround happening faster.

So your late supply of the figures caused me a real issue. Next time when I ask for something by a particular time just do it by then, right?'

'Right. Sorry'.

'So am I' and he walked off.

On Friday he ignored her except at a couple of meetings when he had to speak to her and for the first time since starting this project with him she was glad when Friday night came and she could leave the Hardys business for the weekend.

As she was tidying up her desk ready to leave Travis looked in. 'Doing any thing special this weekend? Maybe something to cheer yourself up. You've had a rough couple of days haven't you?' he asked kindly.

'Yes they've not been the best two days in my business life. I don't know why Steve's got so ratty?'

'Oh it ain't just you. We've all had a thumping from him over the last few days. Still the week's over and we've got two days to relax and forget about it, him, Hardys and the bank' and as he smiled his whole face seemed to relax and shine. 'Now you haven't answered my question as to whether you've got anything special planned for the weekend?'

'No I haven't'.

'Fancy a cheer up meal tomorrow? You and me'.

Yes' she smiled 'that would be nice. Thank you. Where shall we go?'

'Well now I ain't boasting but I'm a reasonable cook so how about you come to my place and I'll do something for us?'

'That would be lovely thank you'.

He gave her the address of the cottage that he was renting in Lemwade, a small village west of Norwich and suggested she arrived around seven so she went back to her apartment much cheered and put her frustration and anger at Steve to the back of her mind.

All through Saturday she kept thinking of the coming evening and having checked her car's sat nav for the distance and estimated time it would take her to get to Travis's place she showered and washed her hair ready for the evening.

Dressing in a short white crop top and blue denim very short mini skirt that nicely showed off her long and well tanned legs, she slid on some blue driving shoes and at six thirty set off, following the metallic voice of the sat-nav until it said "You have reached your destination" as she pulled up outside a small semi detached cottage in Travis's village.

Collecting the bottle of wine that she'd brought with her she locked the car and walked up the little pathway to the front door which was open. Peering through she called out 'Travis, hello?' and as she stepped inside he appeared from the rear of the building.

'Hi come on through. I was having a beer in the back garden' and he led her out into the sunlight which in the evening fell onto a wooden decking area at the far end of the garden overlooking a small stream.

'Sit down. Those loungers are quite comfortable. I'll get you a drink. Would you like a beer or I've got some white wine in the fridge. Or red if you prefer …. not from the fridge' he laughed.

'I brought a bottle' she replied holding it out to him. 'I'm happy to have a glass of that. It's not too heavy and as I'm driving I'll have one now and then another with whatever gastronomic feast you've prepared and that'll do me'.

'Sure' and he disappeared inside re-emerging shortly with another beer in hand for himself and a glass of the light red wine which he handed to her. 'Here you are. Cheers and welcome to Badger Cottage'.

'Lovely name. Have you seen any badgers?'

'No can't say that I have. Now are you hungry?'

'Yes. I skipped lunch so I could do justice to your meal this evening. What are we having or is it to be a surprise?'

'No. To start I've done crab timbale and shrimps set on a bed of crisp lettuce and to follow we're gonna have grilled duck breasts in a slightly spicy sauce which is my own creation and couscous. I hope you'll like it'.

'Sounds wonderful'.

They sat in the garden, watching the stream bubbling along, listening to the evening song of the birds and enjoying not only the warm sunshine but also each other's company.

Travis was easy to talk to and fun to be with and the time flew by until glancing at his watch he said I reckon we could eat now if you're ready. Inside or out?'

'Oh out. It's such a lovely evening and in a few months it'll be winter. Let's enjoy this while we can'.

On one side of the decking there was a small table with chairs but insisting that she sat still Travis soon had laid it with a cloth, cutlery and then brought out their starters already plated up.

'Dinner is served my lady' he said bowing and holding one of the two chairs out for her to slide into place at the table.

'Thank you my man' she chucked.

The meal was delicious and Travis was undoubtedly an excellent cook. The crab shrimps and lettuce was wonderful and the duck in his own special sauce was outstanding with subtle and interesting mixtures of flavours bursting onto the tongue.

Finally putting her knife and fork down onto her empty plate she blew out her cheeks as she said 'Travis that was probably the nicest meal I've had in a very long time. Thank you'.

'Oh it was a pleasure and I'm just real glad that you enjoyed it. Now I don't do puddings but I've got some fancy ice cream if you like?'

'No coffee would be fine. I don't think I could cram in any more, not even a spoonful of ice cream ..... fancy or not!'

The sun had gone in by now and it was starting to get dark and feel a little chilly so she suggested that they have coffee inside and helped him to clear the table and carry things back into the kitchen. As she glanced around the cottage he put the kettle on for coffee.

Originally one of a pair of farm worker's cottages it had been gutted and the sitting room and kitchen had been knocked through into one long room which was quite spacious and light while off the small hallway a tiny loo and washbasin had been cleverly fitted into what had once been a large corner cupboard.

It was neat, well decorated and functional and ideal for a single person or a couple.

'This is nice Travis' she said waving her hand around.

'Suits me perfectly as it's small, easy to manage and ideally placed for Norwich. I got fed up with hotels and here I can be me. If I want to just slob out for an evening or at weekends I can do so. Like you I guess in your apartment in the City?'

She sat on the settee and seeing him staring at her legs carefully tugged down her micro skirt to preserve her modesty. He handed her a mug of coffee which smelt delicious having been made from real ground coffee.

'This has been a nice evening. I've really enjoyed it' she smiled.

'Yea me too. Puts the hassles of the week behind us doesn't it?'

'Especially that bloody Steve' she responded vehemently.

He's got a tough job here you know. It's his biggest turnaround yet and he's very keen to ensure that it is seen not just as successful, but stunningly successful. He sees his future career in becoming known as a top flight turn around expert and he needs this one as a success, under his belt'.

'Doesn't explain why he was so nasty though does it? He didn't need to be like that did he? Ok so I was late with his bloody planning schedule but he could have just .... oh never mind don't let's spoil the evening by talking about him'.

'Tell me are you and Steve together?'

'Together?'

'Yes you know, an item, a couple, only I know you've been spending quite a bit of time together, weekends and so on and I just wondered if there was something more to the row than just some late figures?'

She looked at him for a minute or two and then said softly and slightly sadly 'If there was some sort of together there certainly isn't now and no there's been nothing in our private life that could have caused him to become so horrid to me'.

'Just wondered that's all'.

'Any rate I said I don't want to talk about Steve' and she closed off that subject of conversation so they talked about music, business in general, politics until just after ten she smiled at him.

'Travis it has been a really and I mean really .... lovely evening but I'd better think about going' and leaning forward she popped a little kiss on his cheek. 'Thanks'.

'The pleasure was all mine Emily'.

For a moment there was a frozen stationary silence as they both looked at each other until as if by unspoken agreement their heads moved slowly towards each other and their lips touched gently, then changed from touching to kissing.

It wasn't forced or passionate just very tender and soft as they stayed there each wanting to kiss harder but both determined not to create a situation that maybe they wouldn't be able to control.

He eased away. 'Are you sure you and Steve are not together?'

She nodded not trusting herself to speak as her stomach was starting to churn and she could feel her heart start to thump.

He leaned back towards her but this time his kiss was harder as his lips pressed firmly against hers. Immediately she responded with equal firmness until she pressed her tongue forward and forced his teeth apart to explore the inside of his mouth and he reciprocated.

They kissed for a long time just holding each other and stroking heads, hair and necks until his hands moved down to her top and stroked her breasts lightly and very gently. She in turn found one of her hands running up his jean covered thigh.

As their lips moved apart he said so softly that it was almost unable to be heard 'Shall we go upstairs?'

Her reply was a whisper. 'Yes ……. please'.

On his bed, naked they kissed and she asked if had any condoms?

'No sorry …… can we still continue?'

'Yes but I'm not on the pill so when you're about to come you'll ……'

'Don't worry I'll be very careful' he promised interrupting her as he pressed her onto her back and kissed her fiercely.

Although still a bit worried as to whether he'd be able to control himself, she gradually relaxed as he was kind, tender, considerate, took time, and she lay there shuddering as he, buried deep within her and moving very skilfully, gradually brought her to the brink of orgasm and then let her down, before doing it again. Several times she thought she was about to climax but he inhibited her from doing so whispering 'Wait, come later'.

Thrashing around in perfect ecstasy she finally gasped that she couldn't hold back any longer so panting and grunting with increased ferocity as he moved more strongly within her suddenly the damn burst and she screamed as her orgasm at last rippled through every sinew of her body. Still he moved and she felt a second wave approaching which also exploded throughout her.

Groaning, gasping almost unable to speak she clung to him her nails digging sharply into his shoulders until suddenly she exhaled deeply and relaxed. She wanted to tell him how wonderful it had been but he was still kissing her fiercely and starting to move within her much more quickly. Suddenly he jerked his hips backwards and rolled away and off her.

'Here let me help finish you' she said sliding down the bed and wrapping a hand around his erection started to rub him. 'Is this alright?'

'Yeah but grip tighter and go faster'.

She did as requested and a few seconds later he jerked, grunted and shot semen all over his belly and her hand.

'Keep going but slower now' he muttered and following his demands she gradually slowed until he stopped spurting, then running her thumb and forefinger in a ring shape from root to tip a couple of times she saw that he was finished.

Wiping her hand on the sheet she lay back with one arm behind her head as turning onto his tummy he faced towards her and said 'Thank you'.

'Travis I'm sorry that you had to finish like that but …….'

'It was fine. I quite understand. No problem' he drawled then pausing he looked up at her 'was it ok for you?'

'Perfect …… quite perfect ………thank you'.

Pulling his head onto her chest she could feel his day old stubble against her breasts as she stroked his hair and lay feeling calm, satisfied and relaxed.

'It was good wasn't it?'

'You said it just now. Perfect'.

'Couldn't have been perfect for you having to finish like that?'

'Oh as I said, it was no problem. Long time since I …….'

'Had a girl wank you off?' she interrupted laughing softly.

'No well yes. No, that wasn't what I was going to say. I was going to say that it was a long time since I made love with anyone, so I'm glad it was ok for you'.

'Really. You surprise me a good looking guy like you? How long?'

'Hell let me think. Well I guess it must be five months, maybe even a little longer?'

'I'm glad I broke your drought then'.

'So am I. The problem I have is that going from project to project like I do and country to country as well, it's difficult to form longer term deep and meaningful relationships and I don't usually go for a quick one night stands. Tonight though was different somehow'.

'What was different about tonight then?

'You honey …… you. Don't ask me what it was but somehow it just seemed that we both needed one another'.

'Yes I think we did'.

Cuddling together they relaxed with each other and it was much later when she leaned over to drop a kiss on his nose. 'It's time I was going' she said quietly.

'You can stay if you like'.

'No I'll go, but thanks. Now I need the bathroom' and sliding out of bed she padded around in darkness opening another door upstairs and finding a second bedroom which she saw Travis had set up as a study so retreating she tried the third door and found what she was looking for.

When she went back into the bedroom it was still dark as he hadn't put on the lights but the moonlight was streaming into the room and she could see to find her clothes.

Having pulled on her panties she sat on the bed with her back to him as she fastened her bra then tugged her crop top down over her head and finally stood to pull on her little skirt. She saw him staring at her legs as she did do.

'My shoes are downstairs as is my handbag. I need my comb'. She walked out of the bedroom, found a landing light switch and trotting downstairs retrieved her shoes then pulling a comb out of the bag quickly got her hair into some semblance of order. Checking a mirror she deftly applied a trace of lipstick, ensured that there was none on her teeth and turned to see Travis watching her with an amused expression on his face and dressed in a multicoloured dressing gown.

'Wow that's some robe' she laughed. 'Just like Joseph's multi-coloured dream coat in the musical'.

'Christmas present from my Mom. She wanted to send me something that was expensive and this is pure Thai silk; useful and I'd told her I'd lost my robe somewhere; and light to post. She seems to have hit the spot on all three counts' he grinned. They looked at each other as he asked. 'Sure you won't stay?'

'Yes I'm sure but it has been lovely. All of the evening Travis not just the upstairs part. I can't remember when I've enjoyed myself so much'.

He smiled, nodded, muttered 'Me too thanks ….. well if you're sure?'

'Yes, I'm sure. Bye' and leaning to him she kissed him. He put his arms around her and kissed her back before walking with her to the door and down the little path then stood by her car as she got in and started the engine of the Mini.

'Nice car. Pleased with it?'

'Yes. What do you drive?' she asked knowing that although she worked with him she had no idea what car he drove.

'An old Jag-oo-ar' he replied pronouncing the word in the slightly odd way that Americans do. 'XJS Cabriolet. I'll give you a spin in her one day. Lovely old classic car'.

She nodded realising that it was just the right choice of car for him then blowing a kiss and mouthing 'Thank you' she drove off.

He went back indoors and poured himself another beer which he took outside to the decking and sat listening to the night and the stream.

She, once back at her apartment, ran a hot bath and while waiting for it to fill poured herself a glass of wine which she took into the bathroom with her then when the bath was full she lay back in the hot water slowly sipping her drink thinking about the evening.

Amazing she decided. When she'd gone there tonight she had no thought of sex and no idea that they'd finish up in bed together and she believed neither had he. It was just one of those things that happened but now that it had, she had to consider the implications.

Her boss with whom she'd almost been having a proper relationship seemed to have turned against her but she'd have to go on working with him. Now she'd slept with another colleague with whom she worked closely and suddenly a thought struck her which made her giggle.

If she now bedded Greg then she'd have had all three of the men with whom she was working on this turnaround project. She told herself not to be naughty and to put such sluttish thoughts away. Besides on a practical point not only did she not remotely fancy Greg at all, but also he was married.

Getting out she dried herself and selecting a fresh clean white nightie from her chest of drawers was soon in bed part curled up into a ball as she drifted happily off to sleep thinking of Travis.

Next morning she woke up relaxed and happy, unlike the previous couple of days where she'd woken upset and fed up as a result of Steve's unpleasantness.

She fixed herself some fresh fruit and juice for breakfast and then decided to clean and tidy her apartment. An hour and a half later it was spick and span so she showered, put on her leotard and tracksuit and drove to the gym.

After signing in and leaving her things in her locker she was just about to get on an empty running machine when she spotted Kelly who waved frantically at her from the other side of the gym.

'Oh bloody hell' she muttered but calling 'Hi' she smiled and waved to the little marketing girl.

It wasn't long though before Kelly came over and getting on a vacant running machine next to her said 'Hello'.

'I didn't know you were a member here?'

'I've just joined. It's my first day here today. Do you come here every Sunday?'

'Most and some evenings too'.

'I love the colour of your leotard'.

'Thanks. I got it in London'.

They chatted off and on and Emily tried to maintain a balance of politeness, while remaining a little aloof to avoid encouraging the other young woman in any way. To her relief after ignoring her for about half an hour as she moved from one piece of equipment to another, Kelly said that she was leaving now as she was going to her parents for Sunday lunch.

When she finally finished her workout Emily showered, dressed and drove back to her apartment.

A salad for lunch and then she spent the afternoon catching up on some magazines and the Sunday Times and Sunday Mail newspapers which took her till early evening, where she decided that what she'd really like now was a nice girly evening chatting, drinking some wine and perhaps watching a weepy movie on tv but as she didn't really have any girly friends locally she concluded that she could have the wine and watch an old movie without the chat. That was one of the drawbacks of this nomadic life of the turnaround executive. Constantly away in new places and difficult to build or maintain friendships as Travis had found.

Sipping a glass of wine she knew that actually what she really wanted wasn't to be curled up on the settee having a girly chat, but to be curled up on a settee or in bed with Travis and for a moment she thought about calling him then put the idea out of her mind.

'Don't be silly' she said out loud 'it was just a one off event'. It had been great but that's all it was. And then there was the Steve thing.

Whatever had happened she wondered? Until last Thursday they'd got on well, slept together with increasing frequency, seemed happy with each other and she'd once or twice caught herself wondering if this was a relationship that could develop into something permanent?

He was good looking. Not drop dead gorgeous but handsome, interesting to talk with, fun and generous. In bed he was kind, thoughtful, considerate and pretty good at sex.

So what had suddenly gone wrong? She had no idea. Maybe he'd gone off her. Found someone else? Perhaps in time she'd find out but she wasn't going to chase after him. If there was to be any sort of reconciliation then it would have to be up to him.

Yes she decided he'd have to be the one to say 'Hey look I'm sorry. Let's talk about things and try and sort it out'.

But now there was Travis in the picture too, so did she want Steve to say that?

***

William was now wholly immersed in the stable re-build project and seemed to spend every spare moment on it. He was also re-designing the pathways leading to the emerging stable block and starting to decide improvements to the staff and tack rooms when they were built including possibly a shower as well as a toilet.

It was Sunday evening when Janie was bathing before going to bed that he appeared and sitting still fully dressed on the edge of the bath started chatting before running his hands over her neck and leaning down dropped a kiss on the top of her head before walking out of the steamy room.

Janie relaxed in the huge old fashioned bath then sat up as he had come back in stark naked.

'Shove over' he grinned 'plenty of room for two in here' and stepping in sat facing her.

It had now been over a week since they'd had sex and from the expression on his face that was about to change. Well ok. It wasn't that she didn't want

401

to make love with him it was just that she didn't really want a husband who had changed to wanting it every day. That was alright years ago but not now. However the abstinence of these last few days had in fact started to make her feel the need herself so if he wanted to do it tonight well she'd be ok with that.

They sat smiling at each other for a while then he knelt up, leaned forward and kissed her. The kiss went on for some time and he ran his hands to her breasts where he tweaked her nipples as he pushed his tongue deep into her mouth.

Janie had always had sensitive nipples and it wasn't long before they went hard a fact that he noticed as he stopped kissing her.

'Ah ha getting a little excited are we?' he grinned. 'Well so am I. Up periscope' and taking a deep breath he laid back submerging himself completely and holding his now erect prick vertically so that it poked up out of the warm water.

She knew what he wanted so changing to a kneeling position she waved her hands to shake off the water then holding her hair behind her neck leant forward and licked and nibbled him before swallowing him completely.

She knew he enjoyed her doing this and although it wasn't one of her favourite activities she didn't mind doing it occasionally as she knew it gave him much pleasure.

Unlike with Harry where she'd sucked and licked and chewed his cock for ages and loved doing it for him. That was different somehow though.

Tonight though she guessed it wouldn't be for long as he'd soon run out of breath which he did sitting up spluttering and chuckling.

'Come here' he commanded as he slithered forward on his bottom and lifting her onto his lap waited while she squatted either side of him before lowering herself down. 'That's it now …….. fire torpedoes' and he lunged up into her pussy.

Janie leaned forward and kissed him as she started to move up and down while he gently squeezed her nipples and responded to her kissing. Fortunately the bath was so big and deep that their increasingly energetic activities didn't cause the water to slop over the side and they both moved towards their climaxes as they grunted, gasped and kissed each other.

'Nearly there' he muttered so clenching her pussy muscles and thinking of her own pleasure she soon brought herself to the point of climax holding there until his deep groans and slowing movements told her that he'd come but it was then only a matter of seconds until throwing her arms around him she orgasmed, her groans of pleasure echoing loudly in the bathroom.

As she came down from her peak she kissed him again, smiled and asked 'Alright darling?'

'Oh yes very alright, thanks'.

They uncoupled and lay one at each end of the bath facing each other and smiling.

Now that actually had been rather good and she had to admit she'd not only needed it but had enjoyed it.

They lay for some while chatting and stroking each other's feet and lower legs, topping up the bath with more hot water from time to time until the last top up ran only cool water into the bath as they'd obviously emptied the hot water tank. She also sensed that his stroking of her leg was moving higher and he seemed to have a bit of a smile on his face and a quick glance showed that his prick was getting bigger again.

Oh Lord once was fine, rather good actually but let's not get carried away!

Standing up she said that she was getting a little cool now and was going to go to bed. He too stood and yes she had been right as although not erect, he certainly wasn't flaccid, so grabbing two towels she threw one at him and used the other to dry herself.

When they'd finished drying he stood behind her pushing his naked body against her back and she could feel his erection starting to press against her buttocks as his hands slid around her waist and up to her breasts which he started kneading gently and sensuously.

God he did want it again.

She watched his hands in the large mirror which for a moment reminded her of Harry's mirrored bathroom and bedroom as they worked on her breasts lifting, stretching, squeezing and gently pulling her nipples which started to harden again. Then she saw him lower his chin onto her shoulder before twisting to enable him to lick her ear while one hand made its way down her front and she was fascinated to see it move into her bush before sliding towards her pussy.

It was intriguing and quite erotic seeing herself being worked on like that, so in spite of herself what one of his hands was still doing to her left breast and his other to her pussy along with him slowly starting to rub his erection up and down against her bottom she couldn't stop herself from starting to breath more quickly.

They stayed there for several minutes and her pussy quickly got very wet as she watched herself being stimulated.

Twisting her head round she found his lips and kissed him then turning to face him pressed herself against his front.

'Come on' he muttered taking her hand and soon they were on the bed, with him plunged deeply within her and her legs wrapped around his back and her arms around his shoulders as they made love quickly and passionately.

He took longer this time before he climaxed which enabled her to control her own rise to orgasm but when it happened to her surprise and delight it was extremely powerful. She groaned loudly and for a prolonged period of time as he squirted inside her, stopped moving and flopped down on top of her.

Time to be magnanimous and say thank you to him. No now stop kidding yourself. It was bloody good and it's nice that you've had two orgasms with William in one evening.

'Thank you darling. The first time in the bath was good but that was wonderful' and she unwrapped herself from him as he slid to her side.

'Yes good wasn't it? Maybe I'll ravish you in the bath again if that's what it leads too'.

Oh yes? We'll see!

'Umm lovely. Now come on cuddle me and let's go to sleep'.

'Hang on I just need to put my shorts on'.

'William don't disturb such a lovely post lovemaking moment. I'm going to sleep naked tonight .... and so are you' she whispered as she took hold of his now almost flaccid prick and stroked it. 'Good night'.

There now that was ok wasn't it?

On Monday morning Janie was reflecting on her dilemma about William. There was no doubt that she'd enjoyed their lovemaking last night. It had been fun, erotic and satisfying and she recognised that

William was quite good in bed. Not a patch on Harry's abilities but perfectly adequate and she'd want to make love with him again. Just not every night. Oh well she sighed to herself just have to see how we can handle it.

Going into the hall she'd heard the post van drive up a few minutes ago so collecting the pile of letters and packets from the floor she started sorting it into two piles.

As usual one for William and the other for those addressed to her. Her heart bumped as she saw that one of the letters had a postmark **HM Prison Service** and with trembling fingers she slit it open.

Extracting the two sheets of paper she read that he'd agreed to see her and said that he was looking forward to it. He suggested Thursday of the following week.

Further official information was included regarding the procedure to be adopted on arrival and when visiting prisoners, advised that she would be subject to being searched on arrival and departure and given dire warnings over any attempt to smuggle in any unauthorised materials.

As the date for the visit was a week and a half away she picked up the phone and rang Jackie to check whether she would still come and whether she could make that date.

After checking her diary she said that she could.

'Great and are you still ok to then come on to the cottage in France with me?'

'Yes I'd love to see it. Do you know if it's still yours?'

'No I'm hoping that Harry will tell me. Assuming it is we'll stay there Thursday night but shall we stay on for the weekend? It's a lovely area of France and we could come back Sunday. What do you say?'

'Hey that's sounds good. Let me check with Mathew and I'll get back to you'.

It was only ten minutes or so later that she called back. 'I rang Mathew at his office and he's fine for me to go away with you so yes that sounds lovely. What happens though if the cottage isn't yours any longer?'

'I guess we don't go still let's keep our fingers crossed eh?'

Ringing off she then logged onto Easyjet's website and booked two return tickets to the south of France. Finally she rang Pierre and asked him to have her car ready for her when she arrived. He said that it wouldn't be a problem if she was late arriving as he'd leave the car outside the garage with the keys hidden in the exhaust pipe.

***

At Hardys, work on trying to develop product ranges that could be run on quickly modified machinery was going on apace and Greg was in detailed discussions with some of their customers who were keenly interested in a possible retro range provided the quality was high and the price to them sufficiently low that they would be able to make a big margin from their sales.

What was encouraging to Greg was that two of their customers who over the past couple of years had deleted and stopped stocking most of Hardys products had both committed themselves to not only stocking the new range but also promoting it heavily.

One of them had asked whether the pickles and sauces could also be developed into the retro look and he undertook to find out and revert to them quickly.

Fortunately Geoff Hawkins thought that they could, so when Greg called the customer back and said yes they could do it they committed to supporting and stocking that range as well.

Greg also obtained some further export orders and when Emily asked if the proposed new retro range was going for export, Greg said not at this stage. He wanted to establish it in the UK first but he did think that there could be interest from Japan who seemed to like upmarket quality well packaged products from yesteryear.

It was interesting to observe around the whole business how the knowledge that lots of new business might be coming had seemed to galvanise almost everyone into action and doing that little bit extra.

In fact Steve described it at a Board meeting as being like a bee hive full of positive and co-ordinated activity, all working for the common good.

Attending the Wednesday Board meeting were Frank Gold and Barry Field from the bank and although they were pleased with his description they reminded him and all the other senior management present that positive activity was one thing but what they wanted was positive numbers on the bottom line.

'You seem to be making progress I'll grant you that but what we want is definite evidence that the business is starting to turn the corner.

'I think it hasn't yet turned the corner but the good news is that the corner is now in sight' smiled Travis. 'I believe that previously Hardys was heading in one direction only .... down. Now if we can continue the progress we are making then we might be approaching a point where we have some choices leading to survival and then further down the road we might head into calmer waters of profits'.

He smiled again 'Sorry about all the mixed metaphors but you know what I mean'.

The two bank men looked at him and nodded. Travis was impressive and Steve had done well to get someone of his competence into the company. Actually in spite of their somewhat gruff approach they were appreciating the efforts that were being made and also they were impressed with the team managing the turnaround especially Steve but their approach remained as appearing to be unsatisfied and they felt this was the best way of keeping the management on their toes.

'We'll actually turn a profit when this month's results are published you know' said Travis. 'First time for a long time. Now that's good news for you fellas to take back to your bank colleagues'.

The meeting finished at lunch time and after the two Bank men had gone and everyone was leaving to go back to their own offices Steve asked Emily to stay on for a moment.

'Yes what is it?' she asked coldly when they were alone.

'I wondered if you'd like to come for a drink this evening, or tomorrow maybe?'

'No thanks'.

'Oh. You sure?'

'Yes I'm quite sure thank you. Is that all?'

'Yes'.

'Right well if there's nothing else I'll be getting back to my office then'.

Watching her walk out of his office Steve felt some disappointment and even a little annoyance. What's the matter with her he wondered? She'd been offish with him since that little bust up over late production of some figures. Oh well she'll get over it he mused as he called up his e-mails on screen.

Emily though was cross. No apology just a suggestion that they go for a drink. Well no thank you Mister.

The rest of the week went by as they continued to make progress on the new product ranges. One line in production Hall two had been converted and they were ready to trial the old packing line and filler. Even the engineers had pulled their fingers out and made things happen quickly, adopting a *"how do we make this work"* attitude rather than their usual alternative of *"it'll never work"*.

Steve and Emily remained icily polite to each other and both Travis and Greg noticed that there was an atmosphere between them but they were sensible enough not to mention it and equally the two protagonists were sufficiently professional to ensure that it didn't inhibit their work individually or when they had to deal with an issue together.

The production trial on Friday failed. The disappointment was clear to see and felt keenly by everyone who had worked together to try and make it work.

The only one who remained cheerful though was Operations Director Geoff Hawkins who admitted that he had expected problems with kit that hadn't been used for so long, but as it appeared that the main problems were electrical control issues of the filler's timing device, then they were probably solvable. He persuaded two engineers to work overtime at the newly negotiated reduced overtime rates for the weekend to see if they could fix the problems.

Steve spent the weekend in his office or the factory while Emily went to her cousin. Travis drove to London to join a stag weekend for an old friend. The marriage was one week away and he, the groom and six other men had an extremely boozy two days. Greg explored Norwich with his wife who'd come up for the weekend.

William and Janie held a dinner party on Saturday evening after which they went to bed and made love. It was the first time since last Sunday's double session and was quite good. In fact as she went to sleep afterwards her description of it to herself was that it had been comfortable.

Work at Hardys had progressed over the weekend and the engineers and production people had managed to produce some product and run it down the line. Slowly and only a small quantity but it was a start as Geoff said to Steve first thing on Monday morning.

Next month's figures were also looking positive and Travis thought that for the second month they'd make a profit.

'You just keep getting the business Greg my man. Emily will find a way to plan it in and Geoff will produce it won't you fella?' Steve boomed at a meeting where the four of them were present. Greg agreed that he would.

Apart from the still frosty relationship between Steve and Emily all was working well at Hardys now. William had a reasonable amount of ambassadorial things to do for the company which kept him fairly busy and back at home he continued to drive the builders frantic with his continual checking and double checking, questioning and interfering.

Janie though got more and more nervous as Thursday approached. She'd told William that she was going to see Harry in prison to try and find out if he had actually sold the cottage on from under their feet.

'Would you like me to come with you when you see him?'

No, no, no. Definitely no. I need to see him on my own. It's not just the cottage - it's him. I want to see him. Be honest - I want him, his mind, his information but especially his body. Yes there I've admitted it. I want sex with him again.

'Umm well you can't darling. I've got what's called a Visiting Order and it is just for me. Irrespective of that, afterwards I'm going to fly onto France and see the cottage. If he has stolen it away from us I want to find out about getting our furniture and other possessions back somehow. If it's still ours then I'd like to spend a little time there. Might be the last chance before Christmas. I've invited Jackie to come with me. Hope you don't mind?'

'No good idea'.

Nothing is so different as deceiving oneself.

Ludwig Wittgenstein.

CHAPTER 23

Thursday morning, the day of Janie's planed visit to see Harry at Wormwood Scrubs dawned wet, windy and miserable.

'How appropriate' she muttered as she pulled the curtains and looked out of their bedroom onto the gardens.

'What's appropriate?' asked William as he knotted his tie.

'The weather. It's today that I'm going to see that Harry Norton'.

'Oh yes I'd forgotten. Then you're going off to France?'

'Yes that's the plan, but I'll ring you and let you know what I'm doing'.

He nodded approval and then they both went downstairs to have breakfast together before he set off for Hardys and she drove to collect Jackie and then onto the prison.

She'd seen prisons on tv, in films and in newspapers but nothing quite prepared her for the looming menace of the place standing forebodingly in front of her as she drove towards it.

Driving into the visitors car park she parked, checked that Jackie was going to be alright, suggested that she locked herself in the car while Janie was away and clutching her bag with its visiting order walked up to the door where several other women were standing waiting.

Janie checked her watch and saw that she was about ten minutes early so opening her umbrella against the light rain she stood and waited feeling somewhat self conscious but also wondering what the husbands, boyfriends or partners of the waiting women had done.

At ten thirty the door opened and the small group of about fifteen women filed in and produced their documentation to the prison staff checking them in. Janie left her handbag and umbrella where instructed, was thoroughly searched, then led past a drug dog which sniffed her. She then followed the other women as they were led by prison officers to the visiting room.

Harry was incarcerated in B Wing where the prisoners on remand were kept separate from those criminals who had been convicted.

She found a table and chair and sat suddenly nervous as she glanced around at the other women visitors. Some seemed relaxed and she guessed that they'd been before but a young woman who was probably no more than eighteen was wringing her hands and looked terrified.

Suddenly a door at the back of the room opened and Harry walked in alongside a prison officer. She stood as he walked towards her.

'Janie how nice to see you' and he smiled but it was not the infectious engaging smile she remembered but one marked by sadness and something else. Embarrassment possibly she wondered?

'Yes it's err nice to see you too Harry. How are you?'

'Oh just great thanks. I'm having a wonderful time here with all these nice people. It's like a five star luxury hotel, stunningly good food, a most excellent selection of fine wines, interesting people to talk to, wonderful views and scenery. In short it's got everything that a man could want' and momentarily a brief grin flicked across his face but it was gone in an instant.

'Oh Harry I am so sorry you're in here'.

'So am I' he said with feeling. 'Still that's life. It'll all get sorted at the trial when I'm found not guilty, if not before'.

'So you are innocent of all those awful things that the police said you'd done?'

'Of course. I admit that my accounts got a bit mixed up, well completely mixed up actually. We put in a new computer system and something seems to have gone wrong with the programming of it, so it kept deducting things it shouldn't have, and slotting monies into the wrong accounts or locations. Made it look as though the money had disappeared.

However if the bloody police had let me stay there and straighten it out then all would have been sorted out. I wouldn't be stuck in here, you wouldn't be sitting there worrying about me and everything would be fine'.

That long hair lock dropped forward and she longed to stroke it back into position but didn't know if she could touch him or not.

'Harry the police said some awful things to me about you and what you'd done'.

'Allegedly done. I hope they said that. Alleged accusations until proven guilty ….. which I won't be. Any rate how are you?'

411

'Yes I'm ok but what the police said was that you'd stolen my money and lots of other people's as well'.

'Bollocks. I said just now that I got my accounts mixed up and certain monies went into the wrong accounts. Bit like filing things in the wrong drawer. Simple but I can't resolve it in here and so we'll have to wait until I get out and then as I said I can straighten everything out'.

'Oh I do hope so for your sake as well as the sakes of all the people whose money you've..........'

'I've what?' he snapped. 'Look I've just told you it's all a big mistake but if you're going to go on and on about it then I don't think I want to stay here and talk to you. Remember I can walk out of here back to my luxury five star hotel suite any time I want'.

'Sorry. Don't do that please. Stay' and she stretched out and took hold of his hand. 'It is so lovely to see you again. I do miss you'.

He seemed to relax and smiled. 'And I miss you too my darling Janie'.

She knew that her breathing was getting quicker so deliberately taking a deep breath she steeled herself to ask some more questions.

'Harry please don't get angry or walk out but I need to know something else'.

'What?'

'The cottage. Our cottage in France where we spent those wonderful days together. The police' and she saw him stiffen 'look I must ask'.

'Go on' but he seemed to have spoken through clenched teeth.

'The police say that the documents that you made me sign are false. Worthless and that effectively I've given the cottage away to you and that William and I don't own it any more. Is that true?'

He looked at her for a long time before he replied. 'Whatever may or may not have been right or wrong with the papers you signed, I don't think that I did anything with your cottage. There wasn't time. I was going to implement the protection from French death duties that I explained to you but things kind of caught up on me and I am sure that your papers are still in a file somewhere, no doubt now in Scotland Yard'.

'So the cottage is still ours?'

'I imagine so yes'.

'But would you have sold it?'

'I told you it wasn't a question of selling it. I was trying to protect you and William from those complex French laws. Now let's change the subject'.

'Alright'.

'What colour knickers are you wearing?'

'Pardon?'

'Come on Janie, what colour? There's little enough to get excited about in here and I'd like to go to bed and think about them and what you've got tucked away inside them' he chuckled.

'Blue' she replied. 'They're blue'.

'Dark or light?'

'Light, very pale light blue'.

He nodded. 'Nice. What sort?

'What do you mean what sort? They're women's knickers'.

'Big knickers, small, French style, shorts, thong, frilly, plain?'

'Oh I see. They're fairly plain ordinary style and fit snugly around me'.

'Umm I bet they do .... wish I could see them' he laughed, 'and touch them'.

'Harry there's something else I'd like to ask'.

A look of annoyance crossed his face. 'Now what' and he spoke quite angrily.

'Please don't get cross with me. I have to know. It's something else the police said about you .... err about what you'd done'.

'Oh for fucks sake Janie. If you're going to keep on.......'

Now it was her turn to interrupt and she held up a hand as she spoke.

'The police say you slept with lots of your lady clients not just me. Did you?'

Again he stared at her for what seemed a long time before replying quietly and with obvious sincerity.

'Over the years then yes, there have been a couple of occasions where I've had an affair with a client of mine. I will admit that, but nothing for a long time and certainly no-one since I met you'.

'They ...... the police that is say that you were sleeping with lots of your clients right up to the end including several women older than me .... some a lot older ..... one even in her seventies I gather'.

'In her seventies? Oh come on Janie. I'm thirty five and although I say it myself I'm a reasonably good looking sort of bloke. Why the bloody hell would I want to have sex with an old bag in her seventies. Christ that's the same age as my grandmother. Do I look as though I'd need or want to do that?'

'No of course you don't. So it's really true that you didn't do that? I so want to believe you. Can I?'

'Yes you can. Really'.

She let out a deep sigh of relief and said quietly 'Thank you'.

He leaned forward a little and taking both her hands in his looked deep into her eyes. 'Janie you were .... you are, very special to me. Very special indeed and I think that we could have made it together. I dreamed that you'd leave William and we'd go and live together. I planned in my mind to sell up and then I was going to take the money and buy somewhere abroad and ask you to come and live with me.

Maybe we'd have got married I don't know but we'd have been together, just you and me and we'd have been very happy. I would have made you happy and you would certainly have made me happy. In fact I could imagine lying in the sunshine with you, kissing, loving and just being us. No one else, just you and me and it would have been so wonderful. Perhaps it can be again one day when this is all cleared up'.

She looked at him and tears started to run down her cheeks. He squeezed her hand and more tears came.

'You are so precious and so special Janie. You are the most special woman I have ever met'.

'The police say you slept with men too' she snivelled.

'The bastards. What an absolutely dreadful and wicked thing to say. Do I look as though I'd do that? Well do I?'

'No'.

'Well there you are then. Forget the lies you've been told. Forget the accusations. Forget all of that and remember our time together in my apartment, at that lovely hotel in Newmarket and at your sweet cottage in France. Janie you have to believe me when I tell you that I am innocent and that you mean a very great deal to me'.

'Harry' she whispered. 'That is so ....' but she couldn't finish what she wanted to say. She gulped as the tears and sobs came faster and stronger.

'Hey come on dry up. I want to see you looking happy and beautiful not crying your eyes out. There's enough misery in here. You bring a ray of sunshine, beauty and hope to me. Do you know that tonight all the other blokes here will ask me who was the stunningly attractive woman that visited me today? I'll tell them that you are someone who I am privileged to know and who I hope one day soon, to see again outside this dreadful place.

We'll go to that hotel in Newmarket and have the same room as we did last time. We'll spend days in bed, loving each other and being together. We won't leave the room. We'll eat there, we'll sleep there and most important of all we'll make love there over and over again'.

They sat looking at each other in silence as she dabbed away at her eyes, sniffed hard to stop crying and all she could say was 'Oh Harry'.

'Will you come and see me again?'

'Yes if you'd like me to'.

He said he would then asked what she'd been doing recently and they talked generalities until she said 'I thought you'd be in prison uniform not in your own clothes'.

'No here on remand you can wear your own clothes. It's only when you've been convicted that you have to wear prison garb. Would you do something for me?

'Yes if I can. What?'

'You'll think it's odd but visitors are allowed to bring in fresh changes of clothes for remand prisoners'.

'You want me to bring you some clothes?

'Yes ..... well some special clothes. Would you bring me some underpants please?'

'Yes of course. What sort? You wear boxers don't you? At least you did every time I saw you undress' she smiled.

'Yes but I want you to do something special with them for me'.

'What?'

'I want you to wear them before you bring them here'.

415

'Wear them! Wear them? Then bring them to you? Why?'

'Because then I'll be really close to you in a very special and private way. While I'm in here I can't touch you intimately but it will be the next best thing. It will be our special secret. Will you do it for me? Please …. darling Janie?'

'Yes if that's what you want'.

'Thanks. Something else. When you come next time can you wear something a bit more sexy, more revealing. You're all wrapped up from neck to toe and I can't see an inch of skin from your lovely body'.

'Oh yes. I actually thought that it might be better not to, erm….. not to wear anything too revealing as you were locked up in here. I thought that it might upset you ……. sort of excite you seeing me …… but not being able to touch'.

'No I'd like to see you. I mean just look around you. See that old slag over there talking to that black fella. Got her tits practically falling out of her blouse and that little blonde over there …… see her bloke's got his eyes on stalks looking down her dress top. He must be able to see right down to her belly button'.

Janie nodded 'Ok, sure' and smiled.

'Have you got any pictures of yourself you could send me?'

'Photos? Yes I'm sure I have. I've got some nice ones ….. well I think they are, which were taken on holiday in Corfu last year'.

'Got any sexy ones?'

'No' she laughed 'but I might be able to find one of me in a bikini. Would you like that?'

'Yes that would be great. Thanks'.

'Right I'm getting quite a list aren't I? Pants that I've worn, low top dress and smutty pictures' she laughed.

You've got it' he grinned. 'Need something to keep cheerful in here'.

Suddenly a bell rang.

'Time's up I'm afraid'.

'No it can't be. We've not had long'.

'Visiting is from nine thirty till eleven. You didn't come till ten thirty'.

'Sorry I didn't know'.

'Of course. Will you come to see me again?'

'Yes if you'd like me to?'

'Oh yes I would. Please?' and he stood as a burley prison warder approached them and said 'Come on Norton. Time's up. Don't hang about'.

'Right coming' and turning to Janie he said 'I'll look forward to your next visit' then he leaned down to whisper 'remember bring me some pants you've worn and put on something more revealing next time' and with a grin he walked away alongside the prison officer. At the door he paused, smiled and blew her a kiss.

Janie felt tears start again as she stood and went to the back of the room to be escorted out of the prison.

'She seems a really nice lady' the prison officer said to Harry.

'Nah stupid bitch ..... gullible like all the rest. Get their knickers off and your tongue in their pussy and they'll do anything for you. She wasn't bad at giving blow jobs and when she got warmed up she was a damn good fuck. In fact I'd say she was probably the best fuck I've had in a long time and I've had a few recently I can tell you mate' he laughed. 'Yeah a real mix. Young, middle aged, and a couple of real oldies and in some ways you know the old ones they are the best. They may not look much but they're so bloody grateful they'll do anything for you .... and you can always keep your eyes shut!' he guffawed loudly as he was led back into the deeper confines of the prison.

Janie left the prison in a state of shock, happiness and sadness all rolled into one as she walked back to the car and tapped on the window for Jackie to unlock.

'Well how was it? Did you seem him? How did he look?'

Janie looked at her friend and then leaned forward and burst into tears. 'Oh Jackie it was awful. He looked so .... I don't know, so trapped.

But the good news is that he said that it was all a mistake. Something to do with a new computer system putting everything in the wrong place and making it seem as if the money had gone whereas in reality it was still there but in a different place. I didn't quite understand it all. Computers are a mystery to me but he's very confident that he'll be acquitted when it comes to trial. He said he wants me to leave William and live with him when he gets out'.

'You won't though will you? Surely not?'

417

'I don't know. He is ……..'

'Oh look don't be stupid. You've got the boys to think about as well as William, and your friends, your family. Good God Janie what will your Mother say and your Father?'

'I don't know. It was just that seeing him again I felt such intense feelings for him. Jackie what am I going to do?' and she leant forward and flung her arms around her friend and sobbed for a long time.

Jackie made soothing "there there, come on it's not as bad as all that" noises while stroking and patting her friend's back but this only seemed to set Janie off crying again but eventually she stopped and sat up and pulling down the sun visor opened the mirror.

'God what a sight I look' and reaching for her bag she found her handkerchief, wiped away some mascara that had run, blew her nose then took a deep breath before re-applying her lipstick. 'The good thing is that he said he hasn't done anything with the cottage. It's still ours'.

'That is good news. So are we off there then?'

'Yes come on let's get away from this horrible place. You can't imagine how awful it is inside there' and starting the engine she tapped her sat-nav unit, entered Stansted Airport and set off following the instructions.

On arrival they checked that the flight was on time then went for a coffee. The airport was busy and Janie seemed to have cheered up a great deal much to Jackie's pleasure as the last thing she wanted was to spend two or three days with her friend grizzling and crying all the time.

In fact she'd been looking forward to the little break as not only was she nosey and wanted to see Janie and William's cottage, but also she wanted to find out a lot more about the affair Janie had been having with Harry and she was sure that relaxing away from the uk her friend would spill the beans in a great deal more detail.

When the flight was called they made their way to the gate indicated, boarded and enjoyed the short flight landing a few minutes ahead of schedule.

Janie led the way to Pierre's garage where the old man was just closing up for the night but he beamed when he saw her, led her to the car which was all ready for her with Jacques standing shyly alongside.

'Oh that's lovely' smiled Janie handing the boy a five Euro note. 'Here buy yourself something nice' and giving him a dazzling smile she winked at Pierre, took the keys he proffered, unlocked the car and slid behind the wheel as Jackie got in the passenger side.

'Right anything from forty minutes to an hour and a half depending on the traffic. As it's such a nice evening we'll have the hood down shall we?' and pressing the button she waited while the mechanism whirred and buzzed until everything clicked into place and they were an open top car.

'Right off we go. Au revoir Pierre' and putting the car in gear they set off. Traffic was alright and it was just over an hour later when Janie drove slowly into the little village.

'I feel nervous' she confessed 'in case something really has happened to it' and Jackie could clearly see the concerns that Janie was expressing. They stopped at the gate and Janie got out, took the key to the padlock and taking a deep breath turned it. The rusty lock opened.

Turning and giving a thumbs up Jackie she pushed open the two gates and then skipped back to the car and drove to the front of the cottage.

'It must be alright mustn't it? she asked getting out of the car and going to the front door where she selected the door key. 'Surely the first thing someone would do is change that padlock and this lock …….. but it's opened. Oh Jackie I think it really is alright. Come on in'.

Her friend followed her and wrinkled her nose at the musty smell. Seeing her Janie grinned 'Don't worry about that dusty musty smell. As soon as I ……… open some of ……… these ……….windows it'll soon go' and as she was speaking she was undoing the window bolts and flinging them wide open.

Turning she hugged Jackie. 'It's alright. I am so relieved. I must ring William straight away' and rummaging for her mobile phone she dialled then gave a little grimace. 'Gone to voicemail, I'll leave him a message' which she did.

'Come on let's get the stuff in from the car, unpack, have a swim and a cup of tea. No to hell with tea, let's have some wine, lots of wine. I am so happy I feel like getting blotto tonight'.

Her enthusiasm and relief was so palpably obvious that Jackie couldn't help being caught up in her friend's happiness as they brought in the two small bags with which they'd travelled.

Soon unpacked Janie changed into a bikini and going into the garden rolled back the pool cover to feel the water temperature, then walked to the little shed took out two loungers and cushions. As she set the second one in place Jackie appeared also in a bikini.

'Is it warm?' she asked.

'Yes' and as she spoke Janie scooped a handful of water and flung it at her friend.

'Rotter' but before she could do anything, Janie had slithered into the water and was swimming. Jackie jumped in holding her nose sending a great swoosh of water over Janie and slopping over the side.

They laughed together and swam for a while until clambering out Janie padded indoors trailing water as she went to the fridge, collected a bottle of local white wine, opened a cupboard for two glasses and returning to the garden plonked down on a sunlounger. Soon she'd poured the two glasses of wine and raising hers called out 'Cheers' to the other woman who was just clambering out of the pool.

Towelling herself dry Jackie stretched out on the lounger, took a large sip of her wine and smiling said 'So it's all alright then?'

'Uh huh, at least with the cottage. We'll have to see about the rest and although it's quite a bit of money it's nothing like the value of this' and she waved her hand around embracing the cottage and garden 'so if this is still ours the financial damage will be relatively light'.

'So how many times did you bring Harry here?

'Just the once but it was for several days. It was so lovely ....
magical almost. Not just a few stolen hours but day after day, night after night. We went into the village to eat. We'll go to the same restaurant tonight. Very local French village type of place but it's really nice and amazingly cheap.

When Harry was here we swam, talked, loved. In fact we made love on one of these loungers right here by the pool and on the grass just there' and she pointed. 'Naked, uninhibited and the most amazing passion, you wouldn't believe it'.

So he's good in the sack then?'

'Good? He's unbelievable'.

Fascinated and more than a little jealous Jackie probed carefully, gradually getting Janie to lay bear all the details of what she and Harry had done. Although when Janie had sat in Jackie's kitchen and conservatory a few weeks ago and first talked about her affair with Harry she'd said quite a bit, but she hadn't been nearly as open and uninhibited about the relationship as she was now as she openly explained her feelings for and about him, how she felt about him then and now, where they'd been for their illicit love sessions, how she felt about having cheated on William and how she now felt about him.

The two of them talked or to be more accurate Janie did most of the talking with Jackie simply providing points of challenge, opportunities to explain and continuity. The sun had gone down and although she was feeling chilly and had wrapped her towel around herself she didn't want to break the spell of listening to Janie opening her heart.

It was almost seven thirty though when Janie's mobile could be heard ringing and running indoors she snatched it up, peered at the screen, pressed a key and said 'William hello. Yes I'm fine' she continued as she walked back into the garden. 'Yes we're here at the cottage. William it's alright. Harry didn't do anything with it. It's still ours. Isn't that good news? Yes really' she went on.

She listened to him for a moment or two then said 'Yes I saw him. He's still the same irrepressible person but he denies everything. Says it's all a big mistake. Something to do with a new computer system he installed'.

She listened again. 'Yes of course but do you know I believed him. Well at least I think I did. Still whatever the outcome we've still got the cottage. Now what have you been up to darling?'

She listened again for some time making the odd comment such as "really" or "they haven't" or "that's good then isn't it" until she turned to look at Jackie. 'Yes she's right here glass of wine in hand, her second actually. We're going to go to that nice little restaurant in the village for supper'

More silence as she listened until she smiled and said 'Yes and I love you too darling. Sleep well. See you Sunday. Bye .... bye'.

Putting the phone down she shivered. 'I think we ought to go in. It's getting chilly. Nice bath and then eat. Ok?'

They enjoyed their meal but every now and then Janie couldn't help losing herself from today's reality as her mind drifted away to when she was here with Harry but she was able to put him aside and carry on chatting, eating and drinking with her friend.

She drank a lot more than she usually would have done, so by the time they paid and the proprietor had insisted that the ladies had a glass of local brandy 'Sur la Maison' to complete the meal, as she stood up from the table she wobbled and had to grab it for support.

'Hey you're plastered' Jackie laughed but also found that she too was none to steady on her feet either. 'So am I' she giggled a moment later so linking arms they held on to each other as they wobbled their way back through the village to the cottage. Every now and then one or other of them would say 'Schh' loudly to the other which brought on a paroxysm of laughter.

Back in the cottage Janie flopped onto a settee while Jackie collapsed into an armchair.

'We'd better have some coffee I think' giggled Jackie getting up with some difficulty.

'No I'm going to go straight up to bed' but as she spoke Janie stood and wobbled the wrong way. 'Oh shit' but with a great effort she made it to the stairs and holding tightly onto the banister rail hauled herself up, along the short landing and into the main bedroom where she stumbled around undressing before staggering to the bathroom, emerging after a few minutes, made her way back to the bedroom and tugging the covers aside collapsed into bed and lay there.

Going to sleep straight away she woke up in the middle of the night. Not having any idea what was the time she lay there aware of a slight headache so getting out of bed she went downstairs where she knew some paracetamol were kept in a kitchen cupboard.

Getting a glass of water she went back upstairs got into bed swallowed the tablets and half the water and then lay down but she couldn't go back to sleep. All she could think about was Harry. Harry making love to her in this bed. Harry and her naked on the sun lounger. Harry getting out of the pool with an erection poking ahead of him. Harry in prison. Harry and her in the beautiful hotel bedroom in Newmarket.

'Oh Harry. Is it all true, or are you really innocent?' she whispered. Try as she might she couldn't go back to sleep and all she could think about was Harry. He made love to her so beautifully and she wondered when, or if, she'd ever be able to experience that lovemaking again.

'We must' she whispered into the darkness.

They both felt a little the worse for wear the next morning and decided to take it really easy. Janie walking down into the village to get some fresh bread, croissants, butter and some juice nodded and smiled at the locals many of whom she recognised and they recognised her.

Friday and Saturday passed lazily and happily. She spoke about Harry from time to time but also about William and how in finding a new lease of life supervising the stable re-building he seemed to feel more fulfilled again and so wasn't pestering her for sex so much.

'God you are lucky' exclaimed Jackie on Saturday evening over dinner in the same restaurant again. 'You've got a lover who obviously shagged you senseless; a suddenly horny husband who wants nookie all the time; you're healthy and in great physical shape. Probably all the shagging that does that' she laughed loudly.

'I mean look at you' she went on. 'You're thirty eight …....' but after she'd been corrected went on 'all right thirty nine then. You are trim, neat and look fantastic in a bikini. No wonder men are drooling for you. I'm thirty six and starting to go to seed. My boobs are dropping, I've never really got rid of the stretch marks, and I've put on weight so my waist has expanded a couple of inches and my bum is definitely getting bigger' then she laughed 'ah well we can't all look sexy at your age can we?'

'Do you really think I look sexy?'

'Yes …... why?'

'Erm …. Harry asked me if I'd send him a photograph of myself in a bikini …... while he's in prison'.

'Never mind you in a bikini. You ought to send him one of you in your underwear. Now that'd be sexy for him' she chuckled. 'Mind you we both know what he'll do while looking at the picture don't we' and raising her eyebrows she grinned.

Janie smiled back. 'Maybe?'

'Not maybe. Definitely'.

After they'd drunk too much on Thursday they'd both been careful how much they consumed since but when they were back at the cottage and Janie was sipping a small gin and large tonic while Jackie was slowly drinking a malt whisky, Janie looked intently across the room at her friend.

'Would you take some pictures of me for Harry? Sexy ones ….. me in my undies?'

'God you have got it bad for him haven't you? Yes if that's what you want but are you sure you know what you're doing. Shouldn't you be forgetting him? You are married. You've got two lovely boys, a wonderful house, a good marriage.

As your friend I'm telling you to forget this Harry. You've had a narrow escape. You've still got this lovely cottage but probably if he wasn't in clink you wouldn't have it. You don't know whether he's telling you the truth or not. He's in prison and if convicted will probably be locked away for years. You're not his only woman ….. or man ….. remember what the police said. They don't make those sorts of mistakes you know.

Harry may have convinced you, but you want to be convinced. You are seeing him through rose coloured glasses. You are definitely not being objective about this. Now be sensible. Forget him. I thought you had'.

'So did I till I saw him on Thursday and now I can't get him out of my mind. Jackie you are right in everything you've said. I can't argue with any of it ……….. but I still want him ……….. desperately'.

'When you say want him ……………..'

'Yes want. Sex. I want sex with him again'.

It was no use thought Jackie. Janie was hooked. 'Ok if you want someone to take some dirty pictures I'll do it. Tomorrow morning?'

'God no. I've only got a few bits of stuff here. Next week back home where I've got all my nice underwear …… thanks' and she smiled at her friend.

Better not tell her that I'm going to buy some men's boxers and wear them before taking them to Harry for him to wear then had I?

It was mid afternoon on Sunday when Janie dropped Jackie back at her house, went and had a quick look at her horses, agreed that she'd phone in the morning to fix a time for the photo session, then zoomed off home where William was waiting for her.

He kissed her and said 'Welcome back'.

Dear, darling, dependable, trustworthy, honest William.

Over supper they talked about the cottage, prison, Harry and what might be the eventual outcome of the case. He was interested to hear how Harry was protesting his innocence but somewhat dampened Janie's enthusiasm that it might all be alright when he spoke.

'Well he would say he was innocent wouldn't he?' Stands to reason doesn't it? He isn't going to tell you and any one else he's guilty, although he probably is, as it might affect his trial somehow. Not me gov, it's a stitch up. That's what they say in films isn't it? No Janie my love he'll keep on saying he's innocent until they lock him up'.

'Do you really think that? That they'll lock him up?'

'Yes. Look the police don't make mistakes like that. Didn't you say that they had lots of other clients of Mr. Harry Norton who'd all been defrauded? We seem to have been lucky. We've still got the cottage and the amount of money he's stolen isn't going to bankrupt us'.

'That's what Jackie said. The police wouldn't make a mistake'.

'Well there you are then. No. The best thing to do my love is put this Norton chap right to the back of your mind. Forget about him'.

'That's also what Jackie said' she smiled ruefully. 'Look I'm tired. I'm going to have a bath and then I want to go to bed and get to sleep. I haven't slept well the last couple of nights'.

'Good idea. That's odd though as you usually sleep like a log down there don't you?'

Next morning, Monday the beginning of a new week started with a phone call from the Metropolitan Police to arrange a date for Janie to come to London and make a further formal statement regarding Harry and she agreed Friday wondering if she could get authority for another visit to him by that time so she could combine a trip to Wormwood Scrubs and the police.

As soon as the phone call was finished she wrote a letter to Harry and asked if he'd see her on Friday.

Walking round her lovely old house and peering out of an upstairs window at the progress that had been made on the stables she sighed as she again juggled in her mind Harry and William who'd left early that morning for three days in Paris at some Trade Fair and Conference centre where he was representing Hardys.

Next she drove into Norwich and bought three pairs of men's boxers and returning home slipped off her own panties, flapped some talc onto her bush and around her pussy, then pulled on the first pair. They felt slightly strange but she soon got used to them and happily wore them all day. At night as she undressed she put on her nightie then on an impulse pulled the boxers back on and slept in them all night.

Next morning she carefully folded them placed them in a plastic bag, showered then dressed in the second pair, rang Jackie, agreed they'd go for a ride and also arranged tomorrow morning for the photo session.

It was drizzling on their ride but they enjoyed the freedom that riding brings as well as each other's company although Jackie avoided the subject of Harry, merely confirming that she'd be over tomorrow to take the pictures.

William rang that evening enthusiastically telling her how he was enjoying playing the ambassador role at the trade Fair and was being taken out to dinner that evening by some exporters. He'd spoken to Greg, got a clear brief of what was wanted and hoped to be able to get some tangible result to help his own business although being run for now by others.

This still rankled with him but he accepted that he had no choice as these days banks ran businesses; at least they did when a business got into difficulty.

Wednesday morning dawned bright and sunny and Janie who'd worn the second pair of boxers all night as well, put them into the plastic bag with the first, showered and then sat on her bed looking through her underwear drawer.

She decided that obvious though it was, she'd use black for most of the shots and possibly a couple of her in the red stuff she'd worn that day to London and sat on his desk flashing herself so brazenly at Harry.

Jackie arrived just before ten armed with some women's magazines and also a selection of men's top shelf girlie magazines.

'Here thought you might get some inspiration from these if you are really going ahead with this' she chuckled. 'After all you don't want just to stand there and have me photograph you do you? You need to be sexy, pouting and sultry don't you, so have a look through those while I make us some coffee.

It was about half an hour later when Janie took a deep breath and said 'Right come on then. Let's start my career as a porn star' and giggling indicating nervousness as well as excitement, picked up her digital camera and led the way up to her bedroom.

Altogether they took a couple of dozen photos, all topless. Three were of her in her red panties, fishnet stockings and suspenders while in the rest she wore various black panties and stockings some fastened to suspenders and others hold-ups. In some she was sitting demurely in a chair reading but in others she was sprawled sexily either on the bed or the chair. Only in one was she was without any underwear at all lying on her tummy on the bed facing the camera her head propped on one raised hand so her breasts were on view and with one stocking clad leg lifted at the knee.

Checking them on the little camera screen, Janie pronounced herself satisfied and while Jackie went downstairs to make them some more coffee she pulled on the third pair of boxers safely hidden beneath jeans and a thin sweater.

Together the two women giggled as they downloaded the pictures onto Janie's computer and decided which the best were.

'Now all I've got to find out is how I get them to Harry. I mean can I just post them to him en-bloc or should I send one a week so he builds up a collection? But then maybe it would be best if I take them to him when I next see him?'

'Hang on. Did you say you're going to see him again?'

'Yes. I must'.

'No you don't. Look ………'

'Please don't go on at me. I know what you think but I'm going and that's that' and her voice and face clearly indicated that she didn't want to talk about it any more but seeing the expression on her friend's face she finished 'sorry but there it is. I simply have to'.

Jackie said nothing, just hugged her misguided friend then said that she had to go but not being able to wait until she got home rang Pauline from the car and started the conversation with a question.

'Guess what I've been doing?'

Alone, Janie looked again at the pictures on the computer, then smiling printed off the ten they'd selected, deleted the ones they'd decided not to use and finally created a file and password protected them. Not that there was any real need as William never used her computer and even if he did he'd never dream of looking at her private files. Still she did it all the same.

427

William returned Thursday evening bubbling with enthusiasm and chatted non-stop about being wined and dined, hosting, meeting, networking and generally enjoying the role as Chairman although none of the people he met realised that his position was a sham.

Taking a torch he wandered around the stable building site for about half an hour then came back indoors where they had supper and chatted.

'So what have you been up to then?' he asked.

Not a lot. Did some gardening, rode, went shopping. That's about it. Oh yes I nearly forgot. I've been wearing some men's underwear to impregnate it with my smells for Harry in prison; posed for a bunch of nude and raunchy photos also for Harry; and got another letter from him saying he'd love to see me on Friday, but apart from that not much.

'Oh the usual, riding, some gardening, bit of shopping and catching up on correspondence'.

Not wholly untrue, just somewhat incomplete!

It was getting on for eleven when William smiled said that he thought it was time they went to bed and that he'd really missed her these past few days.

Oh well we all know what that's signalling don't we and I have to agree that I think I'm up for it tonight in spite of constantly thinking about Harry! Maybe it's because of thinking about him!

Their lovemaking was pretty good and they both cuddled together as they dropped off to sleep.

Next morning William was out at the stable block at eight as the work men arrived and it was now possible to see real progress as they were beyond the eaves and working on the roof.

Janie having told William she was off to London to see the police again zoomed away in the Porsche and was sitting in the visitor's room at the prison at ten o'clock when Harry was brought in.

Her carrier and its contents had been x-rayed and also sniffed by the drug dogs as had the envelope with two of her photos before she entered the visiting room and waited for Harry.

'Here you are some new boxers for you' she said as soon as he sat down, then dropping her voice continued 'William's been away abroad on business this week so it's been easy to do what you want. I've worn

each of them for a day and all night so I hope they're alright err ....
what you want?'

'Thank you they'll be great and I'll think of you all the time I'm
wearing them, and where they'd been before I've put them on' he
chuckled.

She blushed slightly but then more deeply when she handed over
the envelope. 'Some pictures for you. Of me, like you asked. There's
two in there but I've got ten altogether, all different. Do you want me
to send the rest to you all together in one go or shall I send one or two
a week?'

'Send them all at once. I won't open them now, I'll save them for
when I'm back in my cell. Thanks, you've no idea how much I shall
enjoy these. Other blokes in here will be so jealous'.

They chatted about nothing and everything. She told him that she'd
been to France and confirmed that the cottage seemed fine at which he
nodded and said that was as he expected.

She didn't say that after leaving him she was going to Scotland Yard
to make a further statement about him which might be another nail
in his case.

This time after she left and got back in her car she didn't cry just
felt somewhat sad that he was still in that horrid place but happy that
she'd seen him again.

*When you get out I don't know what will happen with our lives but
I do know that I am going to take you away somewhere for several days,
maybe to Newmarket, maybe to the cottage again and we are going to
spend hour after hour making love and being together. Just the two of us,
alone and .... and what? In love? No surely not? Run off together? No
of course not. Really?*

She drove to London, found a parking bay close to New Scotland
Yard, booked in, met with Sergeant Maggie Wagstone who took her to
a small well lit, but impersonal room then got her a cup of tea from a
machine and sat down across the small table.

'Now Mrs. Hardy in your own words please tell me everything
from the time you first met Mr. Harold Norton. I know you've done
this already but we need to go over it again in case there's anything that
you forgot'.

***

While she was sitting there recounting yet again to the police the details of her involvement with Harry, he found another prison inmate for whom he'd been looking.

'Hey Winston. How long since you had some real pussy?'

'I bin in here for nine months man and de last time was de night before I was picked up by de cops'.

'Well have I got a treat for you' and he quietly explained what Janie had done for him with the boxers.

'No kidding man?' asked the big black man taking a pair of boxers.

'No it's for real' smiled Harry suddenly clamping his hand on top of the other man's fist 'but there's a small price'.

'What might that be then?'

'There's a fella on your landing named Shiv? I think he's an Iraqi. Pretty boy. Got nice lips and a really cute little bum. I understand that you kind of look after him'.

'What about him?'

'I'd like to have a little time with him …. alone in my cell ….. if you get my meaning?'

'Loud and clear man. I'll see what I can do for you. If these' and he tapped the plastic bag 'are as good as you say then I'm sure something can be arranged'.

'Thanks' smiled Harry as he released the other man's hand before adding 'enjoy them won't you' as he tapped the boxers.

'I will man and ….. you'll be able to enjoy Shiv won't you?'

'I hope so. I really do'.

Hold faithfulness and sincerity as first principles.

Confucius.

CHAPTER 24

It was nearly a year since the turnaround team had taken over the running of the business from William.

Results had been good and the bank after their initial concerns were now convinced that Hardys really was on a recovery path.

More new export business had been secured over the months and three of the major supermarket chains in the UK were now stocking a number of Hardy products including the newly launched retro range which was proving to be a success with customers and consumers alike.

Hardys had also used the same style of packaging for a range of pickles and sauces and they too were proving successful.

***

The stables were nearly re-built and William was now finding little to involve himself in with that project. Still inhibited from doing much at Hardys he was bored and Janie had found that he was turning again to her for sex much more often.

Until she had her brainwave.

She was listening to the radio one morning where a discussion about charity work was taking place and one of the contributors in the studio said that a big problem charities had was getting top class management to work for them because apart from one or two people at the top who were reasonably well paid others were either paid nothing or only a pittance and this was especially true in regional offices.

She stopped what she was doing and listened intently to the rest of the discussion and the point came up again about charities needing management who were prepared to work for little or no remuneration, so when William came back home around tea time from playing golf she sat him down and raised the subject with him.

'It could be something that's not only important but really interesting for you to do and think how they'd benefit from your business experience and skills?'

431

'Darling' he snorted 'the Bank think it was my lack of skills that almost bankrupted the company'.

'That's because they didn't understand the problems that you were having at that time and their refusal to help. It's alright for these hot shot turnaround people they've put in, as you've said that they seem to be able to walk on water as far as the bank is concerned.

No forget about that. People in the Chamber of Commerce don't fully understand what's going on at Hardys do they? To them you are still Chairman. It's just that you've got a new management team working with you.

I bet if you started to tap into your contacts and connections you'd find lots of opportunities to get involved in charity work. You'd be just what they need. Furthermore what about getting involved in small business start-ups where entrepreneurs especially young ones could do with a wise older experienced business man to give them some help and guidance.

I think you'll find a really rich seam of opportunity to use your undoubted talents in those areas my darling'.

Now fingers crossed. If he did then he could get really busy and involved, work lots of hours, get tired out so we can return to occasional sex, rather as was starting to happen now where he had a glint in his eye most nights and often some mornings as well. Well – would he take the bait?

'You could be right you know' he mused with an interested expression on his face.

I am, oh I am. Go on say you'll do it. Yes. Go on ….. please.

'Jackie's husband Mathew was saying just the other day that he'd been approached but he hadn't got the time and at that dinner I went to in Norwich last week for local businessmen, opposite me was a chap from some charity or other bemoaning the fact that they needed management help but couldn't afford it'.

Hold your breath. Are we there? Are you going to say yes?

'God yes Janie. I think you might have a really good idea there. I'm still not really needed at Hardys. I mean they keep finding things for me to do but it's like throwing crumbs out to the birds, just scraps really and nothing of any real substance. The stables here are almost done now and don't need much involvement from me so this could be it. I could really get involved in charity work and also I like that suggestion of helping young entrepreneurs'.

Whey hey, brilliant. Yes, yes yes.

'Exactly darling I knew you'd see the logic in it. When will you be able to begin? You'll need to start networking and put out feelers won't you? Draw up a proper plan of action maybe?'

'Yes I will. After we've had supper I'll start to sketch out some ideas tonight. You won't mind if I put in a bit of study time will you?'

Mind? Oh boy. Hook, line and sinker. Fabulous.

'Well I'd rather you were spending the evening with me, but I think this is so important, both for you and the possible recipients of your involvement, that it is worth you striking while the iron is hot. Now supper is almost ready so get some wine and come and sit down. Kitchen alright tonight?'

William was enthusiastic as he started to talk about possible roles that he could see for himself. Janie gently encouraged him along however she was careful to sound an occasional word of warning or raise a question about the likely issues that might arise as she didn't want him to get any hint that she was deliberately pushing him too hard into this new area of activity. But nothing dented his keenness to start his new sphere of activity.

When William did finally come to bed she was still awake and sensing that he was leaning towards her she quickly started some deep slow breathing. It had the desired effect as after a moment or two she felt him first of all move back to his side of the bed and then secondly from the wriggling and grunting realised that he was pulling his shorts and tee shirt on.

Phew that was a close run thing!

***

The turnaround team at Hardys were more confident by the week.

Travis had got cash completely under control and they were no longer having to rob peter to pay paul, or having to delay payments beyond their agreed payment terms to their suppliers. They were also now cash positive.

Secondly Greg now had sales increasing and building satisfactorily both at home and in their export markets.

Thirdly they had a serious expression of interest in their new retro look products from a potential Japanese importer who claimed that he would be able to gain them distribution of the products throughout that country's major retail outlets and possibly in other Far Eastern countries. They'd sent samples and now anxiously awaited the outcome.

Steve was relieved that the bank was no longer constantly on his back and had settled for a weekly telephone update and a formal face to face monthly review.

The Unions were pleased that the future of the company looked more secure and hence their members jobs would be safe however they constantly reminded Steve and Rod Jackson the HR Director that they were expecting the company to honour its promise to start the process of restoring the wage rates back to where they had been as a first step and then to a higher level to reflect proper market conditions.

As Emily looked at the latest planning schedules she was satisfied with the future plans although she did have a worry as to how they'd cope with this potential large Japanese contract if they got it. Still she decided that she'd cross that bridge if and when it came. In fact she thought that everything was pretty well ok except one thing. Steve.

Relations between them had improved somewhat and they no longer snapped at each other and indeed had moved more towards normality but they were a long way away from where they had been and extremely far from a relationship, with definitely no possibility of any resumption of any form of intimacy.

She'd been out for a drink with Travis on a few occasions but they hadn't slept together again.

One evening though he took her to an Indian restaurant after which he drove her home where she invited him in for coffee but it wasn't long before they left the coffee untouched and went to bed, making love properly this time utilising her supply of condoms.

Another time he'd invited her for Sunday lunch at his cottage and afterwards they spent the rest of the day and evening making love.

She was musing on this on the Monday morning when Travis stuck his head round the door and asked if she was going to go to the company annual dinner and dance?

'Oh I don't think so'.

'Aw come on it'll be fun. It's fancy dress you know' he grinned.

'Even more reason not to go. What's the theme? Let me guess? Vicars and Tarts ...... where you blokes just wear a suit with your collar the wrong way round but you expect us girls to parade around in stockings and suspenders with a stupidly short skirt, a low cut top and our boobs hanging out?'

He grinned. 'Hey that's sounds like a great outfit' then added 'no sadly not. It's movie themes. Characters from movies, or I guess tv maybe? I'm going and I know that Greg and Steve are as well. Even William's coming and I think Janie his wife is going to judge best dressed character. Now can I persuade you?'

'Oh all right. When is it?' and making a note on her screen diary she smiled at him as she said 'now I'll have to think of a character. What are you going as?

'Wyatt Earp'.

'Yea that's good. American character played by a real American. Good now leave me alone as I've got lots to do' and waving him away she looked at her screen and moved her mouse.

***

William had embarked on a series of lunches in East Anglia to network with various people to see if they knew of charities that might benefit from his input.

Often he was asked how he'd find the time but he'd developed a storyline to cover that question explaining that although during the previous couple of years his business had found trading tough over the last few months since his new management team were in place, things had started to turnaround satisfactorily and he was comfortable leaving the running of the business more in their hands while he was able to take much more of a back seat Chairman's role rather than being so hands on in the company. Hence he was wanting to do this charity work.

Each night he excitedly regaled Janie on how that day's networking meeting had gone before going into his study to update his list of contacts that he'd seen, others still to see and make a note of any new leads which he'd been given. A couple of times a week they made love.

She was happy with this frequency of sexual activity, felt that it kept William satisfied and she had to admit that it fulfilled her own needs in the absence of Harry to whom she wrote twice a week.

She also visited him from time to time and noted that his mood varied between sometimes upbeat but on other occasions he seemed depressed.

William had reminded her about the company's annual fancy dress party and she'd willingly said she'd go as in previous years it had been quite a fun occasion. He was going as Henry the Eighth and she thought that she'd go as Mary Queen of Scots.

***

The latest meeting with the Bank had gone really well even though it had dragged on until nearly seven o'clock. After the bank men had gone, Steve had a round up review in his office.

'Well done everyone. Their comments at the end that they were prepared to move to a bi-monthly face to face meeting from now on providing we continued the progress we're making, with in-between monthly conference telephone calls and of course the weekly quick telephone update calls is a real vote of confidence in us you know'

The four of them chatted for a while before Greg, Emily and Travis left Steve alone while they returned to their own offices.

It was around seven thirty when Emily left the office and running through the pouring rain trying to stop her umbrella getting blown inside out by the gusting wind sighed with dismay when she got to her car and saw that one rear tyre was flat.

'Oh bloody hell' she groaned standing looking at it. She decided to ring the AA and ask them to come and sort it out for her but just as she was about to unlock the car to get in and make the call a voice said 'Problems?'

Turning she saw Steve pointing to her flat tyre.

'Yes I'm going to ring the breakdown people'.

'Oh they'll take ages to come on a wet night. I'll change it for you'.

'No Steve. I couldn't let you do that, you'll get soaked'.

'Well I'm not going to drive off and leave you here with a flat tyre and I don't want to sit around for an hour or more till the breakdown truck comes, so stop arguing. Now these cars don't have a spare tyre do they?'

'Normally no but I never did like the idea of not having one so I bought one when I got the car. It's in a cover behind the passenger seat'. Seeing his look of surprise she went on 'Well it takes up quite a lot of space in the boot which I use regularly for shopping and so on, and as I rarely ever have more than one, possibly two other people in the car that's the best place for it'.

'Right well you get into my car and keep dry. It's over there' and he pointed to his green BMW 'and I'll fix this. Now where's your locking wheel nut key?'

She looked blankly at him. 'Where's my what?'

'Locking wheel nut key? You've got fancy alloy wheels and it stops them being stolen?'

'Sorry, no idea'.

'Right. Owners manual?'

'Err ….. glove box I think. Will the key be in the book?'

'No of course it won't' he laughed 'but it'll tell me where the hell it is. Go on get into my car out of the rain. Here's the keys'.

The rain was now pelting down so hard that it was bouncing off the tarmac car park surface. She sat in Steve's car and felt really sorry for him labouring away in the wet but it gave her the opportunity to rethink her feelings for him.

It was surprising that he'd volunteered to change the wheel for her. Most men on a night like this would have either made sure she'd got through on the phone to the breakdown outfit and then left her alone, or maybe kept her company till the breakdown people arrived but to willingly struggle away on such a horrid night was really chivalrous.

'And they say women are difficult to understand' she muttered out loud twisting to look across the car park where he was still working on her car but as she watched he straightened up, seemed to gather up some tools and put them in the boot along with a wheel, presumably the flat tyre and shutting the boot and car door he ran across to her in his car.

'There all done' he said pushing his wet hair into place as he got in.

'You found the locking thingee then?

'Yes'.

God you're absolutely soaked. I'm so sorry and really very grateful. Thank you'.

'No problem. I'll soon be home and can dry off and this suit needed to go to the cleaners in any case. Right I'll be off then. See you tomorrow' and as he turned the key to start his car she opened the door, got out, looked back in, said 'Thanks again' and ran back to her little car.

It only took a few minutes for her to drive to her apartment and once inside she stripped off her business suit and changed into jeans and a sweater, ran a towel over her slightly damp hair, combed it and went into the kitchen to see about fixing some supper. Then she stopped, thought for a moment, picked up a jacket and her car keys and was soon back in the car heading to a Tesco Express store where she quickly collected some ready meals, a bag of pre-packed salad, a pack of cherry tomatoes, the last crusty baguette on the rack and finally a bottle of white wine.

Back in the car she checked **NOTES** on her mobile found the address she wanted and programming the sat-nav set off arriving about ten minutes later where she ran through the rain and rang the doorbell.

It opened to reveal Steve clad in a white dressing gown, legs bare, rubbing his still wet hair with a towel.

'Em hi. Problems with the wheel?'

'No the car's fine. I err ...... came to cook you supper .... to say thanks. Well cook is a bit of a euphemism as I'm a crap cook but I am a dab hand at putting ready meals in a microwave or a warm oven' and she held up the Tesco bag.

'Come in' he laughed. 'I've just had a bath to warm up. Kitchen's through there' he pointed 'I'll go and put on some clothes'.

She walked through from the all in one sitting room/diner into the kitchen which was small but had everything that one would need. Steve had finally moved out of the hotel a few months ago and bought this little one bedroom starter home.

He'd explained to Travis one evening over a beer that although he already had a house in Reading, having moved out of the hotel rather than renting a flat or a house for the next few months till the project finished, it had seemed a good idea to buy something as an investment. When this project was over he'd rent it out as he'd learned that there was a good market in Norwich for these little one bedroom starter houses mainly wanted by young couples getting onto the housing ladder but unable to raise the necessary deposit or afford to purchase and so having to rent.

Rummaging around she found plates, dishes, cutlery and opening the surprisingly large microwave pierced the film lids to the two ready meals, and put them inside.

'There that's better' said Steve when he joined her. 'You didn't need to do this you know'.

'Actually I think that I did. I can say thank you properly and also it'll give us a chance to talk. We need to do that Steve'.

He said nothing just nodded. 'Have you found everything you need?'

'Yes. Now when they're ready do you want Lasagne or Chicken Jalfrezi? You choose'.

'I'll have the curry please'.

'Fine by me. Now get a couple of glasses and we'll have a drink' she smiled holding up the bottle of wine that she'd bought.

He pulled the cork, poured, raised his glass and said 'Cheers'.

She smiled and said 'Thank you for doing the tyre. Women still need men you know. We may be all equal rights, emancipated and politically correct but something like a flat tyre reminds us that we are still the inferior sex'.

'Rubbish. Glad I was able to help'.

They enjoyed their meals and although Steve tucked into the wine she said she only wanted one glass as she was driving.

'Steve what's happened between us? We were getting on great. Well at least I thought we were then suddenly you turned all horrid and cold on me. If I've done something to upset you, tell me. I know I screwed up getting those figures to you that time but surely you didn't need to be so nasty about it, or be so cold and disinterested in me since did you?'

'No you're right. It was wrong of me to take out my concerns on you. I can't excuse myself. I'd had a bad previous session with the Bank and they were really pushing and threatening to bring in someone else to oversee the project. That would have been a disaster for me personally and I was upset, irritable, angry, nervous ……. all of those things and wanted to really prepare thoroughly for that next discussion.

The fact that your numbers were late just added to my tension and I guess I just took out my feelings on you. The trouble was having done that things just seemed to escalate and I couldn't find a way to get them back to normal'.

'You could have said sorry' she replied softly.

'Yes I could …… and I should have done' he responded looking straight at her. 'I know it's too late now but ….. sorry'.

She looked at his face, his eyes, his mouth and nodded. 'Apology accepted' she said quietly, 'but don't leave it so long next time ….. if there ever is a next time'.

Now it was his turn to nod. They looked at each other for a little while until he relaxed the moment by asking 'Coffee?'

It was around eleven o'clock when she said that she needed to leave and after thanking her again for coming round and cooking supper he took her hands and said softly 'Will you stay the night so I can say sorry properly?'

Looking at him she gently extracted her hands from his and spoke quietly. 'No Steve. Thank you for asking ….. but no. Not tonight. Maybe another time'.

'Sure?'

'Uh huh. Yes quite sure'.

He nodded. 'Fine. See you tomorrow in the office?'

'Yes. See you tomorrow. Goodnight Steve'.

As she drove home she was glad that she'd cleared the air with him. He was an attractive man and previously she had thought they might be able to find something deeper in their relationship but since the row she'd forgotten that. But he was nice really and perhaps they could find a way to get it together again.

Steve finished off the bottle of wine and he too was glad that they'd cleared the air as he really did fancy her. No he corrected himself. It wasn't that he just fancied her, he really liked her and now perhaps they could get back together. Sleep together again maybe?

***

The fancy dress party held at a hotel in Norwich was two days later and Travis checked what time Emily wanted to be collected as she'd arranged to go to the party with him so promptly at eight thirty she heard him ringing her door bell.

She'd not told anyone what her costume was to be, so flinging open the door she stepped forward and hissed loudly.

'Hey man that's a great outfit' he acknowledged as his eyes travelled from the top of her head to her feet and back again.

'Is it alright?'

'Alright? It's amazing. Well your carriage awaits you' and smiling he stood aside as she picked up a small black handbag and stepped outside into the communal hallway of the block of apartments.

Her arrival at the party created a palpable rustle of excitement as she walked confidently through the large crowd of people already there. Her decision to arrive well after the event had started had been deliberate as she hadn't wanted to stand around waiting for the bulk of people to arrive and so now about an hour and a quarter after the official start time she guessed that over a hundred people were already milling about in various fancy dress outfits some simple, others elaborate like hers.

Her choice of Catwoman had come to her one evening when she'd seen that Sky tv were showing the film and although she didn't watch it all she saw enough to decide that was what her outfit would be.

It had taken a bit of searching on the internet but she'd found a site that specialised in leather gear. As well as the black bra, hot pants and mask that she'd ordered they also had an extensive collection of other more extreme leather gear including bondage and domination items but she'd ignored them and was happy with what she'd chosen but having tried it all on she decided that she needed something to slightly cover her top and so she'd gone into a dress shop in Norwich and bought a one piece black see through body stocking.

So now with her cats ears mask covering the top half of her face and head, her black leather bra and hot pants, her body stocking providing a modicum of decency to her above the waist together with a little warmth, wide mesh fishnet tights and knee length black high heeled fashion boots she strutted around fully comfortable with herself, envied by many of the other women who were jealous of her long legs, neat tightly covered bum and lovely figure and openly drooled over by most of the men.

At nine o'clock William took to the microphone and announced that anyone who wanted to enter the competition for the best outfit should come forward after which the buffet supper would be served followed by dancing till one o'clock to the disco.

Several people suggested she should enter the competition so after swallowing a quick gin and tonic she did so along with about a dozen others.

The judging panel consisting of William, Janie, one man and one women factory operatives who were on the Company's social committee and Rod Jackson the HR Director were unanimous in their decision as to the first, and eventually agreed on second and third prize winners.

'Right ladies and gentlemen if I could have your attention' boomed William the mike squawking slightly strangely 'the judges have made their choices and my wife Janie will make the presentations. So in third place is Tracey Miller for her outfit as Maid Marion'.

There was applause as the little factory operator came up to Janie, cheek kissed and took her shopping voucher for five pounds.

'In second place is Harry Simmons as Hannibal Lector'. He shook hands with Janie who'd almost dropped the envelope containing his ten pound voucher at the mention of the name Harry.

'But although the judges may have had to work hard to agree on those two runner up places there was no disagreement at all as to the winner tonight so please will .... Catwoman come up here'.

Emily grinned cheerfully; cheek kissed Janie, lip kissed William and took her twenty pound voucher.

'Right everyone, supper is served but before you tuck in may I just say that you all know that two years ago, one year ago, indeed even as recently as a few months ago Hardys was in real financial difficultly but I am glad to be able to say that thanks to your support, hard work and financial sacrifices by giving up some wages together with the hard work and skills of the turnaround team of Emily, Travis, Greg and Steve, we are now in a much stronger financial position, are no longer under the cosh from the Bank and look to be in calmer waters and heading for some real future prosperity once again.

It's been a team effort extremely well led by Steve, who now has some very good news to give you'.

'Thank you William' smiled Steve stepping forward and taking the microphone. 'Yes everyone, I want to add my thanks to William's for everything you've all done to help us in this turnaround. We're not fully out of the woods yet but at least we can see the edge' and he smiled.

'I am also able on a practical point to say that with effect from the start of next month although overtime will remain within the new more stringent rules, we will restore basic wage levels to what they were before we had to cut them and I would hope that within six months from now, provided …….' and he held up both hands to emphasise the next point 'provided we continue to recover and make progress then we will look to improve those overtime rates.

That's all I wanted to say, so now tuck into the buffet, drink what you want but those that are driving be careful, enjoy the dancing and have a great evening'.

There was a warm spontaneous loud and prolonged bust of cheering and clapping. The team had agreed that this party event was the appropriate place to announce the restoration of the wage rates. They'd debated long and hard about whether to do it now or wait a few more months, but had decided that it might provide a real motivational shot in the arm to the workforce and it looked from the reactions tonight that the decision had been well judged.

Emily was constantly approached by lots of people who wanted to talk to her. One of the first was Kelly who told her that she thought she looked quite stunning. Emily smiled her thanks and said that she thought Kelly's own outfit of Little Bo Peep was delightful and that she looked very pretty thus sending the little marketing girl away blushing with happiness.

Most of the young men there, whether they were on their own or even with female partners found excuses either to walk close by her, or stop and talk to her or just look at her either openly or surreptitiously but it was ages before Steve approached her.

'Hi. A well deserved win. You do look stunning and you'll have a lot of young men, oh and maybe older ones too, having erotic dreams about you tonight'.

'Really well to all of them I have one thing to say' she chuckled.

'What?'

'Miaow' then looking at him from under her long eyelashes she asked coquettishly 'will you have them about me?'

'What erotic dreams? Yes lots of them' he laughed and they started to chat until he asked 'Does this incredibly sexy and beautiful Catwoman dance?'

They did for a while but he couldn't monopolise her for long as so many others wanted to get close to her on the dance floor and as it was quite small and crowded most of them got to hold her really tightly.

After a while she excused herself from one of the young finance managers who'd taken the crowded dance floor as an opportunity not just to hold her tightly but to start pressing himself against her, especially his crotch, and run his hands over her leather hot pants. She found Travis and danced with him for a while then took a breather and pushed to the bar where William bought her a drink.

Easing away from the bar and turning round she bumped into Steve who grinned as he said 'Well at last. Since that first dance I haven't been able to get near you all night. Want to get something to eat and sit down to chat for a while?'

'Umm good idea'. By now the food queue was quite short as most people had already selected their food so it didn't take long before they'd filled their plates from the cold selection. They found an empty table and once they started they talked non stop and it was as if suddenly once again they were happy and comfortable with themselves and with each other.

They danced again and had another drink and time seemed to fly past until the DJ warned that there were only a few minutes left before the bar closed at midnight although dancing would go on till one o'clock.

Steve smiled as he took her hand and asked quietly 'Can I take you home?'

'Steve I came with Travis'.

'Oh'.

He'll be expecting to take me home'.

'Sure' and he said nothing more just looked at her as he continued to hold her hand.

Her heart was starting to pump a little faster and she wanted to take him up on his offer but there was Travis to consider.

'Wait here' and she slid out of the chair and walked across the room carefully avoiding the dance floor, to the bar where Travis was drinking a soda water.

'Hello cat lady. Having a good time? When do you want to go? I'm ready now if you want?'

'Travis would you be awfully hurt if I didn't leave with you? I mean if it would upset you then yes let's go now but ....'

'But you want to go home with someone else?

She nodded. 'Sorry'.

'Steve?'

'Yes. Sorry' she said again.

A slow smile broke onto his face. 'No honey that's fine. Really it is. You go and have a good time with him. Glad you two have got it back together'.

'You sure?'

'Yep, sure I'm sure. See you Monday. Nite Emily'.

She whispered 'Thanks' and gave him a little kiss on the forehead and although he smiled when she turned away to go back to Steve the smile went and he looked disappointed.

'Ok come on then' she said taking Steve's hand and pulling him up.

'Is Travis alright about it?'

'Yes ...... yes he's fine about it'.

In the car he looked at her then said softly 'I'd like to take off that mask and kiss you. May I?'

'Uh huh, yes Robin Hood you may'.

It was a long deep and increasingly passionate kiss and when they broke apart he muttered 'Oh God what a stupid man I've been. Come here' and he pulled her to him again.

They stayed in the car for ages, kissing and whispering until they heard the sound of several revellers as they left the party shouting and whistling, not specifically at them but at the night and each other in general.

'Come on let's go' said Steve starting the car. 'Your place?'

'Yes it'll have to be mine as I can't make my own way home like this at this time of night can I?' she laughed. 'Yes take me to my lair' and extending her fingers like claws she growled 'Grrrr'.

'Do cats growl? I thought they meowed' he queried laughing as they drove out of the car park.

'This one does' she said softly buckling her seat belt into place. Not much more was spoken until they arrived at her apartment.

'Drink, coffee, before you go?' she queried.

'Coffee as I'm driving would be great thanks' and following her in he first plonked down on her settee but as she started to bustle around in the kitchen still in her outfit but without the mask he went and joined her.

'That really is an incredible outfit' he said standing behind her putting his arms around her waist and kissing her neck then as she turned to him he kissed her lips as his hands squeezed her bottom.

This time there was real passion from them both as they tongue fenced fiercely and she pushed her body into him continuing until the kettle boiled.

'Kettle's boiling' she said quietly.

'So am I'.

Laughing she pushed him away and made two mugs of coffee which they took into her sitting room.

They kissed again and he gently squeezed her breasts.

'You know' she whispered running a hand up and down his trouser leg 'your outfit is pretty good as well but I had hoped that as you were Robin Hood you'd be in codpiece, doublet and hose showing off your bulging manhood to all us horny maidens' and her hand came to rest in his crutch which she pressed firmly and deliberately.

'Horny maidens?'

'Oh yes very ….. so do you think you could do something about it?'

'I would if I could just work out how the hell I get inside all this lot' he chuckled running his finger down from her neck to her thigh.

'With difficulty' she laughed getting up. 'Alright I'll direct your efforts. First boots and then the hot pants', so he knelt and took off the three suggested items of clothing. 'Now the tights' so still kneeling he rolled them down and off. 'Now the body stocking which undoes beneath the crutch'.

He popped the three poppers then standing said 'Arms up' as he hefted it off over her head and down her arms whereupon she turned her back so he could unclip the leather bra.

'Panties' she next commanded and still behind her he knelt down again and slid down the black thong, eased it over her feet and planted a large kiss on each buttock.

'There' he chuckled 'that's better as although you looked great as Catwoman you look even better with nothing on'.

'Thank you kind sir. Now I'm going to the bathroom and you Mr. Hood, loved by the poor and feared by the rich, get yourself into my bedroom undress and be ready for me. We have got some time to make up haven't we? I think that tonight might be when we should do that' and blowing him a kiss she walked unselfconsciously out of the sitting room.

When she returned smelling of toothpaste, talc and perfume she looked at him lying naked on her bed, mewed 'Miaow' then leapt onto him. Pinning his arms down she climbed on top and rubbed her bush along his prick which reacted by rapidly erecting. 'Grrrr' she growled softly.

They kissed, stroked and whispered until she said 'Stay there' and getting out of bed went to her chest of drawers, extracted a packet of condoms, put it on the bedside table, took one out, opened it and rolled it onto him.

'Umm oh baby' she groaned loudly as she lowered herself onto him. They took time with and for each other with her hitting a groaningly loud and deeply satisfying orgasm which acted as a trigger for his climax.

Over the next couple of hours they kissed, hugged, cuddled and made love once more after which he suggested that maybe it was time to go to sleep.

'Yes I think so Mr. Hood. In any case I'm right out of condoms now so that's your lot for tonight'.

'I'll get up early and get some tomorrow' he muttered.

'Will you now .... good idea .... oh and I suggest you get a jumbo pack as seeing it's the weekend and if you've nothing arranged we could spend quite a bit of it here in bed ….. if you'd like to do that. Kind of getting re-acquainted'.

'I didn't know cats were so randy' he whispered.

'Oh yes incredibly so' she giggled as she put her hand on his cock and balls and gave them a little squeeze. 'Good night'.

They both woke early and as he leaned over to kiss her she felt his morning hard-on poking into her leg.

'Well well well what's this down here?' and sliding down the bed she licked and kissed his erection then moved back up the bed and popped a little kiss on his lips. 'Put the kettle on then go and get some rubbers' she instructed softly. He nodded and got out of bed to go to the bathroom. She waited until he came back then watched him re-dress as Robin Hood.

'I'll go home first and get out of this lot and be back as soon as I can' he said smiling. 'You know you are very lovely in the morning'.

'Only in the morning?'

'No all the time, but I like to look at you and especially make love you in the morning'.

Throwing back the duvet cover she rolled onto her tummy and grinned. 'I'll be waiting impatiently ……. very impatiently' she breathed sexily.

It was about forty five minutes later when he rang her bell and she let him back into her apartment. Moments later she let him into her bed.

'Got what we need?'

'Yep lots. Ten packs of three. The checkout girl in the petrol station looked at me a bit strangely so I said that I was meeting my girlfriend this weekend and thought I'd need quite a few as she was insatiable' he laughed.

'We'd better make a start on them hadn't we? Come here' and she held out her arms to him as she lay naked and inviting on the bed. He stripped off quickly and was soon lying on top of her kissing and stroking but as soon as he was hard he pulled away and grinned.

'Now there's some unfinished business from earlier on my lass' he chuckled rolling a condom onto himself.

'There is' she said looking puzzled.

'Definitely' and taking her head he pulled it down to his erect prick.

She enjoyed hearing him grunt and gasp as she licked and sucked but suddenly he pushed himself forward. From the twitching of his prick and his grunts she knew he was almost there, so gripping his balls with one hand while the other squeezed the base of his prick she sucked hard. He jerked, arched his back and she felt the condom fill with warm liquid but she continued working on him until he relaxed and said 'Thank you'.

Taking that as her cue to stop, she let him slide out of her lips and slithered up the bed to lie next to him. 'You sounded as though you enjoyed that' she said quietly.

'You know I did you sexy lady. As I said .... thanks'.

'I'm glad it was good for you but when you've got your breath back there's something I need you to do for me' and a little later after assuring her that he had definitely got his breath back he proved that he had.

They spent the rest of Saturday and all of Sunday together. He finally went back to his house very late Sunday night where he reflected on the weekend and was glad that he and Emily were now back as a couple, while she lying in bed alone realised that she actually had quite deep feelings for him and started to speculate on what a future might hold for the two of them.

***

The new week started well. There was a great atmosphere around the business as the news of the improvements to the wage rates had ricocheted around over the weekend and since the morning shifts started at six o'clock on Monday.

Travis asked Emily if she'd had a nice weekend and when slightly shyly she said 'Yes very nice thanks', he smiled.

'Good. You and Steve back together now then?'

'Yes we are'.

'Well that's real nice ain't it' and his comment was obviously sincere.

'Thanks and sorry ..... that it didn't work out with us'.

He nodded, smiled again and picked up a pile of computer sheets off his desk and started to study them.

'Travis you are a really nice man, did you know that?'

'Yep. But the really nice man doesn't get the girl does he?' he said slightly sadly she thought.

***

William was also looking forward to the morning as he had a meeting with a charity concerned with deprived children. They needed help with their administrative organisation and then in the afternoon he was seeing someone that the Chamber of Commerce had recommended to him who was involved with business start-ups especially with young people.

***

Janie re-read Harry's last letter to her.

> *Hi Janie*
> *It was really great to get your last letter with all your news. I do miss you but at least having some pictures of you helps pass the time. Any chance of some more? If so could you make them a bit saucier!?!?!?!*
> *When are you coming to see me again? Your lovely presence makes life here bearable. Keep in touch please.*
> > *Harry.*

She thought for a moment then typed a reply.

Harry,

Thanks for your letter – and its request – you naughty boy!!! I'll have to see what I can do for you won't I?

Do you have a date for your trial yet? I miss you and can't wait till you're out and we can get together again.

In the meantime keep well. I thought you looked

a bit down last time I saw you so is there any way you can get some exercise to tone you up. After all we don't want you going to seed do we?

Cheer up, chin up and I'll come and see you again soon.

Lots of love

Janie xxxxxxxxx

As she drove to post it she wondered how she was going to get some additional photos taken of herself and what did more saucy mean? After all she'd been topless for the first lot and there'd been that one full nude shot. Did he want more full nudes?

She also pondered whether she could ask Jackie to take this next lot then it struck her like a flash of lightening. Wasn't it possible to put her camera onto delayed taking or something where you pressed the button and then positioned yourself in front of it before it went off?

She was sure that William had done that last year on holiday to get himself, her and the two boys into a photo and as soon as she got home she took out the camera and to her great relief the little instruction book was still in the back of the camera case.

Half an hour later she'd mastered the technique but didn't dare to go into action today as she didn't want William coming back in the middle of her raunchy photo shoot. Tomorrow though she knew he was playing a golf match in Surrey so would be leaving home early and not back till late.

She drove to Jackie's and they rode then Janie treated her friend to lunch at a nearby pub.

Back home she pottered around until William returned around four thirty full of excitement that the charity had said they could use him straight away and could he start this week so he'd agreed to do three mornings a week from then on. The business start up advisor had also accepted his offer with alacrity to assist budding young entrepreneurs and he was scheduled to start that next week.

All evening he chatted on about it and how he felt this would be a really good use of his time and when they went to bed he pulled her on top of him. Looking down as she bounced on his erection she smiled and either blew kisses or leaned forward to press her lips against his or her tongue into his mouth, but her mind was on tomorrow as she tried to decide on poses that she'd adopt.

***

The Board meeting that took place two months later was attended by a large team from the bank as well as the Hardys turnaround team. It was challenging, very businesslike but satisfying.

The bank formally acknowledged that all their outstanding debts had been repaid and that they had restored Hardys to the status of a normal client, although they said that they would keep a close watching brief on things and instructed William that if there was the slightest hint that problems might start to arise he was to contact them immediately.

William had also agreed to the Bank's request that while he could be re-instated as Chairman they had insisted that he appoint a Chief Executive who would run the business properly for him and with Steve's help he was well advanced on the search using Nigel Charlesworthy to find a suitable candidate.

Steve speaking for the turnaround team thanked the bank on Hardys behalf for their support during the difficult times that the business had been through and said how much he, Emily, Travis and Greg had enjoyed the project.

Greg formally confirmed that he was accepting the permanent position as Sales and Marketing Director of Hardys and advised that he and his wife had found a house in Brooke a few miles out of Norwich which they were buying and expected to move in shortly.

Steve stated that he and Emily would be moving to another project to help a plastics and chemical manufacturer that was in trouble and which the bank had asked them to go and sort out. This was a much bigger company than Hardys and both of them saw it that they'd earned their spurs properly now and were being entrusted with some really big projects.

Travis said that he'd wrap things up at Hardys within a month and was then going to go back to The States but he felt that the number two in Finance could step up to Finance Director providing the new Chief Executive had a financial background.

So with much shaking of hands and mutual backslapping the meeting finished and the attendees departed on their various ways.

Steve invited Emily to go to lunch with him and they went to the Walpole Arms, the restaurant with an excellent reputation of good food and as they were drinking their coffee he leaned forward and took her hand.

'Em this new project we're going to. I reckon it'll take at least a year, maybe longer. I wondered.........' he paused for some time as he looked into her eyes.

'What did you wonder?' she replied softly.

He took a deep breath. 'I wondered if it might be a good idea for us to get a flat, or cottage or a house or something ...... together? What do you say?'

'You mean live together full time?'

'Yes. Work together and live together. I think it would be nice'.

'Do you?' and she smiled cheekily at him. 'Why do you think that?'

'Because ...... erm ...... because ..... well I just do'.

'So do I'.

'Really!'

'Yes. I think it is a lovely idea but we'll have to sort out some house rules as I'm not washing your dirty socks or pants! We'll share the chores, housework and bills. Deal?'

'Deal' then putting on what he hoped was a suitable Norfolk country accent and adopting an expression of leering lust he continued 'but I'll be happy to wash your dirty undies'.

She roared with laughter. 'Pervert. No chance. I'll do my own smalls thank you'.

Trials teach us what we are; they dig up the soil and let us see what we are made of.

Charles Haddon Spurgeon.

CHAPTER 25

Eight months had passed since Emily and Steve's lunch at the Walpole Arms and the formal ending of the turnaround team's activities.

William now back as Chairman was more than comfortable leaving the bulk of the running of his business to James Marsh his new Chief Executive who came to the business not only with a wealth of experience of difficult trading in manufacturing businesses but also a strong financial background.

James and Greg got on like a house on fire and he also fitted well with the rest of the team. Interestingly he also seemed instinctively to know how to get the best out of William without making him feel belittled or sidelined.

William in fact was enjoying himself as James asked for and listened to his views, involved him in the strategy of the business and William realised that he now had the best of all worlds.

He was Chairman in name and in part practice, was still drawing his very substantial salary from the business, remained well respected by all the local business community as well as their friends, but was now working part time with three charities which he found satisfying and rewarding as he also did assisting young people with their ideas on starting various businesses.

The one thing he no longer had was the problems of the business just all the benefits with few, if any of the worries.

***

Janie though had a whole lot of worries as this week she'd been told to attend court for Harry's trial and warned she would be called as a witness. She'd spent many hours with the police and with the solicitors for the Crown who were prosecuting Harry and she'd had one somewhat perfunctory meeting with the prosecuting barrister.

Knowing roughly what to expect and how things were done as William had insisted that she attend with him at Norwich Crown

Court some months ago when the man who'd burnt down the stables, set fire to the box store in the factory, planted the dummy bomb and sent the blackmail letters was sentenced.

She could still see the shock on his face when the judge spoke to him in solemn tones after the jury had returned guilty verdicts on all the crimes of which he was accused.

'Frederick Albert Harding you have been found guilty by the jury of all the terrible crimes that you committed and it is my duty in passing sentence to ensure that not only does it reflect a suitable level of punishment but also acts as a deterrent to others who may misguidedly consider committing such dreadful acts.

What you did was wicked, dangerous, despicable and awful and so you will go to prison for a total of fifteen years and you will not be eligible for consideration of probation until you have served at least three quarters of your sentence. Take him down'.

To ensure that she wasn't late for the trial she decided to travel down the night before and stay in an hotel which she did but she couldn't sleep and tossed and turned for most of the night.

Arriving at the court she was directed to a waiting room. The trial had been going on already for three days and she knew that she was one of the early witnesses being called by the prosecution to give evidence against Harry. Knowing that she couldn't avoid doing so, she'd decided in her mind to simply stick to the facts regarding the money she'd handed over to him and hoped that their affair wouldn't come to light.

'Mrs. Hardy please?' asked a black gowned usher breaking her reverie as she sat in the waiting room.

'Yes that's me'.

'This way madam' and he led her into the court, directed her to the witness stand and asked her to take the oath which she did feeling extremely nervous. After she'd spoken the words swearing to tell the truth the whole truth and nothing but the truth and confirming her name and address she looked around and smiled at Harry.

He was sitting in the dock and smiled back at her as he brushed his hair lock back.

The questions from the barrister leading the prosecution were simple, straight forward and not difficult to answer as they dealt with the investments that she'd handed over to Harry to look after and to her relief after about half an hour he thanked her then turned to the judge and said 'No further questions my Lady'.

Her honour Lady Beatrice Melrose nodded then turned to the defence barrister 'Yes Mr. Goodchild?'

'If it please you my lady' then he looked at Janie and smiled.

'Mrs. Hardy would you tell the court in your own words how you first met my client Mr. Norton'.

'At a ....' she paused to clear her throat 'sorry, at a wedding. My husband and I were guests at a wedding and Harry, umm Mr. Norton, was on the same table'.

'And you got on well did you?'

'Yes'.

'Then what happened?'

'Nothing'.

The barrister raised his eyebrows. 'Nothing? Didn't you arrange to meet?'

'Oh yes. Sorry I see what you mean. Yes, Harry ..... Mr. Norton explained that he was a financial adviser and suggested that if I wanted him to, he'd he happy to check out my investments for me'.

'Check out your investments?'

'Yes'.

'And did he? Check out your investments?'

'Well not then but we arranged that I would to go down to London to see him. William, my husband, produced a list of my financial affairs which I took with me when I met Mr. Norton'.

'Will you tell the court what happened at this meeting in London please?'

'Yes certainly. Harry looked through the information I took with me and as I remember it he said that some of the investments were ok but he thought others could be improved to give a better return'.

'Thank you. Did you agree with his proposals?'

'Well he didn't make any then. He suggested that I leave him to consider alternative investments and that he'd contact me in a week or so to discuss different options'.

'So did you meet him in a week or so?'

'Yes. I went back down to his office in London and he ran through his proposals. There were some significant changes and I said that they looked alright to me but that I'd need to check with William'.

'And did you check with Mr. Hardy?'

'Yes and he said they looked interesting and that he was happy if I went ahead. So I arranged another meeting with Mr. Norton'.

'Ah I see. Now can you tell the court what happened at this third meeting?'

Careful now.

'Harry ..... err Mr. Norton had several papers all ready for me to sign, so he asked me to read them through, explained what was what and then I signed them'.

'Then what happened?'

'Nothing. It was quite a short meeting and afterwards I went home'.

'Just like that? A short meeting, you signed the papers and went home. Haven't you forgotten something Mrs. Hardy?'

Oh no please don't raise it.

'I don't think so'.

'I think you have. Allow me to refresh your memory. Didn't you go and have lunch together?'

Phew!

'Oh yes. He suggested that we went to lunch to celebrate me becoming a client of his and the increased financial return I was going to get in future as a result of him taking control of my investments'.

'Then what happened ..... after the lunch?'

What did he know she wondered? Maybe nothing.

'I went back home to Norfolk'.

'Mrs. Hardy I believe that you seem to have some sort of selective memory. You forgot just now that you went to lunch with my client and now you appear to have forgotten something else. Is it not a fact that after lunch you went back to Mr. Norton's flat?'

'Umm oh yes. For coffee and a glass of brandy'.

'For coffee and a glass of brandy? How nice'.

'Yes it was'.

'Is it also not a fact that at Mr. Norton's flat that afternoon you seduced him?'

Oh my God. Surely not? Please don't go into this.

'Objection my Lady' interrupted the prosecuting barrister. 'I do not see that this is in any way relevant to the offences with which the accused is charged'.

'On the contrary my Lady' reposted Mr. Goodchild 'it is entirely relevant as I intend to establish the importance and somewhat special nature of the relationship between Mrs. Hardy and my client. It is one of a number of key factors relating to special relationships between Mr. Norton and his clients and as such is wholly relevant to this case'.

Janie's heart thumped as the Judge looked at her, then at the prosecuting barrister before staring at defence barrister. 'Very well Mr.Goodchild please proceed, but kindly ensure that all questions in this matter are wholly relevant'.

'Thank you my Lady. I will of course do as you request'.

Oh no.

'Mrs. Hardy I will ask you again. Did you seduce Mr. Norton that afternoon at his flat?'

'No'.

'Mrs. Hardy may I remind you that you are under oath. Now please answer the question again. Did you seduce Mr. Norton that afternoon?'

'NO. I've just told you …….. I did NOT seduce him'.

'But did sexual intercourse take place that afternoon in my client's flat?'

Janie stared at her tormentor. She knew she was blushing and her knees started to feel week. She could also sense sweat starting to appear on her forehead.

'Mrs. Hardy will you answer my question please. Did sexual intercourse take place at Mr. Norton's flat that afternoon?'

'It wasn't like that …….'

'Mrs. Hardy it is a simple question for which a simple answer is required. Did you and Mr. Norton have sex that afternoon? Yes or no?'

There was a long pause before looking down at her hands Janie whispered 'Yes'.

'I'm sorry Mrs. Norton will you please speak up so the court can hear your answer. Did you have sex with Mr. Norton that afternoon?'

'Yes I did' she said more loudly blushing furiously and now feeling sweaty under her armpits as well as her forehead.

'Thank you'. He paused and fiddled with his papers in front of him before looking up at her his gaze steely and his eyes unyielding 'That was the start of a secret passionate affair between you and Mr. Norton wasn't it?'

A frisson of interest whispered around the court as everyone waited for her to answer.

'I wouldn't put it quite like that'.

'Oh well how would you put it then?'

'I don't know'.

'Mrs. Hardy enough of the semantics. You had an affair with my client didn't you?'

Yes'.

'And it started that afternoon didn't it?'

'Yes it did'.

'Did you subsequently meet Mr. Norton in his flat on other occasions for sex?'

'Yes but ....'

'Did you also meet my client at an hotel in Newmarket for afternoon and evening sessions of sexual intercourse?'

'Yes I did'.

'Did you have sexual intercourse at my client's office?'

'No never'.

'But you tried to didn't you?'

'No'.

'Oh come on Mrs. Hardy. Is it not a fact that you sat on my client's desk in front of him, undid your blouse and exposed your breasts to him and wearing a very short skirt opened your legs wide apart to blatantly and quite shamelessly flaunt yourself at him? Flashed might be a better phrase'.

Please floor open up and swallow me. Let me go from this horrible place. Just let me get away. Now. Harry why have you told everyone all this? How will it help you especially as you say you are not guilty? Why make me go through all this?

'Look you make it sound dirty like I was some sort of harlot or something. It was just in fun. The sort of thing ......'

'The sort of thing that a woman, harlot or not, might do when trying to seduce a man?'

'I suppose so. But look if you'd let me ....'

'So would you agree with me that you and Mr. Norton were having an extremely robust illicit sexual affair?'

'Yes I've just told you. You don't need to keep raking it up like this. You're making it sound awful. Dirty. It wasn't ....'

'Mrs. Hardy did you take Mr. Norton to your cottage in France for several days'.

Oh God is there nothing that he doesn't know and isn't going to ask?

There was a long pause before she replied quietly 'Yes but I didn't take him. We met down there'. Now she could feel her back was wet with sweat as well as her armpits, forehead and face.

'Ah I'm sorry. You didn't take him but you just met him there. How fortunate! By chance? A lucky encounter? Walking along a road in France and you just happened to bump into each other did you?'

'No of course not'.

'So how did you meet there?'

'My Lady I really do feel that this is getting further away from the real issues here in this case?' interjected the prosecuting barrister.

Yes it is. Thank you. Please make this man stop asking these awful questions.

The Judge looked at him but from the way that she then looked at Janie it was obvious that she wasn't going to let her off the hook.

'I don't agree. This line of questioning may continue'.

You rotten cow, you're not wearing a wedding ring so you're obviously a miserable frigid old spinster who's getting off on all this detail about sex.

'Thank you my Lady. Mrs. Hardy as it wasn't by chance will you please tell this court how you and my client happened to meet at your cottage?'

'We arranged to do so. I flew down one day to open it up, air it and so on. Harry came down the next day'.

'I see. I believe that I am right in saying that this particular sexual interlude in France lasted for several continuous days didn't it?'

'Yes we were at the cottage for a few days'.

'So for several days you and my client were spending every moment that you could in these sexual activities?'

'No, not every moment …. of course not'.

'But you did spend a very great deal of time together indulging in carnal pleasures?'

'Yes' she replied looking straight back at him but then her courage failed and she looked down at her feet.

'Including having sex naked in the open air in a field on the edge of a wood ……. within sight of a village?'

Harry. Have you really told them absolutely everything we did? Why?

'Yes but we were hidden away. No-one could see us'.

'I'm pleased to hear it Mrs. Hardy!

There was silence for a few moments as the barrister stared unblinkingly at Janie before he continued his inquisition.

'When you returned to this country did you continue to see my client for the purpose of sexual relations?'

'Yes but …….'

'How often?'

'I don't know. I didn't keep score! We just met whenever we could'.

'You just met …… whenever ….. you …… could' he repeated very deliberately looking at the jury.

'Yes'.

'Even though you didn't keep score would you agree with me that the meetings were frequent events?'

'Yes I suppose so'.

'You suppose so? Oh come on Mrs. Hardy. I think we both know that you and my client met with a regularity that would be called frequent. Didn't you?'

'Yes'.

'Thank you and now I'd like to turn to some financial issues'.

Oh thank heavens he's moved away from the sex.

The next few minutes were taken up with his questions and her answers about the financial performance of her investments before she handed control of them over to Harry and after she'd done so. He went over some of the answers that she'd given earlier to the prosecuting barrister, checked and clarified some points.

461

Although the questions were complex and detailed she started to relax as they were no longer dealing with intimate and embarrassing matters as had been brought out into open court a few minutes ago.

Janie was even able to start to wonder how she was going to talk to William about this as it would be bound to be reported by the press.

As he came to what transpired to be the last question on the financial section Janie thought that in a moment or two her ordeal would be over especially as the barrister seemed to adopt a less aggressive stance and seemed more relaxed.

'Mrs. Hardy thank you for clarifying those points' he said quietly then smiling continued 'I would now like to turn to the time after my client was arrested. I believe that you visited him in Wormwood Scrubs prison is that right?'

There was another definite frisson of excitement rustling around the court.

This should be alright.

'Yes I did'.

'May I ask why?'

'The police said that he had probably stolen our cottage in France as well as my money and I wanted to find out if that was true'.

'Stolen your cottage? How could he have done that?'

'He told me that French inheritance law was complex and that if I or William died, the cottage might not go to the survivor but by putting the ownership into one of his offshore companies then we would be protected from that eventuality'.

'Does that not sound rather farfetched?'

'With hindsight yes I suppose it does but at the time I didn't really think about it. He suggested it. I had no reason to doubt him or what he said'.

'You had no reason to doubt him or what he said' he repeated slowly. 'Perhaps you were so besotted with my client that you didn't understand what he was saying to you?'

'Objection my lady' snapped the prosecuting barrister.

'I withdraw the comment. Did your husband agree with this decision to transfer the cottage into one of Mr. Norton's off shore companies?'

'I didn't tell him'.

'You didn't tell him? Isn't that rather strange? Surely it was an important decision? You thought that you were protecting yourselves in some way against some French Inheritance Tax laws. Wouldn't it be reasonable to expect that you would discuss this with your husband?'

'Yes. I don't know why I didn't tell him. I just didn't'.

'I see. So you visited my client in prison to discover if he'd transferred the ownership of your cottage into this off shore company? Is that right?'

'Yes'.

'Was it a complicated discussion you had with my client in prison?'

'No. He said that he didn't think that he had done anything with the ownership of the cottage'.

'You must have been relieved'.

'Yes I was'.

'But that was all you needed to discuss with him?'

'Yes'.

'So Mrs. Hardy can you please explain to this court why you visited my client in prison again after that first visit? In fact you saw him altogether eleven times?'

Shit. What the hell could she say?

There was further significant rustling of interest around the court as Janie thought furiously.

'Mrs. Hardy?

Still she remained silent. Her legs started to shake and her whole face and forehead were now covered in sweat.

'Mrs. Hardy let me suggest an explanation to you. Was not your need to visit my client driven by the fact that you were sexually obsessed with him and that was why you constantly pestered him even when he was locked up in jail?'

'No. I didn't pester him........'

'But you were obsessed with him?'

'Not obsessed ..... no'.

'But you went time and time again. Why?'

'Look I didn't instigate it. He asked me to go and see him'.

'He asked you to keep going to see him?' the barrister said in a tone of incredulity. 'Isn't the opposite true Mrs. Hardy? Is it not a fact that it was you that kept insisting on seeing him?'

'No'.

'So why did you keep going?'

'I just told you. He asked me to and I felt sorry for him in that awful place, so yes I did visit him several times'.

'You felt sorry for him?'

'Yes'.

'How sympathetic of you' he sneered. 'And so feeling sorry for my client no doubt you decided to try and cheer him up?'

'Yes I did'.

'So Mrs. Hardy would you please take a look at this photograph and then describe to the court what it shows'.

The usher handed her a plastic folder inside which could be clearly seen one of the photos that Jackie had taken of her.

No no no please don't bring this up.

'Please' she whispered.

'What does the photo show Mrs. Hardy?'

There was a long pause when Janie blushing bright red looked round the court; looked at Harry who winked at her; looked at the two barristers; looked at the judge and finally looked at the jury. Her blouse beneath her jacket felt soaked with sweat.

'It is a picture of me'.

'Yes Mrs. Hardy. It can be clearly seen that it is you but in something of a surprising pose shall we say. Could you tell the court how old you are please'.

'Thirty nine'.

'Thirty nine' he repeated. 'An extremely attractive thirty nine if I may say so Mrs. Hardy. However as a married woman approaching middle age, attractive though you undoubtedly are, you would not I assume describe yourself as a model?'

'No of course not'.

'Of course not. A married woman approaching middle age with two sons but not a model'.

'No'.

'So Mrs. Hardy will you kindly explain to the court what this photograph shows'.

'Please don't ....' and then her legs felt really wobbly and she slumped down on the chair. 'Sorry could I have a glass of water?'

An usher brought it to her and she sipped gratefully trying to think what to say and how to explain what she'd done which had been an act of compassion but here in this bleak forbidding court would just sound smutty. She glanced at Harry and he had almost a sneering expression on his face.

'Are you feeling better Mrs. Hardy?' enquired the judge.

'Yes thank you' Janie replied standing up again.

'Do you feel able to continue now or would you like a few more minutes to compose yourself?'

'No thank you. I ...... I err feel able to continue'.

Continue? I suppose I must until we come to the bitter end.

'Good then you may proceed Mr. Goodchild'.

'Thank you my Lady. Mrs. Hardy would you please explain to the court what the photograph shows please'.

'It is a picture of me at home'.

'What are you doing in this picture?'

'I'm on my bed. Lying on my bed but do we really have to go into this detail?'

'Yes we do Mrs. Hardy. But it is a little more than you just lying on your bed isn't it? Is it not a picture of you lying on your tummy completely naked except for a pair of stockings, exposing your breasts and bottom to the camera? Isn't that what this photograph shows?' and his voice rose.

There was now considerably more rustling and sounds of feet moving and people could be openly seen whispering around the court room. Several people also leaned forward as if to get closer and hear or see more of Janie's discomfiture.

'Yes' she whispered.

'And here are some other photographs all showing you in various states of undress' and he handed her another folder which she flicked through and saw were all the pictures that Jackie had taken. 'Would you say that this is a normal thing for a married woman to do? Send semi naked pictures of herself to someone else in prison?'

465

'Objection!' The prosecuting barrister leapt to his feet.

'I withdraw the question my Lady' said Mr. Goodchild looking at the other barrister. 'Mrs. Hardy who took these pictures of you?'

'A friend'.

'Another man friend?'

'Objection!'

'I will rephrase the question' he said looking at the judge 'was it a man or a woman friend who took these intimate pictures of you?'

'A woman, my friend Jackie'.

'Did she take all of the pictures of you that you sent to my client?'

'Yes she took all these' she said tapping the folder'.

There was a pause as copies of the photos were handed to the jury.

'Ah so she took all of those …… but there are some other photographs which you also sent to my client aren't there Mrs. Hardy?'

Christ this is getting worse. Surely he's not going to show these in Court is he? Not those I took myself?

'Yes …… yes there are'.

'So who took the others which are more explicit …. bordering on pornographic even?'

'I did'.

'You did? How?'

'My camera has a button which enables you to set it onto a delay time mechanism then pose in front of it before it goes off. I used that'.

'Oh of course. The sort of thing that people would normally use for taking family snaps of themselves and the children'.

Sarcastic bastard!

'Possibly'.

'So you posed in this highly revealing way and personally took these much more explicit pictures of yourself?'

'Yes'.

There was another delay while copies of this second batch of photographs were handed to the judge, the jury members and the prosecuting barrister who glanced through them then put his head in his hands for a moment before looking up at Janie.

Janie watched the judge's scornful expression as she slowly turned over photo after photo. She looked at the jury of eight men and four women as they also studied them. Some just flicked through but one young man on the front row who was probably mid twenties studied each in great detail and then looked up at her obviously comparing the lewd picture with the sophisticated fully dressed woman in front of him. He repeated studying the picture then her with each of the subsequent pictures. His actions alone made her feel ashamed every time he looked at her.

'Mrs. Hardy I now wish to turn to another matter. Would you tell the court if you recognise this?' and a plastic bag was handed to her.

She looked at it, her heart thumping and her self esteem hitting rock bottom.

This was probably the most awful thing that was now to come out. How can I explain that I did it for ..... well what did I do it for? Love? No. Felt sorry for him? Yes. To cheer him up? Yes. No-one will ever understand. I'll never be able to explain it properly.

'I think so'.

'You think so? Can you please then tell the court what it is?'

'Underpants'.

'Underpants? What sort of underpants?'

'Mens .... boxers'.

'Yes men's underpants of the type known as boxers. Is there anything special about them Mrs. Hardy?'

'No I don't think so'.

'So why might you recognise them?'

'Because they are the same colour and type that I gave to Harry' she replied quietly looking at her feet.

'You gave my client some underpants?'

'Yes'.

'How strange! Now why did you do that?'

'He said that it was horrible not being able to change his pants every day and having to wear them for two or three days so I got him some extra ones'.

'Very magnanimous of you Mrs. Hardy .... but that's not all is it? There is something rather special about these underpants isn't there? Will you tell the court what it is?'

'I'm not sure that I understand what you mean? They're men's boxers'.

'Oh I think you understand perfectly well Mrs. Hardy. Now tell the court what is special about them?'

'Do I have to?'

'Yes you certainly do Mrs. Hardy'.

'I'd rather not'.

'Answer the question' instructed the judge staring hard at her.

Cow! No one will understand they'll think I'm some sex crazed slut.

Janie looked at Harry who was now openly smirking at her discomfort.

Oh Harry why have you told them all this? All these intimate things between us? Surely they were just you and me things ... special things ...our things .... weren't they?

'I wore them before I gave them to Harry'.

'You wore them before giving them to my client? Isn't that unusual?'

'Yes I suppose it is'.

'You suppose it is? I think it would be classed as extremely unusual Mrs. Hardy. I assume that as you are a woman of not insignificant financial means, you are able to purchase normal female underwear'.

'Yes of course'.

'Yet you bought some men's underpants and wore them before giving them to my client? Sort of shared them as it were?'

'Yes' she whispered.

'I assume you laundered them before passing them onto my client?'

There was a long pause as Janie sought a way to explain why she'd done what she had without it sounding dirty and smutty.

'Mrs. Hardy I asked if you laundered the underwear before passing them to my client. Did you?'

'No'.

'So please can you enlighten the court as to why you wore these male underpants before giving them ...... unwashed to my client in prison? I thought that he'd asked you to bring him clean underwear'.

'Yes he did but he asked me to wear them before giving them to him'. Janie glanced again at Harry who now looked as though he was actually laughing at her.

'He asked you to wear them Mrs. Hardy? Do you really expect the court to believe that?'

'Well you have to as it's the truth. Harry asked me to wear them before I gave them to him'. She looked over at her lover again where he was now wearing a serious expression while slowly shaking his head from side to side almost as if in disbelief at what he was hearing from her.

'But why? If you'd worn them then it wasn't clean underwear was it?'

'No, not in that sense'.

'Is it not a fact that it was entirely your idea to bombard my client with dirty photographs and used underwear?'

'No! I've just told you it was his idea. He asked me to have the pictures taken. As far as the boxers are concerned he said that it would be an intimate thing between us and a way we could kind of be together in a highly personal and secret way'.

'Oh how very touching! So how many pairs of underpants did you give to my client which you had …. umm shall we say ….. treated ……
in this way?'

'Three'.

'Three ….. I see'.

There was a long pause while David Goodchild glanced through his notes, looked around the court and then taking a deep breath glared aggressively at Janie and raised his voice.

'Mrs. Hardy I put it to you that you are deluding yourself and trying to delude this court'.

'No I'm not. I've told you the whole truth!'

'I hold a different view and so I put it to you that although my client constantly tried quite properly to discuss details of your financial investments, you persistently refused to listen or discuss those matters with him'.

'No'.

'Furthermore I suggest that you didn't bother with documents that he presented to you and just signed anything without bothering to check what it was, as you were more interested in having sex with him than having his financial advice'.

'No that's just not true'.

'You wanted his body not his financial experience'.

'No I didn't'.

'You ignored his perfectly correct and reasonable attempts to warn you of the risks in any investment process, refused to read documents and simply indulged your uncontrollable urge to have sexual intercourse with my client whenever and wherever you could'.

'NO!'

'Yes Mrs. Hardy. YES! Furthermore I put it to you that your actions in constantly pestering my client by visiting him in prison; bombarding him with vulgar pornographic photographs of yourself; sending him underwear that you had previously worn is not the action of a normal person who feels that they have been wronged, misled or swindled but rather the action of a sexually obsessed woman utterly besotted with a lover who would do anything to throw herself at him'.

'No. Look you've got it all wrong. Twisted things round. It wasn't like that. It wasn't like that at all'.

'It was exactly like that Mrs. Hardy' he snapped loudly as he stared at her then at the jury. 'That is exactly .... how ...... it .... was'.

Tears which she'd struggled for so long to prevent now started running down her cheeks as she said softly 'No it really wasn't. It simply wasn't like that. Not like you've made it all sound. You just don't understand'.

'Oh I understand perfectly well Mrs. Hardy' he said loudly. 'You are a voracious, predatory, insatiable, sexually fixated woman who latched onto my client and wouldn't leave him alone. You weren't interested in financial matters. You just wanted sex with him constantly'.

'NO!'

'YES. Any time, any place, anywhere. His apartment, his office, your cottage, open fields, hotels ...... you weren't fussy were you? You just wanted to constantly indulge in sexual activities with him'.

'I didn't!'

'Yes you did. You were utterly obsessed with having sex with my client'.

No .... no I wasn't. I'm not ...... I'm not like that at all'.

'Yes Mrs. Hardy. I am afraid that you are exactly like that ....
no more questions my Lady' he said looking up at the judge.

'Thank you Mr. Goodchild' then Lady Melrose looked at the prosecuting barrister who half stood, shook his head and sat down again.

'You may go Mrs. Hardy' she directed with obvious contempt.

Janie glanced at Harry who smiled back but suddenly she realised that the smile wasn't friendly but a cynical charade and in that sudden illuminating moment it finally became blindingly clear to her how he had used her, humiliated her and possibly destroyed her.

Feeling almost physically battered and conscious of loud discussion in the courtroom she nearly fell down the steps from the witness box as her legs were so weak and wobbly, but when she reached the bottom she turned for a final look at Harry who sneered, then blew her a kiss.

Summoning some strength from somewhere she walked head down out of the court. Once outside she ignored the people milling around her and pushed through to the exit where several reporters shouted at her and someone pushed a microphone into her face.

She was also vaguely aware of a tv camera poking towards her but giving a little cry she started running away from them down the street.

Fortunately she spotted a taxi and hailing it scrambled in as soon as it stopped moving while still being pestered by reporters.

'Where to love?' asked the taxi driver turning round to look at her.

Giving the car park address she slumped back into the seat. The tears poured down her face as she realised once and for all just how cynically and cruelly Harry had tricked, conned and used her. She continued crying until the cab stopped and the driver said 'Here you are love. That's eleven pounds forty please'.

She paid, got out, went into the multi-story car park, inserted her ticket, then her credit card, waited for the receipt and made her way to her car.

The Porsche started first go of the button and letting it burble away she took out her mobile phone and dialled William's number.

'Hello. How did it go?' he enquired.

'Oh William it was so awful, you just can't imagine. Look I've got something to tell you. Something that is so dreadful it is beyond your imagination. Can we meet somewhere please?'

'Aren't you coming home tonight?'

'Yes …… well maybe. I don't know. That will depend on you'.

'On me? Whatever are you talking about?'

'William I need to see you and talk to you straight away. Can we meet as soon as possible, perhaps part way between London and Norfolk?'

'Yes' he responded sounding puzzled. 'Newmarket? How about the Swynford Paddocks?'

'NO!' she screamed. 'No …… not there ….. anywhere ……. anywhere but there'.

'Alright. Bedford Lodge Hotel in Newmarket? It's this side of the town. What time?'

'I'm leaving now, so I'll be there in about an hour and a half or so'.

'Fine see you there. Janie are you alright?'

'No. No I'm not alright at all. I'll talk to you when I see you but William will you promise me one thing?'

'Of course. What is it?'

'Will you promise me you won't listen to the radio, to the news, watch tv, or talk to anyone till you see me?'

'What?'

'Please William it's essential that you do as I've asked. Vital. Please don't listen or watch any news?'

'Ok if that's what you want. I'll see you when you get there then'.

Janie couldn't remember anything about the drive to Newmarket. She had no recollection of which route she'd taken from London or at what speed she'd driven. Everything was blank from leaving the London car park until she pulled into the Bedford Lodge Hotel where she saw William's Range Rover.

He hadn't noticed her as his car wasn't facing the entrance driveway so she parked, walked over to him, knocked on the window and clambered in when he opened the door.

Soft music was playing. Beethoven she thought one of his favourite composers. He had several cd's of his music in the car.

'Hello there. I did as you asked and haven't listened to the radio or news. Bit of an odd request though. Now what's up?'

Dear, darling, dependable, loving, honest, kind, trustworthy William.
How am I ever going to be able to explain this to you without it destroying
you and us? Will you understand that it was ..... well what was it? What
had that horrible barrister called her? A sexually obsessed besotted woman?
Total madness. Utterly stupid. What I'm about to tell you will embarrass
you, hurt you, humiliate you. It might even destroy you. It will probably
finish us as a couple. I know that this could be the end for us, for everything
that we've worked for, for everything I have, for everything that I have ever
wanted. But I have to tell you myself rather than let you find out some
other way. I couldn't let that happen to you.

It has to be me ..... and now.

'William I want you to know that I love you very deeply and whatever
may have happened, whatever I've done I do love you. Remember that
as I speak and please believe me when I say that I do love you. I mean
it even though you may find that very hard to believe when you hear
what I have to say to you.

I realise that what I'm going to tell you now will hurt you terribly.
I also know that what I say will feel like an arrow piercing right into
your heart but somehow you've simply got to believe me when I say
that I love you.

Please hold onto that thought while you listen to me. Will you
do that? Promise me that and remember and cherish the fact that I
genuinely do love you .... because that is the truth?'

He nodded, so taking a deep breath she looked at his kindly face
now creased with lines of worry, traced her fingers down his cheek but
as she spoke the tears started to run down her cheeks.

'William, my darling, I've done something awful and I am so
sorry'.

THE END

Adultery is the application of democracy to love.
                    H. L. Mencken – British novelist and playwright

Love is all we have, the only way that we can help each other.
                    Euripides – Greek Playwright.

Two other titles by Mike Upton and available from AuthorHouse.

AMBITIONS END©

Mike Upton's first novel is a story of Ambition and one man's quest to avenge his father.

As a teenager Mark Watson sees the devastating effect on his parents when his father's business is bankrupted and he vows to get even with the industrialist who caused this event.

The book follows Mark's early years, schooling, his entry into the business world and his single minded climb up the corporate ranks until he becomes Chief Executive of a multi-national conglomerate.

His marriage, affairs and tangled love life are interwoven throughout the story which moves between Britain, America and Europe. He ruthlessly exploits and discards people, manoeuvres, manipulates and plots as he seeks to achieve his overriding ambition to gain revenge for his father.

The question is – will he reach the end of his Ambition?

WINNERS NEVER LOSE©

Winners Never Lose is Mike Upton's second novel and a sequel to Ambitions End ©.

This time it is set in the Oil and Pharmaceutical Industries and covers the wheeling and dealing, complex new product development, cut throat competition, selling off of unprofitable companies and acquiring of competitors that goes on in those industries.

Mark Watson is again the central character and his tough minded approach to the problems, challenges and opportunities that emerge as well as the continued betrayal of his wife with a string of affairs all contribute to an interesting and absorbing story where the action moves from Britain to America, India, Europe finally finishing in Australia.

Winners Never Lose, like his first novel Ambitions End, draws on Mike's extensive knowledge and experience of large multi-national corporations. His first hand familiarity with the way that big business operates is fully utilised in this exciting and fast paced novel.

==============================
To learn more about Mike Upton visit his website
www.mikeuptonauthor.com
==============================

Printed in Great Britain
by Amazon.co.uk, Ltd.,
Marston Gate.